Idolized

A HOLLYWOOD STARDUST NOVEL

By

Kim Carmichael

ALSO BY KIM CARMICHAEL

The Series

Hollywood Stardust Series:
Typecast
Supporting Roles Giselle & Wilson
Limelight
Idolized

Seductively Ever After Series
Façade

Stand Alone

On the Dotted Line

Trifecta

Novellas

Closure
Eternity

Shorts

Interchangeable
The Promise

Children's Book

My Daddy Wears His Art

Published by Rebel Romance,
An imprint of Irksome Rebel Press
Los Angeles, California

KIM CARMICHAEL

Idolized

A NOVEL

Published by Rebel Romance, an imprint of Irksome Rebel Press

Dedication

*To everyone who has ever been idolized,
never allow yourself to be typecast
and always enjoy your time in the limelight.*

Acknowledgements

To my husby who lets me live my dream.

To my sons and fur children who never mind sharing me with my characters.

To Tamara Eaton, my amazing editor, my best friend, without you these stories wouldn't be half of what they are. You are my beacon of sanity.

To Julia Clare, my amazing PA, you are always there to support me, it's now time to hand this one over to you and let you bring it to the world.

To Teresa Neeley-Martin, oh, comma whisperer, do your best, thank you for everything.

To Traci Hyland and my amazing street team, thank you for always being there to mention me on social media!

To JR, MV, AM, without you in my other life, I wouldn't be able to be Kim Carmichael!

To Roxy, William, Steven and Charles, no one ever had a better supporting cast.

Mostly to Logan, Ivy, Erin, Drew, Ryder and Cora, thank you for letting me have you and tell your story.

Short Glossary of Film Terms

Cut
A change in either camera angle or placement, location, or time.

Director
The principal creative artist on a movie set. A director is usually (but not always) the driving artistic source behind the filming process, and communicates to actors the way that he/she would like a particular scene played. A director's duties might also include casting, script editing, shot selection, shot composition, and editing. Typically, a director has complete artistic control over all aspects of the movie, but it is not uncommon for the director to be bound by agreements with either a producer or a studio.

Dissolve
An editing technique whereby the images of one shot is gradually replaced by the images of another.

Exterior
AKA: EXT
Used in a slug line, indicates that the scene occurs outdoors.

Fade
AKA: Fade To Black, Fade In, Fade Out
A smooth, gradual transition from a normal image to complete blackness (fade out), or vice versa (fade in)

Filtered
Post production term to add a filtered sound effect as over the phone.

Idolized
To regard with blind adoration or devotion. To worship as a god.

Interior
AKA: INT
Used in a slug line, indicates that the scene occurs indoors.

Limelight
The center of public attention, interest, observation, or notoriety.

Off Screen
AKA: O.S. Dialogue spoken off screen and is heard by the character.

Producer
The chief of staff of a movie production in all matters save the creative efforts of the director, who is head of the line. A producer is responsible for raising funding, hiring key personnel, and arranging for distributors.

Slug Line
A header appearing in a script before each scene or shot detailing the location, date, and time that the following action is intended to occur in.

Stardust
A naively romantic quality

Step and Repeat
1. (sometimes a step and repeat wall or press wall) is a publicity backdrop used primarily for event photography, printed with a repeating pattern such that brand logos or emblems are visible in photographs of the individuals standing in front of it.

2. The action of having talent "step" onto the red carpet, pose for the photographers and leave, while the next person follows and "repeats" the process.

Typecast
1. to cast (a performer) in a role that requires characteristics of physique, manner, personality, etc., similar to those possessed by the performer.

2. to cast (a performer) repeatedly in a kind of role closely patterned after that of the actor's previous successes.

<u>HOLLYWOOD STARDOM</u>

FADE IN:

EXT. HOLLYWOOD, CA - OUTSIDE NEWLY RENOVATED
HOLLYWOOD STARDUST THEATRE - DAY

Crowd has gathered around the theatre.

ROXY - late thirties beautiful woman dressed in
a flowing dress and a hat holding a handful of
pictures. As she makes her way through the
crowd, a woman bumps into her and she drops the
pictures.

                    ROXY
               Oh.

ROXY kneels down to pick up the pictures.

WOMAN - typical middle-aged woman wearing a
Hollywood Stardust Theatre t-shirt.

                    WOMAN
               I'm sorry.
               (bends down and helps Roxy.
               She lifts one of the
               pictures to her face.)
               Is that you?

CLOSE UP on picture of ROXY, STEVEN, WILLIAM and
CHARLES at graduation.

ROXY leans in and smiles at the picture.

                    ROXY
               Yes it is.

ROXY runs her finger over the picture, stopping
at each person.

                    WOMAN
               And do you even remember
               the ones in the picture
               with you?
               (laughs)

                    ROXY
          (points across the way)
           Actually, the three of them
           are right there.

                    WOMAN
           Oh my gosh. How do you
           know them?

ROXY takes the picture from the woman and stares
down at it.

                    ROXY
          (she inhales)
           They are my loves, my
           hates, my life.
          (Blinks and looks at the
          woman.)
           Sorry.

WOMAN puts hand on Roxy's shoulder.

                    WOMAN
           Don't be sorry.

                    ROXY
           I better go.

                    WOMAN
           Wait.

ROXY turns to her.

                    WOMAN
           Before you go, tell me who
           you ended up with.

                    ROXY
           How do you know I ended up
           with one of them?

WOMAN widens her eyes

ROXY closes her eyes

FADE OUT.

Chapter One

THE LIMOUSINE STOPPED in front of the Beverly Garland hotel, and Ryder Scott held up his hand, a silent command telling the driver not to unlock the door quite yet. No one should ever enter a battle zone without a plan of attack, and he needed a moment to get centered and take in the lay of the land.

While the set up was always the same, the players always changed. As usual, the red carpet trailed from the crowded curb on Sunset Boulevard all the way to the door of one of Hollywood's trendiest hotels. In between point A and point B, a step and repeat emblazoned with the *Hollywood Starburst* movie logo provided the perfect background for the stars to stop, strike a pose, and answer a question or two before heading into the after-party celebrating the movie premiere of the sequel to *Hollywood Stardust* that had waited over twenty years to be told.

After several deep breaths, Ryder lowered his hand, giving the go signal. The second the telltale click of the limo doors unlocking echoed through the vehicle, a nameless uniformed person opened the door into the war zone.

His strategy firmly planted in his mind, Ryder put one foot on the red carpet and paused, allowing the rest of him to remain in the shadows of the car interior. All too soon, the focus of the photographers would pull away from the step and repeat to find out who was in the last limo, though they knew the answer. All his co-stars had already arrived.

At times like this, it was critical to stay hydrated and ensure his pH was optimized, so he downed the last of his alkaline water before achieving his desired result.

At last two photographers turned toward the limo, and once a third followed suit, Ryder took his time exiting the car.

In one fluid motion he stood, flashed the one-sided smile that made him a star, and waved. Once the roar of the crowd gathered around the front of the hotel amplified, the smile became a bit more sincere, and he took his place in line behind his co-stars. All the better to remain in a defensive position as well as provide the much needed grand finale of arrivals. He lived by the motto, last in, first out, and above all else, leave everyone in a state of want.

Logan Alexander with his wife, Ivy, by his side and his kid, Curtis, in his arms went first. The once villain of the group, Logan turned his reputation around when he not only fell in love with the woman interviewing him, but resurrected and helped direct the sequel to their genre changing movie, *Hollywood Stardust*.

"Logan." One of the female news reporters came forward. "What did you think of the final cut of *Hollywood Starburst*?"

"The sequel turned out exactly as we envisioned, and we stayed true to the story." He nodded, and his little toddler reached for the microphone, eliciting a chuckle from the reporters.

"When does the filming of *Hollywood Stardom* begin?" The reporter let the little boy hold the microphone handle with her.

In a startling twist to the *Hollywood Stardust* story, there was a third and final movie planned, *Hollywood Stardom*. Even more surprising was that the four original actors would be reprising their roles. Of course, Ryder would be the penultimate star. He was the one with the body of work, the career to be envied, the one who was even making and producing his own movie. Yes he was the actor and director combination. "We will begin next month, and it's sure to be the perfect wrap-up for this set of characters." Logan took his wife's hand.

"Ivy, what was it like making your acting debut with your husband?" The reporter turned the mic to Mrs. Alexander.

The once camera shy woman not only did some cameos in *Starburst*, but would be taking a full-fledged role in the next movie. She faced the camera head-on. "I couldn't have asked for a better director." She turned to her husband.

In a moment tailor-made for the Hollywood royalty they had become, the couple kissed and Logan led her into the hotel.

The couple in waiting, Drew Fulton, Ph.D. and Erin Holland-Fulton, took their position next. At long last, fans of the elusive happily ever after could rejoice. In a fairytale come to life, the geek and the leading lady from the original movie, reconnected after twenty years and tied the knot in a gala fit for any princess.

The happy little couple struck several media-friendly adorable poses, including several which included having Drew place his hands on Erin's barely visible baby bump.

Ryder gave a quick glance behind him, swearing he could still see the smoke trail on the bullet he dodged when he didn't end up with her. While years ago Erin taught him many things on being an amazing lover, of utmost importance was her lesson on birth control. Don't enter a woman without it.

"Erin, you are positively glowing," the reporter noted.

"It's a Hollywood Glow." Erin held on to Drew. "Among other things."

Well, no one could say Erin wasn't a sales person through and through. Within her first four words, she plugged her and Drew's line of nutraceuticals. Not that she needed to, the stuff was sold out on the high-end shelves where it reigned as the crown prince of supplements. With a sneer, Ryder reached into his pocket and made sure he had his late night dose. Hell, the stuff worked.

"Exactly." The reporter nodded. "So Erin, as the original Roxy, how do you feel the new cast did taking over for this installment of the story?"

Only someone who knew Erin as well as Ryder did would have noticed her grip tighten on her husband, and the slight quiver of her lower lip. Of all of them, Erin had the worst time allowing the role she defined be taken on by someone else.

Erin leaned forward. "They all did magnificent, but I can't say I'm not thrilled to have Roxy back."

Her answer was gracious and truthful, and Ryder gave her a thumbs-up, even if she hadn't see the gesture.

"Your fans are going to be thrilled." The reporter beamed at her and turned her attention to Drew. "Dr. Fulton, how does it feel to return to acting?"

"It feels right." Ever the serious one, Drew lifted his chin at the reporter and then took Erin inside.

Ready for his turn on the front line, Ryder no sooner stepped over to give these reporters a true photo opportunity than a stripe of black lace rushed in front of him, tripped and stumbled right into the center of the step and repeat.

When the woman stopped, clenched her fist and straightened up, two things happened. First, one luscious tendril of auburn hair tumbled free of its updo into her eye giving the woman a sexy "just-got-out-of-bed-and-ready-to-get-back-in-it" look. Second, he recognized the woman. In fact, one could say she was one of his many benefactors, though not in his traditional sense, meaning he hadn't slept with her...yet.

Still, the woman media-blocked his entrance, and though he made sure to have no expression on his face, he waited to determine whether he needed to fight.

"Cora Caine." The reporter tiptoed toward the intruder. "Welcome to the red carpet."

Yes, Cora Caine, the CEO of Chargge.com.

When her web portal/search engine/multimedia site was purchased three years ago by the same company that owned the studio that produced *Hollywood Stardust*, she became a billionaire overnight. She also seemed to be the one pushing for the Stardust movies to continue.

Rather than answer, Cora glanced around and as if she finally realized she was in front of reporters and photographers, she struck her version of a pose.

More accurately, she put her hands on her hips and pursed her lips. "What was the question?"

Inside, Ryder winced. The reporter hadn't asked a question. However, Cora's demeanor gave him some much needed intel. Apparently Ms. Caine hadn't intended to sabotage his moment in the limelight, but simply took the wrong way.

"Were you always a fan of the *Hollywood Stardust* movie? Is that why you became involved with the sequel?" Where the reporter was smooth with his costars, at having her flow disrupted, her voice shook.

"The original movie is one of the most beloved of all time. When my team ran our algorithms, we decided it would be a good investment." Cora crossed her arms over her chest, setting up a barrier to the reporter and covering up one of her best assets.

Ryder wasn't sure if she even answered the question. He was still stuck on the word algorithm. What the hell was an algorithm? Did anyone know?

"Oh, well, yes." The reporter's smile faded. "Your dress is gorgeous. Who are you wearing?"

Ah, the old standby question. It was also a gift on the reporter's part. Hopefully, Cora would take the hint and lower her arms, because no one should be allowed to miss that body. All her curves were made for exploration. Instead of revealing the designer, Cora returned to that pursing her lips thing, making her look like an inexperienced actress trying to impress. Not the appropriate look for a corporate bigwig.

Sometimes the best battles were won purely on opportunity and coincidence. It was time for a surprise attack. After a quick check of his tie, Ryder swooped in and came up right behind Ms. Caine. She gasped, but that didn't stop him. He put one hand on her waist, and with his other hand, he pulled the back of her dress, got a quick glimpse at the label and leaned into her ear. "Owen Blakeney, Blake Designs."

"Ryder Scott, what a surprise!" The reporter smiled again.

Cora twisted around to see him, her lock of hair hitting him in the face.

He corralled her hair and decided the best course of action was to take over. "The gorgeous Cora Caine is wearing an Owen Blakeney dress that fits her better than any glove I've ever seen, and as luck would have it, I have one of his tuxedos on tonight."

"Are you ready to reprise your role as William?" the reporter asked.

"I think the more accurate question would be, is William ready for me?" He chuckled and slid his hand down. Hey, since he saved her ass, he might as well get a little touchy-feely.

"Ms. Caine, are you pleased with the outcome of the second movie?" As the reporter asked yet another question, Cora tensed like she wanted to walk.

In an effort to keep the media monstrosity in place, he tightened his hold and continued to speak for Ms. Caine. "With all the unique circumstances, I think this was a perfect way to tell the story. Now I believe it's time to walk the rest of the red carpet." He gave the reporter a wink and with his arm around her waist, guided Cora toward the hotel entrance.

"You can let go of me now, Mr. Scott." She put her hand over his.

"Why would I do that? It feels like it belongs here." They continued toward the doors, and he nodded at no one in particular.

The doormen did their jobs, but before she entered she turned to him. "I can guarantee that no part of you belongs on any part of me."

"I don't think anyone, let alone you, can guarantee that." To prove his point, he let his hand skim down to the swell of her backside. The angle of the curve let him know if he delved a little deeper he would get quite the magnificent handful.

Her green eyes darkened, and they stared at each other.

"What are you looking at?" She didn't walk away, but she did narrow her eyes.

Though he had met Cora a few times, he never had the opportunity to be this close up to her. In fact, she was quite attractive, actually beautiful, with feminine little features in complete contrast to her harder than steel attitude. Part of him wanted to take a bite, but the other part was afraid he would chip one of his teeth and his caps were damn expensive. "Why don't you use one of your algorithms and figure it out?" He purposely lowered his eyes to her copious cleavage. "Instead of snapping at me, maybe you should thank me for saving your ass out there."

She raised her chin. "My ass did not need saving."

"I think that's where you and I need to agree to disagree." With a quick glance back to ensure at least a few of the cameras were on them, he gave into the temptation from earlier and finally let his palm graze over the aforementioned body part. Oh, he was spot on, her ass was perfection.

Her eyes ablaze, she dramatically grabbed his hand and plucked it off her. "My algorithm tells me this is done." She spun on her heel and stomped into the hotel.

Once more, Ryder looked back at the media. Even more people were focused on him, and he gave them a slight bow. Those gathered let out a collective *awww*. "I better get inside." He widened his eyes to garner any last bit of sympathy and paused to allow the photographers to get their shot before following his impromptu date. Tomorrow's stories would have him plastered everywhere. Job well done, Ryder. Job well done.

AS FAR AS CORA WAS CONCERNED, the only good part about hanging around celebrities was the minute she entered a room, people didn't stop and stare at her.

In fact, she barged through the party in search of her employees, and no one gave her a second glance, everyone focused on the stars. All she needed to do was make her appearance and corral the cast of the next movie for a quick meeting before she could leave and go get some real work done.

Of course, she already had quite a run-in with Ryder, but he caught her at an unusually weak moment. She never intended to end up on the red carpet, but got sick of sitting in a line of limos and left the car out of order. The stupid ushers guided her right to the scene of the crime, or in this case, the step and repeat.

Thus far, her idea to capitalize on the Hollywood Stardust franchise was paying off and putting her in prime position for what she was truly after. The stars' affiliation with her website entertainment portal, Chargge.com, increased her numbers and made her even more relevant. By casting a younger set of heartthrobs in the sequel and returning to the original cast for the finale, everyone from thirteen to sixty was panting to see how the famous foursome would end their story.

She glanced around the party, finally finding the star cluster she was after. Logan, her so-called business partner in this endeavor, his wife, who worked for Chargge's entertainment productions, the scientist, and the bimbo all stood huddled around the first of the offspring to come from their galaxy. All Cora was missing was the super nova leading man, and that was fine by her. From the way they all orbited each other, any news would get back to Ryder, the who didn't seem to belong in their solar system.

With enough astronomy comparisons under her belt to create an entire sci-fi movie, like an asteroid she shot forward. Fine, she had one more simile in her. It was just too easy.

"Cora." Logan spied her and lifted his hand.

She swore not to smile when the little boy with his hair pulled back in a matching tiny ponytail to his father did the same thing.

Though she might be the checkbook behind the movies, every time she entered their circle, she still felt as if she were standing out of their orbit.

For a moment they all remained silent.

Logan cleared his throat. "What did you think?" The man seemed to hold his child a bit tighter and wrapped his arm around his wife.

Erin held onto Drew, and Cora swore Drew almost shielded his wife's eyes, but instead, his hand went to her stomach.

Since the day Chargge went public, everyone reacted this way to her. Well, it wasn't a surprise, since she made people money, a lot of money, including herself. She opened her mouth and those around her leaned toward her.

"Hey, thanks for keeping her warm for me." Out of nowhere Ryder handed her a glass of sparkling wine. He tapped his glass against hers. "I didn't mean to leave your side, but I stopped to get your favorite."

She glanced down at the glass. "My favorite?"

"Yes, love, your favorite." He bent down and spoke in her ear. "You love a Muscato wine, a little sparkle, a little sweet and a little unpredictable for you. I would have pegged you a dry wine girl. What other surprises are you hiding?"

All right, the wine was her favorite. Her mouth suddenly became dry as the wine Ryder assumed she should prefer. She took a sip of the effervescent liquid. "You never know what I'll do next." In truth, she didn't mean her statement to come out as suggestive as it sounded, but maybe he didn't notice.

Ryder sidestepped, his arm pressing against hers. "I hope that rings true for later as well. Maybe right around the time you tell me all about algorithms." He tapped his glass against hers and faced the rest of his friends. "So, what are we doing?"

In a need to recapture control over this meeting, she stepped forward, right into the eye of the storm. "I believe you were waiting for my critique of your film."

Evaluation was never easy, as she knew from experience over and over again. Everyone froze in place.

Well, everyone but Ryder who took to sipping his wine, giving Erin's stomach a thumbs-up and high-fiving Logan's child.

Before answering, and frankly enjoying the way the rest of them trembled, she reached into her handbag for her phone. She put Ryder to work by handing him her glass of wine while she quickly assessed some data. A few clicks told her what she needed to know. "Well..." Out of the corner of her eye, she spied Ryder taking a sip of her wine and shrugging.

Rather than watch him, she forced herself to continue. "The rumble already is promising. We made the right decision to give the green light on the last movie." She scrolled down to get the rest of the report. "The public does want to see the four of you reprise your roles, but we knew that. I am sure *Hollywood*

Starburst will go down as the middle child of the group. The first being the classic and the last being what people want to see. It will now forever be known as the filler, but we had to have a bridge."

Without taking her eyes off her phone, she reached over and took another taste of the wine. Since she had their attention she might as well say what she came here for so she could go and get out of this too tight dress and into forgiving stretchy leggings and work.

Once again she handed Ryder her glass. At least the living coaster was good for something. After reading the rest of the data, she lifted her head. Ryder stared right at her and deliberately took another sip of her drink. Fine, the man was good for two things, holding glasses and standing there and looking pretty. She best get to her task at hand. "Because of Erin's situation, I have an announcement."

"Drew and I have a pregnancy clause in our contracts." Breathless, Erin shot the words out.

"As do Ivy and I." Logan nodded.

"Thank god I need no such clause," Ryder huffed.

"You are not pushing the movie back." Logan's jaw tightened. "We'd lose momentum. We can work around Erin's special situation and whatever else comes along."

"Drew." Erin hid her face in her husband's shoulder.

"What's going on?" Drew patted his wife, but stared Cora down.

Cora waited to ensure their collective hissy fit was over. "You know, only because you are stars is this type of behavior tolerated. If you would have let me take a breath, I would have told you that we are fast tracking the movie and would like to move the production up two weeks. Of course, if Erin goes into labor, we will honor the contracts and pause until she and Drew return from paternity leave. This way we have a bit more time built in." Before nodding, she rewound her words making sure they were all politically correct. Once certain, she took another sip of her wine and returned it to her human cup holder.

The smile on Erin's face had a domino effect on the rest of the flock.

Thankfully, she managed to avoid asking Erin how her timing could be so perfectly bad to add another person to the earth, but it was now her time to bid her little sheep *adieu*. "We want a smooth shoot that can be wrapped up quickly."

Logan stepped forward. "There is one problem."

Oh, a confrontation. Her blood rushed, and she lifted her chin. "What might that be, Mr. Alexander?"

"What about the end of the movie?" His voice hardened.

Cora couldn't stop her smile. Until the day the last scene was shot, none of them would know the end. Though movies were often shot out of order, the final scene would purposely be shot last. "As we have discussed numerous times, the end of the movie won't be revealed to anyone until the day we shoot it."

"Do you know the end?" Ivy asked.

"What do you think?" Of course she didn't know the end. No one, not even the screenwriter knew the end. She gave them each another nod and turned to leave.

"Cora." The smooth sound of Ryder crooning her name made her stop.

"If you have any further questions Mr. Scott, you can call my office." Apparently these people didn't understand some of the unfortunate ones like her, needed to do actual work for a living.

He held his hand up to stop her. "Ms. Caine, I definitely need to ask you a question before you depart."

As if he lived his life perpetually in a movie, the music for the party began. The alternative pop from the *Hollywood Starburst* soundtrack echoed through the space.

"Now I have a question and a statement." He held out her almost emptied glass and corralled her back to the group.

"All right." She downed the damn drink and waited.

"Well, there goes my question. I wanted to know if you wanted to finish you wine." His smile lit up the room. "Of course, now I should offer you some water, it's critical to stay hydrated when you drink alcohol."

Not knowing what on earth he was talking about, she tapped her foot. "What else did you need?"

"It's not what I need, it's what you need." He swooped her glass away and put it on a table with his.

"You have nothing I need." Her getaway would be easy.

"That's what you think." He grabbed her hand and pulled her in. "You need at least one dance before you depart."

With no time for these shenanigans, she tensed. "Mr. Scott."

"Watch it Miss Caine, the cameras are on you. Rumor has it you want a promotion, and it isn't your lack of smarts that won't get you the gig." He wrapped his arm around her and guided her toward the dance floor.

Fine, there were rumblings that the CEO of Ultracom Consolidated, the huge conglomerate that owned not only Chargge.com, but also the studio that produced the *Hollywood Stardust* movies, would be replaced, and she was on the short list of candidates. There were also louder rumblings about how she was the proverbial dragon lady, unapproachable in every way.

"How do you know all this about me, Mr. Scott?" At spying the cameras and other partygoers lifting their cell phones to get the picture, she allowed him to take her into his arms and sway in time to the music.

"For someone all technology, I thought you would have guessed." He pressed his hand to the small of her back and leaned into her ear. "I consulted the Cora Caine Wiki. Now I know everything."

She leaned back and caught yet another glimpse of him. No doubt his looks not only got him the leading man roles, but led many women to his bed.

"So tell me, why are you here with no date?" He twirled with her.

"I thought you had the Wiki, you tell me." With the flashes going off, she plastered a smile on her face.

"Don't fake smile, you're not an actress." Like earlier, he ran his hand down to her waist. "I would say that was a trick question, cause it's more than apparent to everyone here, you have a date."

Above all else, she refused to acknowledge the little flutter in her stomach at his words. Everything tonight was for show, as it should be. In fact, the flutter was nothing except indigestion from the fact she had nothing to eat before arriving here.

Before she could offer a comeback, the music changed. The song that defined the first movie, *Hollywood Stardust*, came on. The partygoers began to clap and Logan, Ivy and their offspring joined them on the dance floor as did Drew and Erin.

"You know, this dance didn't belong to me in the movie, but every woman always wants me to perform it with them." He pulled her in even closer. "How does it feel to live out the fantasy?"

"I have no idea, it's not my fantasy." She faced him head on.

"Don't tell me you haven't seen the first movie." His eyes seemed to sparkle.

"Of course I've seen it." The man was a fool. "I live on the planet."

"Then it has to be your fantasy."

Like all her conquests, now she would win. "Well, contrary to popular belief, nothing about the movie is my fantasy. In order to have a fantasy you have to be a fan first." She matched his smug look with one of her own.

"Not a fan of the movie." He stopped his dance.

Sometimes no answer was the best answer of all and she simply stared at him.

"That really turns me on." Without as much as a warning, he leaned down and kissed her.

Yes, he kissed her, a real kiss, not a peck or even what one would call a movie style kiss, done for effect only. In less than the time it took Ryder Scott, leading man, to tangle his hand in her hair and open his mouth, her body betrayed her, her knees went weak and she had no choice but to hold on for fear she would fall into some bizarre fandom.

Still, she couldn't help but soak up the attention he lavished on her. She relished in how his tongue caressed hers, treating her to his sweet taste combined with the tang of wine and how every inch of her warmed as if she drank a bottle of a deep red vintage.

For the first time since she could remember, she lost herself, did something without thinking of every repercussion first and even found herself kissing him back.

He pulled her in tighter and bent her back slightly. The way their bodies contoured together allowed her to take in his long, lean body with bulges in all the right places.

All the right places.

Yes, she thought that twice.

As suddenly as he kissed her, he broke the kiss and pressed his forehead to hers. "I'll make a fan of you yet."

"You're not that good," she blatantly lied. The man could turn her into a downright fanatic. Once her knees found their strength, she spun on her heel and headed for the exit.

<u>HOLLYWOOD STARDOM</u>

FADE IN:

EXT. HOLLYWOOD, CA - BACKSTAGE AT A CONCERT HALL
- EVENING SUNSET.

WILLIAM - late thirties, dressed in jeans a
leather jacket goes to Roxy and puts his hands
on her waist, pulling her in for a kiss.

>   WILLIAM
>   Tell me to break a leg.

>   ROXY
>   Break a leg.
>   (Wipes her lipstick off his
>   lip)
>   You'll be perfect as always.

WILLIAM smiles, raises his eyebrows and gives
her another kiss, this one more intense that the
first one.

>   WILLIAM
>   Tell me again. If it
>   wasn't for you I wouldn't
>   even be here. You got me
>   singing you told me to
>   audition.

>   ROXY
>   You had the talent.

>   WILLIAM
>   So do you.

ROXY shakes her head and looks down.

WILLIAM hooks his fingers under chin and makes
her look up at him.

                    WILLIAM
          Come on you know it's true.
          (winks)

                    MAN (O.S.)
          Will, three minutes!

                    WILLIAM
          Roxanne, look at what we've
          built. We have the dream.

ROXY stares into his face.

                    ROXY
          We do, we have everything,
          who would have ever thought
          we would end up here, but -

ROXY toys with WILLIAM'S collar.

                    WILLIAM
          But nothing.

                    MAN (O.S.)
          Two minutes!

WILLIAM grabs her hand and kisses it.

                    WILLIAM
          I know you're nervous with
          everyone coming to the
          concert, but this is your
          chance. You're a star, my
          star, maybe not in the way
          you thought, but this is
          it, we made it.

                    ROXY
           Do you think so, really?

She presses her palm to WILLIAM'S cheek.

                    WILLIAM
           I do.
           (Takes her chin in his hand
           and sings.)
            Since the day we met I knew
            it would be us two. The
            love we have together is
            experience by so few.
WILLIAM kisses her.

                    MAN (O.S.)
           Will, now!

                    WILLIAM
           I have to go.

WILLIAM runs onto the stage.

ROXY looks from the sidelines, plasters a tight
smile on her face, and watches him perform.

Chapter Two

THE WAY THE ELEVATOR DOORS parted was not unlike a velvet curtain opening to a grand movie premiere. By the time he stepped into the hallway on the twenty-fifth floor at the prestigious Sierra Towers in Los Angeles, Ryder had his plan in place. The question wasn't if he and Cora were going to have sex, the only variable was how well he was going to perform, and that really wasn't a variable.

Though the famous building that housed Cora's condo was known for being as discreet as it was opulent, rather than ravaging her where any A-lister tenant might spot them, he took to ensuring the electricity between them remained charged and full of potential. The simple act of keeping eye contact and rubbing his palm up and down the contour of her waist, stopping short of the swell of her backside or breasts guaranteed she stayed right where he wanted her, hot and ready to go.

Neither of them spoke as they went to her door. The moment she took her keys out of bag, he plucked them away. At last he allowed himself some forward momentum and went up behind her, wrapped his arm around her waist and slid the key into the lock. Instead of a mechanical mechanism, the lock lit up. Without taking her eyes off him, she reached behind her and put her finger on a little pad. Like magic, the door popped open.

He expected nothing less from his little high-tech sex kitten, but he needed to stay on task. Thrusting the door open, he grabbed her arm, and in the ultimate movie move he turned her around, kicked the door closed, and pushed her up against the nearest wall. As an added bonus, he managed to sneak his hand behind her head, providing a little cushion.

"Finally." He breathed the word, leaned down and kissed her like he owned her, because soon he would.

At the premiere party, he went easy on her. Everyone was watching, and it was their first kiss. However, he had her on her own turf, a place where he could let loose and only hope she did the same, so he used his free arm to pull her in tight as he crushed his lips to hers.

Her breath caught, but rather than freeze, she instantly opened her mouth.

Their kiss for cameras back at the hotel netted him a welcome, yet uncomfortable, erection. Wanting relief and wanting her, he followed her as she made her way out and let himself right into her limo. Though she resisted at first, he took the role of strong leading man and doing away with unnecessary conversation, kissed her again.

The kissing continued, only taking a break for the whole business of getting out of the car and up to her place, and here they were, in the midst of heating up each other up and getting ready to join in the most primal way. This woman was instrumental in having the studio back the *Hollywood Stardust* franchise, and in only a few orgasms, he would hopefully have some support for his own move from the lady who could definitely afford it.

However, even with his goals set firmly in his sights, he took a moment to relish in the way she kissed him back, wasn't shy in tangling her tongue in his, and how she ping-ponged between allowing him to lead, and then taking over.

Yes, she was full of surprises. Pleasant, pleasant surprises.

Before he realized it, she reached for his tie. When it came to disrobing, he was accustomed to making the first move. Luck on his side, he ended up with a little vixen. While he let her unknot his tie and work the buttons on his shirt, he peeled off his tuxedo jacket, and then kissed her.

Since she made it a point to switch things up on him, he did the same and broke their kiss, moved his lips to her ear then her neck, while his hands admired her ample breasts—much more than a handful—with already hard peaks grazing his fingertips, and purely *au naturel*, he had no choice to put to indulge.

As she pulled his shirt open, he reached behind her and inched her zipper down. Much to his delight, she took it upon herself to shimmy her designer dress to the floor. Even better, he discovered she didn't stuff herself into a contouring garment.

"The second I saw you at the premiere I wanted you." Perhaps a little dialogue was in order. He took her hand and guided it to his belt buckle.

Rather than answer, her fingers worked the belt, then went further and unbuttoned his pants.

He skimmed his lips down to her chest and unclasped her strapless bra. The garment dropped, revealing a gorgeous set of breasts ripe for the tasting. In an effort to savor her, he first skimmed his fingertips over her. When he couldn't take it anymore, he dipped his head down, guiding her delectable, hard nipple between his lips and alternating sides to make sure he kept everything even.

A low purr escaped her throat, and she raked her fingers through his hair.

"Did you ever think we would end up here?" He did them both the favor of removing her panties and buried his face between her mounds. After all, he was always used to being surrounded by greatness.

"None of my calculations would have predicted this." In a welcome invitation, she moved her legs apart.

One to always take direction perfectly, he snuck his hand exactly where she wanted. At finding the evidence of her need, he glanced up at her. "By my calculations, I think you know you want to be with me. I'm everyone's fantasy personified, and I'm all yours."

Before he had the chance to delve into her depths, she tightened her hold on his hair. "Listen gorgeous, don't think too much of yourself. I can buy and sell guys like you every day from the interest I make in just one of my savings accounts in one month, and still have change left over to buy a private jet."

"Fuck, that turns me on." Wanting her to feel what he did, he used his fingertips to tempt her a little more.

Her knees slightly buckled, then she grabbed his arm and pulled him up until they were nose to nose. "I thought it might."

Oh, she was a little firecracker. "I can hardly wait to know what a billion-dollar pussy feels like." With his focus solely on her, he retrieved his wallet out of his pocket and then kicked his pants aside along with his shoes, allowing his more than ready erection to make its appearance. The woman seemed to match him in every way, and he had to find out if that held true in the most important way.

She reached between them and stroked his hard-on. "As much as I anticipate what a superstar cock can do."

The woman, the words, her touch all served to excite him further, and in a move fit for any leading man, he picked her up. "Then let's go see if we live up to the hype." With her in his arms, he made his way through her apartment, taking only a quick look around at her top-notch furnishing and accessories, which included a bizarre collection of movie musical memorabilia scattered throughout. Instead, he went in search of the bed. His arousal grew the moment he located what he was after.

Ever the gentleman, he made sure to move her undoubtedly expensive comforter and decorator pillows aside as he set her down. Before joining her, he ripped the condom open. Just to let her know what she was in for, he stood at the side of the bed and stared down at her as he sheathed himself.

"You do like to put on a show, don't you?" She slid to the center of the mattress and lifted one knee.

"You're the one watching." Protection fully in place, he got on the bed, took her into his arms and kissed her as he positioned himself between her legs.

Instead of simply thrusting into her, he rubbed his erection over her, a little taunt, a little tease, a lot of build-up.

"Have we had enough of the trailers?" She curled her legs around his waist, giving him full access.

"Finally ready for the feature?" His own need off the charts, he entered her at last.

He earned the tight, hot welcome he received, but for the first time since he could remember, he was also faced with the fact it would be way too easy to lose control. No matter the circumstances, he had to remain in control.

Not wanting to give the impression he was off his game in any way, he began with slow strokes while he used a breathing technique to regain his balance.

"Oh." The tense, harsh woman beneath him let go, wrapped her arms around him, and kissed his neck.

"Yeah, baby." His voice came out unnaturally low, and he closed his eyes, trying not to focus on how she sucked on his skin using just the right amount of pressure, but visualizing her orgasm, and how he would make it incredible for her.

However, once more she proved to be a formidable match, and rather than simply play the role of receiver, she met him move for move, squirming under him, kissing him, and bucking her hips as the sensations intensified.

Every time their bodies met his desire grew, pushing him closer and closer to his end, but damn, he didn't want to finish. In an effort to prolong the experience and give her more of a show, he pushed himself up on his knees and spread her legs further apart.

From her vantage point, she should get an excellent view of a movie star drilling into her. The only issue was it also gave him the most amazing scene of a gorgeous woman with her copious amount of hair sprawled out around her who writhed with his every stroke.

"Oh god, don't stop." She gave him a show of her own when she squeezed her breasts together.

Her breathy plea and sexy action was nearly his undoing, and his balls tightened as his impending climax began to materialize. He had to get her to come immediately and he slipped his hand between them, finding the one magic spot certain to give her a grand finale. "I want to watch you come."

"Ah." She ground up to the source of the pleasure.

"That's right." The moment she succumbed, he would have no choice but to join her. Even now he fought the urge to simply plunge into her and find release. "Scream my name."

As if she were staving off the inevitable, she bit her lip and shook her head. At last she gasped. "Ryder!" With her outburst came the pulses around him that indicated his success.

Unable to hold back as her body drew him further into hers, his muscles tensed, and he let loose. "Yes!" He slammed into her as his orgasm hit, actually bowled him over. At the first surge of ecstasy, he couldn't move, at the second, his arms gave out, and he collapsed against her, but by the third, he was left a quivering mass of pleasure that could only pant and hold her. What had he become?

With him still inside her, she rubbed his back and let out a low chuckle. "I take it you enjoyed?"

Somewhere, he found the strength to roll off her. "With the way you screamed my name, I know you did." On weak legs he got up, and stumbled through her bedroom to the bathroom and dealt with the condom. He glanced at his reflection, nodded and splashed some water on his face before rejoining her in the bedroom to find her twisted up among her blankets looking as sultry as ever.

"Do you want some water?" he asked. Where on earth did that question come from? Shouldn't she be getting him water or an award statue or something?

"There's some bottles in the refrigerator." Her voice strained when she stretched. "Will you turn off the lights?"

"Sure." Still in the buff, and planning on staying that way, he strolled through her place, this time truly getting a chance to see her items. Among the modern furniture and electronic everything, were framed old time pictures and other memorabilia from famous movie musicals, the kind where people burst into song at a moment's notice and nothing made any sense. Interesting. He didn't think she was the type.

After retrieving the water and cutting down her electric bill, he returned to her. He opened the water and held it out. "Here, hydration is very important."

"Thank you." She took a drink and handed the bottle back to him.

He gulped down some of refreshing liquid, put the bottle on the nightstand coaster and slipped in bed next to her. Hell, he even did the thing where he gathered her up into his arms.

"I take it you're spending the night?" She turned her back to him, but pressed her body against his.

"Isn't that what would happen in one of your musicals? They would never orgasm and run." At his own joke, he laughed.

"What would you know about that?" She flipped her hair back.

Once corralling her hair and getting it out of his face, he spooned her. "I see you like musicals."

"Well, in the musicals they would have had the decency to take the hard stuff behind closed doors. The romance would have been in their eyes and their actions." She yawned.

At her words, he frowned. "I'm no stranger to romance, and though I don't normally sing or dance, I'm sure I can think of something else to tickle your fancy."

"I have to get up early tomorrow. Make yourself at home if I don't see you." With a sigh, she hugged her pillow.

He stared into the darkness. Maybe she would have had better luck with romance if she turned over and actually looked him in the eyes.

HOLLYWOOD STARDOM

FADE IN:

EXT. HOLLYWOOD HILLS, CA -OUTSIDE IN A
RESTAURANT OVERLOOKING THE LOS ANGELES CITY
LIGHTS. - NIGHT

The party is going on STEVEN and his date,
CHARLES and his wife are there, everyone is
talking.

ROXY is drinking a glass of wine and staying on
the sidelines.

STEVEN is in his late thirties blond, wearing
expensive designer clothing. Has a model-type
blonde in a tight dress hanging off him. He
looks over at Roxy, pushes the blonde aside, and
approaches.

                    STEVEN
             Long time.

STEVEN tilts his glass in her direction.

                    ROXY
             (Sipping her wine)
              Some would say too long,
              some would say not long
              enough.

                    STEVEN
             I felt that.

ROXY shrugs.

                    STEVEN
             I have to say this is quite
             a turn of events, I always
             thought it would be you up
             on stage.

                    ROXY
              (staring into his eyes)
          Sometimes you have to know
          when to let go.

                    STEVEN
          Subtlety is not your strong
          suit.

                    ROXY
          Maybe that's why I'm not
          the performer.

STEVEN nods.

WILLIAM joins them and puts his arm around ROXY.
He raises his chin in STEVEN'S direction.

                    WILLIAM
          Good to see you.

                    STEVEN
          Likewise.

WILLIAM faces ROXY.

                    WILLIAM
          Come on, baby, the reporter
          from the paper is here
          covering the story. I need
          my girl by my side.

                    ROXY
          I'll be right there.

WILLIAM looks at STEVEN and kisses ROXY'S cheek
before walking away.

                    STEVEN
          I never pictured you to be
          the type on the sidelines.

                    ROXY
          Who says I'm on the side
          lines, I'm just behind the
          curtain.

FADE OUT.

Chapter Three

THE THREE ILLUMINATED SCREENS on Cora's office desk allowed her to pinpoint the moment her life went wrong, awry, spiraled out of control. If her life were a musical, this would be the point where the main character sang a solo about how low they had sunk.

She started her analysis left to right.

Everything was fine on the screen from a major national news site. The report outlined the *Hollywood Stardust* franchise, spoke of the successful debut of the sequel, had quotes from Logan Alexander, and ended on a positive note speaking of the third installment of the trilogy and the return of the original actors.

All good.

All fine.

Exactly what she wanted.

Cora took a sip of her espresso and diverted her attention to the second screen.

Stock prices were fine. In fact, some might say excellent. She would say everything could always do better. Still, the number was steady.

She exhaled and said a silent prayer the number would remain in its happy place, especially now that she needed to face the third screen.

Chargge.com. Her own website, her baby, her creation betrayed her. The first story at the top of the feed didn't outline the movie, other celebrities or even the premiere party per se. Instead, it gave quite an accurate catalog of her night with Mr. Ryder Scott.

From outside the hotel with his hands on her waist, to some fictional argument they had which left Ryder looking dejected, to their kiss on the dance floor and lastly to him sneaking into her limo with her. There was no doubt that everyone on the planet knew where they were headed.

Orgasm aside, she single-handedly might have destroyed her CEO chances and all because she couldn't keep out of Ryder's pants. Her only saving grace was there wasn't a fourth screen outlining the rest of her illicit night with one Mr. Scott.

What was he doing now?

She could only hope he had the decency to leave early and throw the sheets in the hamper.

Before picking up her phone to call the house cleaning crew, she glanced over at the stock numbers once more. Wall Street must take a while to respond to entertainment news.

She lifted her phone then put it down again. What would she say to the housekeepers anyway? In need of any distraction from the unwanted publicity, she quickly clicked over to her favorite on-line auction site and placed a couple of bids on some collectibles from some old-time musicals. All right, she admitted, she put in a crazy amount, so she wouldn't lose. Everyone had his or her vice, and today she needed the comfort of her little addiction. With that thought, she took another sip of espresso.

A quick knock on her door made her jump. "Come in!" No doubt she would now be updated on her *faux pas,* and she might as well get it over with.

The door opened and in marched Viktor, part assistant, part big brother, part protector. A Russian foreign exchange student who came to their family when she was only seven years old, Viktor ended up being a permanent part of her family after his mother passed away only a year later. A formidable man, he was a wrestling superstar through school, and then learned the ins and outs of technology with her. Without him, she would have never have had her business.

"You see Chargge?" He took what would always be designated as his chair–an antique oversized monster that looked like a throne and completely out of place in her glass and chrome office. She found it at an antique store and bought it for their first office in an old warehouse.

"You know the site is the go-to entertainment hub." She purposely avoided looking directly at Viktor. Her post coital haze wouldn't bode well with the big brother part of him.

"Fine." Viktor lifted his tablet. "So I also assume you were not looking at auctions and saw, Webatainer, Intertainment and every other entertainment site worth anything."

Truth be told, between tiptoeing out of her place as to not awake the sleeping star in her bed, getting her espresso, and then writing Ryder a note threating him within an inch of his life if he touched her espresso machine, she sort of overlooked rule number one. Checking the competition first. Her heart rate accelerating and trying not to move more than necessary, she inched her fingers over to her mouse.

"Cora!" Viktor pounded his fist into her desk.

"I know!" She gulped her espresso back like a shot of whiskey and covered her eyes with her hand, breaking yet another one of Viktor's rules about never looking at the truth head-on. "Let's get some crisis communications specialists in here and see how we can contain the damage."

"Cora." Viktor stood.

Oh Lord, he stood. Actually hoisted himself off his throne. The situation was at DEFCON 12. She matched his stance, shooting up out of her chair with her hands on her hips. "I will fix this, I had a lapse. He was there, and he's beautiful, and he says these things and..." Only years of training allowed her to stop her mouth before she spoke of penis size and magic lips.

"Cora." Viktor put his huge hand over her mouth.

She stopped and stared into his eyes, hoping to absorb any wisdom he would impart.

"The Internet has spoken." He moved his face closer to hers. "They love you with Ryder. Good job." After a pause, he removed his hand from her mouth.

"The Internet likes me with Ryder?" As she heard herself say the words she tried to absorb them. The Internet was basically the world, the universe. If the Internet liked her with Ryder, it could really help her major issue...the fact she was unlikable.

"To quote the competition you did not read. They said Ryder made you look like a human." Viktor raised his eyebrows.

She resumed her seat and stared straight ahead. Human was good, she'd never been called that before. "Well, that's good to know. Now let's get to work." Once more her mind wandered to what Ryder was doing at this moment.

"Here." Viktor reached into his suit jacket pocket and brought out several envelopes then placed the invitations in front of her. "You need to choose some to attend."

"Let's just write checks to whatever we need to." Invitations. The bane of her existence. No one liked her, yet everyone insisted on inviting her to functions upon functions. As if they were covered with bugs, she flicked the pile away from her beloved computing devices. After another quick check of the stock numbers, she went to Chargge's main competition. Sure enough, there she and Ryder were under the heading of unlikely coupling.

"If you want to be the CEO of something other than Chargge, you need to get out there." Viktor said. "We discussed this. Your lack of social functions contributes to the fact that most people out there think you are either a robot or a—" Rather than finishing his sentence, he grabbed the stack of invites and began separating them into piles.

"Robot or what?" She scanned the rest of the article which speculated that Ryder got the kinks out of her chain, while she made him get serious.

Viktor didn't respond, only hummed a little tune.

"Robot or what?" Now she strummed her fingers on her keyboard.

Viktor finished off his piles and stared at her. "Bitch."

"Did you just call me a bitch?" Heat ran through her body, and not the good kind like last night.

"You know you're a bitch. I know you're a bitch. The world knows you're a bitch." He slammed a pile of those dreaded invitations in front of her. "We need to prove them wrong, or at least give them an illusion."

"When I was nice, I was soft and couldn't run a corporation. Now I'm a bitch and too hard. The world needs to make up its mind." She snatched up the little pieces of time sucking waste and spread them out in front of her. "Babies, animals and the environment." All three options were sticky, messy and gooey, and she wrinkled her nose.

"Try this one. It's for tonight, this way you don't have to think about it." Viktor picked up the one for the pet rescue. "Also it allows for a plus one."

"Do you have your tux?" At the thought of another wasted night, she ground her teeth together. CEOs needed to work more than they needed to fritter away time at a nonsense event.

"Mine is at the cleaners, but I'm sure Ryder Scott may have one at the ready." Again, Viktor stood.

"I'm sure the man is booked." How could she even entertain the idea of asking Ryder somewhere? Yesterday was merely a fluke, but they couldn't plan anything. Also, he might be involved with one or one hundred women and that just would not work for her. Even considering considered this insanity didn't work for her.

"I think you're forgetting one major thing." Viktor headed toward the door.

Out of the corner of her eye she glanced at him. "And that would be?"

"At the end of the day, you are Mr. Scott's boss." Smiling, the man opened the door.

Her muscles tensed. Would Ryder consider it a date? Would they have sex again? Would he even accept? He wasn't the type who would sing her a romantic song, but he was likable, at least with her. "Get Mr. Scott here for a meeting." She glanced at the invitation then turned to her computer screens to run some algorithms and check the stock numbers again.

Ryder wrapped one of Cora's towels around his waist, draped another around his shoulders, and gave himself a thumbs-up in the fogged over mirror. The only thing wrong with last night was he didn't get to work off his morning hard on with the feisty CEO.

He ran his hands through his still damp hair and made his way back into her bedroom to enjoy the floor to ceiling windows overlooking the city.

Cora's place was truly magnificent, one he could get used to, as easily as he could get used to diving into the billionaire in more ways than one.

He stretched, allowing the towel around his lower half to fall to the ground. As he walked through her place, he tossed the one around his neck aside and entered her kitchen, first spying a note by her espresso machine.

Help yourself to anything in the
refrigerator. Please do not touch the
espresso machine.

-CC

So much for a love letter. It was too soon anyway, she wasn't privy to all his charms yet.

He put one finger on the machine, laughed and the opened her fridge, nodding at her selection of organic juices. After choosing a carrot orange blend, he found a pen on the counter and added a message to hers.

No worries gorgeous, never touch
the stuff, but hopefully I'll be touching
you later.

Satisfied his words were sufficiently seductive, he gave her an autograph and with his juice in tow gathered up his clothes and communication device and returned to the bedroom.

Once redressed, he ignored his various messages and texted his driver.

At the Sierra Towers, need a pick up ASAP.

In less than a minute, he received his response.

Fine, but you still owe me.

Ryder chuckled. His bill was mounting. He needed to throw his buddy a bone.

If you take me to the Bu I will give you a role in my movie that's better than any cash.

He polished off his juice and waited for the reply.

For Malibu the role better be more than a walk on walk off.

Though he wanted to tell his friend that no role was too big or too small, he knew that was all bull.

I'll make sure you get your SAG card.

Be there in ten.

Strange what people would do for a star. They would stop just about anything to help, pay or not. Ryder shrugged, put his juice bottle on the nightstand and went to head out, taking one last look around the little bit of paradise.

At the moment, Cora's castle appeared more like paradise lost.

Surely little miss money bags had some sort of staff to help her with the inconveniences of day-to-day life. Still, he couldn't have her thinking he was a pig. With a little time to spare, he picked up the towels and stripped down the bed, tossing all the linens into the hamper. As he made his way out, he threw away his juice bottle and straightened out the comforter. Hey, no one could say he didn't have what it took to be one of her musical heroes. Voice or not, orgasms and cleaning up had to bode well for him. Of course he did take the time to grab one little souvenir before closing the door behind him. It was always important to commemorate the big moments in one's life.

While the patrons and employees of the building might be movie star friendly, chances were the bushes and area around the famed apartments didn't abide by the same code of ethics. As he headed into the elevator, he took on the typical star stance, lifted his collar, and put on a pair of dark glasses he kept in his suit jacket pocket at all times. Yes, the world could still tell it was him and that was exactly what he wanted, he only needed to appear as if he didn't want to be noticed. They didn't call him an award winning actor for nothing.

He made his way out and into the sunshine, he stopped, shielded his eyes in search for the car right in front of him. He paused and posed to make sure whatever paparazzi lurking around got a good shot and then rushed to the car, disappearing behind the tinted windows.

"Which villa are you populating today, Mr. Scott?" His buddy, driver, and clean up boy, Ben, started the car.

Ryder leaned back on the leather seat. "Ms. Tuttle." He needed to get a car and some clothes, and at this time of day it was unlikely he would run into her.

"So what kind of part do you have planned for me?" Ben maneuvered the vehicle through the Los Angeles traffic.

"Don't worry it will suit you perfectly." He pulled off his sunglasses and reclined on the seat. If he told the truth, he would tell Ben he didn't have the looks of a star, but of a waiter wanting to be a star, or in the case of how they met, an extra wanting to be a star. Still, women might like him with his sweet blue eyes and blonde hair. Hell, the man had more hair than Logan.

"I can hardly wait to get on set. How is the movie going?" Ben fired another question at him.

His movie. His amazing movie. Once completed, it would be an epic tale or adventure and romance that didn't change genres but redefined them. Of course his movie also gave new meaning to the words work in progress. His tale of the human condition had been in production for well over a decade, and it took him the decade before that to write the screenplay. The poor thing had more starts and stops than Los Angeles traffic.

"I'm working on an alternate funding source."

"Dude, you are always working on an alternate funding source. Shouldn't a star like you have plenty of funding?" Ben glanced at him in the rear view mirror.

Lord, he needed to get himself a real limo so he could raise the panel between the driver and the star. Maybe Miss Caine had some insight to such a service. Until then he had to deal with conversation.

The simple answer to Ben's question was yes, he should have plenty of funding. The true answer to Ben's question was he didn't have any funding. He opted for his own creative answer to Ben's question. "You never use your own money for such ventures. Plus, I'm starting a film. I need to check something." With the answer given, he stopped the questioning by shimmying his cell phone out of his pocket.

He scrolled through the message from Logan, and the one from his agent, Brian, and right before he gave up, he hit pay dirt in the form of one Cora Caine. Well, not exactly the woman herself, but close enough.

Mr. Scott, this is Viktor Bobrov, I work with Ms. Caine. She would like you to meet her at her office at 1:00 pm sharp for a meeting. Please confirm.

Points deducted for using her assistant, but points given for making the first move. Now he really needed to get his car. He looked at the time, if he hurried he would be on time, if he went at his own pace, he would get there on California time.

Viktor, please inform Cora I'll be there. Tell her I'm always ready for an impromptu business meeting.

No sooner had he hit send on the message than his phone rang. In this day and age of texting and messaging, an actual call jolted him. He took one glance at the caller ID and fought the urge to hit the dismiss button.

He knew if he didn't answer it would only begin a series of phone calls until he spoke, or worse yet, they would track him down.

Without second-guessing his next move, he answered. "Yes."

"How are you, Ryder?"

The man's voice rattled his eardrum. "Fine, getting ready to go to a meeting."

"I hope it's a meeting about finishing a movie." Glen Orlando, one time friend of his father, businessman, organized crime boss, and general thug, barked into the phone.

Before answering, he turned away from Ben and cupped his hand around his mouth. "I've told you before that I'm working on the movie, I need some more time. Trust me no one wants this movie finished more than I do." If Ryder ever spoke one truth, that last sentence was it. His desperation to finish the flick was what brought him back to the life that killed his father and ruled Ryder's life.

The day he stepped over the threshold into Glen's office five years ago, his chest tightened, but he had to move forward. At that point, he had exhausted all his traditional funding sources including himself, Logan, and banks. His father made him promise that no matter what he would follow his passion.

"Ryder, come in." Tailored suit, cigar hanging out of the corner of his mouth, grey hair combed straight back, Glen motioned to the chair across from his desk. "May I offer my condolences on the passing of your father."

Though it had been several months, the words still cut through him. He felt defective every time someone acknowledged the facts. It was so much better to live in the land of make believe. "Thank you."

"He was a good man." Glen nodded.

Ryder swore he was walking through a old time noir movie set, complete with the one hanging lamp in the center of the room, a couple of thugs strategically standing in a couple of the corners, and even a dame sitting at the edge of the desk.

"Look, it is him." The woman pointed at him. "Will he give me his autograph?"

"Of course, darling." Glen patted her knee and tilted his chair back as Ryder took his seat.

For a moment Glen rocked his chair back and forth and stared at him.

Trained to control his every action, and no stranger to this arena, Ryder put his script in his lap and waited. The man was simply sizing him up, and Ryder couldn't appear to be too anxious. He had to wait until he was asked.

"So, tell us about your movie." Glen continued his rocking.

By this point, his elevator pitch had been perfected. "It's a movie where fact and fiction converge. A time travel fantasy where the hero and heroine visit several different settings taking on several different roles in order to collect the different pieces to create what they feel is a machine that will supply a supreme energy source for the world."

A slow smile grew over Glen's face. "Roles like in movie roles?"

Ryder straightened up. "Exactly.'"

Glen stayed absolutely poker-faced. "What's the title?"

"Working Title." Ryder grinned.

"Well, what's the working title?" Glen asked.

"That's the title." Everyone always reacted the same way. That had to make for excellent publicity." "The title is Working Title."

"Oh, I get it!" The woman clapped.

Glen rubbed his chin and looked around the room.

A couple of the men nodded.

"Here's what we want to do." Glen resumed his rocking.

What Ryder wanted was money, but he needed to bide his time. The checkbook had to be in the drawer. Maybe they would just hand him cash, even better.

"Unlike most who come to us, you have a name." Glen pushed himself out of his chair and stood. "Of course it's a name that we were instrumental in creating."

Though his muscles tightened, he didn't flinch. His father created him, none of these people. Everyone came out of the woodwork the second a celebrity was involved, and he knew better than to contradict him.

"Rather than write you a check and make you pay us back with a small service fee, we have instead decided to go into business with you." Glen came around to the front of the desk and peered down at him. "Your movie will be our first foray into launching a more legitimate business, if you will."

Everyone around the room let out a small chuckle.

"We want a movie, we want your name attached to it." Glen reached into his suit jacket pocket, pulled out a check and held it out to him. "Consider us your producers."

They wanted a movie, he wanted a movie. Their funds would allow it to finally happen. After only a moment's pause, he plucked the check out of Glen's hands. "Consider me your director."

"Then go make something happen." Glen returned to his seat. "Let's discuss the details."

Ryder glanced at the amount. It would be a start. He came there for money and walked out with business partners.

It all seemed so easy.

Didn't everyone say that once they had the check in their hands?

"Ryder, no one said this would be easy." Glen's voice bore through his thoughts, bringing him back to the present. "Here's the deal Ryder. We want to see progress or we want the rights to the movie."

Ryder tightened his grip on the phone, waiting for the "or else." When none came, he took it upon himself to end the conversation. "Our agreement was for a movie and you will get a movie." In no lifetime would he give his movie up.

"Your agreement has deadlines, none of which has been met on your part."

"If you spent a little less time calling me, maybe I could finish." He shut his eyes and saw nothing but black. At the moment he didn't have any sort of movie, he only had movie parts. Long ago he started the age old tradition of robbing Peter to pay Paul, but there were about fifteen other people he robbed, paid, borrowed and lent that created a spiral he didn't really know how to escape except by his charm and good looks. Hell, it worked all these years.

"Ryder." Glen growled into the phone.

He cleared his throat. "Glen, I want to make a movie. I'll call you next week and give you a progress report."

"You better stay in contact." Still without the proverbial "or else" Glen hung up.

"Seems as if the world wants your movie." Ben wound the car through the canyon and around all the multi-million dollar homes until they drove through the gates of one Ms. Tuttle.

"You act as if you're surprised." He ran his hand through his hair as he got ready to face yet another situation.

"Never, boss." Ben stopped in front of the house. "Do you want me to wait for you?"

"No, grabbing some wheels and some clothes, then have to bolt for a meeting." He high-fived Ben. "Catch you later."

"I'm starting to keep a tab of your promises." Ben lifted a tattered notepad.

"Remember, ninety percent of anything is who you know, and you know me." He gave Ben a pat on the shoulder, got out of the car and sauntered around to the side entrance, letting himself in with a key that wasn't nearly as grand as Cora's.

The lack of the security system beeping to be turned off could only mean one thing. Someone else was in the house, and he stopped. "Damn."

Maybe it was only the cleaning crew. He couldn't remember the days they came.

"Ryder, is that you?"

All right. The cleaning crew wasn't here. He would have to face Teresa Tuttle and he plastered his role-winning smile to his face and headed toward the front of the house.

On the divan by the window, with the ocean as her backdrop, lay Teresa Tuttle, not quite a MILF, Ryder would classify more as an OSILF or older sister I'd like to...

"Ryder." Teresa sat up, jolting him out of his acronym.

"Turtle Shell." He began his trek across the room, only to be halted by Ms. Tuttle holding up a tablet computer and a set of car keys. His car keys. Well, her car keys. Actually, the car she bought for him to drive. He didn't want to get too hung up in technicalities. "Ah, my keys, I've been looking for those."

"My keys." She slid the key ring in the cleavage of her dress. "Come take a look at what was all over the Internet today."

Though he already knew, he appeased her, went to her side and plucked the tablet away. "Did you know that Ms. Caine is CEO for Chargge.com?"

"Everyone knows that." Her voice hardened.

He decided to make his small talk even smaller and scanned the story of him and Cora on the front page of her own website. "I think I look all right in that picture. The lighting could have been better."

"Maybe if you would have taken the picture solo, the light would have found your angles," she snarled.

If small talk wouldn't work, he would have to go for big talk, especially since he was on a time constraint. "Cora is the reason the third film being backed by the studio."

"And that is why you were giving her a friendly peck at the party?" Teresa jutted her jaw out.

While the end of this whole thing with his turtle shell had been sitting on the horizon for quite some time, suddenly it sped toward him. The moment they got possessive, it ended, but at the moment, he also needed some wheels and threads. Rather than small or big talk, he went with a different strategy. "What do you want me to do?" Ah, the passive aggressive question, a good old standby.

"I don't know. I knew what I was getting myself into." She sighed and shook her head.

"That's not the Turtle Shell I know." He kneeled down by her feet, slid the tablet under the furniture, and plucked the keys out of her cleavage. "The Turtle Shell I know would know exactly what she wanted."

"I'll tell you what I want, Ryder Ignatius Scott." In a move that even impressed him, she snapped the keys out of his fingers.

Though he wanted to lunge for them, he stayed perfectly, still primed to act. Plus, his reaction time was off as he was still swallowing back the sour taste in his mouth at the use of his middle name.

"I want you to pick a door." She dangled the keys above his head. "Choose the bedroom and the keys and the rest of the trappings are yours to keep, or choose the back door and get the hell out of here with anything that wasn't charged to one of my accounts."

"That's quite a game show." His first thought was to ask if there was a door number three, but he managed to hold back.

The grandfather clock at the far end of the room chimed as if timing his choice. He needed to leave soon to make it to the meeting with Cora, and he stood. "Let's play a game shall we?"

Something told him he was going to be late.

FADE IN:

INT. HOLLYWOOD, CA – ROXY AND WILLIAM'S HOME –
NIGHT.

ROXY – Lies back on the bed with the remote
control in hand. The television flickers in the
background. She glances over and looks at the
time. It's after 2:00 a.m. and she turns off the
television and tries to shut her eyes.

O.S. The sound of a door opening and closing.

Light shines through the room and WILLIAM
enters.

                    ROXY
              Oh!
          (She shields her eyes.)

                    WILLIAM
              Sorry baby, rehearsal ran
              late.
          (He takes off his jacket,
          jeans and pulls his shirt
          over his head.)

                    ROXY
              How did everything go?
          (She sits up in bed.)

WILLIAM joins her in bed and takes her into his
arms.

                    WILLIAM
              It went well, I think we're
              finally making headway on
              the new material.

                    ROXY
          (Sighs)
          Back in the day when we
          were out here trying to
          become actors, who would
          have ever thought you would
          have ended up a rock star?
          Strange how things work
          out.

                    WILLIAM
          It wouldn't have happened
          without you. You were
          always there in the
          sidelines waiting for me.
          (He rubs her shoulder and
          kisses the top of her head.)

ROXY looks up at him and WILLIAM gives her a
deeper kiss.

                    WILLIAM
          (Pulls back and presses his
          hand to her cheek.)
          Tell me that you'll always
          wait for me.

                    ROXY
          Would you wait for me?

                    WILLIAM
          I did and always will.
          (He kisses her.)

FADE

Chapter Four

"I SAY WE TAKE ADVANTAGE of this good fortune." Heather Lewis, Chargge's Director of Corporate Communications, typed away on her laptop. "We have momentum now."

Cora wasn't sure if she would call the Ryder situation good fortune, but her team certainly seemed excited about it, and she and Ryder did have momentum, though she didn't think that needed to be discussed in their meeting. She also wasn't sure why they were having a meeting. The only meeting she needed was with one Ryder Scott to keep...well, to keep the momentum. Where was he anyway? He should be in the waiting room by now.

Giving into a moment of self-indulgence, she opened up a new window on her browser and checked one of her on-line auctions. One of her favorite auction sites just opened up a whole lot of memorabilia from her favorite musical, *Kiss Me Slowly*, a little fairy tale of a story, not much plot, some comedy, memorable tunes and an unlikely love story. She was still the high bidder on all the items, not that she doubted it for a second, but she did wonder what Ryder Scott items were worth. Maybe she could sell him, since he was proving to be useless.

The door to her office shot open and her secretary, Rodger, burst in. "I have your cold brewed coffee. I'm checking the auctions, don't worry." He held up her cup. "Also the Caine-Scott story is still trending on all media, and two of the network stations are covering it tonight on their entertainment shows, and the *National Reporter* just put up a picture of Ryder Scott leaving your place this morning. I called over to Chargge for them to pick it up."

Rather than focusing on momentum, she focused on the missing man who left her apartment, and she stared at the clock with her mouth half open. The world seemed to be flying by her in weird streaks of color. Viktor said Ryder would be here, then where the hell was he? With a sigh, she set her sights on her coffee, resisting snatching it out of her secretary's hand.

"The key here is that there are about three people on the radar to take over the CEO position of Ultracom." Viktor said and stood up to pace around the table. "First, we have Franklin Kryson, the typical choice, Ultracom's CFO, a lifer with the company. Done good things, in fact he was instrumental in having Ultracom buy Chargge. He got married later in life, no kids, has a parrot."

Though she knew this by heart, Cora nodded.

Viktor hit the remote and the screen changed to a plain looking man next to his plain looking wife in a smart pants suit. "Then we have Albert Feiss, CEO of another purchase of Ultracom, News Now. While this man didn't create News Now, he was the one who put the company in the black, is known for being conservative. He has 2.5 kids, a dog, a cat, a wife, and his belt holds up his pot belly."

Cora glanced between the pictures of the two men. There was no reason either one of them wouldn't make a sound choice to lead a multi-billion dollar conglomerate. Honestly, this should be more than a popularity contest.

"Then we have the wild card." Viktor stopped and motioned toward her. "The young woman who redefined how we receive entertainment news. The person who transformed the Internet. The girl whose roots lie in technology."

With Viktor's description, she sat up a little taller. That was right, she changed how people received information, and she deserved to head up such an enterprise. It didn't matter that she didn't have a husband and kids and a resume ten pages long. Actually, it also didn't matter that she started a company in a garage and built it into something grand. Right now all that mattered was the fact she slept with a star. A star she hired. Technically, what she did was completely unethical. How could she live with herself?

"Up until last night, the only thing we had in our way was the lack of connection to the elusive woman," Viktor said. "Her reputation as a straight-laced hard boss preceded her, made it difficult for the world to relate to her. However, now that she has proven she has a life, is like the rest of us, she will be the woman who changes how we view corporate America." Viktor made his way behind her and put his hands on the back of her chair. "Here we have the makings of a superstar CEO."

A shudder went through her and she shot out of her chair. "I had sex with someone who I'm not sure is technically an employee of mine and suddenly the world had opened up for me." She spun on her heel to face Viktor. "I started my business from a blog about Hollywood movies and musicals and earned three degrees to create my company, but because I took Ryder Scott home with me last night and it somehow got documented all on a system that I help put into place, I'm worthy of a job that people would wait a lifetime for?"

Viktor held his hand out, and Rodger handed him her beverage. "Drink," Viktor ordered.

She took a sip of her cold pressed coffee. "I really don't think this was steeped for over twenty-four hours."

"Drink again." Viktor held the straw.

Fine, she took another sip.

"Cora. Listen to me." Victor gave her the cup. "The world wants to have sex. The world wants to have sex with Ryder Scott. You lived the fantasy. Women want to be you, and men want to have sex with the woman who had sex with Ryder Scott. And if in the process that helps the world relate to you and get you the job you deserve, then just like everything else in business, we take advantage of it."

She pursed her lips around the straw and drew up more of the liquid. At most the barista steeped the drink for twenty-two hours, definitely not twenty-four. "Well, we may have to go with some of my other attributes. Ryder is late."

From behind her, Heather gasped.

If the man didn't show, she would personally make his filming experience a waking nightmare, and that thought was exactly why she shouldn't be sleeping with her sort of employees. "What else can I do besides have sex?" She stomped her foot.

The room took on an eerie silence.

Rodger took the drink from her hand. "I'm going to go downstairs and get you a fresh cup and ask Bruno to show me the timer on the coffee."

She stared Viktor down.

"Golf," Heather whispered.

Both she and Viktor faced her communications expert.

Heather swallowed and turned her laptop around.

On the screen was an image of George McAllister, current CEO of Ultracom, in golf clothes on a golf course with golf clubs. Not miniature golf either.

"It is known that Mr. McAllister is going to help choose his predecessor," Heather said. "You know those others are going to get him on the golf course. I think you need to do the same. Play in his sand box, so to speak." Heather pushed her computer closer but backed away.

"I'm more likely to end up in a sand trap." Over the years she tried to learn the game, until the last time she ended up having to pay to have the green repaired after she got a little...competitive.

Without a word, Viktor went to the back of her office and opened the door to the closet, pulling out her clubs and her practice putting green.

After one more glance at the time she stomped over to Viktor and took the putter out of the golf bag.

He smiled and dropped a couple of golf balls at her feet.

"Get out of here and go find a tux. You're my date for tonight." She lined up her shot.

"I don't do charity events." Viktor chuckled.

"I'm done with stars." She slammed her club into the ball. It careened forward and hit the far wall, leaving a mark. "Also call building maintenance."

Viktor leaned down to her ear. "He operates on movie star time. Don't worry."

"I'm not worried." She hit the second ball and created a second mark on the wall. Maybe she needed to envision something other than Ryder's head when making her shot. "Go worry about how to keep up the momentum."

IF THE SKYSCRAPER IN CENTURY CITY that housed CC Enterprises could be the perfect stock photo of a high-rise in late afternoon, Cora's office could easily be a movie set. A perfect representation of the successful young CEO, it was complete with a huge door to get inside, ultra-modern furniture in the waiting room, and a petite cute receptionist at the oversized desk.

The little spinner looked up the moment the door shut behind him, and she bit her lip.

It wasn't every day Ryder Scott walked into any old office building, this much he knew. He struck a bit of a pose and did his best to catch his breath without making it appear as if he ran though the building to get here.

At last he sauntered forward to the long marble counter, the great separator from us and them, leaned over and peered at the girl over his sunglasses.

"May I help you?" Her voice shook and she let out a giggle.

Under different circumstances, he could get this girl back to one of his discreet hideaways and spin away the hours. However, this little one would net him nothing except a great orgasm. Considering he could have that and then some with the woman whose name was on the door, he took his smolder down to mere charming. He needed to save the heat for the woman who would most likely take him down for being two hours late. "The presence of my company has been requested by one Cora Caine."

"Of-of-of course." With her hand trembling, the girl lifted her phone. "We have a visitor for Ms. Caine."

Not used to waiting, he strummed his fingers on the counter.

The girl glanced at him and her cheeks turned an even deeper red. "Yes, it is." She nodded. "All right."

Perhaps he should ask the gatekeepers if they knew how Cora actually meowed when she came, because he did, then maybe they would let him back into the inner sanctum.

Finally the woman hung up the phone and pointed. "Go straight back through the doors, Viktor will take you to Ms. Caine' office."

Really? No request for an autograph? No acknowledgement besides a blush and a giggle? He pushed his sunglasses up and opened his own door only to be met by a man who, if he wasn't in the industry, should definitely consider a life as a character actor. The character: the guy that would quite literally beat the holy shit out of anything that got in his way. In fact, he might be perfect for the action adventure sequence in *Working Title*.

Tall, muscular and tall, wait he thought that already, but this person was large, huge, gigantic. He held his hand out and went with his gut. "Viktor?"

"Mr. Scott." The behemoth glanced at his hand and turned. "Ms. Caine was expecting you two hours ago."

"I got unexpectedly detained." After all the hoops he jumped through, over and under to get here, he didn't need or want to offer an explanation. Exhausted, he didn't understand why Cora couldn't just tell him what she wanted on the phone or text. Wait, there was one thing. The smile that faded in the lobby reappeared, and making a guest appearance, his erection. Thank god he had the foresight to restock his wallet with condoms. Her work had to be stressful and she probably needed at little relief. He let out a chuckle.

Viktor stopped in front of a gleaming black wood door even larger than the one in the entryway, then the giant turned back to Ryder, narrowed his eyes and gave the door one knock before opening it.

Rather than acknowledging a star walked into her office, Cora was bent over with her backside facing him. Well, that could be good too.

"Go in." Victor stood to one side and stared him down.

Fine, he might have rushed past the mammoth and into the room, and he might have exhaled once the door closed behind him leaving him with a much better behind to view, and without Cora seeing him, he might have rubbed his hands together and licked his lips. "I usually don't respond to summons." He stalked toward her.

"I find that hard to believe." She remained hunched over what he recognized as a putting green with one of those little artificial golf holes with a club in her hand.

"Do you golf?" At his question he shook his head.

"I think the answer to that is more than obvious by my current activity." Her abundant hair hung down all around her. She swung the club back and tapped the golf ball. It veered off to the left of the little hole.

"Do you like golfing?" He watched her.

Before answering, she hit the ball once more. This time it not only went left, but way past the hole. "Not particularly." She corralled a third ball.

If nothing else, the woman was extremely focused. A laser was dull compared to her.

At eyeing his opportunity, he did the guy thing went up behind her, pressing their bodies together and placing his hands over hers on the club. "Try to relax."

"Isn't that what golf is for?" Rather than relax, her muscles tensed. "If you tell me to keep my eye on the ball I don't have to tell you where the ball will end up, right?"

"Seriously, you need to relax, you're like a golf robot, and it doesn't work that way." He let go of her hands only to wrangle her hair and hook it over one shoulder.

"Do you know how it works?" As if trying to comply, she tilted her head from side to side.

"By the way someone yelled out my name last night, I didn't think you needed to ask that question." He ran his lips from her ear down to neck. "I have a great way we can both relax."

"Ryder." She shivered.

"Watch this." At the same time he took her earlobe between his teeth, he pulled the putter back and tapped the ball.

His luck intact, the little white ball complied with his wishes and rolled dutifully into the hole. "I'd never tell you to keep your eye on the ball. I would tell you to keep your eye on the prize."

"And just what is that prize?" She scooted another ball over.

"I'll let you have one guess." As he helped her take another shot, he gave her a light kiss in the junction between her neck and shoulder, a particularly tasty spot, especially with the way her perfume swirled around him, a clean scent that reminded him of a fresh breeze.

Again, the ball hit the mark.

"Are you a golfer, Mr. Scott?" At least her voice waivered a little.

He opened his mouth and gave her a more intense kiss. With her, his body took off with only the aid of thoughts and kisses, a much more welcome occurrence than having to rely on concentration and porn to perform. "I played a businessman a couple of years ago in this romantic comedy, you know the type, the thirty-something billionaire, and I had to golf in a few scenes. I went on the course a few times, it's part of my method." He moved his hands to her waist. "I can show you some other methods." Suddenly he had to have her.

"Did I ever tell you about my method?" Right as he slid up to cup her magnificent breasts, she dropped her club and caught his hands, halting his progress.

"I am happy to have you demonstrate your method anytime." Maybe she wanted to set the pace. More than fine by him.

"My method involves having a superstar escort me to a charity function tonight. I need to be seen being nice, apparently acting like a human." She kept a firm hold on him.

"I am even better at making women look good at functions than I am at golf, but not as good as other things." While she might not surrender, he wouldn't give up and kept his hands as far up as she allowed.

"I think your true strong suit lies in charming smiles and a pretty face, and that's exactly what I require tonight." She tapped her foot. "That and not being one minute late. Do I need to repeat myself?"

"Well, if you don't want me to be late, I'd suggest you avail me of a car and or a driver, since due to some unforeseen circumstances I had to take a taxi here." After choosing door number two at Ms. Tuttle's, he gathered up some clothes and walked a couple of miles in order to get a cab. However, the taxi driver didn't charge him, even though Ryder had to make a stop along the way to stash his stuff at his storage facility.

"Tell Viktor what you need. The invitation is on my desk. Be back here at seven. The attire is black tie. I assume you have a clean tuxedo at your disposal." She shook her head.

"I have more tuxedos than you have Internet passwords." He left out the part about the fact he had many tuxedos on permanent loan from various designers when he did photo shoots.

"Good. Then you best be on your way. I prefer my men groomed to perfection. Get rid of the scruff." With her demands out, she swiped his hands off her and walked toward the door.

Wait. Stop the truck. Was he just dismissed? "Cora."

"I have a meeting. Don't be late." Without even a glance in his direction, she left.

No one dismissed him. She basically just called him down to her office to tell him to shave and put a tux on. Not cool.

She could take her function, her driver and her summons and shove it. The next time she called his name it better be because she wanted him back in the bedroom.

He spun on his heel and headed out the way he entered, almost making it to the door before his phone vibrated. With a huff he slid the phone out of his pocket and glanced at the number. Even though he talked with him hours earlier, Glen was calling again. This time Ryder wouldn't answer. The sting of bile rose in his throat, and he hit dismiss before backtracking to her huge glass desk.

He swiped up the invitation and headed out, he needed to go find Viktor and get his of his tuxedoes out of storage.

HOLLYWOOD STARDOM

FADE IN:

INT. HOLLYWOOD, CA - CLUB ON SUNSET BOULEVARD -
NIGHT.

WILLIAM and ROXY sit together at one of the
tables watching the band up on stage and having
a drink.

The set ends and everyone claps.

                    WILLIAM
          Whenever you want we can go
          backstage.

Two girls come over to get WILLIAM'S autograph.
WILLIAM signs their papers and takes a couple of
pictures.

                    ROXY
          It never gets old, does it?
          (She takes a sip of her drink.)

                    WILLIAM
          What doesn't get old?

                    ROXY
          The fans, the people
          wanting you? The
          performance.

                    WILLIAM
          (Takes of gulp of his drink
          and sits back in his chair)
          No. No it doesn't. I see
          now why you wanted a life
          in the spotlight, but the
          spotlight is ours, believe
          me on that.
          (He grabs her hand and
          kisses the back.)

                    ROXY
          I know, I do believe you,
          but it's not the same.

                    WILLIAM
          (Looks into her eyes)
          I want you to try again.

ROXY shakes her head.

                    WILLIAM
          Don't say no. This is the
          life you want. Sometimes I
          feel like I'm living your
          life. Do it now when we
          have the connections.

                    ROXY
          I don't want to live on
          your coattails.

                    WILLIAM
          We're married, we're
          together, you let me
          realize my dream, now I
          want you to do the same.

                    ROXY
          (Pauses, runs her finger
          along the rim of the glass)
          Do you really think I have
          a chance?

                    WILLIAM
          Years ago, I didn't think
          we had a chance and we
          found our way back to each
          other, and look at us now.
          (He leans in and kisses her)
          I think there's always a
          chance.

                ROXY
 Thank you. I'm going to
 try one more time.
 (She gives him a deeper
 kiss.)

Chapter Five

FOR THE SECOND TIME in two days, Cora shoved herself into a dress that though it technically fit still felt like some sort of strange torture device. She supposed breathing was optional when having to go to these events.

After she sent Ryder on his way with Viktor as an insurance policy, she assigned the Rodger the task of going back to her place and retrieving her dress while she got some actual work done.

"You look perfect." As she headed out of her office, Rodger handed her a bejeweled evening bag.

"Thank you." She forced out the words.

Rodger ran ahead and pressed the button for the elevator. "I cleared your schedule for the morning so you are not due in until ten."

Both she and Rodger slipped into the elevator. "Why did you do that?" Rodger really was an excellent assistant, or secretary as he preferred to be called. Actually, the man was magic. Somehow he always seemed one step ahead of her. She opened her bag, where he had supplied everything she needed from her phone to business cards to mints. Wait, there was an extra thing inside. She narrowed her eyes and pulled out a condom.

"Well in case..." The elevator doors slid closed and before she could reach it, Rodger pushed the button. "You know in case..."

"In case of what?" She held the condom up between two fingers and stepped in front of her secretary.

"In case you need to use that." Rodger lifted his chin. "It's my job to anticipate your needs and if last night was any indication, you may need that. In fact, if you don't mind me saying, you do need that."

"I have this aspect of my life handled." She shoved the condom into his hand.

The elevator doors opened. She pushed ahead of Rodger and stomped through the building lobby. In the daytime, the space was jammed and alive, but in the evening, it took on a soothing silence as the energy of the workday dissipated, leaving the area calm and serene.

Without hesitation, she shoved the door leading to the street open and nearly tripped on her own two feet at the sight before her.

Her car was exactly where it should be awaiting her arrival.

However, Ryder wasn't where he should be.

Rather than staying in the car, he was outside in the cool night air leaning against the vehicle with a slight smirk on his face and twirling a single daisy between his fingers.

The scene could almost be one out of a musical. In a perfect world, he would start a song about nothing and everything, and she willed the flutters in her stomach away. There was no doubt about it, the man was truly beautiful.

She turned back to Rodger.

Without looking her in the eye, he passed the condom back to her. "You should have got two." She snuck the now critical accessory back into her purse and went toward the car.

As she approached, Ryder held up one finger.

She stopped and raised her eyebrows, waiting to figure out why they were being detained. Honestly, she simply needed to sit down.

He held out the daisy for her. "I heard this would match your dress perfectly. I picked it myself."

She glanced down to her form fitting yellow dress with silver accents and the flower and took the token, or maybe in Ryder's case, the prop. "Thank you."

"Take a feel." He leaned in and pressed their cheeks together.

Beyond her control, she gasped as his skin grazed against hers.

"Nice and smooth, no scruff," he whispered in her ear. "You'll also notice that I'm early."

At the moment all she noticed was the way shivers coursed through her body.

"Shall we go?" He skimmed his hand down her side and took her hand.

"All right?" Yes, they should go or perhaps they should go to her place and use the tool Rodger gave her. She tugged him toward the car and lunged for the door.

He pulled her back and opened the door for her. "Allow me."

No wonder the man was an actor, since the show he put on was utterly incredible. Finally, she sat down and took a breath, only to have Ryder shimmy in next to her. His cologne swirled around her and she clutched her purse to try to ground herself in some sort of reality with the king of make believe.

Ryder kept hold of her hand, and Viktor gave her a wave. Her mind reeling, she leaned her head back on the headrest and tried to figure out all that happened from yesterday until this second.

"Hard day at the office?" Ryder put his head near hers and faced her.

"Different day at the office." Out of the corner of her eye, she glanced at him. That might be a better way to take him all in.

"So, tell me what my role is tonight."

Role, yes, of course. Fine, she turned and looked at him head on. Big mistake, he was way too gorgeous. Instead of asking what he meant and sounding as if she expected something more than a role, she remained silent.

"You can choose." With his free hand, he moved an errant curl off her forehead. "Is our relationship new? Are we deeply involved? How long have we been together?"

Her mouth opened but she had no words. The fact these thoughts flowed so freely from him concerned her, but of greater concern was the fact she wasn't shocked or horrified. In fact, she was actually considering his questions. Nowadays this was how things worked. There weren't any grand gestures of love, no breathless romance, songs of love and devotion, only deals and orgasms.

"According to all the major news outlets, including your site, we had a little tiff yesterday. Well, I made it look like that." He shrugged. "I think we should go for lovey dovey. We don't want people to think we argue too much."

Seriously, she had nothing to say. Nothing. She barely managed to blink her acknowledgement. At least he thought things through.

"As you know, I have my method. So let me get into character." He licked his lips and without pause curled his free hand around the back of her head and pulled her in for a kiss.

Her strength gone, she didn't even try to resist. The way his lips brushed against hers for a soft kiss left her tingling by the time he pulled back. "You look delectable tonight. I can hardly wait to ravish you later."

And there they had it. The definition of this evening. Some role play for work with the expectation of sex tonight, and hell if she wasn't thinking the same thing.

If nothing else, this beat her other so-called relationships. Those pretended to be something they weren't, and at least she and Ryder had things mapped out and planned, the way she liked it.

Before the whole situation fully sunk in, Viktor pulled up in front of yet another hotel for yet another event. Thankfully, this one didn't have a step and repeat and fanfare. She huffed and reached for the door.

"No." Ryder caught her hand. "Viktor will get it and let me help you out."

She ground her teeth together, but waited for Viktor to put the car in park, get out, come around the car, and open the door on Ryder's side.

"I can get out of a car."

"Well, I beg to differ, since you're doing it all wrong." Ryder got out of the car then reached his hand inside for her. "No more touching doors, Miss Caine."

She dropped her hand in his and let him quote unquote assist her out of the car.

"Smile." He put his arm around her waist and led her toward the hotel entrance.

"There's no one even here except for the hotel staff." Of course, the hotel staff and some other passersby stopped to look at them the second they spotted Ryder. "And gawkers."

He nodded at the people and continued on his trek inside the hotel. "It doesn't matter if there are people around or not, now that we're together and you're up for your big mondo job, always assume there is someone around every corner with a camera."

As she considered his words, she nodded.

"Do you know the charity for tonight's function?"

At his question, she glanced up at him, but didn't speak.

"We're at the California Animal Partners." He guided her around. "Always know the name of the charity, you never know who will ask."

She pursed her lips and narrowed her eyes. The man was right.

"And get rid of your resting bitch face. You're with me, and you should be thrilled or euphoric." He glanced down at her and winked. "Just envision the orgasm you are going to have later."

Her cheeks heated, and she stared straight ahead.

"Ah, resting orgasm face, much better." He whipped the invitation out of his tuxedo pocket, put his hand on the small of her back, and handed it to the woman at the doors to the ballroom. "Cora Caine and Ryder Scott."

"You certainly are." The older woman beamed at him, giggled and stepped closer to them. "May I tell you what a huge fan I am?"

"I give you my permission." Ryder chuckled.

Cora swallowed back the sour taste forming in her mouth.

The woman let out another giggle. "I'm a huge fan, and I can hardly wait to see you as William again."

"Both William and I thank you."

The woman went into another round of nervous laughter and held out the invitation. "Do you mind?"

Though Cora wanted to grind her teeth or tap her foot, she made sure not to move. She didn't want to have any bitchy face or whatever Ryder called it.

"It would be my honor, Mrs...." He drew out the word, giving the woman a place to fill in the blank.

"Mrs. Laura Parson." The woman shifted her weight from one foot to the other as if she needed to go to the restroom.

Ryder swiped a pen out of his magic tuxedo pocket, signed the back of the invitation, including personalizing it, and gave it back to the lady. "I think we should head in now."

"Thank you, of course." The woman hugged the invitation. "Table thirty-one."

Without missing a beat, he kept his arm around her and entered, glided toward table thirty-one, doing his nodding thing, shaking a couple of hands along the way, and finally pulling out her chair for her.

The rumbles around their table started the second Ryder took his seat. He signed a couple more autographs and made a little small talk before settling down with his arm around the back of her chair. The man was nothing, if not personable. In fact, one of the best things about being with Ryder, aside from the orgasms, was she didn't have to do any of the things he was doing, like talk or be nice. This was great.

With newfound time on her hands, she opened her purse and reached in for her phone. Might as well check her email and such.

Ryder put his hand over hers, pushed the phone back inside its confines, and continued his conversation.

Cora listened to the chatter, becoming lost in the rhythm of Ryder's voice, and the way his fingers played with hers.

The talk died down and with his nose, he moved her hair away from her ear. "How am I doing?"

Before answering, she rewound the last few minutes. "I actually don't know how you do it."

"How I do what?" He punctuated his sentence by kissing her earlobe.

She crossed her legs and clenched her thighs together. The man knew exactly what he was doing on many, many counts. "Be so gracious with the constant clamoring for your attention and the interruptions."

"This is part of life in the public. If you don't do these things, you get labeled as a jerk or a bitch, and we can't have that. People like you and I need other people to do our bidding." As if on cue, the dinner service started and the waiter placed a plate of the traditional rubber chicken with sauce in front of them, complete with limp vegetables and some sort of starch.

Now acutely aware of her own facial expressions, Cora fought the urge to wrinkle her nose or make any other sort of face, but honestly even the thought of a Ryder induced orgasm couldn't blunt the meal. No doubt Ryder would dig right in as if this were some great delicacy.

"Excuse me." Ryder lifted his hand and no less than two waiters rushed to his side.

"Sir, is there something I can help you with?" One of the servers leaned down.

"Not only is this a charity function for animals, but I happen to be a vegan. Might you have something else?" He glanced over at her. "For both me and the lady?"

"Of course, sir." Within an instant the waiters cleared their dishes and dashed away.

"Vegan?" She realized she never really ate any food with Ryder. Truth be told she could have gone for a steak.

"I'm going to get us a couple of drinks. No phones and smile." He let go of her hand and left, straightening his tux as he walked away.

Fine, she sort of didn't want him to leave, and she spent a lingering second watching him as he stopped and signed yet another autograph then even posed for a picture.

A touch on her shoulder interrupted her reverie, and she turned, gasping at some woman with way too much jewelry and orange lipstick smiling at her. "Yes?" Where was Ryder to speak when she needed him?

"So tell me, is he as wonderful in private as he is in public?" The woman's smile grew, reminding Cora of a pumpkin or maybe a clown.

Under normal circumstances, she would have nodded and not answered, or maybe even lifted her phone. How dare anyone ask about her personal life, even if somehow her personal life became public. Still, what kind of question was that?

Before she opened her mouth, the day she had replayed in her mind. How people liked her with Ryder, how she was human and more likable. Humans spoke, that's what they did, and she took a breath. "Even better."

The woman laughed and motioned for to come closer.

Curiosity and the need to comply with everyone's wishes made her lean in.

"So, if you don't mind me asking, how much does a man like Ryder Scott cost?" The woman elbowed her.

Something told Cora this woman wasn't after what it cost to cast the star in *Hollywood Stardom*. "Cost?"

"Rumor has it that he's always bought and paid for and he's well worth it." The woman cupped her hand around her mouth. "I say whatever you had to pay was a bargain."

In order to process the information, she turned away to find Ryder walking toward her with two glasses of wine.

He returned to the table, handed her a glass, and tapped his goblet against hers. "Something not nearly as sweet as you."

With her eyes fixed on him, she took a sip of the fruity wine.

He sat next to her, kissed her cheek and once more began speaking to the others at the table.

She tore her focus away from him and glanced around the room. A couple of people lifted their cell phones and snapped pictures, exactly like Ryder said they would. No doubt those snapshots would end up on her own website tomorrow.

With him she was liked, human and relatable. The woman who had it all, and he made it easy.

After taking another taste of her wine she turned back to the lady. "Nothing worth having is cheap in this world." She laced her arm in Ryder's. No, nothing was cheap, but the one thing she learned since her company went public was that everything was for sale, especially today's leading men.

HOLLYWOOD STARDOM

FADE IN:

INT. LOS ANGELES, CA – WILLIAM'S AGENT'S OFFICE
– DAY.

A secretary leads ROXY into a posh office lined
with awards and gold records.

KAREN, WILLIAM'S AGENT – Middle aged stylish
woman stands when ROXY enters and the two women
hug.

                    KAREN
          Good to see you.

                    ROXY
          You too, thanks for seeing
          me at such short notice.

Both ROXY and KAREN sit.

                    KAREN
          (Smiles and types something
          on a computer)
          William said you wanted to
          try again.

                    ROXY
          It's my dream.

                    KAREN
          (Typing in the computer)
          It's everyone's dream, you
          just have a one up on
          everyone.

                    ROXY
          (Reaches into her bag)
          I have my updated resume.

                    KAREN
(Shakes her head and points
to the computer screen)
 I can get you booked as a
 streetwalker on Crime Today
 or there is a position
 opening up as a plaintiff
 whose little boy got bit by
 a dog on one of those court
 shows. Of course, in a
 couple of months we're
 going to start filming your
 husband's video, and you
 always have a part there.

                    ROXY
(Shifts in her seat)
 Just like that I can have a
 part?

                    KAREN
 For William, of course.
 Anytime. Just let me know.
 I know it's hard to be the
 wife. These little roles
 will keep you busy and give
 you some pocket change.
 I'm surprised you didn't
 come to me sooner.

                    ROXY
(Shrugs)
 Lately I just wanted
 something more.

                    KAREN
 As I said, I understand.
 The wife plays the ultimate
 role, but William made sure
 I would take care of you.
 This business is all about
 who you know. Just let me
 know where you want to
 start.

                    ROXY
(Looks down at her resume
and then crumples it in her
hand)
 I'll take the streetwalker,
 it seems to fit me better.

                    KAREN
(Laughs and types into the
computer)
 It's all yours.

Chapter Six

ONCE AGAIN, RYDER had been summoned to the office of one Cora Caine after waking up in her bed alone. All he had to guide him was another reminder note not to touch her espresso machine and a cryptic text that she wanted to see him at eleven sharp to discuss a proposal. Of course, that came after the not so cryptic text from Glen reminding him that he better be making some progress on the movie.

He chose to delete the message from Glen and focus on the task at hand, so to speak. That task being that if he and Cora were going to continue on like this, he didn't want to have to use his hand in the morning. She needed to get with the program. Yes, she might be running the Internet or whatever she did, but his morning glory needed attention, then she could go do her thing.

"Do you think you can sort of skirt around the traffic?" Ryder clenched his fist and called to Ben from the back seat of the car in a forced singsong voice. Something told him he couldn't be late for this meeting. That something was Cora yesterday when she told him not to be one minute late.

"How would you like me to do that?" Ben scooted the car up like two inches to be stopped by a red light. "We're in Los Angeles."

"Well, Los Angeles is the land of magic. Transport us there that way." Ryder barely got the words out between gritted teeth. He ran his hand through his hair. "Seriously, as a professional in the transportation area, a cornerstone in making this great city what it is, can't you do anything to make sure I show up at this very important powwow during my lifetime?"

"I'll get you there." The second the light turned green Ben hit the accelerator. "How was the event last night? I saw you on the Internet."

The event. What struck him most about the event was the copious amount of checks written. Cora's check alone was five figures. The rich loved to give money as long as there was a photo opportunity and tax write-off attached. He chose to focus on the woman by his side rather than the utter waste of monies. Hell, he should start a charity for his movie.

"Let's get a move on." Ryder sat back as his minion wove through traffic, ran yellow lights, honked and cut off a pedestrian. The man was nothing if not dedicated.

"We're here, boss." The car bounced when Ben skidded to a stop in the underground parking of the building that housed Cora's corporate headquarters.

Lights flashing, a police motorcycle pulled up behind them.

"You did a great job." Ryder glanced at his watch. With minutes to spare, he opened the door himself and got out. He nodded to the police officer getting off the motorcycle.

"You're Ryder Scott." Pen in hand the officer pointed to him.

"I am, and I'm sorry about my driver. He's a little enthusiastic to make sure I get where I need to be." He flashed the man a smile, plucked the pen out of his hand and found a piece of paper in his pocket. After checking the paper didn't have any sort of incriminating evidence, he signed his name. "I take it I can get to my meeting?" He returned the pen to the officer and handed him the autograph.

"Go ahead." The officer clipped the treasure to the clipboard and made his way to Ben's side of the car.

"Boss!" Ben cried out.

Checking his watch once more, he figured he could spare ten seconds. He leaned back in the car. "If you can talk your way out of this one, I'll get you an even bigger part in my movie." With a wink and smile, he patted the top of the car, made his way into the building, and snuck through the crowd of people sliding ahead into one of the elevators.

People stopped and stared, but because this was a building used for high-end deals in the entertainment industry, people didn't bother him, only pointed and whispered. At least the ride up gave him a moment to collect his thoughts. No doubt this would be the so-called meeting where Cora admitted her feelings for him.

The elevator doors opened and he smiled. Miss CEO and he made a true power couple. Compatible in bed, mind, and prestige, if they put their energy together, they could light up a city. In truth, he wouldn't mind taking her out on a non-business related function and showing her off.

He would let her blush and stutter, but in the end he would give her what she wanted, because hell, he wanted it too. For once in his life, he wanted it. Sure it was fast. He blamed it on high-speed Internet access and he was on the fast track.

A spring in his step, he made his way inside CC Enterprises.

Instead of the spinner at the door, he was met with a man around his age, tall, with slicked back brown hair, who he sort of recognized from the night before.

"I was instructed to lock the doors at one minute past the hour. Good job, you're thirty seconds early." The man held his hand out. "Rodger, Cora's secretary."

Ryder shook the man's hand. "Don't you mean assistant?"

"Is there anything wrong with being a secretary? That's what I am." Rodger led him through the office.

"No not at all. It's sort of refreshing." Ryder filed that little tidbit away.

Rodger knocked on the Cora's door, opened it, and tilted his head.

Ryder gave Cora's secretary a nod and went inside the inner sanctum.

The door closed behind him.

Talk about refreshing. His mouth watered at the sight of her behind her desk with all her monitors, her hair flowing down around her and in a tight, low cut, but work appropriate, knit top. Strange, as powerful and smart as this woman was, he never felt like more of a man these last couple of days.

"Come here." Without glancing at him, she held her hand up and motioned him over.

"You know, one of these mornings it'd be nice to wake up with you." He crossed the room, took her hand and kissed the back.

"Well, I'll take that under advisement." A small laugh actually escaped her throat. Who knew the woman had it in her? "I want to show you something." She pulled him down.

He knelt by her chair. On the screens were Chargge.com as well as the sites of two top competitors to the massive website. All had stories about Ryder and Cora.

"We have been trending two days in a row." She clicked to another site that showed a graph.

"The movie star and the money star, what isn't fascinating about us?" Though he didn't really get all the bars on the graph, it seemed impressive, and he nodded. "Seems the public likes us together, I must say I concur."

"For once, Mr. Scott, I must say I agree with you as well." She slid her hand away from his and pointed to the chair on the other side of her desk. "Sit down."

Fine, she was going to play it cool. He could follow suit. Rather than complain, he decided to remind her why she conjured him and gave her a soft kiss on the cheek, grazing the corner of her mouth, before taking his seat.

She continued studying the computer screens, clicking her mouse hither and yon, and right before he was about to clear his voice, or say something, she slid her chair over and stared at him.

It seemed fitting he stared back, only he added a wink and crossed his legs.

With her eyes slightly narrowed, she picked up a letter opener on her desk, twirled it in her fingers and rocked her chair back and forth.

He raised his eyebrows. "I did a movie once where the heroine killed the bad guy with a letter opener."

"I promise you I would never use such a messy weapon." A low chuckle escaped her throat.

"What would you use?" Watching her was better than any action-adventure flick, except for *Working Title* when it finally made it to the big screen.

"My mind." She put the letter opener down and leaned forward. "I can see why you're a star."

The first break in her armor appeared and he could hardly wait to see her crumble. "Aw shucks, ma'am I may make a fan out of you yet." He used his best southern drawl.

"So, let's get down to business." She never faltered from her hard facade.

Here it came. He waited. At last his tough chick would crack her shell.

"Tell me exactly how it works." Rather than the letter opener she picked up a pen.

He opened his mouth to tell her he wanted to be with her too, calm her and soothe her, then realized he had no idea how to respond because she didn't follow the script. Was this her way of saying she wanted an afternoon delight? "I have to tell you that you're a master of how it works, but if you need a little refresher I'm happy to demonstrate." Grinning, he stood. Pushing her right over her desk should do the trick.

She held up her hand, stopping him. "I already know how well you do in that arena, and while you're phenomenal, I don't need a reminder at the moment. What I need to know is how this works. Is it a formal arrangement with a contract, or do we do the civil thing, discuss what we want and go on the honor code?"

Was she asking him to marry her? He looked up at the ceiling. Her text did say proposal, and he considered the possibilities. Gorgeous home, gorgeous girl, great sex, lots of money. He already wanted to date her and be with her, so they might as well go for it. At last he found a match. "What do you think?"

"I would rather not go into contract negotiations, that smacks too much of a job. However, I do need a man and the public loves us together. On my end, I want you to take me to my events...satisfy me." She stood and paced along the back of her office. "What do you want on your end? Clothes, credit cards, country clubs?"

And now he understood. A sick calm overtook him. Apparently his reputation preceded him. Before reacting, he weighed his options, whether to walk out, jump like a kid a Christmas as he had done so many other times, or take advantage as he had done more times than jump.

First, he took a moment to mourn the woman he wanted to ask on a date and actually pay for the meal. The one he almost considered taking a walk on the beach with, and doing those things simply because he wanted to. In fact, she did him a favor because he would get to do what he wanted and benefit as well.

"How much time do you need?" He chose his path, the most obvious route. *Why did everyone always make it so incredibly easy?*

She stopped her trek back and forth across her office, blinked, took a breath and returned to her desk. "Do you have a menu of services?"

"You're a special woman, so why don't we create a deluxe package for you?" He put his hands behind his head and his legs up on her desk.

"All right." Once more she got up, this time coming around her desk, sitting at the edge and pushing his feet off. "I want it all, with two major rules."

He kept his eyes on her, waiting to hear her conditions.

"First." She held up one finger. "No philandering, flirting, or anything else with anyone else. The second I suspect or prove a suspicion, all bets are off."

If she only knew what he thought he was coming here for. If she only knew that yesterday he walked away from a pretty sweet deal all because it felt wrong to sleep with Ms. Tuttle and her at the same time. If she only knew... Rather than speak, he lifted his chin.

"Second." A second finger joined her first. "You will do nothing that will hurt my chances of becoming CEO of Ultracom. Don't think I won't know. I'm a technology goddess with thousands of people, the best of the best, at my command. You are duly warned."

Her words sent a slight shiver down his spine, but he preferred to call it a tingle of excitement, a challenge. "I thought my job was to help you get your job."

A smile lit her face up. Dare he say she looked gorgeous?

"I have no problem with everything you want." Though he wondered how good her technology really worked. Good thing for him people like Glen lived beyond technology. "Especially, since I'll be so busy with *Hollywood Stardom* and the fact that you'll be funding my magnum opus." His father always said things just happened to him out of nowhere, and once again, his father was proved right. Things were happening all over the place.

"Your movie." She nodded. "Is that before or after the clothes and the country club?"

"Sweetheart, I know you want to dress me up, and we both know the country club is for you as well as compensation for my help in fixing your..." he motioned toward her, "fixing you."

Her jaw jutted out, but she didn't argue.

"It will be after the car." If he smoked, it would be the time to take a long drag and relaxed.

They stared at one another, after quite a pause, she put her hand out. "Does a shake suffice?"

He took her hand and pulled her to his lap. "This is more than a gentleman's agreement." He curled his arm around her and kissed her. His erection swelled when she kissed him back, took the lead and slipped him the tongue.

Right as he went to sneak his hand between her legs, she pulled back. "Before we solidify our relationship, I think you need to go clean up any messes you've made and cut any ties. I assume it's all right if I tell the studio to deliver your latest script to my place."

"Don't you mean our place?" He chuckled and brushed his lips against hers. "We live together now, it's more than all right."

"I'll have keys and cards for you tonight." She got up off his lap and pressed a button on her desk. "Until then."

The door opened and Rodger entered, carrying her iced coffee. "Yes, Cora?"

"Mr. Scott needs some help moving into Sierra Towers with me. He needs to run some errands and close some doors." She returned to her chair behind the desk. "Please help him take care of anything he needs."

"Of course. I'll be ready in ten minutes." Rodger nodded and put the cup on her desk. "I personally checked the brew time." As fast as he entered, he left.

"I'll work on your car issue and do some research." She sipped her drink and turned to her monitors. "Be done by six, I'm sure that's enough time."

"All right." He went to her side.

"Get me a script to your movie." She typed away at the keyboard.

"I need to make some revisions before you see it." When faced with the last person who could help dig him out of the hole, he needed to make sure his script was in tiptop shape. "Anything else?" He stared down at her gorgeous hair.

"I need to get back to work."

For a few moments, he watched her click around the screens and lifted her letter opener. "May I have this?"

Her brow furrowed, she tore her focus away from her machines and glanced up at him.

"I love souvenirs." He winked.

"Sure." With a shrug she returned to her technology.

He kissed her cheek. "Later we'll celebrate." As he left, he grazed his hand down her arm and shook his head.

"Still trending." Her voice echoed through the office.

He put his hand on the doorknob and stifled a laugh. Normally women approached him wanting more. Even if they called it an arrangement, they still wanted the relationship. He always bested them and got what he wanted.

Why did he feel that this time he might have been bested?

No, couldn't be. He was the best of the bunch. This time it was just more of a challenge. "See you at six, dear."

<u>HOLLYWOOD STARDOM</u>

FADE IN:

INT.HOLLYWOOD, CA – STUDIO SOUND STAGE – DAY.

ROXY, dressed like a typical streetwalker, walks
around a set of a swanky hotel room with an
actor dressed as a police officer.

> DIRECTOR (O.S.)
> Everyone on their mark.
> Action!

> STAGEHAND (O.S.)
> Hooker take three.

O.S. Clapperboard snaps.

> POLICE OFFICER
> Miss Murphy, all we are
> asking is where you were
> right before you walked
> into this hotel room.

> ROXY AS STREET WALKER
> (Puts hands on her hips)
> I know what you're getting
> at. Why would I call the
> police if I was trying to
> hide something? I told you
> I was with a boyfriend
> that's it.

> DIRECTOR (O.S.)
> Cut! Roxy!

ROXY presses her lips together.

                    DIRECTOR
          (Joins them on stage and
          goes to ROXY)
           Roxy, I need you to have a
           little bit more attitude.
           I really want hooker to
           come across in your
           delivery.

                    ROXY
           If she were trying to be
           discreet would she be so
           overtly a prostitute?

                    DIRECTOR
          (Steps closer)
           Listen here, we expanded
           this role because the
           producer's a fan of your
           husband. We were supposed
           be done filming this tiny
           segment two hours ago and
           you're still in two more
           scenes. You don't
           understand how much work
           goes in to getting
           everything. Deliver the
           line as I told you and
           you'll get your acting
           credit. Understand?

ROXY pauses and then nods.

                    DIRECTOR
           I know you've heard this
           one before, but I can't
           tell you how many people
           would die for this chance.

ROXY nods again.

                    DIRECTOR
          Great!
          (Pats ROXY)
          All right everyone, let's
          get going.
          (Director steps O.S.)

ROXY motions to stagehand passing by.

                    ROXY
          Do you have a piece of gum?

STAGEHAND hands her piece of gum.

ROXY shoves gum into her mouth and starts
chewing.

                    DIRECTOR (O.S.)
          All right everyone, action!
          Action!

                    STAGEHAND (O.S.)
          Hooker, take three.

O.S. Clapperboard snaps.

                    POLICE OFFICER
          Miss Murphy, all we are
          asking is where you were
          right before you walked
          into this hotel room.

                ROXY AS STREET WALKER
          (Puts hands on her hips,
          snaps her gum and taps her
          foot)
          I know what you're getting
          at. Why would I call the
          police if I was trying to
          hide something? I told you
          I was with a boyfriend
          that's it.

                POLICE OFFICER
          Because you're smart enough
          to cover your tracks.

          ROXY AS STREET WALKER
            Prove it.
          (She flips her hair and
          walks off stage.)

                DIRECTOR (O.S.)
          Cut! Print! See Roxy?
          You just have to play the
          game.

ROXY turns back, looks at the soundstage and
shrugs.

Chapter Seven

IT WAS THE PAUSE that caught Cora's attention first.

A slight pause occurred the moment she hit enter on one of the programs for Chargge.com's backend maintenance, something not many would have noticed, but it was a pause nevertheless.

Her software didn't pause. At least it didn't pause unless she authorized it to pause. The only reason for such a delay would be someone working on the system, something else she didn't authorize.

Just to make sure she wasn't still foggy after her Ryder extravaganza last night, she closed the program, reopened it and attempted to run a statistical analysis on hits.

She hit enter.

The screen should flash and in less than two seconds she should have her graph.

One Mississippi.

Two Mississippi.

She gulped down some coffee.

Three Mississippi.

Four Mississippi.

The screen finally began to reload.

Five Mississippi.

By the time she got her report, she could sail down the Mississippi river while she leisurely sipped a cocktail.

She stopped counting, tossed her empty cup aside, and hit her intercom. "Viktor!"

In less time than this damn report was taking to generate, Viktor rushed inside her office. "What is it?"

"Look." She leaned back and pointed at the screen. Still, she wasn't treated to a graph. "We are going on almost thirty seconds."

"Not possible." He moved in and went to the other computer on her desk. "Let's run a password report."

Viktor's huge fingers flew over the keys. With a bit of a flourish, he hit enter. A groan escaped his throat and he shook his head. "Someone is trying to hack Chargge."

Though she suspected the same thing the second her program paused, at hearing Viktor voice her fears, her face heated, and she broke out into a sweat. She gathered up her hair and held it up away from her neck. "I want to go to Chargge."

"We can fix it here." Viktor put his hands over the keyboard as if ready to type. "I can call over."

"No, in person is always better." She kicked off the heels she wore for Ryder's benefit and slipped on her flats. "People have years of emails, everything on our servers, and I want to be right there at ground zero until it's fixed."

"Let's go." Viktor led the way.

No sooner did she slide into the front seat of the car than her phone rang. "Ryder is calling me." She hated the way her chest tightened. What if he wanted out of their deal? They hadn't even begun.

"Are we going?" Victor put the key in the ignition.

"Didn't I just say that?" She motioned forward and answered the phone. "Cora Caine." Yes, she purposely used her work voice and greeting. Truth be told she didn't have any other voice or greeting.

"My, my aren't we official?" Ryder chuckled. "Since our social status has changed, and I know what you look like gloriously naked, you can just answer hello with a little breathy undertone."

With his words she allowed herself to exhale. She gave a sideways glance to Viktor. "I will take that under advisement."

"Oh, you're at work. Okay, no sexy talk, I get it. I had a question."

"All right. Ask." She rubbed her hand over her eyes.

"May I drive the car? Rodger is, how shall I say this? Driving a little slow." He lowered his voice.

"No, you may not drive the car until you're on our insurance. Sit back and enjoy being driven by a professional." Did they really need to have this conversation?

"Rodger is a professional driver?" Ryder asked.

"Yes. Is that all?" At the pounding taking residence in the center of her forehead, she squeezed the bridge of her nose.

"You sound tense, well more tense than normal," he continued. "Everything okay there?"

"I just have to take care of some things over at Chargge." Why they were talking about this was beyond her.

"I think you have a headache. I'll get rid of it for you later. If you can't wait, take two aspirin, but only aspirin until I get you the proper remedies, including me." His tone was sexy, almost hypnotic.

Only because they were stuck three red lights from her other office, and he somehow knew she had a headache did she ask the next question. "How do you get rid of headaches?"

"It's an art baby, one that you will be privy to later. I'll let you go."

She only hoped it involved some sort of sex. "Get your tasks done. Goodbye."

Before she even had a chance to take a breath, they pulled up to the Chargge.com offices. "I need to get Ryder mobile or Rodger will run him over, but he's just going to have to wait until I have time." She didn't even want to picture what her secretary's day would be like doing whatever Ryder did.

"I will put that on my to-do list." Viktor got out of the car.

She followed. "We also need to get him a key to the apartment and on the fingerprint scanner, and let security know he's a resident now."

Viktor got out his cellphone and began taking notes.

"Also, I need to know what he likes to drink and eat." They ran through the lobby of the building. "What else do you need to keep a human alive?"

In a sudden move, Viktor stopped and spun toward her.

Though she tried to skid to a stop, she banged into him anyway.

He caught her by the shoulders and held her at arms' length. "You can't keep a plant alive."

"I can keep my business alive." Through everything, she needed to keep Ryder alive as well, and it all seemed a bit overwhelming. "I wonder if he uses any special male things. I never lived with a man before."

They both looked each other.

"Let's go to work." She broke the uncomfortable silence.

"Good, I really don't want to think of Ryder's special male things," Viktor mumbled.

Unsure how she felt about knowing about Ryder's special male things, she rushed in front of Viktor into Chargge's main office. Ryder or not, she had work.

All three of her employees in the front shot up.

One of the girls dropped some papers. "Miss Caine, we weren't expecting you."

"You should always be expecting me, then you won't be startled when I arrive." She shook her head. "I'll be in the war room. Send Matthew Sumner to me and find out if Ivy Alexander is in the building." Without waiting for a response, she continued on her march. Out of the corner of her eye, she saw her employees stand or freeze, heard them gasp or whisper. She wished they would just continue their work.

At last she came to the war room, the room off the warehouse that housed their servers, where the main programming meetings took place. She sat at the small conference table and pulled her personal laptop out of her bag, logging onto the main system right as Matthew Sumner, their lead programmer, ran inside.

"Cora." Laptop under his arm, he shut the door and slid by her side. "I noticed it too. If you check your email, I sent you a report about servers running slow, and I asked for approval to do a password analysis."

Maybe if she had been thinking of work rather than Ryder's male things she would have seen the email. Before she spoke, she logged onto her email. Sure enough right around the time she and Viktor were driving here, the email arrived. He followed the rules perfectly.

"Switch to the backup servers and swipe the main ones clean. We have plenty of redundancies built into the system so the threat of going down is merely that, a threat." She stared up at the ceiling and ran the protocol through her mind. "Have everyone do a password update. Run an IP analysis if anyone was stupid enough to leave any DNA behind."

Both Viktor and Matthew typed away on their respective machines.

"Above all else, make sure nothing is breeched. I refuse to end up in the media with someone leaking emails or anything else." Even making a sex tape with Ryder Scott and posting it on her site couldn't fix that situation. "I'll be staying here until we are safely on the other server, and all the systems have been checked by me."

Matthew nodded and both he and Viktor continued their work.

At a light knock on the door, she held her hand up, stopping the men from moving. She opened the door to Ivy Alexander.

"The girls at the front said you asked for me?" Ivy didn't look her directly in the eye.

"Yes, come in. Close the door behind you." Cora turned on her heel and went to the end of the conference table far away from the men.

Ivy followed and once seated waved to Matthew. Word on the street had it the two used to date or something, Cora wasn't really sure, all she knew was she just received Matthew's wedding invitation to a woman named Bambi who evidently worked for Drew Fulton. Ugh. It sounded like an incestuous soap opera.

"Is everything all right?" Ivy crossed her legs and fiddled with the hem of what appeared to be a vintage 1960s dress.

If Cora had a penny for every time someone asked her that question the second they sat down in front of her, she would have another billion dollars in her account. "Has something happened that would make things not all right?"

Ivy sat back. "Well, considering you have never truly talked to me, and only talked to my husband, I think it's a valid question."

Finally, someone who had a reason for asking. "Fair enough." Cora couldn't stop a slight smile. "Everything's fine." She supposed a little small talk was in order. "Are you ready to start shooting next week?"

"I have only a small part, but yes." Ivy beamed at her. "We're going to cover the shoot for Chargge as well."

All right, enough chatter. "I have a question for you."

Ivy widened her eyes. "All right."

Before leaning in to her new confidant, Cora glanced over at the men. With them still working, she went for it. "Do you know anything about Ryder?"

"Something tells me you know much more about him than I do." Ivy's eyes sparkled.

With a huff, she continued. "Aside from that, is there anything I should know about the care and feeding of him?"

"As far as food, he's a vegan and likes pancakes." Ivy pressed her lips together, then covered her mouth and coughed. "As far as care, I have heard Logan describe him as..."

Cora held her breath waiting to hear what one Mr. Alexander had to say about her new bedmate and her phone rang. Again, Ryder. She held up one finger to Ivy telling her to wait, and answered. "Cora Caine."

"Ryder Scott." His deep voice vibrated through the phone. "I have a question for you."

"Seems to be a theme. What do you need?" She did her best not to glance in Ivy's direction.

"First, I wanted to know what name comes up when I call you. Is it just Ryder? My initials, a heart?"

"This is why you called me?" What was with all the senseless conversation today?

"No, that just popped into my head when I called you. Now I want to know." He laughed.

She quickly glanced at her phone and put it back to her ear. "It says Ryder Scott." Out of the corner of her eye she saw Ivy straighten up. "What does mine say?" At her question she ground her teeth together.

"CC."

Her heart betrayed her and sped a little at the nickname he bestowed upon her and the blunt way he said it. Not that other people hadn't called her that before, or that her business wasn't named CC Enterprises, his way just had more flair. "Very well, what did you need?"

"I'm calling to ask if I can drive the car." His voice turned flat.

"Didn't we have this discussion already?" she asked.

"Yes, I wanted a different answer so I called back."

"Do I sound like a woman who would change her mind?" Though she tried not to look, she did catch Ivy giving her a thumbs-up.

"You changed your mind about me, and look we're moving in together." Another chuckle escaped from the famous man on the phone.

"I have to go. I have work." Without saying goodbye, she hung up and faced Ivy. "Now back to the matter at hand."

"Cora, I need you to authorize the transfer." Viktor interrupted her talk and pushed her laptop across the table.

Thankfully, she stopped herself from snapping at Viktor. Instead, she looked over the work and entered the password.

Again, she turned to Ivy.

Again, her phone rang.

Again, it was Ryder.

"Excuse me." Cora practically hit the phone. "Cora Caine."

"May I please have permission to drive the car?"

The voice that almost made her swoon before now grated on her, and she balled her hand in a fist. "Ryder."

"They say the third times a charm."

"The third time will get you a definitive no." She sighed.

"It didn't last night."

"Goodbye, Ryder I'll see you later." This was whom the public liked?

"How will I know where to meet you?"

At last she smiled. "Rodger will drive you." Again, she hung up and turned her attention back to Ivy.

Ivy gave her a grin. "Logan calls him a high maintenance pompous ass who always gets what he wants."

With a nod, she motioned to Viktor. "We have to get Mr. Scott some sort of car tonight, and I don't have time to go car shopping." Logan's description seemed to be spot on. "Also, find a place that serves vegan pancakes and strong coffee." What had she done?

RYDER HUNG UP THE PHONE and turned to his new nemesis, the slow driving secretary. "Let's go get my stuff then greet my public."

"Your public is at a storage facility?" Iced tea in hand, Rodger followed him over to his space.

"The public is where you find it." Ryder worked the combination on his lock, snapped it open, and motioned toward the roll up door. "I'm ready."

"Do you want me to roll out the red carpet for you? Sorry, I forgot to bring one." Mr. Assistant sipped his tea and huffed.

"Don't worry, I think I have just the thing." Playing to the back of the storage facility, or at least to Rodger, the wonder help, he bent down and swept the door up.

The simple sight of his treasures put a calm air around him.

Inside was his personal stash of memorabilia, memories and other treasures collected over the years. His father always told him to commemorate all every moment, never forget, and his little square of the world held exactly that. Of course, being who he was, and being what the public was, his items were worth plenty. Not that they were for sale.

Among the movie posters and other bits and pieces collected over the years was something to show Rodger up. He reached down and rolled out a piece of red carpet he acquired from a teen awards show he hosted over a decade ago. "Now I can walk inside."

With Rodger behind him, he made his way around the boxes of artifacts.

First things first, he needed to put his newest piece away, and walked over to a filing cabinet. He opened the top drawer, added the letter opener to the pen and little spoon he already borrowed from Cora's apartment.

Once ensuring all his items were in order, he found a copy of the *Working Title* script and grabbed the handles of his two suitcases he packed only the day before. "Do you help with luggage?"

"Only because I want to leave, and we have a schedule." Rodger grabbed one of the suitcases and glanced around. "What is this? A shrine to yourself?"

"I don't believe one should make a shrine to one's self. That would be wrong." However, he would bet money on the fact that there were several shrines to him around the world. On his way out, he grabbed a handful of 8X10 glossies and a marker.

He rolled up the red carpet and locked his little compartment of items that were devoted to him, but definitely not a shrine.

No sooner had they put the luggage in the trunk than the door to the office way at the end of the row opened and the owner and his wife stepped in, followed by three women who instantly went into the fan girl stance. They stood, huddled together with their hands over their mouths, which said they recognized him.

The owner pointed in his direction, giving Ryder his cue.

"What's going on?" Rodger asked.

"Shrine starter kit." After taking a breath, his private signal to morph into the movie star, he went to hold up his end of the free storage rental deal. With a grin and tilting his sunglasses down his nose in the way all women loved, he sauntered toward the little gaggle of girls with glossies and marker that wouldn't scratch the photo.

"Oh my god Ryder, it is you." One woman clasped her hands and stared up at him while the other two simply vibrated with excitement.

He looked down at himself and then back at the little estrogen-filled group. "Well, what do you know, it is me."

His little quip caused all the women to giggle.

"I take it Sy and Dara are taking as good of care of you as they do me." He shook hands with the owners.

"We were just thinking of renting a space for some extra furniture we've accumulated," the spokesperson of the group continued.

"I wouldn't trust any of my accumulations to anyone other than Sy and Dara. He signed three of the pictures and handed one to each of the girls and bowed. "Plus, maybe we'll cross paths again someday, but right now I must be going." Over his sunglasses, he winked.

The women let out a collective sigh.

He nodded at the owners and returned to the car, slipping into the backseat in one fluid motion.

Rodger started the car then twisted around and stared him down.

Keeping the smile on his face, he held one of photos out to Rodger. "I can personalize it if you like."

"I'm good." The man didn't move.

"So I take it I don't impress you." Ryder decided then and there the man was a pain in the ass. His hand wandered to his phone. Maybe the fourth time would be the charm when it came to Cora.

"I work for one of the most powerful businesswomen in the country, if not the world. She impresses me." Rodger jutted his jaw out. "What else do we need to do, Mr. Scott? I have strict instructions not to return until you've cleaned up any messes you have made."

All right, the man was at least loyal and protective. Not bad traits unless it went against him. "What kind of messes are you referring to?" Cora made a similar reference. Rather than argue, he started signing some extra photos to drop off at Brian, his agent, to deal with the fan mail.

"Anything that may end with us needing to go to a discreet medical clinic." The man faced forward once more.

Unbeknownst to anyone, he cleaned up one situation yesterday when he walked out of Ms. Tuttle's life. Everyone thought he was a male whore, but that was such a harsh word for what he was. Serial romantic opportunist would be more accurate. Not needing or wanting to explain this to the assistant or anyone else, he changed the subject. "Now that I think about it, there is one more place we need to go." After a quick scroll through his phone, he gave Rodger the address, and sat back with the professional diver.

Twenty minutes later, they reached their destination.

"This is a supermarket." Rodger slid the car into a parking spot.

"Not just any supermarket this is the organic market. I will not allow Miss Caine and myself to put garbage in our bodies. Also, she has a headache, and I need to take care of that." Ryder got out of the car and paused to get the lay of the land. Off to one side was a huge tent filled with people and a bunch of cages. A sign indicated it was some sort of event for an animal shelter. Eying the crowd, he wasn't quite sure who were the animals. At all costs he needed to avoid that madness.

"Are you sure all you need is a supermarket? We have no more puddles on the floor we need to mop up?" Rodger joined him.

"Not unless there is something dripping inside." The people at the storage facility were one thing, a big swarm was another. Still, the market seemed a great way to torture Rodger, and Cora might need some revitalizing juice after tonight's celebration. "We can go in the side way."

Rodger stood by him. "What, you don't' want to walk into your public?"

"You have a lot to learn since I'll be around." Sunglasses on, shoulders down, he made his way around the cars, almost making it to the far side of the building when he stopped short in his tracks.

In show business, timing was everything. If it weren't for his father taking advantage of some perfect timing over three decades ago, he would have never got his first role as an actor. Some careers were made simply based on walking into a restaurant at a precise moment.

Of course, there was the flip side, when timing was off. Like right now, he spotted Glen and one of his cronies coming out of a little café only a door down from the market. "Damn it." All he needed was Cora's secretary blabbing about this little unfortunate meeting. To make sure timing remained on his side, he spun on his heel and began walking back toward the car. "Maybe we should get my stuff moved into my new place. It's a little crowded here."

Rodger rushed after him. "I thought you wanted to take care of Cora."

"She does have a headache." Instead of using the side door Ryder was certain was just for celebrities, he veered toward the regular entrance. With each step he took, the energy of the people changed, but he made it to the door. Part of him waited for the onslaught, the other dreaded it.

For one second he thought he might enter the store without interruption.

The next second he proved himself wrong.

"Ryder! Ryder!" The woman from the shelter waved to him.

"Is it weird how everyone calls you by your first name, even though they don't know you?" Rodger followed.

"That's called money." Since he was already spotted, ignoring such an obvious photo op would be a sin. Ryder adjusted his sunglasses and walked toward the yapping nightmares and the lady.

"Oh my god." The woman clasped her hands and jumped. "I'm sorry to bother you, but could I get a photo? Maybe it will help some of these dogs get adopted."

"Of course, anything for our furry friends. I was just at a fundraiser for animals last night." He plucked the woman's phone out of her hand, handed it to Rodger and knelt down by one of the cages with the woman. "Take several shots so she has some options."

"Oh thank you, Ryder." The woman kissed his cheek.

He glanced over at the dogs, some puppies, a big strapping setter that reminded him of Drew's dog, and the dog he settled in front of. The floppy mutt was lying in the cage and slowly turned to him with big wet eyes.

"Oh, he likes you. He hasn't moved all day. He's our sad little beagle." The woman thrust a piece of paper and pen in his direction.

"Why is he sad?" On automatic, he signed the paper and continued to take in the canine. He never had a pet, because he figured he would kill it, and he didn't need that on his resume.

"His owner died. Spike here hasn't really recovered. He's going to have a hard time finding a home. He just needs a nice place with some people who love him." The woman sniffed as if she might start crying.

With the gathering crowd, he leaned into the dog and tilted his head to catch the good sunlight. "Listen here, Spike, you need to perk up. You have a lot of competition here, and it's always important to make sure you stand out from the crowd. Find your light, buddy." Right as he went to stand the dog put one paw up on the cage.

The people all around let out a collective "aw."

"Excellent work, now you're getting the hang of it." He stuck his finger in the cage, gave the dog's paw a little scratch and stood.

The dog sat up straight and stared at him with eyes that wanted to bore a hole through his heart.

Ryder forced himself to turn away. "Well, good luck."

"He hasn't really perked up until now." The woman pointed over to the cage.

The focus on him as always, he turned.

Damn, damn, damn. Stupid dog sat there staring at him with those orbs that wanted to absorb him and with his small little paw up on the cage. If that was his version of perky, this dog really needed to take better direction.

"He's only three years old and fully trained. He must see your star glowing, you told him to find his light." She held on to his arm. "You're his light. His beacon."

In a movie this would be the moment where the camera would slowly pan over the crowd waiting for him to make his decision.

Of course, in a movie he would have a script and more than a nanosecond to make a decision.

The dog continued to stare. That was a face that could make money.

Stop everything. Again, his father said things just seemed to happen. An idea formulating in his head, Ryder kept his focus on good old Spike. The sad little dog no one wanted could definitely be the poster animal that would send checks flying his way.

Once more he bent down. "Do you want to be owned by a star?"

When the dog moved his ear and whimpered, Ryder shot up. "Spike has a home!" He lifted his fist in victory.

The crowd went wild and the woman burst into tears.

With a wave of his hand, he silenced the chaos.

Everyone held their collective breath, waiting to hear what he would say.

"Adopting an animal like Spike is only one of the goals of organizations such as Ryder's Rescue." He nodded.

"You're part of a rescue agency?" The woman held out a clipboard and made him sign some papers.

"Yes, I am an advocate to dogs, especially those who have trouble finding a home. We are currently taking donations." This was perfect.

In only what he would call a whirlwind of activity, people began chattering, and the crowd, who now handed him money and checks out of nowhere, surrounded him.

This was more than perfect.

Timing was everything.

Once the money died down, he took custody of the first thing that he owned rather than what owned him.

Leash in hand, he and his four-legged money magnet rejoined Rodger. "I have an alternate remedy for Cora." Everyone who was anyone knew dogs were therapeutic.

Without a word from Sir Secretary, the three of them got in the car.

The dog lay down on his lap. At least he was low maintenance.

"Cora's instructions didn't say anything about an animal. You can't keep him." Lips pursed, Rodger stared at him.

"I think an animal would be good for her reputation. It's all part of my master plan." Surely, the man would understand if Cora benefitted.

They both looked at Spike. Now the dog fell asleep.

"I'll just put him in the corner of the kitchen. He's pretty mellow, Cora won't notice." Even as the words left his mouth, he knew they were a lie. Cora noticed everything, but Spike made money. Ryder couldn't give him up now when they just started.

Rodger gave him one glance, more like a glare.

"Are you crazy? I was never going to keep him, just got stuck in a weird position. The public and all." First, he had to take care of the big dollar signs in the form of making sure Cora was taken care of. He backtracked and patted Spike on the top of his head. "This pooch may have been seeing stars, but it wasn't me. I do need to make another stop to clean up a mess. One may say I need a pooper scooper."

With no doubt Rodger would rat him out, he directed him to the only person on the planet who understood.

After quite a jaunt to Pasadena, he knocked on the door of Mr. and Mrs. Fulton.

Breathless, Erin and her dog, Beaker, answered the door and stared at Spike. "Why are you here?" She backed up and instantly Beaker spoke the universal language of dogs by sniffing his furry cohort. In need of translation, the animal looked back at his mistress for an explanation. "Why do you have a dog?" Erin asked the question of the hour.

Ryder stepped inside. Spike lumbered after him, walked around in a circle and laid down on the throw rug in the entryway. Now he, Erin and Beaker all stared at their fourth waiting...waiting...nothing.

"I have to get back to the city, I'll see you later." He dropped the leash and wished he told Rodger to keep the car motor running.

"Ryder Scott, take one step out that door, and I will kill you with the power of my pregnancy hormones." She narrowed her eyes.

Only the threat of being shot down with anything dealing with pregnancy made him freeze as if he were identified in a line up. "I need a favor." He flashed his made for Hollywood smile.

Erin didn't move. Neither did Spike. They truly were a match made in whatever location people got matched with animals.

"I was on my way to Cora's and stopped at that place in Santa Monica that has all the organic vegetables and stuff. Cora has a headache, and I needed to get some things." Fine, an explanation of some sort was in order, but he chose to leave out the part about seeing Glen out and about as well.

His co-star and long ago partner in crime put her hand on her hip and sighed.

"I never got the stuff, but there was this dog shelter event outside and, well..." He motioned to the dog. "His owner died, and he was all lying there, and one thing led to another, and you have to trust me on this, the dog really wants to be with a star."

"His owner died?" Her expression softened "You're a superstar, take him to one of your other women and have a pet."

Now for the big reveal. "In a major plot twist, I don't have any other women, and I can't bring a pet to Cora's right away."

"Cora." Erin raised her eyebrows. "You have been all over the Internet with her."

"So I've been informed." He wondered if they weren't trending if they would have been normal. Probably not, nothing was normal, and she wouldn't have any use for him. "Can you do me a favor, please? I'll owe you one."

With a huff she kneeled down and held her hand out to Spike. "You'll never repay me."

The dog didn't move.

"He loves you!" Relief washed over him.

She wrinkled her nose. "He didn't do anything."

"Then he's no worse for the wear. He's depressed. Just keep him here until Cora gets used to me. Think of your home as his therapy to be re-acclimated to the world." His face ached from the forced smile.

"All right, but this isn't permanent. At least he doesn't seem like too much trouble." She gave the dog a little pat and backed away with a shrug. "Maybe Drew will be able to bring him out of his shell."

"Maybe Drew needs to design some pet pep pills or something." Again he headed for the exit.

"Pet vitamins." She smiled and turned her attention back to her own dog. "Beaker is perfect the way he his."

Before leaving, he bent down and took some pictures of his newest payroll. "Careful with him, he's the face of Ryder's Rescue." He motioned for Erin to get the shot.

Never one to miss a photo op, she bent down and smiled. "You have a charity?"

"Yes, I was at a function about animal rights. They're very important. Animals don't have a voice, so you have to listen to other things and be an advocate for them." He turned the camera around and got in the shot with Erin. Hey, two stars were better than one.

"What are you up to?" She scowled.

"Nothing. I'm trying to get to Cora." The woman always could tell, but hopefully her pregnancy hormones would throw her off the trail.

"If you have a charity, wouldn't she know about the dog?"

Good point. He had to think fast. "We have to work out the particulars of having an animal at the Sierra Towers. This was a rescue emergency." At his explanation, he exhaled in relief. "I really need to get going."

"Hold on." She dashed away.

In the time it took for him to get a few more shots with Spike, Erin returned.

"Here." She handed him a check. "Give me the receipt next time you see me. Drew was just complaining about how we need more tax deductions."

He glanced at the check. The large check. Thank god, his years of training allowed him not to have any reaction like jumping around and high-fiving her. "You qualify for a free Ryder's Rescue tote bag."

"Wow, sounds official." Erin shrugged.

"Well, I hate to drop off a pet and run, but I have to get back. I'm meeting Cora at six." His relationship turned into a job and for a job, he couldn't be late. Unlike his dealings with Glen and the others, he couldn't turn and walk the other way down the street, he had to perform. He also needed to get some receipts and tote bags.

HOLLYWOOD STARDOM

FADE IN:

INT.HOLLYWOOD, CA - STUDIO SOUNDSTAGE - DAY.

ROXY, still dressed like a streetwalker, is
lying under a lamppost with blood around her.

A ruckus rumbles through the space when William
enters the soundstage.

The DIRECTOR walks over to WILLIAM and shakes
his hand. Other production people crowd around
him, and he signs some autographs.

                    WILLIAM
            (Waves over at ROXY still
            lying on the soundstage)
             I wanted to see my wife on
             her last day on set.

                    DIRECTOR
            Well, we were just about to
            shoot the last scene.

Both WILLIAM and the DIRECTOR walk over to the
shot.

                    DIRECTOR
            Everyone take their mark!

                    WILLIAM
            (Leans over to the director)
                How did she do?

                    DIRECTOR
            Once she embraced the role,
            she did fine. She just
            needed to let go and trust
            me.

                    WILLIAM
          (Smiles and nods)
          That pretty much sums her
          up.

                    DIRECTOR
          I'm not sure if acting is
          all she thought it was
          going to be.

                    WILLIAM
          I didn't want her to think
          she was being held back.

                    DIRECTOR
          I understand.

                    WILLIAM
          I'm glad she embraced the
          role.

Chapter Eight

LIKE A DUEL about to begin, Cora's car and the car carrying Ryder stalked down the alleyway from opposing sides. As the cars came to a stop, Cora snatched up her handbag like a weapon before getting out of the car and standing her ground.

Ryder exited his vehicle and stopped as well.

So the man wanted a battle, did he? Was he still pouting because he couldn't drive the car? Well, this was war, her warriors backing her up, and she wasn't budging.

"CC stay right there." Ryder held his hand up, reached back into the car and with a brown paper bag in his hand sprinted toward her.

She crossed her arms and kept her focus affixed on her enemy as he approached. Her head pounded in time with each of his steps.

"Oh baby, you are tense. I see you still have that headache." Ryder lifted his chin to Viktor as if to say hello, and put the bag on the hood of the car. He pulled a huge bottle of water out of the bag, opened the top and handed it to her. "Alkaline water. I have a case in the car as well. Start with this. Part of your headache has to be dehydration. I'm glad that I had time to stop for some rations after this insane day."

Not wanting to think about what his rations were, she turned her head refusing to take his watered down peace offering. "I think part of my headache has to do with being interrupted multiple times today with inane questions."

"Did Rodger keep calling you? Maybe we should talk to him about that." Ryder put the bottle to her lips. "This water is healing, trust me."

Only because her mouth was parched from the fight did she take a sip of the magic water that shock of all shocks, tasted like...water. "Before we do anything else, we have to set some things straight."

"I think before we do anything else we have to fix your headache." Once more he reached back in the bag, this time pulling out a little container of almonds. He opened that and popped one in her mouth. "Almonds have natural pain relievers."

She chewed the nut while envisioning another nut, the one standing by her side. "Don't think you can ply me with nuts."

"That comes later." He put his arm around her and kissed her neck. "Orgasms do wonders for headaches. I will make sure to deliver one right to you personally once we get home."

"Speaking of which." It was time to fire her weapons, and she spun toward him. Damn gorgeous man.

He grinned. "You already look like you have some color back."

No way would his pretty face and perfect grin deflect her from her purpose. "Did you clean up all your messes?"

He raised his eyebrows. "I wasn't as dirty as you thought, but I'm squeaky clean now."

Though she found that hard to believe, rather than belabor the point, she chose to keep forging ahead. As his smile faded, hers appeared. "Good, you can follow instructions." She reached into her handbag and found her own bit of magic, not in the form of nuts or liquid, but in an envelope.

"Haven't you heard? I take direction perfectly." He backed up as if he needed to get a better view, the lay of the land so to speak.

Well, before the man got laid, he needed to understand. "Excellent, then I don't need to repeat myself to get the desired result." She stepped forward, closing the distance between them and held the envelope up.

"I thought we didn't need any paper." The playful demeanor gone, he stared at her.

"Who needs paper when you can have plastic?" She opened the envelope and pulled out three cards. "I have here, a credit card, a key to the Sierra Towers, and your health insurance card. We'll program the lock with your fingerprints later."

"You're nothing, if not productive." He inched closer and reached out for his prizes.

She snapped her hand back. "I would have been more productive, if I wasn't getting foolish phone calls from a spoiled star. Remember, I have a business to run and a position to win."

"Isn't that why I'm here?" In a rapid fire move, he snatched the cards away from her.

She crossed her arms. "Just as long as we're on the same page."

"I thought we didn't need paper." Taking his time, he removed his wallet from his pocket and put the cards away.

"Or a series of rapid fire phone calls over nothing." She needed to make sure she made her point and therefore would win.

"Sometimes calls over nothing are the best ones." His voice lowered.

Rather than continue, she glanced over at Rodger.

"I'll deliver Ryder's items to the apartment and see you in the morning." Rodger called to her.

She gave Rodger one nod, and even from the distance her gesture was enough for her secretary to salute, get in the company car and drive away.

"He didn't say goodbye, and after we had such a lovely day together." Ryder returned his wallet to his pocket. "Tell me, what are we doing in an alley behind some warehouses? When you said meet you at six, I envisioned a restaurant or something."

"I'm still working, come on." Head held high, she headed toward the warehouse.

"All work and no play." Ryder kept up as they approached the warehouse.

"Keeps my pretty boy in the lifestyle to which he's become accustomed." Again, she reached into her purse and pulled out another envelope.

Viktor ran ahead and gave one knock on the large metal door.

"What is this place?" Playing the role of dutiful significant other, Ryder caught her hand and laced his fingers in hers.

She peeked up at Ryder with his square jaw line and that perfect nose. Some would say she bought herself the ultimate prize. Hopefully, by producing everything he needed she would prove what she could do. "There is one more card you need." She opened the envelope.

In a scene fit for a movie, the door rolled up in a slow movement, revealing a pitch-black room.

Viktor looked back at her, and she lifted her chin giving him the go-ahead. Her protector snapped his fingers and in a flash, the space illuminated unveiling five of the most prestigious sports cars the world had to offer, all in gleaming black and each top of the line with every option. "Car insurance card, but you will leave the company car behind." Not on any planet would she have Rodger made miserable.

"Holy Mother of God." Rather than stomping forth like he owned the place, Ryder squeezed her hand and pulled her closer. "You are amazing."

"What would my pet like to drive to his first day on set?" She swiped her hand in front of them. "You can only pick one treat, so choose wisely."

He leaned down to her ear. "I am really turned on right now."

"I have no doubt." Men were so easily appeased. "Which engine do you want rumbling your loins?"

"I know what I want rumbling my loins later." A chuckle escaped his throat. "If I lick it, is it mine?"

"So to speak." It wasn't the time to remind him who held the pink slip and everything else. She held the power, but he seemed to fall into line.

"Excellent." He wrapped his arm around her, licked her earlobe and turned toward the vehicles once again. "I got the first thing claimed."

Oh, the man was quite an actor, she needed to watch herself. Their banter, his looks, and his loins were way too easy to get lost in. No wonder he had a string of women at his beck and call. "Go choose some wheels, a star of your caliber needs something spectacular."

Not in need of any more prodding, he let go of her and went to the first car, the traditional Ferrari, the car that everyone recognized as the sports car of success.

At least he took his time, walking around the car, sitting inside and putting his hands on the steering wheel.

Viktor came to her side. "With all due respect, are you sure you know what you are doing?"

"Small investment to get what I need." She watched Ryder go to the next vehicle, a Lamborghini, and repeat the same ritual. He did the same with the Porsche and the McLaren. "Good job setting this all up," she murmured to Viktor.

Finally, Ryder made his way to her personal favorite, the Aston Martin. Sporty, classic lines, more unassuming, yet just as grand.

"CC." He walked around the cars once more then held out his hand to her. "Come here."

"What else do you need? I basically brought the dealership to you." Though she made sure her tone laced with discontent, she still put her hand in his.

"First, to say thank you. Second, to say I narrowed it down. I just need to see something." He took her over to the Ferrari and opened the passenger side door. "Please get in."

The new car scent took over each one of her pores as she slipped inside, and she decided that caused her light-headedness, not the fact Ryder said thank you or anything.

He closed the door and went to the front of the car, raising his hands as if framing a shot. After a moment, he nodded and retrieved her from the car, helping her out and leading her to the Aston Martin. "One more time, gorgeous."

Once more, she allowed him to go through his ritual. However, this time rather than getting her out of the car, he got in the driver's side, put his hands the wheel and faced her. "Instead of licking leather and metal, may I just lick you in a more interesting place?"

A minor jolt ran through her. "So is this the one?"

He answered by slowly licking his lips and raising his eyebrows.

"Why?" Before getting on to licking, she needed to know what went on in that pretty little head of his.

"Easy, you look the best in it."

"That's the reason?" She crossed her arms.

"This is the kind of car that doesn't need to scream how amazing it is. Just by being in its presence, you know you came upon something special." He leaned in, brushed her hair off her shoulder and pulled her in for a kiss.

Her insides warmed, and the moment his tongue touched hers, the heat pooled between her legs.

"Every time I kiss you I end up with this raging erection." He took her hand and placed it on the growing bulge in his pants.

Yes, his erection was impressive, indeed. For only a moment, she let her hand linger before pulling back. "Am I to think this is an unusual occurrence?"

He took her chin in his hand and stared into her eyes. "I'm an actor for a living. Usually I have impeccable control in everything I do, and yet this is beyond my training." Once more, he kissed her, this one deeper, his tongue exploring her mouth, her body having an equal reaction to his.

In a sudden move, he broke the kiss. "Do you want to take a ride?"

Silly her. She thought they were already on one. "Are you sure this is the one you want?"

"Absolutely. This one feels right." His eyes never left hers.

She waved out the window, and Viktor jogged over. "Ryder has decided the Aston Martin is to his liking."

Viktor reached into the car and opened the glove box. Inside was the contract and the specialty key that looked more like a cube of glass.

On cue, Viktor handed her a pen, and she signed the contract then gave him the papers. He continued to stand there.

"You would think that they would do away with these ancient writing implements already." She held his pen up. Maybe she needed to invent self-signing electronic paper.

After swiping the pen away, Viktor cleared his throat.

"Oh fine." With a huff, she opened her purse, rooted around in her wallet and handed him a fifty-dollar bill.

"I'll take care of everything else. Enjoy your drive." Viktor plucked the money out of her fingers and backed away.

"What was that for?" Ryder chuckled.

Rather than answer, she tossed him the key and shut the glove box.

"I want to know what bet you lost." He inserted the thing that wasn't a key in the traditional sense into a slot in the middle of the dash and pushed.

The engine revved, the car came alive, and Cora couldn't stop a smile. Modern cars were more like computers with engines. Cars like this one were works of art melded with technology and mechanics at its finest. "Get going."

He returned his hands to the wheel, his fingers running along the contours as if he were caressing a woman. "Tell me."

"I bet you would choose the Ferrari." She pushed her back into the fine leather.

"Well, I'm full of surprises."

They glanced at each other.

"How long are you going to make me wait?" she asked. Though he was more than easy on the eyes, it was easier to look straight ahead than at him, and she focused out the windshield.

"Only until you're ready to burst." Without warning, he hit the accelerator and the car rolled out of the warehouse.

They drove through the back alley. Before turning onto the main road, Ryder stopped and turned to her.

"Don't forget I have to work tonight," she reminded him. The setting sun backlit him giving him an unreal glow.

"We are working." He punctuated his sentence with his deadly one-sided grin, or as Cora now dubbed it, the grin of no good.

Not that she wanted to be good. "How do you figure?"

"We need to be seen, make everything official. I think making it into a few tabloids is in order. We need to keep trending."

Only a few hours ago, she sent him traipsing through the greater Los Angeles area getting rid of his other errant females and now they were official.

"It's not as unusual as it seems. All these things are calculated down to the minute. Nothing in this town is ever by chance." As if reading her mind, he filled in the blanks.

"So now is the time?" In this one arena, he knew more than she did. Not that she really wanted to know.

"It's perfect." He ran his thumb along her lower lip. "Leave your lipstick a little smudged, it's a sure sign we've been kissing."

"Nothing like setting the stage." For the first time in a long time, she let someone else take a small amount of control.

"That's right, baby. Let's go make some sizzle." Once more he punched the accelerator and made his way into the city. "It's our first night together. You showed me what you could do, now let me show you what I can do."

She held on, but let Ryder stay in the driver's seat. Something told her she hadn't won the battle or the war.

Ryder rolled down the windows and weaved his way through the streets of Los Angeles. Neither of them spoke, but he kept hold of her hand as he shifted the gears.

Caught in the rhythm of the car, the breeze, even Ryder, her mind wandered. Chargge, Ultracom, CEOs and servers all faded into the background while she wondered what this night with Ryder would entail.

They drove through Beverly Hills and into West Hollywood, home of some of the most famous restaurants and hot spots. People, dressed in all designer clothes and trying to set the latest trend, lined the streets.

"When we stop, do not get out of the car until I get you. Look only at me, but keep your face in my shoulder as if you don't want to be seen." Ryder pulled up to the valet stand.

"Yesterday you told me to be prepared for pictures and to smile." Cora furrowed her brow. The man had issues about exiting cars, that was certain.

"Right and today I'm telling you to be camera shy because now we're in a serious relationship, and you don't want anyone infringing on our private time together." He put the car in park.

He wanted her to play the role of shy and demure? That didn't fit her.

"Then why are we at one of the most popular restaurants in Hollywood?"

"Exactly." His amazing smile took her breath away.

Before Cora had the opportunity to ask one of the hundred questions that streamed through her mind like a bad feed, the valets descended upon them. The first one opened Ryder's door.

"It's brand new. I trust you'll take good care of it?" Along with a hundred dollar bill, Ryder handed over the key thing.

"Of course, Mr. Scott. Welcome." The valet took the cash and the key and shook his hand.

She watched the exchange as a second valet came to her side of the car.

"Miss Caine." The man stepped back.

What? He knew her name? This wasn't her circle.

"Excuse me." Ryder rushed around the car, and he held his hand out to her.

Her head spinning, she put her hand in his and not only allowed him to help her out of the car, but with the gathering crowd and the flashes already going off, she clutched on to him and gazed up at his face. At least she had a view.

As if protecting her, he put his arm around her. Rather than the charming Ryder who signed autographs and chatted yesterday at the charity event, tonight he held her close, guided them through the crowd, and made his way into the restaurant.

The restaurant was packed, with little room for even standing. Even she couldn't get a table at this hour, but Ryder was definitely many steps above her in the connections department.

"Two please." Ryder leaned over the podium with the host and hostesses.

"Of course, sir." The man lifted his hand, obviously signaling someone, and spoke into a microphone attached to his ear. "Ryder Scott and Cora Caine need a booth in the back for two."

Since she had never been to this restaurant, the fact everyone seemed to know her name unnerved her.

While they waited, Ryder faced her and hooked his finger under her chin, tilting her face up to his. "How are you doing?" His tone low, dreamy, no doubt rehearsed.

Though she tried to resist, she couldn't help but gaze into his dark blue eyes. "How does everyone know who I am?" In her own world she was well known, but seriously, how many people could pick out CEOs among the mix of the population?

He moved his face closer to hers. "Baby, it's their job to know." His finger grazed her lower lip.

Her mouth watered, anticipating his kiss.

"Mr. Scott, your booth is ready." A woman in a skintight black dress that barely covered anything and stilettoes that added at least six inches to her height joined them. "Right this way."

They followed the woman through the crowd.

"Is there anything special you would like tonight?" the woman asked.

Cora glanced around. Everyone's focus was on them, people pointing and lifting their phones.

"We're celebrating tonight. Please bring over a bottle of champagne and an arrangement of appetizers. For desert something chocolate, I trust the chef." Ryder finished their order right as they reached their destination.

He guided her into the tiny booth and slid in next to her, putting his arm around her and staring into her face. "Even after a long day at work, you still look stunning."

Shit, she blushed, she knew it. The heat in her face had to produce some color. She needed to keep her act together, remember what they were. "I have to say, I'm impressed you can pull all this off."

In record time, the champagne arrived. While one waiter poured the beverage, another came and arranged several dishes of appetizers that seemed more designed to provide a decoration for the table rather than give any actual food value.

"You should like this it's sweet and sparkly." After the waiters left, they were alone, well except for the public at large keeping their eyes on their every move. Ryder handed her a glass. "How about we have a little toast?"

"To our new arrangement." Maybe if she said it aloud, her cheeks would cool down.

He gave her a slow shake of his head. "To the dream."

The way he whispered the words made her shiver. Needing to end the moment, she tapped her glass against his and took a sip. The bubbles went up her nose, and she laughed.

"You need to smile more often." He took his turn, tapping their glasses.

They drank again. To abate the heat swirling around her, she finished off her glass.

"Thirsty are we? Let's remedy that." Never taking his eyes off hers, he refilled her glass.

This time she managed to stop, gulping down only half the glass. The man wouldn't stop looking at her. Talk about making someone self-conscious.

He scooted closer and casually moved her bangs off her forehead. "It's our first official date, so why don't you tell me something about Cora Caine?"

"Is it really a date since we moved in together and have an official arrangement?" At her words she polished off the champagne.

In one smooth motion, Ryder gave her some more of the tasty liquid. "Let me ask you a question."

She waited, this time going back to sipping the drink.

"Is that what you want the public to see?" He reached over to one of the appetizers, a mushroom stuffed with something that smelled almost better than Ryder's cologne, if Ryder was a food, of course.

Somewhere between him taking a bite of the mushroom and then feeding her the other half and another glass of champagne, she considered his question. "Absolutely I want the public to see us. Isn't that what I said this morning when we made our deal?"

"That's not what I'm asking. I know what the deal is, but I also know that every time I look at you, your cheeks turn the most delightful shade of red." He brushed his fingertips over the side of her face.

Damn man noticed everything.

"What I'm asking is do you want the public to know we are in a so-called arrangement, or do you want them to think this happened organically?"

After three glasses or was it four of champagne, she didn't know how her throat could be parched, yet she still finished off another glass. At last she opened her mouth to answer him, tell him about his own reputation, and talk about trending on the Internet.

He put his finger over her lips. "I know what people say about me, I know what you want to achieve, but what I want to know is are you interested in merely playing a role or do you want to get into character?"

For a woman with three degrees, she had no idea what he was asking and she shook her head.

"Why don't we stop talking about arrangements and deals and insurance cards and let things happen as they come?" He leaned in and replaced his finger with his lips. "I think the performance will be much more convincing."

Before she even realized it, she found herself kissing him, a light kiss but still passionate, one that made every bit of her tingle. Every bit. "Ryder." Out of the corner of her eye, she noticed people staring at them, taking their picture.

"Now tell me something about Cora Caine." He treated her to another kiss and then sipped some champagne. "Why Chargge? What was the spark?"

The people continued to gawk at them. Was this what his life was like? The obvious answer was yes. "Ryder, everyone is looking at us."

"Of course they are, this whole city has been waiting for us to make our debut since the second they saw us on your website." He put his glass to her lips. "When you created Chargge did you ever think you'd be the trending story?"

"I was always the woman behind the scenes." To keep her faculties about her, she grabbed the nearest thing to her hand, his leg.

A low growl rumbled through him. "So tell me why Chargge?"

"It started as a site dedicated to movie musicals when I was a teenager and then morphed into an entertainment site. There's something comforting and innocent about musicals, yet romantic. Something we lost." Her voice trailed off, and she shrugged. "I wanted to see if I could create a site that would be larger than my mother's, and it was actually one of her customers who gave me my first big feature on a celebrity, even though I was only seventeen." She laughed, but wasn't sure why. Nothing was funny, but she just wanted to giggle.

"Your mother has a site as well? Which one?" With their faces mere inches apart, he fed a different appetizer, a delectable piece of butternut squash tempura.

She nodded and chased the treat down with some more of her new favorite beverage. Once more, she felt her cheeks heat, and she pressed her forehead to his. "My mother is Madame Sublime." At her admission, she closed her eyes. The room seemed to move.

"Madame Sublime as in Madame Sublime will give you and your partner a fine time?" He rubbed his thumb along her neck.

Yes, her mother was one of the first on the technology train and brought sex toys, books and other pleasurable accessories to the Internet and therefore, to the masses, all with free shipping and a twenty-four hour hotline. "She may have been one of the first with a million-dollar site, but mine's worth over a billion."

"You're sexy when you get competitive, even when it's with your own mother." He chose a different appetizer, a delicious date with a sweet spicy nut.

When his fingers grazed her mouth she had no choice but to give them a little lick. Call her the human napkin.

With a low moan, he used his fingers to trace her lower lip.

"You know what else I have that my mother doesn't?" She swirled her tongue around the tip of his finger.

"I can tell you what I have that no one doesn't." He moved her hand to the bulge in his pants.

"She only has a tennis pro. I have a real star." As she leaned back, the whole restaurant seemed to want to go with her, so she stopped and stared into that gorgeous face.

"That you do."

"What else is on our agenda for tonight?" Since she only had a half a glass of champagne left, she finished it off.

"Club, dancing, more champagne?" He put his hand over hers and pushed down. "Maybe you had something else in mind?"

All she wanted was to get this man home, throw him on her bed and have her way with him. No wonder the public flocked to him. They all wanted what she bought and paid for. Still, she paused.

Could they do this, just leave without another stop? Would it be all right to miss the photo opportunity when her career was at stake?

"For once, why don't you let go and do whatever you want." A raise of his eyebrows punctuated his sentence.

"How about we go home?" The words left her mouth too fast.

"I want you right now, and I'm glad we have a fast car." He motioned for the waiter, pulled her in tighter and kissed her.

Dizzy, she held on and went with it, got into the role. With Ryder it was way too easy to slip into the character he wanted, even though she watched him pay with the credit card she gave him earlier.

"HERE, LET ME SHOW you around the apartment." Cora pulled Ryder inside, tripped on the edge of the carpet in the entryway, and fell into his arms.

"All right." Ryder held her steady as he closed and locked the door.

"This was formerly my apartment at the Sierra Towers, and now it is our apartment at the Sierra Towers." She swiped her arm in front of her, the force of her own movement causing her to spin around and face him. "Ryder."

"Cora?" He swallowed back a laugh. For the first time since he could remember, he was looking forward to calling a place home.

"This is the entry way." Her gaze took him in, and she pressed her palm to his cheek. "You are really a handsome man."

"Thank you, you're quite gorgeous yourself." He wrapped his arm around her and pulled her close. After getting her to loosen up and stop worrying about their public audience, they had an amazing time, one he wanted to duplicate again and again. Cora was sexy, smart and sassy. Of course, now he could add smashed to her list.

"Will you kiss me now?" She kicked off her shoes, making her a few inches shorter.

Before giving her what she wanted, he made a mental note to keep champagne on hand at all times. His little drunken CEO was absolutely delightful. He dipped his head down and kissed her. While she proved to be an active participant in their private moments, this time she flung her arms around his neck, opened her mouth and returned the gesture wholeheartedly.

Though a bit less elegant than her normal kisses, he loved the way she guided his tongue into her mouth and took her time sucking down to the tip. Since the restaurant, he'd been struggling with a waxing and waning erection that could use some of her attention.

"Oh my god, I almost forgot our tour." In a sudden move, she broke the kiss grabbed his hand and pulled him into the dining room. "Here is the dining room, we can eat here if you want." She pointed to the perfectly staged glass dining room table even set up with dishes and flowers. "I've never eaten here, but this is where we would eat if we were to eat here."

"What do you do here?' He came up behind her and wrapped his arm around her waist.

"Usually nothing, but it's so hot, I think I'm going to take my shirt off here." She made one haphazard attempt to unbutton her shirt, laughed and placed his hand between her boobs. "I think I need help."

"Let me oblige." With an ease born from years of practice, he flicked open her buttons using only one hand.

He slid the shirt off her shoulders, lowered his face to the crook of her neck, and cupped her more than handful breasts. "Do we need the bra?"

"Do you think we should take that off in the dining room?" She glanced up backward at him.

"I think it's more than appropriate." Rather than waiting for her response, he unfastened her bra and tossed it aside with her shirt. The way the strategically placed lights illuminated the room gave him the perfect view to her hard, ready nipples. He licked his fingertips and skimmed them over the tight peaks.

"Oh." She arched her back. "That feels good."

"I think this is the perfect place to have a little nibble." His mouth watering, he turned her right as she pushed him away.

"I didn't show you the kitchen!" Once more, she grabbed his hand and went the few steps over to the kitchen.

Part of him really wanted to know what she would do next, the other wanted her to return so he could continue his meal.

Totally topless, she held her arms out. "This is where I eat."

Watching her, bouncing boobs and all, he decided this is where he would do his eating as well, and he wasn't the least bit hungry.

"Actually, I don't really eat here, but I do make my espresso." She leaned against the counter and curled her arm around her prized appliance.

Something told Ryder she would be needing a double shot or possibly a triple or quadruple tomorrow.

"I like my espresso the way you like your water." At her statement, she shot straight up and jumped. "Oh! Let's see if Rodger put your water in the refrigerator. That's where it will stay cold."

"Yes, the refrigerator is usually the place for that." Before he had a chance to catch her, she rushed to the stainless steel cold box and opened the door and bent way over.

"Look, Ryder."

Oh, he was looking for sure.

Again he went up behind her. This time he put his hands on her hips and pressed up against her.

She wiggled her backside. "You're not looking."

"Trust me, I'm looking." He slid her skirt up around her waist and pulled down her panties, rubbing his palm over her fine round bottom. "I like what I see."

"What about the water?" Her tone teased him.

"I'm looking at something much more quenching." He snaked his hands around the front of her thighs.

"I can feel how hard you are." She clutched the shelf.

"You did that." He planted a trail of kisses down her spine. Only to get rid of the inconvenience of his pants, he took one step back.

The small gap between them turned out to be enough for her to slip through his fingers and dart through the apartment.

"Cora!" Yet again, he went after her, this time stomping through place, picking up her panties and her skirt along the way to the bedroom. By his calculations...

"I need you now." Sprawled over the bed in all her glory, and everything about her was glorious, she held her arms out.

Perfection.

"Don't move." He stared at her spread out on the bed as he pulled his shirt off over his head, and for the first time, dropping an article of his clothing in his bedroom.

She squirmed, bit her lip and lifted one knee. "Take off the rest."

"Is that what you want?" With over exaggerated movements, he unbuckled his belt and slowly pulled it out of the loops. He held it up and dropped it, letting it make a satisfying clink as it hit the floor.

"Ryder." She rubbed her hand over what would now be designated his spot in the bed.

Raising one eyebrow, he removed a condom out of his wallet, put the little pleasure package between his teeth then tossed away his pants and underwear in one smooth motion.

"Um." She slid her hands over her chest and her stomach until they disappeared between her own legs.

As he approached, he rolled the condom on. "Here, allow me." He joined her on the bed and took her in his arms.

No sooner had he positioned himself and prepared to plunge into her, than she took him by the shoulders and pushed him onto his back.

Damn, he adored a woman who took control, and he gladly surrendered.

"No allow me." She straddled his hips and lowered onto his erection.

Her warmth encompassed him and he sank back among the pillows and forced his eyes to remain open and not miss a second.

In a slow circle, she gyrated her hips. The dim light in the room backlit her in such a way to allow him watch her body, her breasts bouncing with her every movement.

"Oh yeah." He ran his hands up her legs.

"You told me to do what I wanted." She pushed his hands away, leaned forward and braced her arms on his chest, but didn't move.

"What do you want?" Nose to nose, his lips brushed against hers.

"What do you want?" With the tip of her tongue, she outlined his lips.

The woman had barely done anything and already he throbbed. "Cora."

"You're going to have to do better than that." Still, she didn't budge.

Unable to take much more, he grabbed her hips and writhed beneath her. "Tell me what you want, and I'll do it."

"I think I have to make it happen." Without giving him a chance to respond, she kissed him, didn't let up as she finally raised herself up and drove down.

At getting the slightest relief, he sucked in his breath. "Cora."

She never let up, but she alternated between grinding against him and impaling herself on him over and over again. Whenever he thought they established their groove, she switched things up and, he was caught in the most delicious torture somewhere between needing to fling her to her back and pound his way to his climax, and enjoying the buildup. "Cora, please." Had he just begged?

"Oh." She straightened up, leaned back against his knees and tangled her hand in her hair. "Ryder, I'm almost there."

"I'll get you there, baby." His fingers instantly went to her center. As he rubbed her toward her end, her movements evened out, the pressure built at a steady pace. He couldn't last much longer.

"Come with me." She reached back behind her and cupped his balls.

"Cora." He bucked his hips at the unexpected touch. It was all he needed. "Baby, come on!"

"Now Ryder!" She massaged the area just beneath his balls.

"Cora!" The most intense pulses took over him, and he had no choice but to scream out her name.

His orgasm hit him hard, to the point where he was sure he saw stars, and not the Hollywood kind. She collapsed on top of him as her climax crested and rippled around him, only heightening his own pleasure.

The remnants of his release faded, leaving him a weak, panting, mass only able to hold on to the woman.

"You screamed my name." She tickled her fingertips over his chest and slid off him onto her side of the bed.

"I had to, that was amazing." Truth be told, he never experienced an orgasm like that. Actually, if he was going all out, he would say never experienced a woman like Cora. She seemed tailor-made for him.

"That was what I wanted. I knew I could do it." She curled up among the covers.

"Is there anything else you want?" Reluctantly, he got out of bed to deal with the condom.

"We'll see in the morning, if we're still trending." She yawned and turned over.

Again, she bested him. After a shake of his head, he did what he needed, then strolled through the apartment to get their water. He opened the fridge to his water neatly placed in rows and looked out over to the windows at the view of Los Angeles. No matter what, he had to keep them trending, and though he asked her to forget their roles, he never could.

HOLLYWOOD STARDOM

FADE IN:

INT.HOLLYWOOD, CA - WILLIAM AND ROXY'S DINING
ROOM - EVENING.

ROXY brings out a big tray of food to the table
while WILLIAM pours some wine.

                    WILLIAM
               (Lifts his glass)
                To my wife, the actress.

                    ROXY
               (Let's out a laugh)
                I spent most of my time
                playing dead.

                    WILLIAM
                Hey, it takes talent to do
                it well.

ROXY shrugs and doles out WILLIAM'S plate.

WILLIAM stands, takes the dish, puts it down and
grabs her hand.

                    WILLIAM
                Hey, working girl, come
                here.

                    ROXY
               (allows WILLIAM to guide her
               into his embrace)
                Good thing you're working,
                we couldn't buy a box of
                crackers on what I made.

                    WILLIAM
                (Tilts her face up to
                his)
                I have us covered. Always.

                    ROXY
          (Wraps her arms around his
          neck)
                    Always.

WILLIAM gives her a deep kiss.

                    WILLIAM
          (Holds her in his arms and
          sways them back and forth)
           Always know that no matter
           what happens, I'm here.

                    ROXY
          (Presses her hand to his
          cheek)
           I know that.

                    WILLIAM
          (Kisses her hand)
           Do you?

                    ROXY
           Yes.
          (She lowers her head to
          William's shoulder.)

Chapter Nine

A SEMI-TRUCK DROVE OVER Cora's head and when it hadn't done enough damage, it backed up and rolled over again.

"Oh my god." She tried to move and only ended up draping herself over the edge of the bed and staring down at the Persian rug. With so many colors, if she threw up no one would ever notice.

"Well, now I know how to get you to wake up in bed with me." The bed shook with Ryder's movements, and he spooned her. "Feeling a little dicey I take it?"

The only answer she could muster was a groan. Every muscle on her ached, her head throbbed, and her stomach wanted to run for escape.

"Let's sleep it off." He moved her hair off the side of her face and gave her a light peck. "Things won't look as bleak in a few hours."

She swallowed, swearing that some nasty person lined her throat with a combination of knives and gravel. "I have to get to the office."

"Baby, I don't think you'll be any good there today. Even a CEO can take a sick day," he crooned in her ear.

"No, I have to go. I can't not go to work because I was drinking and having sex with a movie star." If one of her employees didn't come to work because of their partying, she would dismiss them post haste. She looked over toward the bathroom. At the moment, it seemed miles and miles away, and when she tried to push up, her every muscle protested. "Ryder."

"All right. This is no worse than having to be on set in this condition. They say all the world's a stage." Once more the bed bounced as Ryder got up. He came around to her side and helped her sit up.

The room spun and she hid her face in his chest. He smelled like a man. Lord help her if she felt better, she might be inclined to lay in bed with him. "Are you sure I'm not dead?"

"Absolutely." He pulled her up, and they took the long walk into the bathroom.

Her reflection in the mirror made her shudder. Hair all over the place, smeared makeup, pale. "Dear Ultracom, here's your new CEO." She put her hand over her eyes.

"Okay, I don't think this is a full hair and makeup day, but I can fix this. At least you give me a lot to work with." He left her by the counter. "Stay right there."

To retain her full and upright position, she braced against the wall and willed it not to move.

He walked around the bathroom, turning on the shower and opening a drawer.

She shuddered when he closed the first drawer and the sound of wood on wood boomed through her head.

"Oh look, I have a drawer for my stuff, and my toothbrush is in the holder next to yours."

Though she had seen a toothbrush before, she opened one eye. Indeed, there were now two toothbrushes in her holder. She closed her eye again. Everything was easier if she didn't have to see it.

"First things first, let's get all this out of the way." After opening and closing another drawer he came up behind her, gathered her hair up and began brushing.

Except for hairdressers, no one else had brushed her hair since Viktor got the brush stuck in her hair when she was in sixth grade. In truth, she wasn't a fan of people messing with her hair.

However, Ryder's hair brushing could only be called an experience or possibly foreplay. Had she not felt as if she were going to pass out, it would have been a mixture of calming and erotic. He took his time, sectioned off her hair and brushed, not too soft, not too hard, just right, and she couldn't help but let out a little moan. Then in an action she didn't anticipate, he proceeded to braid her hair. His hands moved quickly, his fingers grazing her skin as he worked, giving her a delightful jolt even under the weight of her hangover. He coiled her braid on top of her head and pinned it in place.

"Okay missy, hop in the shower. Just stand there, I'll be in there in a minute." He prodded her toward the water.

With no choice, she did what he said, and she didn't budge as the warm water ran over her.

Suddenly the shower door opened. "All right Miss Caine, everything today is about hydration." Ryder joined her and put a bottle of water to her lips. "Drink down like a good girl."

Again, she did as he requested and let the pure, soothing water wash dilute the poison on the inside of her body.

"I take it you're not one who drinks too much." He took a sponge and washed her down.

"I've never done anything like this." She let Ryder tend to her. Fine, she enjoyed Ryder tending to her. Yes, she probably needed to at least glance at her phone, but she was sure she couldn't focus on the words. Were any of her auctions closing? Lost in Ryder's soothing touch, she decided it didn't matter.

"We will watch it from now on." He continued rubbing her back. "So what is on today's work docket?"

His hands slid down her legs. The man expected her to think while he was taking care of her? She knew what those hands were capable of. "I had some issues yesterday I want to make sure are one hundred percent resolved. Also, I wanted to talk to you about your movie."

"My movie?" He took her by the shoulders and turned her.

At last she found the strength to open her eyes. Lord help her. If the man was gorgeous normally, him in the shower wet and staring down at her with his hair damp and in his eyes was off the charts. She couldn't even think about his body. Hung over or not he could arouse her. All smooth and sleek with the right amount of muscle definition and that v that pointed the way to his more than ample...

"What would you like to know about my movie?" He put more soap on the washcloth and brought it to her front.

"Why don't we start with what's it about?" Her voice hitched as he rubbed the cloth over her breasts.

He let out a low chuckle. "I wanted to create something that defied all genres. It's unique, an art piece, it has action and adventure seasoned with paranormal and fantasy undertones. There is also romance and some drama and a bit of comedy."

The alcohol had to still be floating around in her system because she wasn't sure what he said, especially with the way he now skimmed the washcloth between her thighs. "What's the name of it?"

"Working Title." He scrubbed her down to her toes, fed her some more water and then proceeded to skim the cloth over his body.

Fine, she simply stood there and watched as he ran his hands over his chest. Ryder Scott was nothing if not entertaining. Talk about a man who chose his ideal profession. "Okay, what's the working title?"

After rinsing off, he faced her. "It's working title." He shut off the faucet, stepped out, wrapped himself in a towel and then held a huge towel out to her.

"I understand." She let him encompass her in the towel. Feeling a bit more human, she went to the sink, took her toothbrush, and then handed Ryder his. In an effort to repay some of the way he took care of her, she even squirted the toothpaste for him. "Working title or not, I just want to have a name to put with the project."

Together, they both brushed their teeth, then took turns rinsing in the same sink, though she had two.

"Baby, the title of the movie is *Working Title*." He dropped his towel in the hamper and took hers and did the same.

"I need to see a script." She watched him walk by her. After all, it would be illegal not to look his sculpted backside.

"All in due time." The man had a drawer in their bathroom, his toothbrush next to hers, a side of the bed, and now he had his stuff in their closet. Still naked, still feeling like crud, and still confused about his movie title, she went and sat on the bed considering everything as she gawked at him getting dressed.

He slid the hangers back and forth on the pole and finally chose a pair of jeans and a black button down. "I know you prefer your men, namely me, groomed to perfection, but I need to take care of you, so I'll have a bit of stubble. I promise to shave later." After a nice long stretch, he slipped on his pants sans underwear and pulled the shirt on. "Now get dressed. I'll go make you something to put on your stomach, and I'll drive you to the office. Once you tend to you other work we can continue our meeting."

For a few moments, she sat there and stared at nothing. What the hell just happened? Now Ryder was driving her to work? She needed to get her act together, get her own food and drive to work. With conviction, she stood, her head pounded, her knees weakened, and a wave of nausea threatened to knock her over.

Maybe she just needed a ride. No way could she call Viktor or Rodger, she would never live it down. At least if she walked in with Ryder, the attention would go to him. Yes, she needed a ride and an escort.

Again, she forced herself into a standing position and dragged her body to the closet. With her hair already in a braid thanks to her new roommate, she just went with a simple black dress. Maybe no one would notice her. Somehow she managed to slip it over her head and get her feet into some shoes that at the moment felt at least a size too small.

"I went against your rules and touched the espresso machine, but I think you need the caffeine. I also added one of the brown sugar cubes in the little silver dish at the side of the machine." He handed her the little cup and then went behind her and zipped up the dress. "We can take the toast I made on the way. Also, the script to *Hollywood Stardom* arrived. I guess it's really official now that I'm getting packages here. I'll take it to work with us and study."

She sipped the warm brew and narrowed her eyes at the cup. This was the taste she was always going for, but could never achieve. Dark, roasted and toasted with a hint of sweet. The man touched her machine, but he made it better. Was she mad or not?

"Shall we?" He held his elbow out to her.

Caught in her own thoughts from espresso, to mail to everything else, she hooked her arm in his. On the way out, he handed her the toast and the script, took a juice and put a pair of dark sunglasses on her face. "No one will ever know. They'll just think you're trying to hide."

He led her through the building, and suddenly she found herself sitting in the front seat of the Aston Martin. While she knew she should call in or check her phone, the thought of trying to read the tiny screen made her stomach churn and she chose to open the script and flip through the pages. Then it hit her. She was now holding Ryder Scott's script. Once this movie wrapped, they could make a tidy sum off this on the Internet, though she hoped he would never sell it. In many ways this was history, and she ran her fingers over the page.

"All right, Miss Caine I need to ask you something." Ryder put on his own pair of sunglasses and drove out of the building.

"What do you need?" She unwrapped the toast, handed Ryder a piece and nibbled on the corner of the bread. The simple treat was oddly tasty, but maybe it always tasted better when someone else made the toast.

"Will you do me a favor and turn to the last page of the script?" As he drove through the city, he strummed his fingers on the steering wheel.

She did as he asked. "Okay, now what?"

"Will you be a doll face and read me what's on the page?"

"It says Insert Final Scene Here." The words caused her to sit up straighter.

"Yes, about that, I find it is my method to know the end of the movie, so I have my character's motivation straight from the beginning. It makes for a much more convincing performance." At a stoplight, he turned and flashed her a smile. "How about you tell me who Roxy ends up with?"

She raised her eyebrows at him.

"Can I have a kiss." Now he plied her with pursed lips.

"Not if you think that is the way to get the end of the story out of me." The light turned green and she motioned forward.

He continued driving. "Can you give me a hint?"

"No." Her voice fell as flat as their conversation.

"I know what you look like naked."

"I don't care if you post pictures of me on Chargge I'm not telling you the end." She made sure to use her official voice.

"May I ask why?" Once more they stopped, and he faced her.

"Because I don't know the end. No one knows it. It hasn't been written." Oh yes, she bested him, and she crossed her arms, and sat back with her toast.

"So we'll get to know the end at the round table this week when they give us the final script pages right for the first day of shooting, right?" They drove into her office building.

She pointed to her spot. "What do you mean? This is the script except for the last scene?"

"That's just so we basically know what's going on, but changes are always made along the way so we will get new script pages every day." He settled his car in her spot.

Before going into the office she slipped her phone out of her bag, but she had one more question. "What happens to this script then?"

"They'll get destroyed." He opened the door and got out of the car.

Rather than looking at her phone she looked at the script and hugged it to her chest. With the filming of *Hollywood Starburst*, she just made sure the money was there, but this film seemed more personal.

Ryder opened her door, and she came face to face with Ryder's crotch. His well-endowed crotch. The one in perfectly fitting jeans that seemed to show off exactly what he had without being vulgar, and she knew exactly what he had.

Point proven, this movie was definitely more personal. Still, she decided her sentiment had to be because the man knew how to make a tasty slice of toast and braid hair.

He held out his hand. "You never answered my question."

"Which was?" She slid the script under her arm and at last lifted her phone to her face.

"The ending and me, your live in lover, knowing it."

"You won't know it until they shoot it. You know this. By the way it was in your contract."

They made their way to the elevator and stepped inside.

"I thought I had an in." Ryder groaned.

Finally, she hit the button on her phone and her heart seized. Her phone was full of notifications, but the only words she saw was that Chargge was down. "Ryder." Though she instantly began shaking, she tried to get on the website.

Nothing happened. Then again they were in an elevator and even she couldn't control that.

"What's wrong?" He bent down to her phone.

"Chargge is down. Oh my God." This wasn't happening. Not right after yesterday. Her heart threatened to explode.

"Can I do anything?" He wrapped his arm around her.

A weird dizzy feeling took over her, and she held on to him. "Can you make the elevator go faster!"

"Not in this movie." Though he did the thing where he pressed the button multiple times and with increasing levels of force.

At last the door slid open, and she ran into her office to be met by Rodger.

"Chargge is back up." Coffee in hand he dashed toward her. "It's back up. It's okay."

Her entire body trembled and the ill feeling she had all morning only amplified. "It's back up." She should have been there.

"Come on." Rodger corralled her toward the door. "Where were you?"

Ryder came up behind her.

"Never mind." Rodger shook his head and they all went to her office.

"Where were you?" Upon her entering the room, Viktor stood then glanced at her new roommate. "Never mind."

"I believe I'm taking offense at this." Ryder remained by her side.

"Tell me." She gulped down the not exactly icy cold coffee and waited.

"We had a denial of access hack," Viktor reported. "Multiple IP addresses, all clones. It flooded the backup servers, and we went down for seven minutes and thirty-eight seconds. We are back on the main servers, all systems go."

"This is really good stuff. I can use it in my movie." Ryder nodded.

While her heartbeat slowly returned to normal, she sat at her desk and turned on her monitors. "I apologize. I should have been here."

"You have nothing to apologize for." Ryder went and sat in Viktor's throne. "This is why you have a ton of minions. Let them do the minioning while you get your big fancy position."

Without taking off her sunglasses or letting go of her purse or Ryder's script, she refreshed the Chargge's page and breathed a sigh of relief when she saw her familiar purple electric plug logo make its way on the screen.

Viktor stomped over to Ryder. "You're in my chair, but I do agree with you on one thing. This is why she has a staff. I've been telling her that for years."

"Well, if we agree, allow me." Ryder stood and brushed off the seat.

Viktor sat. "Everything is all right now." He turned his attention back to her. "Your focus needs to be on getting this position."

"Chargge doesn't go down." At long last, she got the chance to glance at the screen.

Viktor pointed to the screen. "Maybe you and Ryder sizzled all the cables."

As she got the competition sites up on the other two monitors, Ryder came up behind her.

"Seems as if the savage CEO has been tamed by leading man." Ryder read the story. "The two have been spotted all around town living it up as seen here at this famous LA hotspot."

The picture was of them drinking champagne, looking at each other, and Cora hated the way her heart sped.

"We have to say we like this pairing. They seem to fit." Ryder patted her shoulder. "Your competitors seem to concur. I like the way they are inadvertently giving Chargge more publicity by covering our story."

At Ryder's words, she froze. All this started the second they were spotted together. Was there a connection? What was going on? Had Ryder, the master of self-promotion, anything to do with it? She shuddered at the thought and brushed it away.

"Now, while you all do whatever it is you do with servers, I'll go study until it's my turn to take the savage CEO to lunch." He plucked the script away from her.

She tapped Viktor and frowned at the loss of her little piece of Hollywood history. "Did you know those aren't the scripts they use when filming?"

"Makes sense. They probably have to make changes." Viktor shrugged. "I know it bursts your Hollywood bubble, but everything is a business."

"Let her have her smoke and mirrors." Ryder sat the table and opened the script. "She needs more fantasy, not more reality."

Cora glanced around the room and then back to the computer screens. She needed to keep her eyes open. She failed Chargge and herself today. Too much fantasy might be fun to watch on the Internet, but it could also take her down in the end. Everything around her was an act. Maybe she should look at the auctions and surround herself with some more musical memories. Everything seemed much more simple when surrounded by music.

HOLLYWOOD STARDOM

FADE IN:

INT.HOLLYWOOD, CA – WILLIAM AND ROXY'S BEDROOM – NIGHT.

ROXY enters their bedroom in a long nightgown.

WILLIAM pulls back the blanket. ROXY turns out the light and joins him in bed.

                    ROXY
          (Moves up to his side and
          rests her head on his chest)
           I'm not used to being the
           one who is home late.

                    WILLIAM
          (Wraps his arms around her)
           How was your day being the
           plaintiff?
          (He chuckles.)

ROXY looks up at him.

                    WILLIAM
           Ask me.

                    ROXY
           The first time you took the
           stage, did you know that
           was what you wanted to do?

                    WILLIAM
           It's strange. I joined the
           band when I thought I lost
           you. I felt like I
           belonged there. Then I got
           you back, and I knew that I
           had my life.

ROXY leans in and kisses him, then lies her head on his chest.

                    WILLIAM
          The acting wasn't what you
          expected?

                    ROXY
          I'm glad I did it. I just
          don't know what I wanted.

                    WILLIAM
          Never settle until you know
          what you want.
          (He kisses the top of her
          head.)

                    ROXY
          What if you don't know what
          you want?
          (She closes her eyes.)

Chapter Ten

THE ASTON MARTIN SAILED into the parking lot behind Wilson's Bar, the establishment owned by Logan's brother was a major Hollywood hot spot, and the location for the *Hollywood Stardom* read through. Ryder took the spot normally reserved for the owner and left the engine on a few moments longer than necessary. No one should be denied hearing the purr of this amazing machine. Since he got the car over a week ago sometimes he simply took the car around the block to hear it roar.

In less than an instant, his action produced the desired result when Logan Alexander, and Drew Fulton stepped outside.

Ryder paused, took his time gathering his things, and when he was damn good and ready, opened the door to greet his public. Of course, he backed up to allow the men plenty of room to gawk and stare in awe.

"Well, well, well." Logan skimmed his fingers along the gleaming black paint then came around and stuck his head inside the vehicle. "Complete with new car smell. Am I to guess that one Miss Caine is happy with Mr. Scott's service?"

"It's not a service, but more a mutual admiration society. I just needed some new wheels and picked up this little horse and carriage.", He stretched the truth only the smallest amount, but he had to protect his benefactor. The rumors would swirl around them anyway, especially with his reputation, but he made sure to lay on the romance thick, something that was exceptionally easy when it came to his CC. He just needed to get her to play along, then it would become natural.

Drew nodded and glanced in the car. "Erin and I were considering this model, but it doesn't hold a car seat."

Both Drew and Logan laughed, speaking the secret language of those with offspring and Ryder shuddered at the image. He would take his two-seater just fine. Cora and he could drive off into the sunset with nothing holding them back.

"Speaking of which, it looks like there's just enough room in this car for you, Cora and one mellow dog." Drew went to Ryder's side and patted his shoulder.

"How is Spike?" Ryder gave him a grin.

Drew crossed his arms. "I think he needs his master."

"Oh yeah, Ivy, Curtis and I want a tote bag." Logan pulled a check out of his shirt pocket and handed it to him. "Don't' forget to give me a receipt."

Receipt, right. Tote bag, check. He needed to get on his charity. "Thanks, man, this will do some good."

"It would do better if you had your mascot with you." Drew elbowed him.

"I just need some time. You remember what it's like when everything is new." For the first time in his life, he didn't have the upper hand with this man. The man who also had his dog. He had to try a new tactic, be nice. "I'll work it out."

"All right, but work it out." Drew shook his head.

"Don't we have a read through to get to?" Ryder turned on his heel and ushered himself through the bar, making a mental note on things to take care of to keep the free money rolling in. Decorated like a 1920s speakeasy, Wilson's could almost be a set on its own.

Their director, Edward Andrews, greeted him first. "Ryder."

Ryder shook his hand. With he and Logan both having major roles in the movie, the powers that be brought in a professional director, rather than have either of them direct. Andrews' was known for his work on sequels and continuity.

"Good to see you," Ryder said. Of everyone, he needed to make nice with the director, though he knew he could do the job better than anyone.

"There's the man who needs to take his pet." Erin came over and gave him a hug.

He gave her a kiss on the cheek. "Spike needs more of your healing energy first."

"You are such an ass." She pinched him. "But I'm Roxy, so all is right in the world."

After rubbing his arm, he continued his rounds to Logan's wife. "Mrs. Ivy, always a pleasure." He took her hand and kissed the back. "What do you think of the script?"

"I think thus far, it's on track." She giggled. "I suppose we'll have to see what our screenwriter has in store for us."

At the mention of the only other woman he wanted to talk to besides Cora, Ryder turned to find a mess barreling toward him. A funnel of black curly hair, disheveled clothing and a general swirl of shambles, Madeline Hart would have collided with him, if he hadn't stepped back and avoided the cyclone. However, she was an amazing writer.

"Hi Ryder?" Burdened down with an unorganized pile of paper in her hands, she smiled at him. Ivy personally picked this writer as Madeline was a huge fan of the original film and even helped clean up some things for the second movie, however he did have to wonder how this person ever got through Cora.

Unsure why her greeting was a question, he flashed her a smile and managed to position himself slightly behind Ivy. "Maddie, how are you?" This was the woman who would make or break his lines and one he needed to ask a favor, therefore he had to be especially sweet to her.

"I'll have your first batch of pages to you in a bit." She nodded and then stumbled over to the table.

"Why don't we all get started?" Edward herded them all around the table.

For decades he and Logan took their spot on either side of Erin.

Now he watched Ivy and Logan sit down together and Erin and Drew sit down together. Well now he had his own woman, and his woman owned this whole shebang. Maybe she should have been here for this important meeting. Ever since that whole computer fail thing last week she worked hours and hours, only stepping out with him for a quick photo op, and she left before he woke up every morning. They hadn't even had sex yesterday.

Only one option left, he took his chair next to Madeline. With the opportunity handed to him, he leaned over. "I was hoping I could ask you a question."

She turned to him, giggled, and he was pretty sure she snorted. "Me?"

Ramping up the star power, he stared right in her eyes. "Yes, you." He kept his tone and volume low.

"Well, I want to welcome our stars here." Edward greeted them.

Madeline leaned in and her cheeks turned red. No doubt she could deny him nothing. "What would that be?" She curled her hair around her finger.

He gave her an eyebrow raise. "I have something I want you to take a look at."

"Oh, my." She put her hand to her chest. "Aren't you with Ms. Caine?"

"Yes, I'm with Cora!" Yes, he blurted out the words a little loud. What the hell? "I just wanted to ask you to take a look at a script of mine." More than once Cora asked to see a script, so now he had script fright and wanted to make sure it was as perfect.

Her hand moved from her chest to her mouth.

This was all he needed.

"Maybe we could talk about our script for a few minutes, Mr. Scott." Edward kept the fake smile on his face.

"I'm sorry. I knew you were seeing Cora," Madeline whispered. "I'd be happy to look at your script."

"Thanks." Like a good schoolboy, he faced front. Now that he thought about it, he didn't see her except for a second yesterday, and she certainly wasn't where she should be first thing in the morning. While Edward droned on and on about something, he retrieved his phone and sent Cora a text.

All right, he sent her a heart and a wink face.

The little moving dot bubble let him know she was instantly responding.

Are you trying to tell me something?

Though she didn't use an emoticon, at least she didn't text yell at him for bugging her. She probably missed him too, not that he missed her.

With a bit of a swagger in his typing, he responded. *Yes, I am.*

Get through the read through and you can tell me in person.

In person meant actually seeing her. *Dinner and then maybe we can do some role play.*

I'm no actress.

"Ryder." Edward's voice interrupted his not really sexting with his woman.

He gave a quick glance to Edward, but he really wanted to continue his conversation.

"Ryder," Edward said.

Damn, he better pay attention. He was the good one after all. In a rush he sent one more message. *Don't worry, I have the script.* After adding another wink face he put his phone down on the table. "Yes."

Edward gave him an extended look. "As I was saying, I would rather not have phones during our meetings or on set."

Though his first thought was to ask whether Edward knew where Ryder slept at night, he decided to go a different route. "I apologize. I was just speaking to Cora."

The man's expression did not change.

"Cora Caine." He flashed him a smile.

"Yes, you have made that abundantly clear. Why don't we continue?" Edward lifted the script. "Does anyone have any questions?"

Everyone around the table raised their hands.

Edward glanced around to each of them. "Does this have to deal with the end of the movie?"

With their hands still up, they all gave their director a collective nod.

"Let's discuss it. Madeline." Edward motioned toward her.

At her name, Madeline jumped and all her papers went flying across the table. She gathered up the documents into a crinkled pile. "I think in order to discuss the end, we must first discuss the beginning."

"The beginning of the movie?" Erin asked.

"No, the beginning of the series." Somewhere in her mess, Madeline unearthed a yellow pad with notes.

"We know the beginning," Ryder jumped in. "Four kids, road trip to the Hollywood Stardust Theatre, we have the bad guy, the good guy and the geek, there's a love triangle, ends on a cliffhanger when girl chooses good guy, but watches bad guy leave." Ryder nodded at everyone. That should at least take care of several hours of this day. He needed to get back to the apartment and do some manscaping before the woman of the house arrived home. "In movie number two, the girl drives back home and nothing changes. Fast forward twenty years and here we are."

Madeline faced him. For the woman who only moments before blushed and mistakenly thought he asked her out, the stars in her eyes faded, and she practically shot flames at him. "That's not even remotely what these movies are about."

Whoa. He still needed his favor, and he sat back and went to reach for his phone but stopped when he noticed Edward glaring at him.

"The end of the story hasn't been written, and moreover, it won't be written until we are all ready for it." The woman cleared her throat. Gone was the disheveled mess as she leaned over the table. "Because this story is so beloved, and because we've kept fans waiting for twenty years for the end, we will also wait, but we're going to do something a little different."

No one in the room could pry their focus away from the woman who would write their fate. Actually, their character's fate.

"Because the *Hollywood Stardom* story is told by Roxy reflecting on her life and on whether she would have ended up with each of the three male leads, there's no reason to know the end until the end. During the filming I'll meet with each of you and everyone will make a case for their character's end."

They were going to have to fight for their character? What kind of bullshit script was this?

On the table his phone vibrated and wanting to know what Cora responded he flipped the device over.

Damn, it wasn't Cora.

In fact if Cora had a polar opposite, it would be the person texting him.

Glen.

His chest tightening, he had to find out what the man messaged, and like a kid trying to pass a note in school, he used one finger and inched the phone closer to him.

Don't get too distracted by your new love interest, you still have a movie to make.

When the tool had the audacity to attach a picture of him and Cora the night she got a little tipsy, Ryder gnashed his teeth together.

Maybe you will finally learn to use your connections wisely.

Heat overtaking his body, he snatched up his phone. *Don't ever mention her again.* He hit send and tightened his hold on the damn device

There will be no need to ever mention her again if you do the right thing.

Ryder forced himself to swallow. *Is that a threat?*

From across the table Edward waved his hand. "Excuse me, Mr. Scott?"

"One second." Phone in hand, Ryder turned away from the table and focused on those blasted moving dots.

"Mr. Scott." Edward raised his voice.

Do the right thing and there will be no threats.

If Ryder had ever heard a threat, and he had heard many in his life, this was one. Now what should he do? Answer or ignore?

"Mr. Scott!"

Unable to think about his next move with this incessant chatter, he shot out of his chair. "I said I need a second. This is important." He turned, closed his eyes and attempted to think. What the hell was he going to do? This wasn't the run of the mill threat or maybe it was, and it just felt more sinister.

"And this movie is not important?" From behind him, Edward lowered his voice.

Ryder took a breath and slowly faced the table. "I'm not in grade school, and if I need to attend to important business I will. This isn't even a read through this is a lecture. When you want to actually work, I'll be on point." There was no way in hell he could concentrate on any movie until he figured out what to do next with Glen.

Edward stared him down.

Uncomfortable silence overtook the room.

Logan stood and went to his side. "What is with you? Take it down a notch."

"I have a few things I'm dealing with." Ryder attempted to speak without moving his lips. "I just finished one movie and I'm staring this one, and I have my own movie to deal with, I barely even had a break."

Logan pushed him back away from the table. "Is this thing with you and Cora real?"

With Logan's question, the heat surrounding him threatened to incinerate him. "Is this thing with you and Ivy real?" Was anything real? Was this as real as he could make it?

"It just happened exceptionally fast between you two, and you don't have the best track record." Logan pulled no punches.

"Seems to me I remember someone acting very fast with some reporter and, as I recall, your reputation wasn't stellar either."

Even with sweat breaking out on the back of his neck, he made sure to look his co-star right in the eye.

"Then since we don't start filming until next week why don't you go do something with her and pound it out so we don't have a feud on the set." As if challenging him, Logan lifted his chin.

"Fine." Do something? He supposed they could do something. In fact now that he thought about it, he would love to take Cora to his cabin in Big Bear and wondered if she would even agree to go. Maybe the drive and the air would do them both good. The cabin was the best escape.

Logan elbowed him. "Now go make nice."

"You know, you and I could have directed this, we didn't need a policeman." He sighed.

"This one is going to hit close to home, and we're both leads. We needed him and he's the best. Or that's what I've been told." Logan shoved him forward.

Once more, he looked at his phone. Sometimes the best course of action was no action. The more he argued, the worse it would get. He slid the stupid link to the world into his pocket, returned to the table and held his hand out to the director. "No phones." No way would he apologize.

"Thank you, Mr. Scott." Edward shook his hand.

He and Logan resumed their seats.

"Now. Why don't we go through the first scene and get our sea legs?" Edward motioned toward Madeline. "While our screenwriter passes out the pages, I want to remind everyone to turn in their scripts as they won't be necessary and aren't even complete."

Turn in the script? No. Cora really seemed to like the script, and he told her she could have it.

Madeline handed him papers and reached for his script.

In a flash, he put his hand down on it. "I have some notes in there. I'll give it to you in a bit." Instead, he reached in his bag and gave her his *Working Title* script. Not only would he get his favor, but it was a great diversion.

Madeline nodded and made her way around the table.

No one was taking this script away from Cora, and he wasn't going to make her wait until the film wrapped to have it. When he thought about it, what could he give her she couldn't buy?

He put the papers on top of the script and gathered them all up together. It wouldn't take much to sneak it into his bag. It wouldn't be the first time he stole. The only difference was this little treasure wasn't going into his storage facility, but to a woman who deserved it.

HOLLYWOOD STARDOM

FADE IN:

EXT. HOLLYWOOD, CA - OUTSIDE HOLLYWOOD STARDUST
THEATRE - DAY

ROXY opens her eyes. The camera pans to
WILLIAM, STEVEN and CHARLES in the crowd.

                    WOMAN
          (Points to WILLIAM on the
          picture)
           I recognize him. My
           daughter loves him.

                    ROXY
          The world knows him.

                    WOMAN
          How long have you known
          them?

                    ROXY
          We met in high school.

                    WOMAN
             Really.

                    ROXY
          (Nods)
          We all traveled here when
          they were going to tear the
          theatre down. They let me
          live my dream even when I
          turned into their
          nightmare.

                    WOMAN
          What do you mean?

                    ROXY
          I put them through the
          wringer. I wasn't old
          enough to deal with the
          emotions.

                    WOMAN
          (Puts her hand on ROXY's
          shoulder)
           You never answered my
          question.

ROXY faces her.

                    WOMAN
          Who is it?

ROXY takes a breath.

FADE OUT.

Chapter Eleven

"SIT RIGHT HERE, Miss Caine." Ryder settled her in her chair at the dining room table and leaned over her. "I thought we'd break in the dining room."

"I see this." Cora reached for her glass of wine.

He kissed her cheek. "We're like real people."

"Don't let the dining room fool you." Out of the corner of her eye, she glanced at him. Since she walked in the door, he'd been acting weird. In truth, that wasn't accurate, she would just say weirder than normal. Actually, she didn't know what normal was anymore. However, he did usher her into a nice hot bath and after towel drying her and doing the hair braid thing again, he had her put on a robe, and led her to the dining room table for dinner like a normal person.

Well, it wasn't unheard of.

She guessed.

"Stay right there while I get our plates." He took a sip out of her wine glass, then disappeared behind her into the kitchen.

After learning her lesson about too much alcohol, she reached for her new must have—a glass of alkaline water—and leaned back in the chair, wondering what Ryder could have possibly conjured from the nonexistent groceries in the refrigerator. Did he even cook?

"Here we go." Ryder returned and placed a plate in front of her. "The best of the best from my friends at Karma Cuisine. They deliver."

If nothing else she got her answer, unfortunately it only created more questions. "What is this?" She had to admit everything was pretty, almost too pretty to eat, but it seemed as if something were missing.

"Cucumber and watermelon salad, hummus with gluten free pita bread, a variety of seasonal olives, and a Portobello mushroom steak." He used his fork to point out the different dishes.

And now she knew what was missing. "Don't you mean Portobello mushrooms and a steak?" At saying the word, her mouth watered.

"The mushroom tastes just like a steak. You'll love it." With a lot of vim and vigor he dug into his plate.

She followed suit and took a bite of the vegetable that wanted to be meat. Smoky, hearty, delicious even, but it wasn't steak. Still, his whole display was sort of endearing so she decided to go with it.

The sounds of silverware and dishes filled the room giving the place a little bit of a homey feel that wasn't totally unwelcome.

"So, how was your day at work?" He poured her some more water.

When he first texted her earlier, she thought he would have wanted her to come home and go straight to the bedroom. She had been so busy the last few days they didn't really have much quote unquote personal time. However, with his bland question she had to wonder what was going on and put her fork down.

"How was your day?" She stopped short of asking what sin he committed.

"I brought you a present." Grinning, he took a quick drink of his water and reached over to one of the empty chairs.

She ground her teeth together wondering what he bought her with her credit card. Whatever sin he committed had to be horrible to warrant a present and dinner and no sex.

"I have to admit I sort of took this from the reading today. They wanted them back, but I knew you liked it." He presented her with his script from *Hollywood Stardom*.

Her mouth opened then she closed it as she assessed the gift. He gave her the script. There were only a few of these in the world, and she couldn't stop a smile. As a bonus, earlier she found out she won her auction for an actual prop from her favorite musical, an actual note they used right on stage. Today was a day of memorabilia.

"I signed it too." He scooted his chair over and opened the manuscript.

CC – you are making my star shine brighter. RS

"Oh." She ran her fingers over his handwriting. Fine, his signature topped what she won. "I don't know what to say."

He leaned into her ear. "I was hoping that you would say later I would get lucky."

Though she hated the relief that washed over her, she also relished in it, and faced him. "Trust me, you're getting lucky."

"Excellent." He pulled her into his lap.

At the sudden movement some loose pages fell out of the script.

"Ah." Ryder scooped up the papers. "Now these I cannot give you as these are the ones I need for work."

She glanced at the papers, then at Ryder. "Read something."

"You have plenty of books, go pick one and we can go read in bed."

"Are you shy?" At his reluctance, she had to laugh. "Read something from the famed William, our rock star. Your main part of the story is first." She thumbed through a few pages and stopped at one and pointed.

"I'm not singing for you. You'll have to get the voiceover artist for this scene." He reached for the script.

She held the script back. "Don't tell me my superstar has stage fright."

"Fine, I'll read." He took the script. "But only with the caveat that no matter what you think of my voice, we're still having sex."

"I'll go one further and say we won't have sex unless you sing me these two little lines." At her challenge she raised her eyebrows.

"All right, but only because it's you." He cleared his throat.

She watched as his eyes darted over the page and his demeanor completely changed. The bit of playfulness that always seemed to grace his face vanished. He took a breath and started with the dialogue.

"Roxanne, look at what we've built. We have the dream." His voice came out deep and strong with a bit of longing. He gave her a little nudge and pointed to Roxy's line.

She paused, but having a feeling he wouldn't continue unless she played along she read the line. "We do, we have everything, who would have ever thought we would end up here, but..." Without a doubt she didn't sound anything like an actress.

"But nothing." Ryder continued and sat up. "I know you're nervous with everyone coming to the concert, but this is your chance. You are a star, my star, maybe not in the way you thought, but this is it, we made it."

"Do you think so, really?" Cora read the cue and ran her hand over William's, wait, Ryder's cheek.

"I do." Also keeping in character, Ryder took her chin, and turned her toward him and finally sang.

Since the day we met I knew it would be us two.

The love we have together is experienced by so few.

With his lines out, he gave her gave her a light kiss.

His untrained voice possessed something, something he'd been taught to ignore or stifle, but something that needed to come out.

They pulled back and stared into each other's eyes.

In an instant, William disappeared, leaving Ryder and she bit her lip.

"You look a little star struck." He laughed and brushed her bangs aside. "Actually, you look a little confused. It's my voice I know."

She shook her head. "Did William always love Roxy like that?" The emotion in the words or the way Ryder delivered them made her heart sort of ache.

"What?" He narrowed his eyes.

"That's what I heard in your song." In truth, she felt a little breathless.

He stared into her face. "That's what you heard?"

"Were his feelings always that deep?" She had to have the answer.

"You said you saw the movie, and you made the second one, don't you know?"

When she didn't answer, he stood, taking her with him. "Well, while I planned a different one of my movies for tonight, I think we're going to have to go back to our roots." He brought her into her rarely used living room and sat them on the couch. "I have dessert, be right back."

Still a little taken with the song and watching Ryder act, she didn't have a chance to protest before the man disappeared into the kitchen once more. Maybe they needed to make a musical.

In less than a minute, Ryder returned with an assortment of chocolate covered fruit and joined her on the couch. At last real food. Well, it would have been real food if he ditched the fruit. She still wanted her steak.

In a move straight out of a family made-for-television movie, Ryder settled in the corner of the couch and gathered her up to lay against him. He leaned up enough to retrieve his phone out of his pocket and fed her piece of chocolate covered banana as he took a selfie of them. "Always nice to document the evening." With a little laugh he shoved his phone back in his pocket.

"Let's get this going." Using a remote, he pressed some buttons and put his feet up. "Try to really watch it this time."

Suddenly the apartment was filled with that godforsaken theme music to *Hollywood Stardust* that to this day made more than half of the female population in the world drop their panties.

The credits rolled over the screen and the establishing shots of high school and road maps set the stage, and rather than the first time she watched the movie, where she barely saw any of it due to her giggling girlfriends, or the second time where she spent more time watching her phone and making sure the sequel would be a sound investment, she did as Ryder requested and actually watched the movie.

If she were ever on a game show and quizzed about what *Hollywood Stardust* was about, she would have said four kids in a car, sex and a spoiled brat girl who had three guys panting after her. The reason the movie was a success was every female wanted to be Roxy, every teenager wanted to escape, and the movie came out at exactly the right time.

Then she truly watched the movie.

Watched a girl who wanted to go on a quest to the Hollywood Stardust theatre, but more than that, she wanted to go a quest for her heart, and her place, and her life, but she was a teenager and didn't really know where to go searching. Hell, Cora was an adult and she didn't know the answers either.

She watched the three guys each on their own path of self-discovery. Charles the brain needed a relief valve before he headed into his tests. He knew he wasn't going to get the girl and never even tried, but instead he made a lifelong friend. Steven slept with Roxy. He represented the unattainable guy, and once Roxy attained him she lived out the fantasy.

Then there was William.

The proverbial good guy. The one every girl said she wanted to be with, even though deep down she wanted Steven. The one who, above anyone, loved Roxy.

As the end of the movie approached, Cora sat up. She knew the end—everyone knew the end. The end was one of the most famous endings in movie history. Still, her heart raced. Charles went home, where he needed to be, the right decision for him.

Steven drove William and Roxy up to the Hollywood Stardust theatre and Cora's heart pounded as William took Roxy's hand and led her toward her destination.

Steven went the way of all the bad boys every girl wanted to change and drove off.

William pulled Roxy into his arms, gave her a hug, then Roxy opened her eyes and watched Steven drive away.

The screen faded to black and her adrenaline getting the best of her Cora jumped up. "Oh my god!" At her own outburst she clasped her hand over her mouth and turned toward Ryder.

"I know, I know, Steven drove away. She should have ended up with Steven." Ryder shook his head.

"Are you nuts?" She stomped her foot. Then unable to discuss it, she crossed her arms and paced the length of the living room.

"Wait!" Ryder went to her and took her by the shoulders. "Cora."

Jaw jutted out, heart still pounding, she looked into his eyes.

"Give me your view of the end." His tone came out as serious, as if he were playing a neurosurgeon in a movie.

"I think we should go have sex now." She tried to get away, but he held her in place.

"First tell me." He widened his eyes.

No question, Ryder would bug her until she told him. "William brought her to her goal. I think in many ways he was her goal, but just like any end, you wonder what else could be, but..." She huffed and let the rest out. "...William loved her." Her voice did not crack when she said that last part. Damn, yes it did.

Suddenly, Ryder pulled her in and kissed her, a hard kiss where he wrapped his arms around her and even bent her back. He broke the kiss, leaving her breathless.

"Ryder?" She practically panted.

"Before I have my way with you, I have to commemorate this moment." Once more, he got his phone, positioned them in such a way to give them some great light and snapped a picture. "I'm going to put this up on my social media. It'll be great for both of us."

His fingers flew over the phone, and he even added a little caption.

Regular stay at home night with a private movie screening and yes, she would have picked William. He tagged her and hit upload.

Off in the distance her own phone sounded off, letting her know Ryder mentioned her. By morning, the picture would be all over Chargge and everywhere else, like she wanted, and like she had to remember. Just the regular night with the normal couple.

HOLLYWOOD STARDOM

FADE IN:

INT. ARIZONA – INSIDE STEVEN'S HOME OFFICE - DAY

STEVEN – late thirties, hair pulled back dressed in a white shirt and jeans, is in his office at his computer. Posters from the various movies he has directed hang on the walls.

                    STEVEN
           Roxy!

                    ROXY
           (Enters breathless)
           Did you figure it out?

                    STEVEN
           (Spins the chair toward her)
           Stand right there and
           strike a pose.

                    ROXY
           (Smiles)
           Direct me first.

                    STEVEN
           (Raises his eyebrows)
           Stop. Look me in the eye.
           Give me a pose that makes
           me squirm in my seat and
           hold it.

ROXY licks her lips puts one hand on her hip and the other one on her collar, opening her shirt slightly and stands perfectly still.

                    STEVEN
          Don't move.
          (He spins his chair back to
          his computer and furiously
          types, glancing at her a
          couple of times.)
          All right. Come here.
          (He holds his arm out.)

ROXY exhales and goes to STEVEN taking sitting
on his lap.

                    ROXY
          Did I help?

                    STEVEN
          You always help. We're the
          dynamic duo of film.

CAMERA PANS over the walls. Showing Roxy as the
star in the films that Steven directs.

                    ROXY
          But this is the first time
          you did the screenwriting.

                    STEVEN
          And I have my muse on my
          lap.

                    ROXY
          Maybe then you should make
          your muse official.

                    STEVEN
          Maybe that would break the
          magic.
          (He smiles and kisses the
          tip of her nose)

ROXY leans back and looks into his eyes.

                    STEVEN
          It's coming love, I want
          the timing to be right, and
          now we have to work on this
          picture.

                    ROXY
          It always seems like
          something gets in the way.

                    STEVEN
          That's called life.
          (He pulls her in for a
          kiss.)

ROXY hugs him, sighs, and looks at her empty
ring finger.

Chapter Twelve

PUBLIC LOCATION, PRIVATE LOCATION, indoors, outdoors. Things Ryder always considered anytime he stepped anywhere near the public. Even meeting at a private location could hold many perils for him, especially if it was with a woman who was not the one he was seeing at the time, namely Cora. All he needed was for this to show up on a tabloid. After all, his girl said she had all sorts of ways to find things out. He wondered what she truly knew. In the five days since their movie night, figured out she was absolutely fastidious on anything she deemed worthy of her time. Now she had dissected the entire movie plot point by plot point. Basically, his woman knew a lot.

For this particular interlude, a semi-public kind of private place would be best. If someone snapped a photograph, he could easily explain it away with something that was even foreign to him...the truth.

Supplies in hand, Ryder made his way into the commissary at the studio. At this time of day, the place stood pretty empty, except for the errant grip or production assistant. Showing up early was a calculated move, one designed so he could choose the perfect setting. No one could ever be trusted, and he took a seat in the far corner where the only seat his guest could take was across from him at the other side of the table.

After setting up the table with the requisite pads of paper, pens and as a bonus two bottles of juice, he leaned back and glanced at his phone. Along with a few messages from his agent and Logan, he had to smile at the fact none was from Glen and one was from Cora. She still hadn't really gotten a handle on the whole sexy text thing, but hey, the woman was trying.

Lunch?

All right well, it wasn't much in the great scheme of things, but it was a huge step in the world of Cora. First, she initiated the text. Second, she actually used a question mark, making it more of an invitation rather than a command. Since the night she decided William would be the man for her, he detected a crack in her armor, and a welcome one at that.

He stretched his fingers and decided to show her how this was done.

Only if you are the main dish. At his thought, he licked his lips.

I'm at the office.

Leave it to Cora to state the obvious.

Then get the stuff off your desk, it will make a perfect table.

See you at noon, maybe you can bring your script with you.

Yes, the script. His script. The one she asked for repeatedly. It wasn't an unusual request. What if she read it and didn't like it? What would happen then? If she didn't believe in the movie, would she still back him? Somehow, he had to get back the movie money Glen gave him and actually make a movie. *When the script is ready for Cora consumption you will see it.* All he knew was it had to be perfect and he looked up to see his script whisperer barreling toward him. *Noon it is, be ready with my favorite dish.* He hit send and stood, welcoming his guest of the hour.

"Ryder." Papers everywhere, hair everywhere, clothing everywhere, somehow Madeline managed to thrust her hand out from among all the mess.

After shaking her hand, he helped her plop down in the seat, then catching an errant paper and moving her hair out of his mouth before taking his own chair. "Thank you for coming."

A snort and a giggle later, Madeline settled into her seat. "I read your script."

His stomach twisted into a knot. "And?"

Rather than answer, she opened the document, thumbed through the pages and pulled out what appeared to be some typewritten notes and ran her fingers over them.

"Madeline?" At the moment, she should be squealing with delight, saying how much she adored it, could barely tear herself away, and though it wasn't on film yet, she could totally picture the whole thing replaying in her mind.

"I just want to review my notes." With no emotion, not even a snort, she thumbed through her pages.

Anytime someone had to refer to their notes meant they couldn't remember. What the hell, did he have an unmemorable treatment? That was impossible. He strummed his fingers on the table.

"All right." She nodded.

Ryder held his breath.

"The story is good." She lifted the pages to her face.

"Good?" The word thumped against his chest like the tomatoes they would be throwing at him. In Hollywood, good would get you absolutely nothing, it was almost better to be a flop.

"Yes, good." At last, she put the papers down. In an instant, the disaster zone that was Hollywood Stardom's screenwriter disappeared, as if suddenly the papers arranged themselves, and Madeline became a little less disheveled. "You need to ramp up Marko's character arc, give him some more backstory, up his stakes, you can pepper with some added dialogue."

"What about a flashback?" He leaned over the table to see what Madeline wrote about his main character.

"No, that may work for other movies, but because this takes place over so many scenes and genres and there are a lot of fantasy elements, I think a flashback would only serve to confuse the audience." She turned the page.

After letting her words sink in, he sat back. Was his story confusing? No, the viewer merely had to pay attention. His movie had plot.

"Now onto the plot." Madeline continued.

At least the woman recognized there was a plot.

"I feel there's a hole in the love story. You never get the 'I love you moment.' I really feel you would benefit from adding one more scene of one more genre and letting us have some of that type of fantasy." She turned the page.

"You want me to add a scene?" Just to prevent him from jumping up and screaming, he clutched the edge of the table. Yes, he was prepared for editing, a little I dotting and T crossing, but adding a scene?

"This is your script, you can do what you want, but if this was my script or a script I was fixing, I'd add a scene right here." She pushed the script to the middle of the table and opened it up to a page about three quarters of the way in.

"I already have a romance genre sequence." No way could he add a scene. Did she understand what that entailed? The story was finished.

"I think in this case, a musical scene would illustrate the romance perfectly." Instead of looking at him, she read her notes in his script.

"I don't sing and I don't dance." He growled at her. Did he need to add a scene?

"You're not Marko." Madeline let out a laugh. "But speaking of self-insertion..."

"What?" Self-insertion? Scene adding? No flashbacks? This woman was tearing his script to shreds. "What else is wrong with Marko?"

"It's not Marko, its Lena." A smile grew over her face. "Let me ask you something."

His female protagonist. "Yes." Truth be told, he was still back on scene adding and now he felt desperate for a flashback. Actually, he wanted to vomit, but they were at the studio in a semipublic private place.

"You based her off your past relationships?" She raised her eyebrows.

Not knowing how to answer her, he didn't answer her.

"Marko is clearly you, or what you perceive yourself to be, so Lena clearly has to be the woman you think you want." Madeline's eyes crinkled with her smile.

"Is this a problem?" No way would he confirm or deny her suspicions.

"She needs depth." Madeline handed him another page of notes.

Fine, he was with a lot of shallow people. Depth, scenes, flashback, self-insertion. He wrote a piece of shit. Why didn't she just say it? "What do you suggest?" Head hung low, he put his proverbial tail between his legs and waited for the next knife to go in his chest.

"Don't have her fall in instant love, have her stand up for herself. It's okay if she doesn't agree with Marko all the time. She is more than just an accessory to your hero."

Madeline's words resonated around him. All her words. She was a seasoned screenwriter, an excellent one. Cora hired her, and he went to her for advice. If he allowed himself a moment to step back, he could see the musical scene, get what she said about adding more to Marko, and deep down he always knew Lena needed work. The heroine was two dimensional, flat and boring.

He needed to make her smart, funny, a match for Marko, more like…like…like… "Oh my god." The blood rushed through his veins at his revelation.

"There it is, that spark. That's my favorite feeling. What did you discover?" Madeline shifted in her seat.

"I think I got it." He breathed the words. "Lena is different."

"Your story is different." Madeline clapped. "They say we pull from what we know. Make those changes, and you have a great film. Excellent commercial potential." She handed him the rest of her notes.

"Thank you." He gathered up the papers. "What can I do for you?" Did he pay her?

"A credit when the film is made would be perfect." She graced him with another snort and pulled one last thing out of her pile and held it out, transforming once more into the hurricane. "Maybe a signature."

He took the glossy recently taken of the *Hollywood Stardom* cast. Everyone else had signed it. Once she had his signature, it would make real money, and she deserved it. He grabbed a marker out of his bag, signed his name as not to cover any important part of the picture and personalized it for her. "I have some writing to do."

They both stood and headed toward the exit. He had to get to lunch with the woman who was truly Lena. She was his key to making this movie and having his life back.

HOLLYWOOD STARDOM

FADE IN:

INT. ARIZONA - ROXY AND STEVEN'S LIVING ROOM - NIGHT

STEVEN and ROXY enter their home.

> STEVEN
> (Closes the door)
> We're ready. Filming starts next week.

> ROXY
> (Smiling, she backs up, and motions for Steven to follow.)
> Oh, Mr. Director, I think I need some extra special tutoring.

> STEVEN
> (Crosses arms)
> Oh, is that so? Don't I give you constant attention every day?

> ROXY
> (Kicks off her shoes and lays down the sofa)
> Seems right now I need something more.

STEVEN slowly walks across the room, stops and looks down at her.

> ROXY
> What is it?

> STEVEN
> Did you ever think we would make it here?

                    ROXY
          (Holds her arms out to him)
                    Part of me always
                    knew it, part of me
                    thought we would
                    never be here, part
                    of me thought we
                    would be farther
                    along.

                    STEVEN
          (Joins her on the couch and
          takes her into his arms)
           What if Miss Roxy never
           gets what she wants?

                    ROXY
           I don't think you can deny
           me anything. You made me a
           star.

                    STEVEN
          (Let's out a laugh)
           That's only because I can
           make you into what I want.

                    ROXY
           And you always get what you
           want.

                    STEVEN
           Just like I can deny you
           nothing.
          (He pulls her in for a
          kiss.)
           You'll get what you want
           when I want it as well.

ROXY pulls back, looks into Steven's eyes then
kisses him once more.

Chapter Thirteen

CORA OPENED HER EYES and held her breath before glancing at the clock. After saying a silent cheer, she had at least another hour before Ryder had to get up for the first day of shooting *Hollywood Stardom*, she turned over onto what was fast becoming her favorite sleeping surfaces. Namely Ryder's chest.

With a satisfied moan, he wrapped his arms around her and settled back down.

The last week their mornings slowly morphed into a little quite time they shared, rather than a rush for her to get ready and go to the office. Some said it took two weeks to make a habit. Fortunately or unfortunately for her, this whole AM ritual only took a week. Either she was a fast learner, or she was a fool.

Since the night they watched *Hollywood Stardust*, things changed. It wasn't something she could exactly pinpoint and definitely not something she could describe, but there was definitely something different. They lived together, came home to each other, had sex together, what did she expect?

Then last night they watched *Hollywood Starburst* under the guise Ryder needed to brush on his character's development. Although she spearheaded the movie getting made, she never really watched that one either. Another road trip had Roxy traveling on her way back home. The story itself was deep, moving and held a strong moral about taking time for oneself. However, after getting upset all over again about Roxy and William not ending up together, she might or might not have let out that she preferred Ryder in the role rather than the Ryder lookalike actor hired to portray the character in the sequel.

Rather than teasing her or making her explain further, he simply kissed her, held her hand, and took her to bed where he was especially special.

She ran her hand over the part of his chest she wasn't strewn over. The man was all smooth skin and muscle, maybe they needed to make a movie about that, it would be a blockbuster.

Beneath her palm his heart beat, sort of soothing and hot all at the same time. She hooked her leg over his and skimmed her hand down his side to his hip and his thigh.

Strange how the simple act of touching him aroused her, or maybe it was just because she anticipated morning sex. She couldn't help but sneak her hand between his legs.

His morning erection greeted her, and her mouth watered. Impressive would describe him accurately, long, thick, hard, velvety, but more than that was how he knew how to use what the good lord gave him.

As she gave him some slow light strokes, she lifted her face to the crook of his neck, and right as she went to kiss him, he took her by the chin and connected their mouths.

Her heart jumped with anticipation, and she tightened her hold on him. He turned to his side, deepened the kiss, and cupped her bottom.

With a gasp she broke the kiss, and his mouth instantly traveled to her neck where he sucked and nipped her soft flesh, sending heated shivers throughout her. What about this man made her crazy with need?

In search of his lips, she turned her head. Ryder took his cue and kissed her, a languishing kiss where their tongues caressed against one another and their mouths melded together.

She pressed her body to his and now they gyrated in unison until they both panted in desire.

At last, he reached over her head, got one of the condoms he stashed in the little compartment in the headboard, ripped it open with his teeth and pressed it into her hand.

As soon as she rolled the condom on him, he got her on her back and entered her.

Her breath hitched at the sudden, welcome fullness.

Embedded inside her, he leaned up, stared down at her, and brushed her hair away from her face.

Unable to take her eyes off him, she bit her lip, and curled her legs around his waist. If he didn't move soon, she would explode.

He lowered his mouth to hers, and rather than driving into her, ground his hips in a circle, hitting her in all the right ways.

The sun shimmered into the room, and though he needed to get on set and she needed to get to work, they lay there together as if neither of them had any cares in the world except for how they moved in that delicious rhythm designed only to edge them closer and closer to their end.

Their build up was slow but intense, her climax began to crest, and she held him tighter. "Oh God." It was there on the horizon like the sunrise, but not quite.

He sped up but stayed fluid, gentle. "Let it happen."

She shut her eyes, and writhed beneath him. "Ryder."

"It's so good." Again he kissed her.

"Ryder." She bucked her hips, anything to get him as deep as possible.

Finally, he lost control and rammed into her. "Cora, now!"

In a heated burst, her body gave in to those amazing pulses she craved. They encompassed her, and she dug her nails into his biceps as her climax consumed her.

"Ah!" He held her tighter and tensed with his end. "Damn."

They remained in each other's arms, catching their breath and allowing time for their muscles to relax. This wasn't the morning quickie he wanted last week, everything was different, better and little bit disconcerting.

"Lord." He lowered his face to her chest. "That was so good I swore I saw stars."

"Maybe that's a good omen for the movie." She couldn't stop a smile.

"It's certainly better than breaking a leg." His chuckle vibrated though her. "Let's go clean up, stay with me while I get ready."

"You need help getting ready?" As he moved to her side, she winced as his body left hers.

"I just want you there." He got out of bed, took her by the hand, and took her into the bathroom with him.

Together they took care of their morning grooming, shared a shower and got dressed.

She finished putting on her mascara and watched Ryder simply comb his wet hair straight back.

"Not your favorite look I take it." He came up behind her and brushed out her hair. "From now until this movie wraps, I won't be doing my own hair or making my own clothing choices, unless it's after hours."

"Oh, I suppose that makes sense." The fact he actually put on underwear this morning should have given her the clue.

He wiped a smudge out from under eye, and guided her to the kitchen where he proceeded to make her espresso. "So, what are you going to do with all your morning time now that I have to be on set at the crack of dawn?"

With the movie upon them, she wondered how their lives would change. They sort of had a routine, but along with routine she needed to act like any good company and be nimble in times of change. "I suppose we'll just have to go to bed earlier." She popped some bread in the toaster, and went to the refrigerator to grab some fruit, water and a protein shake.

"I love the sound of that." He gave her a kiss on the cheek and the toast popped up.

While he got down two plates and prepped the toast, she doled out the fruit. He put her espresso by her plate, and she put the water by his. Lastly, he got down two glasses and poured them each some of the protein shake.

They looked at each other. When did they turn into a couple with habits? At least she didn't have to worry about their routine.

"Cheers." He lifted his water.

"Here's to toast." She held her espresso up, and they each took a sip of their respective beverage, shared their quick breakfast, and then left the apartment, parting only to get in their respective cars.

"Come here." He held his hand out to her. "Edward doesn't allow phones on set, so if I don't get to text or call, that's why."

"Break a leg." She gave him another kiss and got in her car.

They both sat in their cars and looked at each other.

More than a minute passed, then Ryder made the motion for her to roll down her window.

She pressed the button and the glass that separated them disappeared.

"What are you doing?" he called over.

Faced with one of those moments where she could lie or tell the truth, and with her head still in a post orgasmic haze, she went with the truth. It was easiest. "I was waiting for you to drive away. What are you doing?"

"I was waiting for you to drive away and since that's a guy thing, can you get going so I'm not late?" He flashed her a grin.

She gave him a thumbs-up, rolled up her window and never admitted to herself or anyone else that she watched him follow her for several blocks, until he had to turn toward the studio, and she toward the office.

Too many times to count, she ended up at the office during these early morning hours. The quiet was welcome compared to walking into chaos in progress.

Yes, they were welcome, unless she had a movie star in her bed. One who knew how to use her espresso machine and make toast, and make love. At her thoughts, she sped into her parking space and let herself the building, walking through the lobby, the click clack of her heels echoing on the marble floor.

This time of day there was absolutely no one else there and probably for the first time ever, rather than heading straight toward the elevator, she walked over to the huge floral display in the center of the lobby and actually looked at the arrangement. The whole coming into office early and staying on Ryder's schedule thing would work right until the time he went on location for some of the filming.

What would happen then?

Of course, the greater question would be what would happen after the CEO position was filled? They never really put a time frame on their situation. Did it last until the decision was made? Was there some other boundary she didn't know about? Maybe they would do as Ryder said and live the role.

Her stomach tightening, she shook her head. These silly girl thoughts didn't belong in her world. No matter if her office was empty or not, she refused to walk inside her sanctum with anxiety over nothing. How was this different than any other relationship, except for the part where they pre-planned a few things and made some arrangements? She had no time to worry and waste time on such silly nonsense that came with a more traditional relationship.

The pound of foreign footsteps interrupted what should have been complete silence.

Startled at the interruption and she spun around to find nothing, no one.

Though it was probably the guard, the shudder down her spine made her feel as if someone was there, watching her. "Hello?"

Nothing.

She wrapped her arms around her shoulders and glanced around in all the corners.

Again, nothing.

Since Ryder and all the disruption with her business, her schedule had been off. She wasn't the woman who was scared to be alone. This was where she worked, where she spent the majority of her time.

Even with her heart still speeding, she forced herself to the bay of elevators, and pressed the button. Solace would be found upstairs.

Out of the corner of her eye, she swore she saw some movement.

"Hello!" She froze and broke out into a sweat. The shaking started instantly, and she swore her knees wanted to give out. "Hello!"

The only answer she received was the ding of the elevator and the doors sliding open.

Her hand on her chest, she scanned between the elevator and the lobby.

Even with her trembling, she managed to retrieve her phone from her purse grinding her teeth together when her first thought was to call Ryder, then remembered he couldn't take phone calls on the set.

"Damn it." Out of nowhere, her world was off kilter. What the hell would Ryder do anyway? What was wrong with her?

Once more, she looked into the empty elevator, but she couldn't shake the sensation like someone was there.

She backed away from the doors and went toward the front of the building. Her shaking vibrated to the point where when she reached the doors leading to the main street, she could barely push them open. At last she managed, and the cool morning air hit her face. She took her first full breath since her mind decided to play tricks on her. Then she saw her favorite coffee cart setting up.

"Miss Caine." The older man nodded at her. "I'm not quite open yet."

"That's fine. Do you mind if I sit here?" She motioned toward the little table and chairs set up around the little courtyard.

The man smiled. "I'll be ready in a few minutes."

Hugging her purse to her, she sat at the table and went to the Internet on her phone.

Chargge was fine. They weren't on the front page, but she supposed that was all right. After a quick peek at her auction sites, she did a quick search for her and Ryder.

The *National Reporter* came up as having uploaded a story about them in the last forty minutes.

At a mention in the sleazy tabloid, she bit her lip and hit the button.

Her throat dried out at the headline.

You Get What You Pay For

Over the last two weeks, we've all be watching in wonder as the romance of the Hollywood hero, Ryder Scott and Internet Ice Queen, Cora Caine, has unfolded in almost picture perfect fashion. We caught this pic of Ryder driving to his first day of shooting the anticipated Hollywood Stardom in a brand new Aston Martin. Either Ryder goes through cars like alkaline water bottles, or Miss Caine bought herself the ultimate Hollywood hunk. We have to say Miss Caine, you got a bargain at twice the price.

In need of that coffee, or a break or a tranquilizer, most definitely an antacid, she hit the speed dial on her phone.

"I'm on my way to the office," Viktor answered. "I saw the *National Reporter*."

"I'm at the coffee stand in front." Her voice came out scratchy as if she hadn't spoken in a year. "We're not going to the office today."

"Where are we going?"

In the background, Cora heard Viktor starting his car.

"We need to go check out what's happening on the set at *Hollywood Stardom*." She hung up and went to the man with coffee. Everything changed too fast.

HOLLYWOOD STARDOM

FADE IN:

EXT. ARIZONA – ON LOCATION IN THE ARIZONA DESERT – MIDDAY

PAN to ROXY standing while the male lead gets down on one knee in front of her. She sighs, shakes her head and turns to STEVEN.

                    STEVEN
          Cut!
          (He gets out of his
          director's chair and goes to
          her.)
          What's wrong?

                    ROXY
          I can't do this.
          (She stomps off set.)

                    STEVEN
          Everyone take ten!
          (He runs after ROXY,
          skidding to a stop in front
          of her.)
          What the hell are you
          doing? I have to get this
          shot.

                    ROXY
          Did you put this scene in
          here to torture me?
          (She tries to move away.)

                    STEVEN
          (Catches her by the
          shoulders)
          We rehearsed this scene,
          you were there when I wrote
          it. What are you talking
          about?

                    ROXY
(Shakes her head)
 Did you know that every
 time we rehearsed this
 proposal I thought that
 somehow you would come
 charging over with a ring?

                    STEVEN
 Why does everything come
 down to this?

                    ROXY
 Because it does. Because I
 waited years for you.
 Because I fought for you.
 Because…
(She turns away.)

                    STEVEN
 Because you gave everything
 up for me.
(He lets go of her.)
 I'm not going to be
 threatened into marrying
 you.

                    ROXY
 I'm done being your piece
 of clay. I quit.
(She walks off set.)

Chapter Fourteen

THE FIRST DAY ON SET always reminded Ryder of the first day of school. There might or might not be some of the same people, the dynamics hadn't been set yet, and there was pressure to be on one's best behavior, look pretty and generally get along with others.

Still in afterglow mode from his early AM session with Cora, he made his way into his trailer. Long ago, he had his own trailer, but he ended up selling it off, keeping only a few select mementos, and afterward made sure these little luxuries and all the fineries were put into his contract.

He nodded at the vanity where he would have his hair and makeup done. The bathroom boasted a whirlpool tub big enough for both him and Cora, and thankfully, he asked for a king sized bed. It even contained an entertainment area, including a big screen television.

Before settling in, he checked to make sure there were exactly twelve bottles of alkaline water in the refrigerator, four bottles of sparkling water from a famed spring in France, and a jar of organic creamy peanut butter. Decorating the room was live bamboo, a Zen rock garden and a water lily in a glass bowl. He needed to add an espresso machine to his rider for his lady.

Yes, there were perks to being on set.

After changing into the costume already hanging in the closet, he heard a knock on the door. No doubt, hair and makeup was there to get him ready, and he opened the door.

"This is yours!" Erin thrust two shopping bags at him, stomped inside his trailer and motioned for the stagehand to follow. "Put him here." She pointed to the floor.

Without a word, the stagehand deposited Spike at his feet.

"Erin, come on," Ryder protested. "It's our first day here." He looked down at his furry friend. "I told you I'd make this up to you."

Spike looked up at him and raised his paw.

"That is the most he has done since you brought him to us. Drew said no more, and I can't stop crying." Her hair up in curlers and in a red satin robe, Erin appeared to be an overdramatic housewife. "I can't work and cry over a dog at the same time."

"What am I supposed to do with him?" Unable to resist Spike's droopy little face, he bent down and gave him a pat.

Spike wagged his tail and did that thing with his paw again.

"He loves you." Erin's voice broke. "I don't know why, but he loves you."

"Hair and makeup!" Two women entered the trailer, shoving themselves in with him, Erin and the stagehand.

"Erin," he growled. Spike did his paw thing. At least they were in sync.

"Inside the bags are his food, his toys, his leash, his clothes, his schedule, the vitamins Drew specially blended for him, and the tablet that has his video pre-loaded, so he can watch while you're working. I also included your monthly supply of Hollywood Glow and another check for your charity." She put her hand to her forehead. "I'm sorry Ryder, but I'm a mother now, and I have to think of my baby first. After buying you that car, Cora can buy a dog sitter, since she obviously needs you for something." With the flourish that only Erin could create, she looked down at Spike, pursed out her lower lip and then ran out, her red robe billowing in her wake.

"What the hell does that mean?" he asked the rest of the people in his trailer. "He watches videos?"

The stagehand shook his head and walked out.

"We're on a schedule, Mr. Scott." One of the women tiptoed closer. "What a lovely little dog."

Spike took one look at the woman and hid behind Ryder's legs.

He took his chair and his dog stayed by his side. His dog. His and Cora's dog. They could have a pet, yes they could. They were normal...sort of.

Even he couldn't convince himself of that one.

The women began working on him. The distinctive scent of theatrical makeup filled the room, and he sat back to allow them to do their jobs. Maybe before he went out into the trenches, he could slip Cora a quick sext.

Before he even had the chance to ask one of the girls to get his phone and his script pages, another knock came at his trailer door. Not wanting to get up with the girls around him, he lifted a finger telling them to stop. "Come in!" He expected either Edward or Logan. If Drew showed up, he needed to ask how a dog watched a video.

The door opened and Glen, his nemesis, walked inside with another man dressed in a black suit.

His skin heated to the point where he was sure the makeup would melt right off him. Asking how they even got here would be a moot point. They could go where they wanted.

"Mr. Scott, I thought we might find you here." Glen nodded. "We brought you a little gift for your first day on set."

If the man kissed him, or gave him a black rose, he was screwed. Wait, that was a whole different movie.

The second thug revealed a long thin box in red wrapping paper.

With no chance of avoiding this confrontation and unwilling to make a scene, at least not one that wasn't scripted for the movie, Ryder smiled up at his crew. "Would you two lovely ladies mind giving me a few minutes of privacy? Maybe you can take Spike out over to that little patch of grass by the commissary and come right back?"

The women put their tools down and one grabbed Spike's leash. When the dog didn't move, the other woman picked him up after looking back twice at him, left.

Once the door closed, Ryder gave his unwanted visitors a grin. "If you wanted a personal autograph session, I could have arranged one."

"Don't you want to open your present?" Glen crossed his arms.

He didn't want to touch anything from them. "I am going to make *Working Title*. I'm finally in the position to be able to make some last adjustments to the script and continue shooting."

"How are you going to do any filming while you're in full production here?" Glen asked.

Fine, the man had a point. "It's a three-month shoot. I won't schedule anything after this wraps and I'll devote every bit of time to Working Title. In fact, I'll provide you with a full schedule by the end of next week." Maybe he and Cora could go on location and get out of here for a while. Hell, he would give her a part. With all the computer knowledge she possessed, she could do her CEO stuff from anywhere, probably even another planet. Actually, that might be a cool thing to add to the script in his sci-fi sequence. "I actually got some polishing advice from a screenwriter and I think the changes will really add to the story."

"You've been promising us progress for over a year now. You're our first foray into film, you are the star we want." Glen took the present and stepped closer. "However, we need a little more on your part."

Ryder pressed his back into his chair.

"All we've seen is unusable footage as too much time passes for there to be any continuity." Glen took the top off the box.

"I think the *Hollywood Stardust* franchise has proven that you can overcome time lapses between shoots." At his own sensible statement, Ryder crossed his legs.

"We don't want any more lapses." Glen tilted the box toward him, showing him a high-end designer pen. "We've decided to let you off easy. We want your movie, all the rights, your name in the credits, and we'll disappear."

The man could have just as easily asked him to chop off an arm. He hardened his jaw and shook his head. For twenty years, he worked on this movie. First writing it then tweaking it, and using his money and other's money to try to get it made. This was the one thing that would make him different. Everyone only knew Ryder Scott, the Hollywood leading man, the one who did some directing, the man who flitted from one thing to the next, the man who might or might not be for sale to the most beautiful women with the most money. This movie was a chance to show everyone his other side, his true creation, something that was purely his. "I'll make your movie. I will."

"If we give you one last break, we'll need a little more collateral on our side." Glen held the pen out to him. "We want the cabin."

Years ago, he swore to his father he would never let the cabin go. No matter what he needed or what happened, his father reminded him what he needed could be found in the cabin, whatever happened could be dealt with there, it was their nest, their safe place. All his life he remembered his father's business associates wanting it. It had since become the brass ring no one could grasp. In fact, his father put the property in Ryder's name on purpose. He said that made it untouchable.

He hit a dead end, the only way out was through Cora. But she shouldn't be surprised if he asked for something for the movie, because it was part of their deal. If that were the case, why was he even hesitating? "How about I just pay you back?"

Glen shook his head. "We want a movie. We want it with you."

They owned him until he produced a film. The money, the cabin, whatever, was nothing but an insurance policy. When the bad guys couldn't be bought off, the stakes only amplified. The money they gave him was gone, and no matter what he needed Cora's funds. "I'll get you some collateral, but I'll need a few days."

"You have until tonight." Glen eyes widened. "Do you understand me?"

"This shoot may go late tonight. First days are hard." Above all else he had to buy some time.

Without a knock, the door opened. His crew and his pet came inside.

"Mr. Scott, we have to get you ready." The woman handed him his dog.

"We'll see you tonight." Glen lifted his chin and then both he and the other jerk left.

Spike in his lap, Ryder stared unseeing, while the women finished their work, transforming him back into the role of William. The twenty years were good to his character. Rather than pursuing his acting career, William went on to be a rock star, some would call it a different sort of actor. His character lived his dream, stood out, had roots, Ryder needed that as well, and that's why he couldn't let go of his movie.

"You're all ready, Mr. Scott." The women backed away from him.

Everything that could have happened before walking out onto set already occurred. There was nothing he could do about Glen until later.

He stood, set up Spike with some food, water and his tablet and stepped outside.

Spike followed him down the few stairs.

"Hey buddy, you have to go inside and watch your movie." He put him back inside the trailer, but Spike came down the stairs again.

Apparently, nothing was going to work out for him today. After two more tries, he gave up closed the door and let Spike come along for the ride. He was thankful for the little walk before reaching the Hollywood Stardust façade, the site of their first scene.

Already Logan, Ivy, Drew and Erin were on set. The crew continued their set up.

"Is that our new prop?" Logan stared down at Spike.

Spike hid behind his leg and lay down.

Drew let out a laugh.

"He's really mellow, his owner died," Ryder said. No matter which direction he moved Spike moved with him.

In full Roxy regalia, Erin stomped over. "Are you dead?"

After this morning, it was a question he didn't know the answer to. Still, he said, "Not that I'm aware of."

"Then his owner isn't dead, because you're his owner." Erin glared at him.

"Hello everyone." Edward's voice boomed behind him.

A charming grin forced on his face, Ryder turned and nodded at the director.

"Is that your dog?" Edward focused on the canine.

"No. I mean yes." Ryder never had so many problems with a director. He normally told them what to do. "It's my therapy dog, I'm giving him therapy."

"We can't have a dog on set." Edward held out his arm and corralled Ryder away from the rest of the group.

Ryder went to run his hand through his hair, then stopped, realizing it would only cause havoc for the hair stylists. "Listen, I can take care of the dog situation, but you aren't allowing phones on set."

"We haven't even begun and already you are holding up production." Edward frowned. "We also have another matter besides the dog that needs to be addressed."

At a total loss for words, Ryder shoved his hands in his pockets and waited for the next anvil to fall.

"Did you *inadvertently* take the *Hollywood Stardom* script?" His director's low tone was soaked with sarcasm.

"Are you saying I stole it?" Be it that he stole it or not, no one would accuse him of such a thing, and he ground his teeth together.

Edward leaned in. "You can take my words however you like, but I want my script returned."

"It's not your script," Ryder hissed in return.

"Actually, it's my script." In yet another surprise of the day, his lady's voice gave the whole situation a welcome interruption.

Though he fought the need to appear as if he were running to her, he ran over to her with Spike by his side. "Hello, baby, I didn't know you were coming today, or I would have made sure I had an espresso maker delivered to my trailer."

She barely gave him or Spike a glance, but with the fire in her eyes, he was sort of glad she wasn't looking at him.

She stepped forward. "Edward what seems to be the trouble?"

In what could only be called a bizarre plot twist, Spike followed her.

"Miss Caine." Edward held his hand out.

The second Cora lifted her sunglasses and crossed her arms without ever shaking the man's hand, Ryder decided whatever she wanted he would give her. Of course the only issue was, he had nothing to give her she couldn't buy herself except that script she loved.

"What's going on?" She huffed and looked down at the dog who was now lying on her shoe.

Ryder knew that huff. It was the huff of the person taking too long to answer, and she had to repeat herself, but ask the question in a different way huff.

"I believe we had a little misunderstanding about the *Hollywood Stardom* script. All the actors were to turn them in and Ryder's is missing." Edward smiled, but it wasn't the fake smile of a seasoned actor, this smile was just a mess.

At last, Cora turned to Ryder. A quick movement that simply let him know she wasn't pleased.

If he was tense from the dog, the thugs that Cora could have easily run into if she were only a few minutes earlier, and his issues with Edward, Cora's look was the cherry on the sundae of crap, the straw that wanted to break his back. Hell, that look was the anvil falling on his head.

She returned her attention to Edward. "I personally asked for the script, and it's in my possession. I'm sure there's no problem with that, is there?"

"No ma'am," Edward whispered.

His co-stars, Madeline, the cameramen and Viktor all gathered around. This was all Ryder needed, a performance before the performance.

"Good. I'm sure Ryder just forgot to tell you I asked for it." She slid her foot away from Spike, but the dog scooted over and resumed his position.

Edward crossed his arms and leaned back on his heels. "I understand how things are going to work."

Ryder straightened up. He wasn't sure if Cora caught this man's inflection, but he did, and no one, absolutely no one would talk to her that way.

As if sensing the fact, he was about to take this man down she swiped her arm out, stopping him. "Pardon me." She and Spike stepped toward Edward. "You understand how things are going to work? Unless that is code for something on set that I'm not privy to, I think we have a definite problem here."

"I wasn't using any code." Edward lifted his chin.

One of the girls gasped, maybe they all did. Everyone definitely held their collective breath.

Everyone but Cora.

His girl licked her lips as if she were ready to go in for the kill.

"Excuse me for one moment." She turned on her heel and stomped away. "Logan, Ryder, Viktor, come with me."

The three of them practically tripped over each other, following her away from the gathered crowd.

Spike came up behind all of them and resumed his position on Cora's shoe.

She cleared her throat, looked down at Spike and shook her head before pointing at Logan. "Can you and Ryder direct this film without it getting in the way of your acting?"

"Yes." The corners of Logan's mouth twitched as he held back a smile.

Ryder fought the need to start cheering and do that dance football players made when they scored a touchdown. Instead, he waited for her to ask him.

"Fine." She went to walk away, but he caught her arm.

"Aren't you going to ask me?" All he really wanted to do was pull her in for a kiss.

Her answer came in her narrowing her eyes.

"I can direct. I would love to direct. Logan and I did Starburst." He went to kiss her.

"We need to talk." She pushed him back and stomped right back to Edward.

Now Ryder understood exactly why girls hated when guys said those words. With his chest tight from all the back and forth garbage, he stayed at Cora's heels. Spike had the right idea, as he was about ready to curl up on her shoe as well.

"Mr. Andrews, the *Hollywood Stardust* franchise is extremely important to the studio. Part of what makes these movies special is the interplay between these actors who have known each other for over two decades. I cannot have anyone disrupt that, least of all the director. Therefore, although this is sudden, we have decided to release you from you contract." She tilted her head in Viktor's direction.

Edward turned positively pale. "Miss Caine."

"Viktor will escort you back to the offices to finalize things and remind you of certain key elements you signed in your contract, including my right to make this decision." As if to prove her power, and there really was no need, she paused. "That's how this is going to work."

Viktor motioned for Edward and the men walked away.

A silence, better than one in a horror movie, overtook the area.

Once more, his woman proved to be the ultimate professional. "I want everyone to listen up," she said. This movie is important, not only to the studio and the actors, and everyone involved, but most importantly, to the fans. Everyone take a break and after lunch Logan and Ryder will get you started."

He listened to Cora. Screw Ultracom, this woman needed to be CEO of the world. No one ever defended him like that. No one. Not even his own father.

With the bombs she dropped, she nodded and once more walked away with Spike as her sentry.

Unsure if he should wait for her summons or go after her, he chose what any good hero would do and dashed her way. If nothing else, he had to find out what she meant when she said they had to talk. He caught her by the arm. "Let's go to the trailer and celebrate your greatness." With the dreadful director out of the way, maybe he could mention his movie and hit a home run all before lunch.

"That wasn't greatness that was a disaster, there's a difference." Jaw jutted out, she shook her head, and continued marching away.

He glanced behind him to find everyone watching, and wanting to get her out of the spotlight, he guided her behind the Hollywood Stardust façade. "Here, we don't need an audience."

"Take your hand off me." She shrugged him away and stared down at the dog.

"His name is Spike." He slowly made his way toward her.

As if she were doing an experiment, she backed up.

Spike went with her.

Again, she backed up to the same results.

"He sort of adopted me the day I moved into your place. Erin had him, but with the baby and everything..." He went to her side and shrugged. "He lost his original owner and apparently he only perks up around us. He needed to find his light and I thought he wanted to be with a star, but I think he's looking for a different kind of light, maybe a beacon."

"Ryder." She let out a sigh.

"I'm sorry. I'm sorry about the dog, the script, the douchebag director." No one else was around, but he still looked for the spotlight blaring down on him melting his makeup.

"Are you sorry about this?" She swiped her phone out of her purse, hit a button, and held the device up to him.

No, no, no not something else. He grabbed the phone and read what the *National Reporter* wrote about them. Nothing unusual, the same old thing about women buying him. "All right."

"That's all you have to say?" She turned her back to him, her shoulders slumped down.

Cora didn't have the years of tabloids behind her. Something he needed to remember. He took her by the shoulders. "I don't think any of what they wrote is a secret. You know what I say?"

She shrugged.

"Let's prove them wrong." He turned her toward him.

"I don't understand." For a woman who normally looked people right in the eye, she focused on his chest.

"It doesn't matter how we got here, all that matters is that we're here." Once the sentence left his mouth, it felt right.

"That sounds like a line from *Hollywood Stardom*." Her unexpected canine friend right by her side, she stepped away from him.

"Let me show you something." Like a kid showing off his new bike, he rushed over to her, pulled her down in a little corner behind the façade, and popped open a tiny door used for electric wires. "Look, baby."

She leaned in to the writing behind the wood panel. "You did this?"

"The four of us wrote what we wanted to be on the wrap date of *Hollywood Stardust*." He pointed at the list. "I wanted to be a rock star, but I can't sing a note."

"Erin wanted to be an actress, that's a stretch." Cora read Erin's entry written in her oversized bubbly writing.

His legs killing him from his funky position, he sat on the ground and pulled Cora onto his lap. Spike came over and curled up next to them. They made a bizarre grouping, but one that fit in a strange way.

"Drew wanted to be an astronomer." Cora let out one laugh.

"The guy is smart." Ryder pointed to Logan's entry. "Well, he said he wanted to be a director, talk about nailing his future."

"The two of you did well on *Hollywood Starburst*. I was advised it was better not to overwhelm you, but I should have listened to my gut." She leaned back against him. "Thank you for showing me this. Make sure no one ruins it now that they're using it as a set piece again."

Should he ask about his movie? Could he after he everything? He inhaled deeply and took his time exhaling. The exercise did nothing to clear his mind. "So, besides gaining a pet and firing the director, and of course seeing me, what brought you on set today?"

She ran her nail down his arm. "Do you ever feel like people are watching you?"

"Only every second of every day, except when we're alone." Her attention gave him some welcome shivers, and he turned his arm over for her to get the flip side.

"Not like that." She turned and hid her face in his chest.

It was unlike her to make such a damsel in distress move. He took her chin in his hand and gently made her face him. "Did something happen this morning?"

She brushed his hand away and shook her head. "I don't know. I guess I'm just not used to all this attention from the media. I usually show up in business journals."

"Why didn't you call me?" A sick sensation overtook him.

"The old director didn't allow phones on set."

"Well, the new directors allow it, especially in the case of the woman who runs the show." His instinct told him it was something more, but it also told him not to push.

"I think I better get to work and let you meet with your co-director." She pushed herself up. "You have a movie to make."

Speaking of movies, this was the perfect in to what he needed. Why couldn't he say the words? "Why don't you hang out for a while?" He took hold of her hand.

Spike wedged himself between them.

"Ryder." She looked down at the dog.

To sweeten the pot, he nuzzled her neck. "Can we keep him?"

Spike lifted his head.

"Is there anything else I can do for you, Mr. Scott?"

Hand in hand, they walked with Spike trundling along with them.

Yes! Though he wanted to yell the word, he stopped. "Can I have a kiss?" Instead of asking for what he needed, he pursed his lips and went for what he wanted.

Before giving in, she wrinkled her nose. Still, she gave him a kiss, tongue and all.

He was just going to have to think of another way to appease the beast, and he hugged Cora to him.

HOLLYWOOD STARDOM

FADE IN:

INT. ARIZONA - LOCAL PUB - EVENING

STEVEN and CHARLES sit together at a table
drinking a couple of beers.

>   CHARLES
>   So, when am I going to get
>   to see some stars?

>   STEVEN
>   (Shakes his head)
>   I could ask you the same
>   thing.

>   CHARLES
>   My stars are right where
>   they belong.
>   (He points up.)

>   STEVEN
>   My star is determined to
>   make me out of my mind.

>   CHARLES
>   There's a reason you're not
>   taking the next step.

STEVEN gulps down his drink.

>   CHARLES
>   This has been going on
>   since you were in high
>   school. She wants more,
>   you don't give it to her.
>   Then you give her a little
>   bit, which placates her for
>   a while before it blows up
>   in your face.

                    STEVEN
              (Tilts his glass in Charles'
              direction)
              Thank you for telling me my
              life.

                    CHARLES
              That's always been my role.
              Historian, voice of reason,
              mediator.

                    STEVEN
              Then mediate this.

The men look at each other.

                    CHARLES
              Once you won her, you lost
              interest, but you don't
              know what to do without
              her. The proverbial rock
              and a hard place.

STEVEN raises his glass to passing waiter.

                    STEVEN
              Is that all you have for
              me? You're not going to
              tell me to marry her at
              last? What's the answer?

                    CHARLES
              Look to the stars. The
              past and future are always
              there.

Chapter Fifteen

"BEN, I HAVE JOB for you to do." Ryder let himself into the gates at his storage facility.

"What is it boss?" Ben's all too cheery voice filled the phone.

"I have a charity, my dog Spike and I started it." He looked at the picture of the dog on his phone. Spike stayed so close by Cora's side she finally acquiesced and took the animal, saying Rodger knew how to deal with dogs.

At his news, Ben seemed to gasp. "Dogs are cool. I didn't know you had a pet. What can I do boss?"

"The charity has really taken off, so I need a chairman, someone who will get a lot of public attention." Ryder hit his head into the car seat. He always was a master of improvisation. "That someone is you."

"Boss, I'm on it." Ben's voice dripped excitement and wonder.

"I'll text you some details, but start with getting some receipts for donations and tote bags." He put his hand over his eyes. "Think of what we can do to raise some funds. Any questions?"

"What's the name?" Ben asked.

At least the guy was sharp. "Ryder's Rescue." He hung up and took a breath at what he now had to do. In truth, he could use some rescuing himself.

Since he and Logan took over, phones were now allowed on set. After putting off the inevitable, he finally texted Glen and made a time to meet at his storage facility. At first thought, Ryder was going to meet him at some far off location. Then he realized it didn't matter. They knew his car, they knew where he lived, they knew his girl. No matter how good Cora was with computers, these people could track either one of them in an instant, and there was no point in hiding.

As he got out of his car, his phone chimed, and he found a text from Cora, not Viktor, not Rodger, but Cora herself. The first one she sent him that didn't involve some command.

In honor of your first day on set, I'll let you choose the takeout, just remember that me and Spike aren't vegan.

Her quasi-homey little message almost made him hurl. What if she saw him now? He went inside the temperature and moisture controlled warehouse and rolled up the door to his own personal stash. This would be the perfect place for them to hide his body.

The setting provided a snapshot of his life. Little bits and pieces collected over a career most would die for. Other actors in his league had millions behind them, he would also if he didn't always want more. After all wasn't more the name of the game? Wasn't that why he wanted to finish his movie? Everything everyone did everyday was in the quest for the elusive more.

Without the fanfare of a red carpet, he walked inside. The entire room was draped round the concept of more. Every last thing, and he would admit it, wasn't nearly enough.

"Mr. Scott." Glen called to him.

Ryder didn't even bother acknowledging the dick and his ass.

"I have to say I much prefer the movie set to this place." Glen entered his domain, crossed his arms and looked around. "What do you have for me?"

He held his arms out. "Collateral."

"You brought me into a room of junk?" Glen tightened his jaw.

The thug beside him stood by the exit with hands on his hips.

It was time to get talking or Glen would never leave. Though his chest threatened to collapse in on itself, Ryder couldn't let them sense anything other than the calm, cool, cocky actor. "This is hardly junk." He reached into his pocket, pulled out a piece of paper he managed to print out between him and Logan piecing their movie back together and pointed to the first item up on his auction block. "This original *Hollywood Stardust* poster is signed by the entire cast, including the director. Last time one sold without Drew Fulton's signature and in less than pristine condition, it went for ten thousand dollars."

Glen glanced toward his sidekick. Both men nodded. "Keep going."

"Here you have the original outfit I wore in *Action Accomplished*, as well as the gun." The character he played in that series might be more beloved than William. Done playing game show host that involved his cash and prizes, he handed Glen the paper.

In a surreal moment, he watched the two men walk around his one completely personal space and collect over six figures from his life.

He remembered when his father made these runs, or collections, as his Dad dubbed them. Hey, everyone had to get their start somewhere.

On one particular night, his father and he drove into the Hollywood Hills to one of those huge homes that didn't appear that impressive on the outside, but once they walked in, even at ten years old, Ryder knew they hit the mother lode. He was taught at a young age to know the value of everything around him. The antiques and other collectibles were worth a delicious dime. His father never said pretty penny, he said pennies were for losers.

Four of his father's so-called assistants followed them inside and surrounded a man who seemed around his dad's age, but a lot smaller and really pale.

"It's always the ones who don't appear as if they need the money who need the money." His father walked around the grand living room.

The man didn't utter one word.

"And they're the ones who never pay their debt." His father stopped at an amazing grandfather clock and pointed.

The man pressed his lips together.

One of his father's assistants opened the front door and more men entered. They wrapped up the clock in cloths and took it away.

"I don't understand." His father continued his trek, this time stopping at some ornate chairs. "We even said we would take payments. You got what you wanted."

The same ritual was repeated, with the chairs, then the sofa, some knickknacks, and even the guy's grand piano. When the movers were finished, all that was left was a portrait over the fireplace of the guy and his family. A wife and two kids, one around Ryder's age.

"Let's have a little chat, shall we?" His father motioned for his team to step outside, but Ryder stayed by his side.

"Mr. Scott." The man's voice shook.

"When I said talk, I meant I do the talking." His father put his finger over his lips. "Don't even think of arguing. You made the deal, you came to us."

The man backed up and took a breath.

"You and I both know what we just took doesn't nearly cover what is owed us." A master of the dramatic pause, his father nodded.

As if to interrupt, the man opened his mouth.

If his father's expression was a bullet, his father shot the man a look that would have blown his brains out.

Once the man closed his mouth, his father continued. "I can help you lessen the load, if you do something for me."

With the next pause the man learned his lesson and simply stared at his father in quiet reverence.

"My son here, he likes acting and takes lessons. We've gone to some auditions but it's a hard industry to break into." In slow, calculated steps his father approached the man. "I think we can make a deal where my son and his vast talent can get a ticket to the head of the line, and I hear you have a film your casting for that needs a boy around Ryder's age."

Without a second of hesitation, the man held his hand out.

His father shook the man's hand. "Now you may speak."

"I'll have the contracts at the studio by ten a.m." The man smiled at him.

"Wise decision. Maybe we won't need to make another trip back here, since I'm willing to give you some more time to come up with the money." His father let go of the man and made his way toward the door.

"Thank you Mr. Scott." The man called after him.

"See you tomorrow." His father saluted the man, then put his arm around Ryder's shoulder and they left. "I told you I'd make you a star."

"Ryder, you are quite the star." Glen's statement jolted Ryder out of his reverie.

His father hadn't lied. The film he was contracted for went straight to number one over the most important weekend in the summer and catapulted him into pre-teen idol status playing the role of an orphan boy.

Ryder's focus landed on the corner of the room where two of the props from that movie used to reside.

"You made a real gesture tonight," Glen said. "I'm sorry it had to come to this. Maybe we went too easy on you because of our connections with your father, may his soul rest in peace." Glen held his hand out. "Get us our movie. Let's work together."

"I made the deal, I came to you." Making this man more of an enemy would do no good.

"That's the Ryder we know. Now go on home to your gorgeous girlfriend. At least now you have some time." Glen patted his shoulder, and he and his goon left.

Rather than a snarky comeback, he took in his room. "Thank you."

Without a list, he knew exactly what was missing and with nothing more to see, he locked up, and returned to his car as his phone rang. CC appeared on the screen. Instinct alone caused him to lift the phone, but he stopped short of answering. He didn't need to check in. This afternoon he should have manned up and asked her for the money, that was their arrangement. The fact he hesitated, didn't take advantage of the deal he made with her made him sick, and he tossed his phone on his seat and took off.

On nights like this, and there had been a few, but none this bad, he usually went into Hollywood and explored something new. Plenty of women would love to shine up a star for the evening, and the thrill of the chase was something that could never be duplicated. Just like the items he gave away tonight could never be replaced.

Without a destination in mind, he rolled the windows down and drove through Los Angeles, letting the lights and sounds of the city work their magic. Though he planned on trolling through Beverly Hills and frequenting some of his old haunts designed for the famous and discreet, somehow he found himself driving into the parking lot at the Sierra Towers.

"Mr. Scott." The valet opened the door for him.

Without a word, he handed the man the key, and he made his way up to his and Cora's apartment. They were going to have a talk right now about arrangements and commitments. Hell, he might have made the deal, but she came to him.

Jaw stiff, muscles tight, he opened the door.

Wait, stop, hold on.

No one was here.

No takeout.

No dog.

No Cora.

Only the strategically lit spaces that made their place feel like a fancy hotel room waiting for its guests.

Among the other pearls of wisdom his father spouted off, he always said, go with your gut. Ryder left the apartment and made his way back down to the valet. He was out of there.

WHEN HER CELL PHONE RANG, Cora's first thought was that it had to be Ryder.

Her second thought was it *better* be Ryder.

After confirming it wasn't Ryder, her third thought was who the hell was calling her after hours on a number she didn't recognize? Not that it mattered, she was in her office and someone in her position worked all hours. "Cora Caine."

"Cora, this is Dane Ellis."

At the man's announcement, her stomach flipped. Dane Ellis, was on the studio's board of directors and a close confidant to George McIntyre, current CEO of Ultracom. She motioned for Viktor and put the man on speaker. "What can I do for you, Dane?"

Viktor dashed over his throne.

"I know it's getting late and you have a personal life, but I was hoping you might be able to come down for a quick in person meeting to discuss the situation with Edward Andrews."

The man's monotone voice caused her to shudder. His insinuation about her private life made her want to vomit. The fact that for one brief nanosecond she thought about Ryder and what happened if he called while she was in a meeting made her want to get her head examined.

"Of course I'm available to come down. This is an important topic. I'm on my way." She hit end on the call and stared at the screen on her phone.

"Let's go." Viktor stood.

"Hold on." With her mind reeling, she needed to slow down and focus. Since Ryder snuck into her life, she hadn't had three seconds to think. "I can't walk in there alone. I have to show him what I have at my beck and call." She broke down and called Ryder.

After the fourth ring, it went to his voice mail. "It's Cora, call me, we have a situation with the studio."

"What are you doing?" Viktor gathered her bag and his items. "We have to get out of here."

"Hold on." Once more, she dialed her phone.

"This is Logan."

At him answering right away, she balled her hand in a fist. Logan wasn't in her bed at night, and if he were available why wasn't Ryder? "This is Cora. Do you have everything under control after today's director change?"

"We had a meeting and reblocked the first scene and—"

"That's all well and good." She cut him off. "I've been summoned to a meeting with Dane Ellis about what happened today."

Viktor motioned for her to get going.

Logan paused for a second. "I'll be there."

"Thank you." Though she wanted to ask him about Ryder's whereabouts, she restrained herself. "By the way, what time did you end today?" Maybe it was the same question, but it sounded better.

"Wrapped." Logan corrected her. "We wrapped a couple of hours ago, thought it best we start fresh tomorrow."

"I'll see you at the studio." She hung up, snapped her fingers, and pointed at the door.

Spike ran to the door, and they both followed Viktor out of the office and to the elevator.

Viktor frowned down at the dog. "He doesn't do anything unless you tell him to."

"That makes him brilliant. Everyone should take a lesson from the dog." She had to admit he was obedient and when he wasn't listening to her, he was laying at her feet. Now that she thought about it, the dog would make the perfect man if he was human. Damn it.

As they made their way through the lobby, she admitted she was happy to have Viktor and Spike with her after she had those strange feelings that morning, as if someone were watching her. The only person better would have been Ryder.

She wrinkled her nose and kept to the task at hand, namely not wrecking her chance at her position, all for the man she hired to get this position.

"Do you ever feel like people are watching you?" Curious, she asked Viktor the same question she asked Ryder earlier.

"No. They're watching you, but now they are watching you and Ryder." He opened his car door for her.

Her mind going off in a million different directions, she got inside the car put Spike on her lap, and they both stared out the window.

In times like this, she had to stay focused and unemotional. Any quiver in her voice would show weakness. By the time they got to the studio, she had a plan in place. In truth it was the same plan she had when they left, but at least it was a plan.

As she and Spike got out of the car, Logan pulled in the next spot.

"Where's Ryder?" he asked.

Not wanting to say she was about to ask him that exact question, she took her bag from Viktor and shot Logan a look.

"Got it." Logan smoothed his hair back and all of them, even Spike, walked into the corporate offices on the studio lot. In Los Angeles dogs were a perfectly acceptable accessory.

After Viktor announcing them to a haggard assistant, they were ushered into Dane Ellis' office. The portly, older man in a well-fitting suit and sporting some grey through his brown hair perfectly represented the type of person normally chosen for the job she wanted. No doubt, he thought her too young, too emotional, too female. To prove him wrong, she gave him a firm handshake before sitting in the chair on the opposite side of his desk.

Logan took the chair next to her, Viktor went to her other side and Spike lay by her foot.

"Cora, thank you for getting here so quickly." As if looking for someone one else, Dane glanced over to the door.

She crossed her legs and forced herself to sit back. Most likely, he was searching for Ryder. Shame on her for positioning her phone face up in her bag to see any possible messages from her missing partner. She needed to be on point with this meeting. Still, she peeked twice.

"I think we can dispense with the niceties and get to the matter at hand." Dane lifted a stack of papers. "No sooner had you terminated the man's contract than I was sent a slew of messages threating us with a lawsuit."

"His contract clearly states he can be terminated at any time," she said.

"Right," Dane said. "What concerns me more than that is the fact that he basically accused you of firing him to protect the man you're in a relationship with." He put the papers aside.

"Dane, the cast of this movie is very special in that the stars are friends and two of the original cast members are married. It's a balancing act and to give a proper send off to the series and pay homage to a beloved story, we cannot have someone come in and disrupt the chemistry." She wouldn't lie, she was impressed by her own defense.

"What did happen with Ryder Scott?" Dane tented his fingers and inhaled.

"The relationship between Edward and Ryder was combative at the beginning." Logan piped in. "It started at the read-through. I know that we all have to work with individuals we don't necessarily get along with, but I have to agree with Miss Caine in this case. Bringing that contention into a group who has tight bonds would've made for too much tension on set and affected the final outcome of the movie."

She resisted her urge to high-five Logan.

"We brought on Mr. Andrews to take some of the pressure off Mr. Alexander and Mr. Scott, so they could focus on acting," Dane countered.

"In hindsight, I realize that this group must lead themselves." Cora took the stage again and lifted her chin. "This movie is a unique case, and they know what they need to do." Another peek at her phone revealed nothing.

Dane strummed his fingers on the desk. "I feel as if we are letting the school children out on the yard with no teachers."

"I'll be there." The words exited her mouth at such speed they would be impossible to get back. Out of the corner of her eye, she saw Viktor turn to her.

"You're going to be on set and do your normal job as well?" Dane's tone was one of sarcasm and disbelief. Maybe even one of a father scolding his daughter.

And this is how it would be played.

With new conviction, she sat up and leaned over into his space. "With all due respect, Dane, this is all part of my normal job." She used both hands to make air quotes. "I committed to these movies just as I have committed to Chargge and the rest of my duties.

Therefore, if my presence is required on set for the studio and Ultracom to be put as ease, then that is my normal job."

The corners of the man's mouth twitched, but rather than smile he nodded. "All right, Miss Caine. I've seen firsthand what you can do, and I'll trust you to do what is best."

She didn't bother with a thank you.

"Did you hear about Franklin Kryson resigning today?" Dane went right into standard business small talk and idle chatter.

Viktor shifted in his seat.

She ground her teeth together. Her distraction led to her missing an extremely important development in the CEO race. With Franklin out of the running, it would be down to her and Albert. Normally, at this point in the conversation she would bid the man adieu and get to her nearest Internet connection. Then she remembered she had to be human. "Is he all right? That seems rather sudden."

Dane shrugged. "He hasn't offered a reason."

"Oh. I see. I wish him well." Hopefully, that was enough small talk. She stood. "I trust this meeting is concluded?"

"Absolutely. The numbers on *Hollywood Starburst* have panned out even better than predicted." Once more, the man held his hand out. "I'm surprised Ryder wasn't here."

Of course the numbers were better, since she purposely quoted them low. She shook Dane's hand. "I don't find it surprising at all." Though she did take another glance at her phone, and it wasn't to find out about Franklin Kryson.

"Point taken, Miss Caine." After shaking Logan's and Viktor's hands and waving to Spike, Dane ushered them to the door.

Even with the disaster averted, she knew she'd be in the crosshairs until Stardom ended, well, wrapped. With each step toward the exit, the knot in her stomach tightened, but not because of what she just committed to, not because one of the front-runners for her position backed out, but at the lack of communication from Ryder.

No matter how tempting, she wouldn't ask Logan.

Then they stepped outside, and she realized she wouldn't have to ask.

The knot twisted upon itself at the sight of Ryder's car parked next to Viktor's.

She stopped.

Ryder got out of his car and crossed his arms.

"I need to get home to Ivy and Curtis." Logan patted her shoulder and without a word to Ryder got in his car and drove off.

"What are you doing here?" Ryder broke the silence.

"I was about to ask you that." Not wanting to create theatrics at a movie studio, she went toward Viktor's car.

"I went home. You weren't there." Before she reached the car he walked forward.

"Well, if someone read texts or took phone calls, you would have received the answers to your deepest mysteries." Why he acted as if she did anything wrong was beyond her, but she didn't need it.

He blocked her way to the car. "Come with me."

"I'll see you at home." In no world would she give in to him.

"I really need you to come with me." His voice softened. "I just need you."

Apparently, she was out in outer space because she walked to the passenger side of his car.

"I'm going to go do some research," Viktor announced before getting in his car.

Ryder rushed over and opened the door.

She pointed to Spike, and he hopped in the car, then she took her seat.

Ryder got behind the wheel and drove away.

Neither spoke. She wasn't even sure how they ended up at odds, but something was definitely wrong, and she didn't need this complication along with everything else. No matter what their status was, she had a right to know what happened to him.

Only when they went the opposite direction from their home, did she finally decide to break the silence. "Where are we going?"

Rather than answering, he continued his drive, and got on the freeway. At this time of night there was no traffic, and he let the car loose as he headed toward Santa Monica.

They winded their way down Pacific Coast Highway. On one side of them lay the earth, on the other the huge black space of the ocean. At the moment, her thoughts could fill that space. What had she done? Why did Franklin walk away? Did she hurt a man's career today? Did she hurt her own? Was this all worth it? At this point in her career, she didn't need to be called in to be checked up on. No one should ever doubt her decisions.

As much good as Ryder did for her with the public, could this little tryst be having the opposite effect where the rubber hit the road? At the end of the day, the public wouldn't choose the CEO of Ultracom.

Worse yet, was she even willing to give him up if it did affect her chances?

She fired someone for him today. Pure and simple, clear as crystal, her claws came out, and she attacked the only way she could.

All this for a man who hadn't bothered to call her back. She pressed her fingers into her temple, willing the thoughts to stop.

Right when she was ready to ask again, where they were headed, what they were doing, or if he had any answers whatsoever, Ryder parked the car in a turnout designed for tourists to take in the view.

"Cora." He crooned her name in that dreamy tone of his, put his arm around the back of her seat and leaned in close.

"Spike needs some air." Before he had a chance to kiss her and make her forget her name, she opened the door, stepped out and snapped her fingers.

Spike bounded out of the car and sniffed around.

She turned her back to Ryder, crossed her arms and stared out at the little bit of light from the moon reflecting off the water. With the salty sea scent, the rumble of the waves and a bona fide movie star getting out of the car, this was the perfect setting for a romance movie, or better yet a musical where the lead would sing some smarmy, yet swoony, love song. Of course, the movie star was really destroying the mood.

"Cora." Ryder walked around in front of her. "Talk to me."

Even in the dark and even when she was pissed at him, the man was a sight to behold. Where the hell was he after the wrap? Maybe it shouldn't bother her, but she couldn't stop herself from thinking the worst. At the end of the day, no matter Ryder's blush producing words about living the role, she had to remember this was an arrangement. Business. A deal just like anything else.

"What were you doing when you didn't answer my text or my call?" Her voice came out strong, like a CEO, a tough professional.

He stepped closer, a smile lifted one side of his mouth.

In her career she'd dealt with worse. She straightened up. "Ryder, answer my question. I needed you before."

"You had Logan." He leaned back on his heels. "What happened? Did you get in trouble for firing that asshole on account of me?"

"I don't get in trouble." Damn him for knowing what happened. Perhaps all those years in movies gave him a sixth sense. "And I didn't fire that man for you."

"Liar." He closed the distance between them, and put his hands on the car on either side of her, caging her in.

She ground her teeth together and stared him down.

"To answer your question, the first day on set is hard enough without getting handed the director's job. I took a break and took a drive, but then I realized all I wanted was you." His fingertips played with her hair.

Ignore him. Be strong. She pressed her lips together.

"If you tell me you only wanted me there to be a lackey in your meeting, then I'm going to tell you that you had Logan, and you didn't need me." He inched in. "But if you tell me you were truly upset I didn't call, and you wondered where I was, and there was a pit in your stomach as the possibilities whirled through that gorgeous head of yours, then I'll promise you that it won't ever happen again and apologize for tonight."

"You're insufferable." Maybe if she didn't look directly at him, she wouldn't be blinded by everything Ryder Scott.

"And you crave it." He looked into her eyes, and his lips swept over hers.

A gasp escaped her throat.

"Just like I crave you." He grabbed her, wrapped his arms around her and gave her a deep kiss.

Their bodies pressed against each other, his taste filled her mouth, the stress of the last few hours washed away with the tide.

"So, I guess we are now on a full phone relationship. That's a far cry from the day I moved in." He pushed her back on the car and slid his mouth down to her ear. "You do care." Once more, he found her lips.

At his words, she shut her eyes. She fired a director for him, she hated not knowing where he was and hell, she even craved him. Her only fear was if she admitted she cared what else would she do for him?

FADE IN:

EXT. ARIZONA – GRANDPARENT'S HOME – EARLY
MORNING

ROXY and STEVEN'S GRANDMOTHER are in the rock
garden.

> ROXY
> Thank you for letting me
> stay here.

> STEVEN'S GRANDMOTHER
> You're always welcome here,
> you know you're one of my
> own.
> (She grabs ROXY'S hand.)

> ROXY
> (Looks down)
> I always wanted it to be
> official.

> STEVEN'S GRANDMOTHER
> Who says it's not official?
> I know what I feel and
> that's all I need to make
> it official.

> ROXY
> I just feel like no one
> ever wants to claim me.

> STEVEN'S GRANDMOTHER
> Love, you have always
> searched for someone else
> to take care of you and
> give you the answers, when
> you have to take care of
> yourself.

                    ROXY
          (Shrugs)
          I don't know how, I don't
          even know where I'd start.

     STEVEN'S GRANDMOTHER
          Instead of asking for what
          you want, demand it, and if
          it doesn't work, then move
          on.

                    ROXY
          (Turns to STEVEN'S
     GRANDMOTHER)
          Are you telling me to move
          on?

     STEVEN'S GRANDMOTHER
          (Pulls ROXY in for a hug)
          No, I'm telling you to be
          with someone who will claim
          you.

Chapter Sixteen

AN ORGASM WAS MOST definitely the way Ryder preferred to wake up. It cleansed him, relaxed him, and helped him focus mentally. In fact, as he reclined on his couch in his trailer reviewing the few minutes of test footage they shot the day before in front of the Hollywood Stardust façade first thing in the morning, he decided that filming or not, he and Cora should start every day with an orgasm.

Yes, as he told Cora at the beach last night, he craved her. Craved her in that way where even if he made love to her before going to bed, he had to have her first thing in morning. Part of the issue with yesterday was he couldn't stop thinking about her. In a small consolation prize, she did say she would be coming by the set. Maybe they could take a break here in the trailer. After all, He did have a king size bed with high-end natural fiber bed sheets that needed to be tested.

A quick glance at the time told him he had to get to going. They needed to make up for lost time yesterday. He stood, stretched, and made his way out. As the first real shooting day, there was already a barrage of people on set. But that didn't include the parade that began the moment he neared the scene of the crime. Well, in this case, the scene of the scene, and he didn't remember casting any roles for this part.

By parade, he meant seriously, it was a parade.

The fanfare started with the baton twirler, in this case, Rodger carrying what appeared to be an iced coffee and a briefcase.

Behind him came a coordinated dance of various people he didn't know who set up a desk, equipment he didn't recognize, but it looked pretty space age, some chairs and even a little canopy.

What he would call the marching band came in the form of Viktor, who inspected the space set up by those who came before him. He nodded and set up a director's chair with the name Caine silkscreened on the fabric.

Then everyone, and he meant everyone, from the stars, to the extras, to the woman manning the catering table, turned to watch the Grand Marshal herself make her entrance.

In an impeccably tailored black business suit with a crisp white shirt, her hair flowing behind her and Spike by her side, Cora marched down the line, nodded at her public, practically waved, then bowed and took her seat in the chair with her name.

The grand finale came when one of the workers hurried over and set up a little dog bed with Spike's name on it. When Spike took his spot, Ryder wondered if he should get the little guy a crown or something. Instead, another person came over, put a silver bowl down, poured some bottled water into the bowl, and handed the dog something to chew on. Ryder figured that was better than a crown, for a dog anyway.

The set took on a silence normally reserved for active filming. He turned behind him toward the crew and then back to Cora. Since he was the one sleeping with her, technically, he needed to be the one to figure out what the hell was going on, and he approached. "Baby?"

"I suppose since the world knows we live together, it's all right you call me baby." She took a sip of her coffee, opened her laptop and stared up at his hair.

"Cora." He tried again.

She continued to stare at his hair. "Yes."

"What's with the set up?" Her absolute fixed gaze on the top of his head made him shift his weight from one foot to the other.

"Last night when I was called to Dane Ellis' office, I told the studio I would be on set, but I have to work, so we brought my office here." She narrowed her eyes as if staring his hair down. "Go on and film and maybe we can go to lunch."

With her whole job thing looming over him, he nodded. The situation seemed reasonable enough, and he got his wish to have her here. Deciding not to tell her they were in for at least twelve hour days on the set, he just needed to know one thing. "Is something wrong with my hair?"

"I don't like it." Now she wrinkled her nose.

"Why not?" He leaned down and lowered his voice.

"It doesn't look like you. I like it how you wear it, that's rock star enough. Maybe we can get someone to fix it." She merely lifted a finger and Rodger ran over.

"Yes, Cora." Since her secretary always had to be doing something, Rodger straightened out her pens.

"Would you mind fixing Ryder's hair? You know how I prefer it." As if it were some disturbance, she motioned toward his hair and refocused her attention on her computer.

Without skipping a beat, Rodger put his briefcase on the table and opened it to reveal not papers or work things, but a whole host of bizarre items, including tools for hairstyling. "Mr. Scott, if you don't mind sitting down, I'll have this fixed for Cora in just a moment."

In addition to the questions of why Rodger walked around with what appeared to be a soldering iron as well as a can of peaches, was also why did this man know how Cora liked his hair?

"What's the hold up?" Logan came over and gave Cora a kiss on the cheek.

Ryder shook his head, now Logan germs were on his girl. Maybe Rodger had a cleansing wipe.

"Is there a reason that you get to have your hairstyle, but Ryder must have some molded thing that makes him look like a doll?" she asked.

Well, if nothing else, this conversation was doing wonders for Ryder's ego. The second he got home, he was washing his hair. For future movies, he would have to have a hair clause in his contract. A few years ago he did a movie where he had to shave his head, what would have Cora done then?

"Cora, it's my goal to keep this movie on time and on budget for you. Now I know you are used to seeing Ryder look a certain way, but I can assure you that on camera it will transform him into William." As if he were teaching a class, Logan spoke slowly. "Plus, all the workers are union workers and we have to have them do their jobs or there could be issues."

"Oh, I understand." She sat up. "Thank you for the education. Don't let me hold you up. Go film. Ryder and I have a lunch date."

Instead of contradicting her, Logan turned, shot him a look and walked back to set.

"I better get to work." Ryder gave Cora a kiss on the lips and followed Logan, reminding himself to ask Rodger for that wipe.

He joined the rest of the cast.

"Let's see if we can make up for lost time from yesterday." Logan stepped back and took in the set done up like the backstage of an outdoor concert park.

They spent the next two hours blocking the scene, getting the lighting and the props correct. Since Ryder's scene with Roxy was first, Logan would take the lead on the direction, and they mapped out some strategies.

He glanced back at Cora. The few times he checked on her, her head was buried in her computer, but now she was standing and talking to Viktor and Rodger. She paced around, shook her head, pointed to that blasted computer she was always glued to, and put her hand over her eyes. A master of body language, he knew something was definitely wrong and tensed.

"Ryder." Script pages in hand, Logan came over. "I thought we'd pan down from the sun into the concert. That will make a great transition to Roxy's dream or flashback or whatever we're calling it."

"Hold on." No way could Ryder discuss anything until he uncovered what was going on with her, and he jogged over to her little tarp tent thing. "Baby, what's wrong?"

Rather than answer, she turned her computer toward him.

"Call to Bring Back Alan Smithee." He read the headline on the *National Reporter* website. "Rumor has it drama is already afloat on the set of the third installment of the Hollywood Stardust franchise. Seems as if Miss Caine made a decision for her sweetheart and snuffed out Edward Andrews' directorial flame less than two hours after production on the anticipated movie began. In a not so shocking move, Logan Alexander and her personal pet, Ryder Scott, have been given the job. Though we loved their work in *Hollywood Starburst*, could this abrupt change be the sign of emotion getting the best of the ice queen? Is the star about to burst? We only hope that they won't have to dig up good old Alan Smithee to direct what may become a vanity film made solely for the stars and their significant others."

"I don't even know who Alan Smithee is." Her voice hardened as if she would fire that man on the spot as well. "Someone look him up right now."

Deciding to play the role of interpreter, he put his hand up, stopping both Viktor and Rodger from going into a round of

Internet searches. "Alan Smithee was a pseudonym used when a director didn't want to be named, so it sort of became synonymous with a flop."

"How does anyone know what is happening? We only filmed a few scenes yesterday!" She put her hands on her hips and faced him.

For the smartest woman in the world, Ryder needed to remember film wasn't Cora's first career. "Can you guys give us a moment?" He went around the table and took her into his arms, putting his face in her hair and finding her ear. "Do you think I would ever let this movie be a flop? I'm in it after all."

"What about what they said? That I fired Edward for you?" With her face in his shoulder, her voice came out muffled. "That's not CEO material."

Damn her job, the job she wanted, the job she had, the job he signed up to get for her. Since they got together, he watched her work like no other, her commitment never wavering. Yes, he had to remember this world wasn't her world. She was real and these things might shatter her. "Listen to me. I promise all this publicity is good." He pushed her back. "Just watch the story unfold today in the tabloids, all right? All this coverage will only have the public clamoring to see the movie."

At last, she nodded. "All right you made it better, you may now kiss me."

Finally, he would reap one of the rewards of having Cora on set. He dipped his head down and kissed her.

Logan tapped him. "Do you think it is possible that you can hold off kissing your girlfriend so we can actually...I don't know...shoot a movie?"

Cora stepped back. "Alan Smithee is not directing this movie." She tilted her chin up at Logan. "And don't think I don't know who he is."

Logan leaned in. "He will be if you don't let us direct something."

"Point taken." Cora returned to her post.

Once more, he and Logan returned to the set. Another two hours and hundreds of adjustments later, they finally deemed them ready to actually film something.

"All right, William, Roxy, let's see you together for the first time in over twenty years." Logan and the rest of the crew went into a round of applause as he and Erin took their positions.

"It's been a long time." Erin winked at him.

"Like a lifetime." In truth, it felt rather strange putting his arms around her, even though they rehearsed several times.

She giggled. "Don't squish the baby."

"I promise." For the tenth time since the *National Reporter* fiasco, he glanced over at Cora. Where she had been working before, alternating between head down at her computer and walking and talking on her cellphone, now she sat back in her chair, legs crossed, watching. Dare he say he had a bit of nerves. He closed his eyes and inhaled. "Don't laugh at my singing. It'll be fixed."

"Deal." Erin raised her eyebrows.

"All right, quiet on the set!" Logan called out.

"William and Roxy Concert Take One!" One of the PA's yelled and snapped the clapperboard.

William encompassed him. The boy now man who loved the woman in his arms. The woman he once fought for, gave up. The woman he wished only for her happiness. Their love spanned decades, and for this part of the movie, he was the one who owned her heart.

He stared into Erin's eyes. "Roxanne, look at what we've built. We have the dream."

Erin studied his face, her eyes even glossed over with tears. "We do, we have everything. Who would have ever thought we would end up here? but..."

"But nothing." He took her by the shoulders. "I know you're nervous with everyone coming to the concert, but this is your chance. You are a star, maybe not in the way you thought, but this is it, we made it."

"Do you think so, really?" Erin pressed her hand to his chest and toyed with his collar.

"Cut!" Cora's voice rang through the set.

Cora, not Logan.

Every person there turned to her.

She barreled toward them.

Logan stood from his chair, faced her, and crossed his arms. "Is there something wrong, Cora?"

Ryder let go of Erin and dashed over. Someone needed to be the human shield.

"When Ryder and I rehearsed this scene, Roxy put her hand on William's cheek. I really feel that was more effective to show their love." Cora stared Logan down.

"You feel that's better?" Logan's jaw tightened.

Ryder opened his mouth. He didn't like the tone Logan was taking with her. She wasn't any run of the mill producer.

"Yes, I do. I quite liked that better," she said. "I have now watched all the films in detail, and I feel the hand on the cheek is a much more personal gesture given this particular couple's history." She stood her ground.

Then again, if someone were telling him what to direct, Ryder might not take it too well.

Logan raised his hands and backed up. "We are calling an hour break while Mr. Scott has a meeting with our producer."

"Break?" Cora looked to him. "You filmed three seconds of film and didn't even do the correct gesture."

"Ryder!" Logan snapped.

"Cora." Ryder grabbed her arm and guided her away. "Let's go check out my trailer."

"You already made a trailer for the film?" At trying to keep up with him, she tripped.

Refusing to be detained, he picked her up, took her into his trailer and dropped her down onto the bed.

"Ryder, I'm in the middle of working, what are you doing?" She smoothed down her hair and sat up.

"You're in the middle of working? What do you think we're doing?" He pointed toward the outside.

"I wanted to ask you about that. It seems as if everyone is standing around waiting to film, but no filming actually takes place. How much have you filmed so far?" She scooted to the edge of the bed and crossed her legs. "The day I spent at the set of *Starburst*, it seemed a hustle and bustle of activity."

"Baby, that day was staged for you and the other bigwigs." He remembered that day she came on to the set with the other higher ups.

At his words, she furrowed her brow.

"Yes, it's like only showing your boss your best work. We knew you were on the way, that day was as much of a performance as the movie itself. We didn't even use any of that footage." There, the great secret was out. Everything in this industry was made up. "We didn't shoot scenes yesterday, we filmed maybe ten seconds of establishing shots. I can't go to lunch, unless you want to come in here, and we eat what the caterer brings us, and we're going to be working long days and many of those days it feels like we are just standing around."

She continued look at him with a dazed and confused expression.

"Being on a movie set is like painting a wall. It is hours of set up for two minutes of film." He sat down next to her. "Now I know you're used to being in charge and running things, but you can't comment on anything during working hours, and you can't be upset over tabloids, and you can't ever, not under any circumstance, never ever call cut or anything else while we're filming."

"I really liked the hand to the cheek better." She let out a sigh.

If nothing else, this was a woman who wouldn't back down. "I think that may be because that's how we did it, you and me."

She looked up at him and put her hand on his cheek.

After giving her a wink, he put his hand over hers.

"I apologize, I thought I was helping. I'll stay quiet. Just with everything that happened with corporate and all, I got a little nervous." She shrugged. "I want to do a good job."

"Then let us do our job and your job will be stellar." To punctuate his statement, he gave her a light peck and pulled her down on the bed. "We're going to make you a great movie." He stared up at the ceiling. For the first time in his life, he cared about something more than what he could get out of it and making sure he looked good. The pressure was on.

HOLLYWOOD STARDOM

FADE IN:

INT. ARIZONA - GRANDPARENT'S HOME - AFTERNOON

STEVEN and his GRANDMOTHER are in the kitchen.
GRANDMOTHER hands him a cold drink.

                    STEVEN
          Thanks.
          (Glances at his watch and
          shakes his head.)

               STEVEN'S GRANDMOTHER
           Are you filming today?

                    STEVEN
           No, another day lost.
          (He gulps down the drink.)

               STEVEN'S GRANDMOTHER
            All your life all you ever
            thought about was what you
            lost.

STEVEN leans back on the counter and looks at
her.

               STEVEN'S GRANDMOTHER
            Maybe you're too afraid of
            losing.

                    STEVEN
           What are you trying to say?

ROXY comes into the room holding her bag.

They stare at each other.

                    STEVEN
          (Stands up straight, goes to
          ROXY and takes her bag.)
           Are you ready to go home?

                    ROXY
          I'm ready to get back on
          set. That's what you
          really wanted to know.

                    STEVEN
          While I want you back on
          set, I wanted to know if
          you're ready to go home.

                    ROXY
          What are you ready for?

STEVEN lifts his chin.

                    ROXY
          (Takes her bag back)
          I'm ready to get back on
          set.
          (She gives STEVEN'S
          GRANDMOTHER a kiss then
          walks away.)

              STEVEN'S GRANDMOTHER
           Don't be afraid of losing.

                    STEVEN
           Maybe I lost it already.
          (He follows ROXY.)

Chapter Seventeen

BACK IN THE DAY, when Cora did her own coding and could sit for hours plunking away at a computer, everyone called her boring.

However, nothing, absolutely nothing, and when she said nothing, she meant nothing, was more horribly boring than being on a movie set.

All the clichés were spot on. Watching grass grow or paint dry or her write code, would be much more interesting than watching a film being made. A strange little plot twist since they were creating something meant to be watched.

Basically, everyone stood around, talked on radios, and complained while they were getting ready to film. When at last they filmed, everyone held their breath for fear of a mistake. If, on the off chance, by some mere stroke of lightning, the actors, the environment, the props, the extras and every other detail passed muster, then they filmed it again. A million takes from different angles, close ups, not close ups, and every other variation one could think of, and then they did some more. She had algorithms that didn't do that much analyzing.

All this netted them to maybe, possibly but maybe not filming one page of a script per day, and they were thrilled about it.

Cora wanted to put her head through a wall.

The only good thing that happened on the film side of things was the whole monstrosity of people moved into a soundstage, which for some reason, seemed easier than filming outside only because they didn't have the weather to deal with. In her entire life she never heard so much talk about the weather. They were in Southern California, they didn't have weather, hadn't anyone received that memo? Lord knew they had enough paperwork for everything else.

On the other hand, Ryder was spot on when he told her several days ago to watch the story about the director and Alan Smithee unfold. The report morphed from troubles on the set to an epic tale of their love affair, and then suddenly the issue about the directors turned into what she did for her man, and how the movie would reflect the love that all the actors and one producer had for the story.

Dane Ellis even called and said she was doing a great job.

Poor Alan Smithee never had a chance.

Aside from the boredom, there was only one small minor little glitch that needed to be addressed. "Rodger, I need to ask you to do something for me." With all this time on her hands, she clicked around an auction site. Some more items from *Kiss Me Softly* were up on the auction block, these from the original Broadway cast.

"That's why I'm here." Her secretary walked across Ryder's trailer and sat on the couch next to her.

"This could be classified as a personal question." Not wanting to make eye contact, she stared at her computer and entered her bids. With the boredom on set, aside from the auctions, she also managed to watch each of the first movies again twice, and read her script of *Hollywood Stardom*. Now there was something missing. Something of vital importance.

"I know the brand of condom you and Ryder use. I've purchased stock in the company. I think I can handle anything else." As he spoke Rodger straightened out her desk.

"Have you read the end of the *Hollywood Stardom* script?" She attempted keep her tone light and casual.

He faced her. "Just ask."

"Rodger." She grabbed the sleeve of his shirt. "I need you to use your vast experience and find out what the end of the movie is."

"I thought you told me that each character was making a case for their own ending." Rodger's expression remained completely blank. He would have made an amazing poker player.

"You and I both know Madeline knows the end." Actually, she didn't know that, she only prayed Madeline did because Cora was about ready to explode. "You have never failed me, get me the end."

"I shall bring it to you on a silver platter." Rodger stood. "Right after I get your afternoon iced coffee. Come on, Spike time for your afternoon ablutions."

Spike stretched and without question trotted to Rodger.

As he walked away, Rodger typed something on his phone. A peek at his screen showed he already had Madeline's picture up. The man was magic.

She returned to her computer and clicked on her work email, flinching when one of the new messages came from a sender named starwatcher. As if on automatic, she opened the email.

Beautiful picture. Mr. Scott is lucky to have someone like you. Maybe you should make stargazing your full time profession.

Even more creepy than the strange message was the picture attached of her and Ryder leaving the studio together a few days ago.

Until she went to type a command into her computer, she didn't realize she was trembling. Ryder told her she needed to get used to the tabloids and the media, but this went beyond. The picture, the words, the feel of the message. What did stargazing mean? Lying on her back looking up at the sky, like dead?

The rush of adrenaline getting the best of her, she jumped up, and dashed toward the exit.

Right before she reached the door, it opened.

At the form in the door, she screamed and grabbed the first thing to meet her hand. She held up Spike's tablet. "Get away from me!"

"Cora!" Viktor rushed in. "What's wrong with you?"

Viktor. It was Viktor. The man who was basically her brother. Her heart beat so loud she could barely hear solid reasoning, and she doubled over and tried to breathe.

"What's going on?" Viktor put his hand on her back and took the tablet away.

Once her trembling subsided enough for her stand up, she took his arm and took him to the computer. "Look." She motioned toward the screen. "How did they get my email, and how did they get that picture? What does stargazing mean?"

"Let me see." Viktor held up his hand. "I'll forward this to me and see what we can find out, but in all likelihood it's one of Ryder's fans. Let's show him, surely he's dealt with this kind of thing before."

"No!" she screamed. "Don't tell him!"

Viktor turned to her. "What's wrong with you? He'll know what to do."

"He doesn't need to know this," she shook her head, "he told me I had to get used to it. You know, some fans can get a little overzealous." She went to the mirror and smoothed her hair down. "I don't want him focused on this. I'll sound like one of those women who can't take care of herself."

Viktor stood beside her. "Either you have it bad, or you don't care."

"What does that mean?" She lifted a bottle of Ryder's cologne and put it to her nose. Spicy, earthy, musky, it smelled like...it smelled like Ryder.

"Between you preferring to work in Ryder's trailer, rather than the one we had brought over for the business, and you smelling his cologne, I got my answer." He plucked the bottle out of her hand.

The sudden need to see Ryder overwhelmed her. "I think I'm going to the set for a while."

"All right." Viktor patted her head. "I'm going back to the business trailer to get some things done and see what I can uncover about the email."

As she walked to the soundstage, she passed Rodger, who presented her with her afternoon pick me up. She gave Spike a scratch and went to the sound stage. The production assistants let her pass, and she took her normal chair now positioned next to the matching one that said Scott.

Ever since her first day on set, she learned to simply sit in her spot and be quiet. Without making any sudden moves, she reached in her pocket and turned off the sound on her phone. She was pretty sure Logan still wasn't talking to her for that one ring at the beginning of the week.

Since they were still shooting the part of the movie where William and Roxy's romance took center stage, the set was decorated to look like their home where they brought everyone after the concert. If it weren't for the equipment and all the people standing around, it would like any other home of two busy professionals.

Ryder and Erin stood in the middle of the room laughing and playing a game of thumb wrestling.

"All right, quiet on the set." Logan called out.

Cora sat up. Her timing was perfect. They were actually going to do something.

One of the PAs rushed forward with a clapperboard. "William and Roxy kiss take nine." Just like in any movie about making a movie, he snapped the little contraption.

Wait. Cora bit the inside of her mouth. William and Roxy kiss, not the quick peck in the concert, but a real kiss. Yes, she read it, but sort of forgot about the part that he would actually have to act it out, and apparently, this was the ninth take of it.

She watched as Ryder curled his arms around Erin, one hand went to the back of her head, the other to the small of her back, and he lowered his mouth to hers.

It took every bit of strength Cora possessed to not yell cut. Instead, she shifted in her seat and watched Ryder give Erin a kiss that he was supposed to be giving Cora.

Stop. She forced herself to clear her mind. This wasn't a kiss kiss, this was a movie kiss. It wasn't Ryder and Erin kissing it was William and Roxy.

"Cut! Print!' Logan yelled.

Print, as she learned, was good. It meant they liked it. Getting something to print was harder than getting a bill to become a law. With this little inconvenience out of the way, maybe Ryder could have a break.

Ryder and Erin stepped back from each other and resumed their thumb wrestle.

Hair and makeup came over and touched up the actors.

In Cora's not vast experience, the arrival hair and makeup only meant more takes. Darn.

"Let's get the close ups." Logan's voice rang through the space.

Again they went through the ritual with yelling and the snapping the thing.

Again Ryder kissed Erin.

Again Cora's mind wandered. Erin and Ryder had been an on again off again couple way back when. Yes, Erin was married, but Cora wondered what kind kiss Ryder was actually giving Erin. Obviously, they had kissed before, had sex, shared intimate moments.

By the time she watched the next take, Cora broke out into a sweat but told herself she was being unreasonable. What did she expect? Actors did kissing scenes, sex scenes, all different kinds of scenes.

On the next one, she glanced around the soundstage for Drew. She found him with his back facing the action, reading something. Smart man.

When they made it to the next take, she decided without any shadow of a doubt she did not enjoy watching Ryder kiss someone else. She also decided that she didn't really want to observe this anymore, and since she didn't have the foresight to bring reading material, she needed to get out of there. Like a good girl, she waited for Logan to call cut, and as silently as she could, slid out of her seat and tiptoed out of the soundstage.

She stepped outside into the sun and stomped over to the trailers. The work trailer and Ryder's trailer. For quite some time she stood in front of the two destinations, trying to make a choice, but all that flashed before her was Ryder kissing Erin.

"Let me make this easier for you." Ryder basically appeared out of nowhere, grabbed her hand, and dragged her into his trailer.

"I have work to do." A fool, she was a fool. She was a fool who was angry and a fool who was angry at being angry.

"I only have a thirty-minute break, but I wanted to show you something. Don't move." He held his hand up and disappeared into the bathroom.

Tapping her foot, she listened while he brushed his teeth.

Shirtless, and with his face glistening from water, he came out, took her into his arms, bent her back and kissed her.

Well, not really. He opened his mouth but didn't treat her to any tongue, he simply moved his lips over hers and contorted his body in such a way that between the way he held her and how he had their heads tilted made it hard to breathe. This, whatever it was, lasted much longer than necessary for no tongue and the amount of her discomfort.

As fast as he kissed her, he pulled away.

"What the hell was that?" She stepped back and put her hands on her hips.

Instead of answering, he tilted his neck from side to side, inhaled and once more wrapped his arms around her. This time when he kissed her, he was Ryder again. The Ryder who tantalized her with his tongue, the one who let his hands wander down the side of her breast the other one cupping her backside.

She lost herself, melted into him, and returned the favor, allowing her hands to travel down his smooth skin. They should make the most of his thirty minutes.

When he broke the kiss, he pressed his forehead to hers. "There is a movie kiss. The kiss that is only an act, the one that generates no heat, the one where you're trying your best to find your light and making sure that you're not blocking the actress so you don't have to do yet another take."

He took her hand and pressed it on the growing bulge between his legs. "Then there's the real kiss that generates this reaction."

He saw her at the set and saw her leave. Her cheeks heated at being found out.

She sighed. "You and Erin—."

Before she had a chance to finish her statement, he cut her off by putting his finger over her lips. "Me and Erin were thrown together for years while she waited for Drew."

"What about you?" At her words, she shut her eyes. Thank god she wasn't near a mirror because she couldn't even look at herself.

"Sometimes you don't know you're waiting until you find what you want." His voice lowered and he backed them up through the trailer toward the bed.

"Don't feed me any lines." She gasped when he lifted her and laid her down on the bed.

"There are movie lines that are scripted." He positioned himself on top of her and kissed her, a quick playful kiss. "Then there are lines that are real."

With his words, he treated her to a deeper kiss, a real kiss, one that made her flood with need and made her want to hold on. When they started, their relationship wasn't supposed to be real, but everything felt way too authentic—from her not wanting him to even fake kiss another woman, to that email and not wanting to tell him.

She looked up at the Ryder recalling the words of that email. Technically, she was stargazing.

Everything was too real.

FADE IN:

EXT. ARIZONA - LOCATION SHOOT - AFTERNOON

ROXY is standing looking at the MALE LEAD down
on one knee in front of her.

                    MALE LEAD
          I love you. I don't ever
          want to wake up and find
          you not there. I don't
          ever want to go to sleep
          without your head on my
          chest. I don't want to
          live in a world without you
          as my wife.
          (He reveals a ring to her.)

                    ROXY
          I don't know if I deserve
          you. I don't know if I
          can.
          (She puts her hand over her
          mouth and runs O.S.)

MALE LEAD clutches the ring in hand then runs
after her.

                    STEVEN
          Cut! Print! Excellent!
          (claps)
          Everyone take fifteen.
          (He walks away and goes to
          ROXY standing over by a
          tree.)

                    ROXY
          (Running her fingers over
          the pattern in the bark)
          Well, no one can ever say
          you were with me because of
          my extreme intelligence.

                    STEVEN
          (Takes her hand but she
          pulls it away)
           What do you mean?

                    ROXY
          The scene. It is us, but
          not like I thought. It
          wasn't a precursor to a
          proposal, I think you want
          me to run away. It would
          make your life much easier.

                    STEVEN
          Never forget I was the one
          who wanted you first.

ROXY faces him.

                    STEVEN
          Why don't you wait until
          the end of the movie to
          decide if it's us or not?

                    ROXY
          I've already read the
          script.

                    STEVEN
          Then what's your verdict?
          I think we have an award
          winner.

                    ROXY
          Maybe we need a different
          ending.

Chapter Eighteen

TICK TOCK, TICK TOCK. Don't think memorabilia bought you all the time in the world.

Staring at his phone, Ryder wiped his forehead and leaned against one of the buildings on the studio lot made to look like a perfect little street in suburbia where William and Roxy resided. Thankfully, his main segment was coming to a close. Unfortunately, his time with the thugs wouldn't be wrapped up quite as fast. Damn, he would finish *Working Title*, he would. Life continued to happen, he had debts and things spiraled out of control. But once *Stardom* wrapped, with Cora by his side he knew he could finish, then he would take her hand, and they'd walk off to do another project together. One with no strings to things he didn't want her even guessing about him or his past.

Fine, yes, he thought about just sailing off with her. Doing more projects, being with her.

Before he turned his life into a romance movie, or heaven forbid, he burst into song and became a happy pappy musical, he needed to finish out his other commitments. First and foremost, he could never have Glen thinking he was ignoring them.

I have an alarm set on my phone. Trust me I'm on it. Ryder hit send, his stomach sinking when he saw that Glen was instantly texting back.

We trusted you before, but maybe now that you are with such an established and gorgeous woman, you will turn your life around.

He balled his hand in a fist and ground his teeth together. Threats on him, his movie, his stuff he could handle. Comments, even seemingly innocent ones, about Cora lit every one of his fuses. She was clean, pure, and he wouldn't have her tainted by these bastards.

Leave her out of this and everything will get done much faster. He pushed the send button hard enough to almost break the damn phone.

If you didn't care we wouldn't either.

"Damn it!" He shoved his phone in his pocket and without even thinking, rammed his fist into the building. Unexpected shooting pain skyrocketed through his arm. These stupid buildings were supposed to be facades. "Shit!"

Cradling his throbbing hand, he doubled over and stumbled forward. His shoe caught in something, and he fell, twisting his leg and hitting the ground with a thud. His breath left him, and he gasped for air right as something hit him in the face and shattered around him.

"Ryder!" Someone yelled his name. "Keep your eyes closed!"

Though every fiber in his being longed to flinch, open his eyes, assess his own condition, he resisted. Years of training to control every movement came in handy at last.

The thump of footsteps coming toward him vibrated through the ground.

"What happened?" Logan's voice rang through next. "Get a medic."

Searing, burning pain, just about everywhere, he turned to his side and when he opened his mouth to try to tell them not to get Cora, something that felt like a shard of glass entered his mouth, propelling him straight into to a fit of coughing.

"Don't move! A floodlight broke over you." Logan grabbed his arm.

He let out a moan. Without opening his eyes, he heard people gather around. Almost as if he were in another world, things happened around him with him in the rare instance as spectator and not actor. The distinctive, distorted voices of people shouting commands over the radio echoed, followed by a siren.

"The medics are here." Logan gave him a squeeze. "Everyone clear a path! Let's sweep this glass away."

"Halt!!" A voice he didn't expect, but recognized, commanded attention.

Part of him wished he could open his eyes and see her coming toward him, the other part of him didn't want her to see him like this.

"No one touch him," Cora yelled out her decree, and her heels clip clopped toward him. "Ryder?" She took his hand.

Every muscle seemed wrenched in some sort of ache, or he was being a wimp. He wasn't sure which.

"Excuse me, Miss."

Someone, he could only assume the medic, came over.

"You are not touching him. I have my own medical staff." Her tone came out the same as when she fired Edward. "Rodger!"

Rodger?

"Miss, only a medical professional is allowed to work on the patient."

"Excuse me, but Rodger is an Emergency Medical Technician and my employee, and I am telling you to back away while he fixes this." For the first time ever, her voice cracked.

"Mr. Scott, do you feel anything cutting into you?" Rodger leaned down to his ear and spoke low. "Your eyes?"

"No." He had a feeling Rodger whispered to keep Cora from hearing.

"Do you trust me?" Rodger asked.

"Yeah." The sick thing was he did trust this bizarre man.

In a move he never anticipated, Rodger lifted him. "Shake your head."

Without question, he did as the man demanded.

Everyone around them started to clap.

No sooner did he finish, than he felt an oversized brush sweep over his face.

"Now don't move while I take a look," Rodger said. "He has a lesion here, but no glass is embedded."

Ryder flinched when Rodger touched the cut on his cheek.

"Now, open your eyes."

As if reentering the atmosphere, he did as Rodger requested. The sun blared down on him, making it hard to focus, and he blinked a few times until his eyes adjusted.

"He's bleeding!" Cora skidded on her knees next to him.

"Watch it." All he saw was glass and Cora, and he didn't need her getting hurt.

"Cora, stay still," Rodger ordered. "I don't want to be doing this to you." With a pair of tweezers in his hand, Rodger plucked away a few extra shards of glass then cleaned and dressed the wound with supplies the medics handed him. "Can you stand?"

Ryder nodded, and Rodger put his arm around him as he got on his feet. "I'm fine!"

Once more, everyone went into a round of applause.

"Does he need stitches, a hospital, do we need to go to the emergency room? I can call Cedars and have them reserve an OR." Cora kept a death grip on his hand. "Rodger!"

"It's a superficial wound. Nothing is broken." Out of his pocket Rodger pulled out a lozenge, and held it to Cora's lips. "Open."

For the first time ever, Ryder watched Cora obey a command without question and open her mouth.

Rodger placed the little tablet on her tongue.

She chewed, swallowed and took a breath. "I want Dr. Duke and Dr. Morris brought to the apartment right now. Tell them to meet us there. Pay them whatever to drop what they are doing." Her voice returned to the woman in charge.

"Are you all right to work?" Logan came over.

Before he had a chance to even open his mouth, Cora held her hand out, stopping Logan from getting any closer. "No, he's not all right, a lighting unit fell on him, we should all be thankful he's up and not hurt worse, and right now we're going home and will resume production when Ryder is well, and not a moment before."

As if everything in Cora's life was planned for perfect timing, Viktor drove up to the scene of the crime, jumped out of the car, and opened the back door.

Rodger ushered Ryder into the back seat, and guided Cora next to him, then got in the driver's seat. Viktor took his place in the passenger side, then, as if this whole thing was normal, they drove away.

"I have the doctors on the way." Viktor typed something on his phone.

"Do you think we should have brought in Dr. Shapiro as well?" Cora asked.

"What else do we need?" Viktor asked.

Cora continued to look Ryder over, her fingertips lightly grazing anywhere she deemed might be hurt. "I need you to call that place Ryder likes and get that vegetable soup. Have them bring a gallon. Then I want those vegan pancakes for him. Ryder loves pancakes." She pressed her palm to this side of his face. "Also, make sure he had his juice. Double this week's order."

Stunned from the accident, and even more stunned from Cora and her actions, Ryder remained quiet.

The rest of the ride she simply stared at his hand holding hers.

As they pulled up to the building, he gave her hand a squeeze. "Hey, are you okay?"

She jolted her head up as if he startled her. "I should be asking you that."

"I'm asking you." If he said he wasn't enjoying the concern in her eyes, he would be lying.

"When I heard you were hurt, I thought my chest was going to explode. I haven't run like that since elementary school."

He stared into her eyes. What if it were she who was hurt? The glimmer of the thought made him shudder.

"Why are you shaking? Are you going into shock?" She dug her nails into his hand.

"Baby, I'm all right." He forced a grin. "Seriously."

"I'll be the one to determine that." At last, she gave him a little smile.

Viktor opened her side of the car, and Rodger opened his. She gave him a light kiss and got out.

Rodger stopped him before he excited. "When we get upstairs, let's wash off your hand." His gaze traveled down.

Ryder glanced at the side of his hand, all scratched up from when he hit it into the wall earlier. "Thanks."

"Whatever it was, it must have been really frustrating." Rodger raised his eyebrows and backed up to let him out.

The two of them locked eyes. "I must've fallen on it."

Cora came around to his side of the car and held her hand out. "Are you all right?"

"I'm the same as I was before." He put his good hand in hers and pulled her in tight. Maybe he wasn't all right. He didn't know.

DOCTOR DUKE LEANED DOWN, adjusted the light, and moved closer. "It's just as I suspected. Dr. Morris?" He motioned toward the patient.

Cora wrung her hands, waiting for the diagnosis on Ryder.

The second doctor went in for an inspection. He even took his penlight to illuminate the wound better. "I have to agree with you. I must say you all did an excellent job of getting rid of the glass."

"What about Dr. Shapiro?" Cora gasped her question and everyone in the room turned toward the third doctor with Spike in his arms.

"Spike is in excellent health. He's thriving, and I updated his vaccinations." The good doctor put the dog down and approached their bed. "I may be a vet, but I have to say I concur with the best dermatologist and plastic surgeon in the country."

Cora went to Ryder's side and rubbed her hand over his shoulder only to be met by a rather painful scratch. "Look at this." She held her hand out revealing the tiniest shard of glass in her palm. "He still has glass on him."

"Those shards will sneak up on you." Dr. Morris shook his head.

"What do you intend to do about it? Look at this gash on his face." She motioned toward her injured actor. Maybe they didn't think much about the accident, but was it an accident as Ryder claimed, or was he stargazing? A shiver ran through her.

Dr. Duke opened a bandage, and Dr. Morris took the it and without much pomp and or circumstance put it over Ryder's cut. "He'll be fine..." Dr. Morris looked at his watch. "...right about now."

All the doctors shook Ryder's hand, and he signed a few autographs.

"Does he need any prescription or anything?" She ground her teeth together. Maybe they needed some more doctors.

"If he's in any pain, just have him take an aspirin." The doctors made their way out.

She followed them. "When should I change his dressing?"

At the door, Dr. Duke turned toward her. "When you feel like it, you can take the bandage off."

"What about sleeping?" Thinking she was done with these hacks, she opened the door.

"If he's tired, he should sleep, if he's hungry he should eat." Dr. Morris stepped outside. "If he's anything else he should do that." He gave her a wink.

"Thank you." She slammed the door and rushed to the kitchen to feed Ryder. Hungry or not, the man was eating. Apparently, these physicians never studied the Internet and therefore couldn't possess her vast medical knowledge. They weren't there to see Ryder lying on the ground basically lifeless, they hadn't seen the blood trickling down the side of his face, they hadn't picked out shards of glass from his hair in the shower.

After collecting their food, tray in hand, she returned to the bedroom to find Ryder in bed with a yellow pad and pen, scribbling something down. "You know, we have computers for that kind of thing." She tried to joke, but nothing seemed funny.

"Oh, now I feel dirty." He chuckled and put the paper aside.

"What were you writing?" She put the tray on the side table and joined him on the bed.

"Some last edits on *Working Title*." He shrugged and put the paper aside.

"Then I may actually get to see it soon." She got his bowl of vegetable soup then handed it to him, along with some hummus and gluten free pita bread. "How long did it take you to write it thus far?"

"I wrote it over the course of several years. I was always doing movies, so it took a long time." He took a couple of bites of the food. "I'm really looking forward to working on it again, finally getting it done."

It didn't take a woman with three degrees to realize that was a hint. With everything going on, she put his movie on the backburner. Maybe she conveniently forgot, not because she didn't want to help, but their arrangement had slipped her mind. Hell, with the way she reacted after his accident, she knew she wasn't playing a role, everything came naturally.

All relationships were built on some sort of deal. He held up his part and then some. Life wasn't a happy musical where people were smitten by a mere glance and a song. Still, she swallowed away the lump forming in her throat. "Where is the first area we need to start working on for your movie?" Not wanting to look at him, she turned and got her meal off the tray. Rodger got her favorite, filet with a black truffle sauce and a baked potato, definitely not Ryder approved.

"The movie is underfunded." He fiddled around with his soup but didn't eat any.

"I figured that much out." Her business acumen kicked right in on that one. "Do you have a budget?"

He turned to her.

His blank expression didn't tell her as much as his silence. "How did you get funding in the first place?" The first thing anyone asked for when seeking money was a budget.

"Cora." He sighed.

"You have to tell me." Her heart sped.

"I thought I knew a lot about this." He took her hand and stared down at it. "I threw some numbers together, then friends funded me, people in the industry. I tossed in some myself. I had some debts and such and the movie would get behind when I was working. It sort of became a mess. I need to get back into production."

All along she wondered how a star of Ryder's caliber could end up needing money, needing her, but without him going further, she saw the whole picture. It was a problem one too many rich and famous got themselves into.

"Cora, I..." He shook his head. "I don't want to be this man in your eyes. Just forget it."

"Ryder." At his words, the lump subsided. "We'll work on the movie together. I want to make it happen for you. Bring me everything, and we'll get a budget. I can hardly wait to see the script." No matter the circumstance or the deal or whatever, she would figure out a way to make his movie.

He took her hand and kissed the back.

"Will you try to eat something?" Her appetite returning, she dug back into her meal.

Out of the corner of her eye, she caught Ryder staring at her. Actually, not her, but her food. "Aren't you hungry?"

"Starving." He scooted closer to her.

In an experiment, she cut off a little piece of the filet, dipped it in the sauce, and held her fork out to him.

Like a true carnivore, he descended upon the offering, plucked it off the fork with his teeth, fell back on the pillow, and chewed with his eyes closed.

"You're not a vegan." She fed herself another bite and then held another piece up for Ryder.

"It's a very hard diet." He leaned in to take the morsel.

Today was a day of revelations. She held it up out of his reach. "Explain yourself."

"It started to be healthier, then the public loved it, and no one ever wondered about me." He grabbed her wrist and guided the fork to his mouth.

Yes, she had heard rumblings about Logan taking the wrap for Ryder's drug use when he was a teenager. His ruse almost made sense, and it definitely made sense in Ryder's world. He was the dream, the good boy, the one who adopted dogs and didn't eat meat.

"So now I'm your supplier?" She gave him some more.

"That's not what I would call you." He put the plate aside and took her into his arms.

Powerless, she cuddled up against him. "What would you call me?"

He turned her to her back, moved over her, and stared into her eyes. "Mine."

She cursed the delightful spin in her stomach.

"I can be me when I'm with you, I can be real, and you're mine." He gave her a light kiss.

Maybe his deceptions weren't intended to deceive her, maybe they were his way of telling her his truth. Or maybe that was what he wanted her to think. In truth, he seemed to be the only one she could be real with as well. Either way she found herself wrapping his arms around neck, only to encounter something sharp cutting into her. "Oh!" She flinched and pulled her arm back, the little sparkle imbedded in her skin, displaying another tiny shard of glass.

"Oh damn baby, I'm sorry." He plucked the glass off her, and kissed the spot. "This glass keeps appearing."

Yes, little shards of glass had a way sneaking up. She hoped they didn't find any more because she cared too much.

HOLLYWOOD STARDOM

FADE IN:

INT. ARIZONA - LOCATION SHOOT - EVENING

STEVEN is in his trailer with the PRODUCER.

                    PRODUCER
          The movie is turning out
          good. I'm happy with the
          progress, especially once
          you got your star back.

                    STEVEN
          (Nods)
          She's hitting her mark now.

                    PRODUCER
          Will you only work
          exclusively with her?

                    STEVEN
          (Leans back on the couch)
          What are you getting at?

                    PRODUCER
          (Leans forward)
          You know exactly what I'm
          asking. If I had some
          opportunities that wanted
          you to work with a
          different lead actress
          would that be an issue?

                    STEVEN
          (Runs his hand through his
          hair and takes a breath)
          What kind of opportunity?

                    PRODUCER
          The kind of opportunity
          that nets the director
          seven figures and little
          gold statues.

                    STEVEN
          We're not married.
          (He turns away.)

The door to the trailer opens and ROXY enters.
Both STEVEN and the PRODUCER face her but remain
quiet. The PRODUCER sits back.

ROXY stops in the door way and looks between
them.

                    ROXY
          (Holds onto the door)
           Is this boys only?

                    STEVEN
          (Glances over at the
          PRODUCER)
           Of course not, we were just
           finishing discussing the
           dailies.

                    PRODUCER
          (Stands)
           We'll talk later.
          (He walks by STEVEN pats his
          shoulder and then nods at
          ROXY on his way out.)

                    ROXY
          (Closes the door and goes to
          the STEVEN)
           What's going on?

                    STEVEN
          Nothing, business talk.
          New opportunities.

(He takes ROXY'S hand and
pulls her down on the couch
with him.)

            ROXY
 What kind of opportunities?

            STEVEN
(Tilts his head.)
 New horizons.

            ROXY
 Opportunities for some.
 Misfortune for others.

            STEVEN
 There are always two sides
 to every coin.

Chapter Nineteen

"YES, I UNDERSTAND you're concerned." Cora paced in the kitchen at Wilson's bar.

Refusing to leave her, Ryder watched Cora retrace her steps over and over again. She had been on the phone for the last ten minutes talking to that Dane Ellis ass who seemed to want to analyze every single thing his woman was doing to make *Stardom* successful.

Yes, she delayed production a couple of days while his face healed enough to put makeup over the cut, and yes, she went over budget in a few minor spots, but the fact was, she had done everything in her power to make the movie a success. A finale for the ages, no jerkoff director required.

His superwoman not only managed *Hollywood Stardom*, but she also was working on an extensive budget for *Working Title*. While this wasn't exactly what he wanted as far as funding went, he knew he would make any movie with her at any time. She was the personification of what a producer should be.

"Dane, we are one third done with the movie. Things will pick up now, and I'm absolutely confident that the final product will be worth it in the end, not only from an artistic standpoint, but a financial one as well." She stopped, faced the wall, and balled her hand into a fist.

Ryder held his breath and held his tongue, but every part of him wanted to snatch that phone away from Cora and tell the not so great Dane where to shove his doubts.

"Yes Dane, I'll be at the meetings. Have a good afternoon." She hit a button on her phone, but didn't turn around.

Now a Cora aficionado, he retrieved her iced coffee off the counter, snuck over to her side, and while he kissed her neck, gave her a sip of her preferred elixir. "Don't let that guy get you down, you're brilliant."

She grabbed the drink and shook her head. "Just make me a blockbuster, so I can rub the reviews in his face." As if envisioning the act, she smiled.

"I'll do my best." Though he kept his tone light, the pressure was on, and he had every intention of bringing this movie in on time and making it a success for her. "Come on let's go join the others." He took her hand and they entered the main room at Logan's brother's bar. Already Logan, Ivy, Drew, Erin and Madeline were there, and Ryder had to admit, he took a little bit of pride when Cora sat down next to him. At last he was part of this elusive coupledom that eluded him, and dare he say, he had the best of the bunch.

"Cora, Ryder, we were just discussing the location shoot in Arizona next week." Logan filled in the blanks.

His co-director's mention of the location shoot made his proud coupledom vanish. Cora had to attend some stupid corporate meetings and wouldn't be able to go with him. It would be the first time they were apart since they got together, and he had to admit he wasn't all too happy about it. Since he was with the queen of the Internet, all he knew was the hotel better have some amazing Wi-Fi because they were going to have spectacular video conferencing sex. Still, at the mention of the trip, he let out a groan.

Cora patted him, but he glimpsed a bit of a glimmer in her eye at his misery. Well, as long as she was happy.

"Now that we're all here, let's get down to it." Cora took out her laptop and tapped away. "Madeline, the floor is yours."

Ryder had never seen anyone type quite as fast as her.

"That's a good one." Madeline laughed, unearthed a yellow pad and jotted something down.

"Did I say a joke?" Cora narrowed her eyes.

"That would be good for a comedy, you know someone says, the floor is yours and another person comes in and hands that person a floor." Madeline cracked up complete with a snort and hitting the table.

The rest of them sat there waiting for their screenwriter to compose herself.

After one last snort, Madeline cleared her throat. "I would like to discuss the end of the movie with each of you in your character's point of view." She opened a file folder. "Ryder let's start with you."

Cora sat up.

For her he had to give it his best effort. "William was the first to love Roxy and he always wanted her happy. They need to end up together because that is the storybook ending, the one everyone is waiting for."

At the slight nod of Cora's head, he knew he hit it and everyone could take that. The boss had spoken, so to speak, and he would get the big ending the world waited for.

"I disagree," Logan interjected.

Ivy shifted in her seat, opened a notebook on the table and pushed it toward Logan.

"Explain, Logan." Pen at the ready, Madeline took notes.

"Steven is the ending everyone wants to see. It's the ultimate comeback story." Logan glanced at Ivy's notebook. "Deep down every woman wants to be with the bad boy and with the way Roxy has continued to return to Steven, it makes the choice evident."

Ivy pointed to something on the page.

Logan nodded. "Additionally, the whole first movie ended on one of the most famous cliffhangers in cinema history where Roxy opens her eyes and watches Steven drive away. The fact they end up together will finally put closure, not only on the entire relationship, but on the movie franchise as a whole."

Madeline looked to him.

In a burst of action, Cora typed something into her computer, hit enter and then turned the screen to him.

Ryder scanned the words on the screen and slid his chair closer to Cora. The woman was brilliance personified. Ivy may have studied the movie, but no one could beat his girl and her furious fingers. "Let me offer a rebuttal to my esteemed colleague's case." Hell, he played an attorney at least twice in his career.

Everyone around the table turned to him, and he stood to make his point. "Roxy and Steven had a passive aggressive relationship, the proverbial cat and mouse, while Roxy and William's relationship was built on mutual admiration and respect. I believe that's the message we should be sending to the women of the world." With a nod, he returned to his seat.

From beneath the table, Ivy pulled out a red leather bound book, opened it to a marked page, and slammed it in front of her husband.

Ryder caught sight of the title of the book. Ivy was reading from her master's thesis. Cora didn't have a thesis. Damn it.

Rather than stand, Logan sat back and crossed his arms. "While you make a point, I believe showing the world that people can change and one can get their dream is what Hollywood movie magic is made of. In her heart, Steven is who Roxy wanted and giving her the Hollywood send off, while showing the world that a relationship can be strong, vibrant and sexy after two decades is what the public needs to see."

"Are you saying William wasn't sexy?" Ryder leaned forward.

"Why did Roxy open her eyes?" A smile took over Logan's face. "Why did she return to Steven time and again? William obviously lacked something."

"There's more to life than awesome sex!" Ryder hit the table, then looked over his shoulder to hear who said that using his voice.

Logan got up. "Everyone is waiting for Roxy and Steven."

Once more, Cora entered something into her computer then motioned for him.

Not to be outdone, Ryder shot out of his chair as well. "The current algorithms state the public is split between Steven and William, with a small percentage hoping for Charles." At least he thought that was what Cora's chart was showing him. No matter, Ivy might have a thesis, but Cora had algorithms. No one knew what the hell an algorithm was or did, so no one could argue.

Madeline jumped up. "Why don't we hear from Charles...I mean Drew?"

Each keeping an eye on the other, he and Logan returned to their chairs. Ivy patted Logan and Cora took his hand as they all looked toward Erin and Drew.

Without any props to aid him, Drew shrugged. "I'm not sure Charles was ever a contender."

Both Ivy and Cora smiled.

"Drew!" Erin burst out. "Why wouldn't you fight for us?"

"Sweetheart, for you would get into a ring with any heavyweight, but this isn't us." Drew shook his head.

Apparently, Drew tamed the savage Erin, and Ryder watched her visibly relax.

"No, you don't understand." Erin's voice lowered.

"Erin, please elaborate." Madeline continued to write her notes.

"Charles played an integral role, especially in the second movie. He was Roxy's best friend with no pressure, and she loved him in her own way." Erin took Drew's hand and held it to her chest.

At his wife's attention, Drew kissed the back of her hand.

Ryder resisted the need to roll his eyes. That was Erin and Drew's story not Charles and Roxy's. Self-insertion much?

"Then again, I always feel like in real life she would have ended up with William, seen the love he had for her, and gone to him." Erin sniffed. "Of course, Steven was the unattainable one, the one in the back of her mind." A tear rolled down her cheek.

Madeline reached out to her. "Erin?"

"This is why Roxy could never choose, and in the second movie it was even worse. How do you choose between the dream, the one, and the unlikely source?" Erin motioned toward each one of the men. "How does one choose?" Her voice broke, and she burst into tears.

Of course, Drew or not, Erin would always be Erin.

"It's all right." Drew pulled her into his arms. "Come here."

Erin planted herself on her husband's lap and cried into his shoulder. "How can Roxy choose?"

"It's going to be okay." Drew rubbed her back.

After wiping her nose on Drew's shirt, Erin straightened up and looked at her husband. "You're like all the heroes rolled into one." She kissed him and hugged him.

"So are you." Ivy kissed Logan's cheek.

Madeline went into a round of applause. "Thank you." She gathered up all her papers. "That's all I need."

"That's it?" Ryder pushed Cora's computer back to her. They needed more magic numbers. "We have more algorithms."

"We have a thesis." Logan held up Ivy's book.

"I have my end." Madeline shoved all her items into some oversized, overstuffed bag.

"What is it?" Everyone asked in unison.

"I have a contract with a strict clause." Madeline patted her bag. "I have to keep my security tight."

"I need to get some work done, Cora said. "I have some meetings I can't avoid coming up." She packed up her laptop then leaned over to him. "You did good, Mr. Scott."

They got up.

"I want to win this for you." He hooked her bag over his shoulder and took her hand.

"I'm not sure if winning is the right word." She laughed. "It has to be what's best for the story, though I admit I am a William shipper, but I guess I'm biased."

He nodded, but his mind wandered back to earlier and her conversation with the bigwigs. She was biased, and he needed to step up and win for her. He only hoped he had a little of the three heroes in him as well.

HOLLYWOOD STARDOM

FADE IN:

INT. ARIZONA – STEVEN AND ROXY'S HOME – NIGHT

With his hand over her eyes, STEVEN guides ROXY
into the dining room. He lowers his hand and
reveals a candlelight dinner.

                    ROXY
          We had our wrap party for
          the movie yesterday.

                    STEVEN
          This is just for us.
          (He pulls out a chair for
          her.)

ROXY sits and watches as STEVEN pours the wine
and lifts a silver dome of her plate, revealing
a fully plated steak dinner.

                    STEVEN
          (Reveals his own matching
          dish then sits down next to
          her)
           This looks delicious.

                    ROXY
           Strange, I smell something
           rotten.
          (She takes a sip of the
          wine.)

                    STEVEN
          Impossible. This was
          delivered by Rodolpho's.
          It's your favorite.

                    ROXY
          (Pushes the plate away)
           It's not the food.

STEVEN looks at her.

                    ROXY
          Just tell me.

                    STEVEN
          I have an opportunity.

                    ROXY
          There's that word again.
          What opportunity?

                    STEVEN
          A movie. Twelve weeks in
          Europe.

                    ROXY
          (Presses her lips together
          and looks into her wine
          glass)
          I take it since I didn't
          see any script, the female
          lead has already been
          chosen?

                    STEVEN
          The film has been cast
          already. Original director
          had obligations. The money
          is phenomenal, but they
          want it fast and clean.

                    ROXY
          Meaning no significant
          others. When do you leave?

                    STEVEN
          End of the week.
          (He reaches over and grabs
          her hand.)
          It will be quick and we
          will profit big.

                    ROXY
          What kind of picture is it?

                    STEVEN
          A drama.

                    ROXY
          (Stands up)
          Strange, I would have
          thought it was a war film
          because I feel attacked.

Chapter Twenty

FOR THE FIRST TIME since she decided she would be on the *Hollywood Stardom* set, Cora drove separate from Ryder. Her move was deliberate because she needed to check in on the office. She needed to go over the *Hollywood Stardom* budget, and Ryder seemed to get upset anytime she was questioned. No wonder he didn't have much paperwork dealing with his movie. That was fine, he had her.

Though she hated the way she smiled at how they fit together, both in mind and body, she couldn't stop it either. She glanced at the clock on her dashboard. If she played her cards right, she could get her report finished, do her conference call and get back to set before the caterer had a chance to make her favorite chicken sandwich for lunch. Fine, she would end up sharing with Ryder in the trailer. His secret on his diet was safe with her. After all, they were a couple.

As she drove into the unground parking of her office building, she sighed. They were a couple she guessed, they did couple things, they had couple plans, even long-term ones. When she allowed herself to put their arrangement on her back burner, their relationship was normal, or as normal as a relationship with a superstar could be. What happened next? Truth be told it was becoming easier and easier to live the role rather than play it.

Her stomach swirled in a not unpleasant way as she parked. She got out of the car and went around to the passenger side where she gathered up her bag, the espresso Ryder made her before they left, and a prop her star took from the set—a statue with a bronze eagle on top. The little knickknack was in William and Roxy's living room set and yesterday appeared in the middle of her dining room table at the apartment. Ever the diplomat, she offered to move it to a more appropriate location, namely anywhere where it wouldn't be a centerpiece in their apartment.

She paused long enough to take a breath. The last time she came to the office at this hour, she ended up with her mind playing tricks on her and feeling like someone was watching her. Instead of focusing on that morning, she used one of Ryder's acting techniques and visualized her next actions. She was going to march through the lobby, get on the elevator, and go right to her office. Her goal was getting back to set and sharing a chicken sandwich.

"Don't most stars fade by this time of the morning?"

At the, strange, almost electronic deep voice, her entire body went rigid. She didn't speak.

The scratch of the person's shoes on the asphalt indicated he stepped closer to her.

Her throat dry and overcome with shaking, she forced herself to focus, look around. If he were right behind her, there was no way out. Whoever this was had her wedged between her car and the exit.

"Is that why you're at work so early? Some of the shine wearing off?"

A shudder ran from the base of her neck down to her spine, and she slid her hand to her purse toward her lifeline to the world, her phone. In no way would anyone take her down. "Back away right now."

"Make one more move and you won't be able to stargaze anymore." The voice came closer. "You should know how to take direction by now."

As if she would ever take direction from this lowlife. She worked with the best and wouldn't ever settle for anything less. Heat, fire, rage, burst through her. With the only weapons she had at her disposal, she spun around, flung her espresso at the man. He was in all black, wearing a matching drama theatre mask. She hit him in the shoulder with the bronze eagle trophy.

"I'm a producer!" she yelled.

The person let out a cry and lunged for her, knocking her down. "You are a bitch through and through."

She fell hard on the asphalt and gasped to keep her breath. Her trophy rolled out of reach and with nothing more to lose, she kicked at the intruder, managing to catch him in the shin.

"Watch yourself or you won't be able to watch the stars." Her attacker stumbled back, then pointed at her and ran.

"Help!" Cora scrambled to her feet, picked up Ryder's prop and hugged it to her chest and tried to remember to inhale. Her heart beat with such powerful force it shook her entire body, but she couldn't move, only stare in the direction her attacker dashed off.

The door to the building lobby opened. "Miss Caine?"

"Help!" Her own cry of weakness echoed around her.

"Miss Caine, are you all right?" The guard she recognized rushed toward her.

"Can you escort me to my office?" Her voice sounded as if someone else far away were speaking.

"Of course, Miss Caine." He motioned ahead. "What happened?"

Rather than answer, she juggled all her items as she got her phone out of her purse. No way would she create a spectacle.

"Would you like me to help you carry something?" the guard asked.

"No! I have it." Cora hugged Ryder's trophy to her and glanced at her list of speed dials before selecting the proper choice and sandwiching the device between her shoulder and her ear.

"What's wrong?" Viktor answered the phone.

"What makes you think anything is wrong?" She followed the guard through the lobby.

"It's five in the morning and lately that time of the day is reserved for another man." He chuckled.

"I'm at the office. Something happened, and I was just wondering if maybe you wouldn't mind coming here. I'll buy breakfast." Though right now she could go for Ryder's toast or Ryder, she couldn't bother him on set.

"What happened?" The little bit of laughter in Viktor's voice vanished.

She charged ahead of the guard and hit the button for the elevator, nearly dropping her prop.

The guard reached forward, but she shot him a look, held on tighter and turned her back to him. "I was in the parking garage and someone came over, said some things about stars and stargazing and knocked me down. Maybe I tripped, I don't know, but I'm fine. He ran off."

"Cora!" Viktor yelled into the phone.

The elevator doors opened.

"I just need help with this report. I have to go." She hung up.

The guard got inside with her. "Miss Caine, if something happened, I need to know. Are you all right?"

"I'm fine. It was nothing, really." She tapped her foot. When the doors opened at last she headed straight to her office.

The guard stayed at her heels. "Miss Caine."

She sat at her desk and turned on her monitors. "Please. I'm fine. Can you just stay until my Chief Operating Officer gets here? He's on the way."

"Of course, Ma'am. I'll be right outside." The guard went to the door, but stayed where she could see him.

With everything she carried in still in her hands, she sat down and scanned the screens. Chargge on one, stock prices on the middle one, the third now the official Hollywood Stardust Franchise website. She slid up closer to the third monitor and clicked around, landing on a trivia game about the actors and chose the one entitled, *How well do you know Ryder Scott?*

If she were a betting woman, she would say she knew Ryder better than most, but something told her that wasn't the type of questions the quiz would ask. At least she hoped not.

"Question one." She read aloud to no one but her trophy. "What was the first film Ryder starred in after *Hollywood Stardust?*" That was an easy one. "*Daybreak Delight.*" She clicked the selection and got a gold star. Only a few days ago she watched that film. It was an avant-garde film where he played the role of a drifter with a heart of gold. He even won an award for his portrayal.

She refocused on the computer screen and read the next question. "What award did Ryder win for his portrayal of Rusty Delight in *Daybreak Delight?*" With a roll of her eyes she clicked the correct answer. "People Select Award."

Another gold star.

Focused on the quiz, she made her way through nine questions.

"Last question." She wondered what she got at the end. "What is Ryder's middle name?" After rubbing her hands together at the easy question, she went to click the mouse.

"Cora Elizabeth Caine!"

At Ryder's outburst, she jumped up and dropped not only her mouse, but her purse and Ryder's trophy. Ryder? Where was Viktor? How did Ryder get here? Also, how did Ryder know her middle name. Wait, Ryder was here.

He was here.

With his face only partially made up for the movie, he burst into her office, made a beeline toward her and pulled her into a hug.

"What's wrong?" She leaned back, mainly to get a glimpse of that glorious face. "What are you doing here?"

"How can you ask me that?" Practically panting, he took her shoulders and held her at arms' length. His eyes darted over her face. "I heard what happened, why didn't you call me?"

She pulled away and wrapped her arms around herself. "It was nothing, just some weirdo in a parking lot. You don't have to be bothered with this."

"For the smartest woman on the planet, what's coming out of your mouth is plain stupid." He closed the distance between them and ran his hands through his hair. "Your life is threatened, and you don't want to bother me on set?"

"I told you, nothing happened." Her body vibrated from her trembling.

"Then why are you shaking?" He turned toward her desk and glanced at her screens. "Why are you playing a game? Why weren't we together this morning anyway? What report did you have to do that you couldn't do around me?"

Trying to figure out which question to answer first, she opened her mouth.

"Actually, I'm not interested in any of those questions. I'm going to say what's on my mind." Again, he took hold of her shoulders. "We're together. Me and you. The fact that I'm not the first person you thought to call when something like this happened cuts through me. When Viktor called..." He let go of her and walked over to the windows.

"When Viktor called," still in sweat pants, Viktor entered the room, "I told him what you told me, and he dropped his phone and came running."

Cora put her hands on her hips. "Why did you call Ryder? I said I was fine."

"Because this belongs to him, not me, and you and I both know that." As if daring her to defy him, Viktor lifted his chin.

Ryder turned to her. "I want to know exactly what happened."

"You know, if we make a big deal out of this, it just gives it more power." She returned to her chair and picked up the eagle trophy. Between the items Ryder brought home and her auction wins, their place was getting overrun by memorabilia.

Viktor sat in his throne and opened his laptop. "We need to file a police report."

"I don't want to do that. Besides, what's there to report? Honestly, we don't need any publicity." Relaying this entire story to the police would only waste time. She took the mouse and finished her quiz. "It's probably just one of your fans. He was wearing a drama mask and everything."

A huge gold star popped up with a banner declaring her a Ryder super fan and giving her a wallpaper she could use on her computer. Probably whoever attacked her in the garage could really pass this test.

"What if it's not?" Ryder resumed staring out the window.

"No, it's the same person who sent Cora that email. They used the same words." Viktor typed away.

At the mention of the email she winced.

"There was an email?" Ryder shook his head.

She ran her fingers along the metal eagle.

"I'm going to go ahead and figure out what to do." Viktor closed his laptop, put it under his arm, and left the room, closing the door behind him.

That blaring silence everyone hated encompassed the room.

After several minutes, she couldn't take it anymore. "You need to get back on set."

"I'm not that good of an actor." Hands in his pockets Ryder rocked back and forth from his heels to his toes.

"Ryder." With nothing to say after she uttered his name, she sighed.

"I'm the one, Cora." His words echoed through her office. "I am."

"What does that mean?" Her heart ached at his longing tone.

"I'm the one you come to first." At last, he faced her. "What are we if I'm not the one?"

Almost beyond her control, she found herself standing and going to him. "Before this all happened, I was thinking about that."

"What was that?"

"I guess about us." At sounding like a girl, she frowned.

"I've been doing a lot of that too." He held his arms out. "I'm going to make sure you're safe. I'm going to take care of everything."

Unable to stop, she went right into his embrace.

"Tell me you're all right," he whispered in her ear.

"I'm fine, really." She inhaled. Since the movie started, his normal cologne combined with studio makeup gave him a unique scent. She could pick him out anywhere with just a sniff. "I don't want this to turn into a circus, we have much more important things to do. Please let's not make this into a big deal. I want us to live our lives."

"Together." He took her chin in his hand and skimmed his lips over hers. "Tell me I'm the one."

"Yes, you're the one." There was no denying it.

"Tell me again you're all right," he whispered.

"I am." She shut her eyes and breathed in that wonderful scent. Yes, she was fine. If she kept repeating the words, it would give them power and make it true.

FADE IN:

EXT. ARIZONA – OUTSIDE STEVEN AND ROXY'S HOME – EARLY MORNING.

A limo stops in front of their home. STEVEN hands his bags to the driver and goes back to ROXY standing in the front doorway.

                    STEVEN
               (Holds his arms out)
                Come on, Rox.

ROXY crosses her arms

                    STEVEN
               (He goes to her and takes
               her in his arms.)
                Baby, it's only three
                months.

                    ROXY
               (Puts her head on STEVEN'S
               shoulder)
                Something tells me it's
                forever.

                    STEVEN
                We've been together
                forever.

                    ROXY
                I think even forever ends.

                    STEVEN
               (Leans back and looks into
               her face)
                How is that possible?

                    ROXY
                It's going to end right
                now.

STEVEN bends down and kisses her.

                    STEVEN
          I have to go.
          (He gives her one more quick
          kiss, lets go of her, and
          backs away.)

The LIMO DRIVER holds the door open. STEVEN
gets into the car and waves.

ROXY closes her eyes.

The LIMO DRIVER shuts the door and gets into the
vehicle and drives away.

ROXY opens her eyes.

Chapter Twenty-One

RYDER PACED AROUND an empty soundstage and glanced at the time. Since Cora's attack last week, he had been away from her all of four minutes and thirty-seven seconds, not including her bathroom breaks. Wanting to take her out and do something special, he ended production early and left her alone in his trailer with a glass of wine he personally poured, his hair and makeup people, Spike and Rodger.

Fine, maybe she wasn't technically alone, but he wanted to get back to her ASAP, but needed to make this phone call. If his life were a film, at this moment, the camera would pan in on his cell screen and the music rose, heightening the tension when he pushed call.

On the second ring, Glen answered the phone. "Mr. Scott, what do I owe the pleasure of this call to?"

"I thought we had an understanding." He rubbed his hand over his face.

"Interesting. For once you and I agree on something." Glen snickered into the phone.

"Glen, seriously. I'm going to finish filming *Stardom* and then I will finish *Working Title*, if it's the last thing I do. Leave Cora out of this. I got the message." Ryder ground his teeth together.

"Oh yes, I heard about Cora's unfortunate incident." Any jocularity disappeared from Glen's tone. "However, you need to do you research better. You may have been sent a note, but it wasn't from me, and frankly I'm offended you think we'd have done such a shoddy job."

From his experience, and unfortunately he was proficient, if Glen's people had done this, they would own it. It was part of the code, the whole honor among thieves thing, but still, something wasn't setting right. "Of course not."

"Well, you're scared and you're moving in the right direction. I almost wish we would've sent a message of our own." Glen chuckled.

In trying to make things better, Ryder made them worse. He broke out into a sweat. "I don't need any messages. I know the script." Needing to return to Cora, he hung up and ran through the studio lot, stopping to inhale and calm down before he opened the door to his trailer.

His empty trailer.

No Rodger being annoying.

No hair and makeup people pampering his girl.

No Spike laying somewhere.

And most importantly, no Cora drinking her pre-approved Ryder wine.

"Cora!" The shout that exited his throat packed, power, strength, and complete and utter panic.

The door to the bathroom opened, Spike trotted out followed by Rodger and lastly, Cora.

"Ryder! Calm down," she called from the bathroom.

His heart threatening to pound its way out of his chest, he backed up and leaned against the makeup vanity. "How come Rodger's allowed in the bathroom with you when I'm not?" With his words, he gasped for air. The morning of her attack, he tried to go into the bathroom while she did her business and was quickly shooed away. Actually shoved away. Spike got to watch her, even at home. The whole thing wasn't fair.

"I just wanted him to fix something on my hair."

Rodger shook his head. "I'm dog sitting tonight. Spike and I have a whole evening of debauchery planned."

The secretary motioned to his pet, and Spike trotted alongside him as they left.

"Don't let him eat only treats and make sure he goes to bed at a proper hour," Ryder called after them. Hell, it seemed like the right thing to say.

The door closed and he turned toward the bathroom again and waited. In an effort to make tonight extra special, he had the hair and makeup crew do Cora up, and he even chose an evening gown from the costume department. "Are you ready *mi Corazon*?" He needed to get back to charming and sexy leading man rather than crazed and paranoid nut case. It might be a stretch, but it was worth a go.

At last she stepped out, a gorgeous vision in a floor-length black dress. The low-cut ensemble presented a plentiful, yet respectable, amount of cleavage, and also showed off her light complexion and shining red hair perfectly. By far, she was more gorgeous than any starlet he had ever seen.

"God, you're beautiful." The charming left him to be replaced with awe.

"So what are we doing tonight?" Even through the makeup, her cheeks glowed.

"One of the perks of being with a man of my star stature is that tickets to the most popular show, where people simply burst into song, are but a mere phone call away." From his suit jacket pocket, he pulled out two box seats for the impossible to get into show in Hollywood, the *Kiss Me Softly* revival, her favorite.

Her first smile since the incident outshone the color on her cheeks. "This is my favorite." She stepped closer.

"Then I say we get going." He returned the tickets to his pocket, took her hand, kissed the back, and led her to Viktor in the waiting company car. On nights like this he didn't want to drive, he wanted to enjoy and simply look at the woman with him.

He let her into the car, slid in next to her, and put his arm around her.

She turned to him and tickled her fingers over his jawline.

Something about her touch, even little ones, drove him up the wall. He kissed her fingertips, then her palm, then her wrist.

She let out a little coo.

"I wanted to ask you something." He worked his way up her arm to her neck. "Hear me out."

"Oh no, what have you done?" She tilted her head to give him better access.

Forbidden from asking if she was all right, he now felt like a bomb waiting to explode. He needed her to voice her feelings. "I don't think I should go to Arizona."

"Then stop thinking." Her words came out terse, but she pushed his face down to her chest.

When presented with bountiful goodness, one had to take a taste. Before continuing his line of questioning, he took the time to kiss the top of each of her breasts, then paid a little special attention to her cleavage. "Cora." He could never get enough of her.

"Unless you are going to tell me about your raging hard on, I don't want to hear it." Her voice took on that corporate tone he hated, especially when she used it on him.

"Cora." He lifted his head.

"Ryder." With her jaw jutted out, she sat up straight. "I wasn't hurt."

"Thank god." He faced her, looking right in her eyes.

"Nothing happened."

"Thank god."

"I'm fine." Her eyes narrowed.

"Thank god."

"Then what's the issue?" Now she let out a sigh.

"I either want to stay with you here, or I want you to go to Arizona with me." Especially with everything that happened, he didn't want to be apart from her.

"I have to go to my meetings. They can't be rescheduled." Shaking her head, she leaned back on the set and faced forward. "I'll come up right after."

"Then let me postpone the location shoot." The more she retreated, the more he needed to push.

"What are you going to do? Sit and stare at me while I work? Trust me, if watching a movie being made is boring, it's nothing compared to watching me stare at a computer screen."

"Maybe it will give us some time to work on my movie." He said the first thing that popped in his head.

"You know I didn't forget, right?"

Even with only the streetlights to illuminate the inside of the car, he saw the muscles of her jaw tighten.

"What didn't you forget?"

"I know I need to make you a movie. I don't forget deals. This is why—" She stopped and turned away.

His chest constricted, and he reached out for her, putting his hand on her shoulder. "Why what?"

"I am going to make good on my end Ryder, so don't you worry your pretty little head over it. But I'm not stupid, I need to do the numbers first. Also, a script would be nice." The car stopped in front of the theatre, and she put her hand on the door handle toward the street side.

In a flash, he grabbed her hand, pulling her over to the sidewalk side. "I'm holding up my end too, look at the nice public place to photograph our love affair. Let's make a proper entrance, shall we?" He opened the door. "Smile pretty."

Star smile practically sewn on his face, he got out of the car to the crowd of people in front of the theatre, and held his hand out to Cora.

She put her hand in his.

Almost the second they appeared, the flashes, points, gasps and screams began.

At least twenty people descended upon him for autographs.

Rather than stand straight by his side, Cora positioned herself a little behind him and took his hand.

Never wanting to put either of them in a bad light, he did his duty, but finally nodded and smiled. They needed to get inside.

"There's the star!" A man lifted his professional camera and rushed toward them.

Cora let out a scream and tightened her hold on his hand.

"Cora." He tried to make his way through the crowd, but the man stopped them.

"We heard about the attack on Miss Caine, do you have any comment?" The man held out a microphone.

The police report must have been posted. No wonder Glen knew about the attack. "I thank god every second she's all right." He pulled Cora in closer. Did she hear his words? They were the truth.

"Do you think it was a fan?" The reporter followed them.

"We have no speculation on who it was. Thank you." At seeing a break in the crowd, Ryder moved forward.

The reporter kept up with them. "Miss Caine, do you have anything to say?"

When Cora didn't respond, he took over. "We have no further comment."

Finally, they made it inside the theatre, were ushered to their box seat, and an attendant brought them both some wine.

Alone, he leaned over to her. "Are you all right?"

"I told you not to ask me that, and I told you I'm fine." She gulped down her wine and turned to him. "And just so we don't do this all night, you're going to Arizona, I'm going to my meetings. You have a movie to finish, I have one to make, and now we'll be all over the goddamned Internet with a story I didn't want out there because we had to file the police report."

The lights flashed, indicating the play would start soon. "Let's feast our eyes on the land of make believe, where people can sing and dance."

"Just not you, right?" She snarled and crossed her legs.

"Right. I only act." He pressed his back into the seat.

"I know." A sly laugh escaped her throat.

This was how they would play? She might own the world, but he didn't have to buy. "After this delightful romp, I'll pack to go on my location shoot." He stared out over the audience. Only a few times had he played on stage, he preferred film. There were too many risks with live acting, and you could never take anything back. It was too much like real life.

HOLLYWOOD STARDOM

FADE IN:

EXT. HOLLYWOOD, CA – OUTSIDE HOLLYWOOD STARDUST
THEATRE - DAY

ROXY turns to the WOMAN.

> ROXY
> (Points to Steven on the
> picture)
> You may not recognize him,
> but in some circles he's
> just as famous as WILLIAM.

> WOMAN
> (Nods)
> I feel like he's familiar.

> ROXY
> Award-winning director.

> WOMAN
> Oh yes!
> (She jumps up and down.)
> He directed that romance
> drama where the woman goes
> off to find herself.

> ROXY
> That's the one.

The camera pans back to WILLIAM, STEVEN and
CHARLES. A crowd gathers around them and they
all three sign some autographs.

> WOMAN
> (Motions over to WILLIAM,
> STEVEN and CHARLES)
> Now the third one I feel
> like I have seen as well,
> but is that him in the
> picture?

                    ROXY
          Yes. That's my best friend.
          He's always been the calm
          in the storm.

                    WOMAN
          So are you ever going to
          tell me?

ROXY smiles.

FADE OUT.

Chapter Twenty-Two

DAY TWO OF NO SLEEP wasn't bad. Nope, not at all. In fact, if Cora could figure out a way never to sleep, she would be caught up at work. She glanced over at the clock. It was now three in the morning. The last time she slept was not yesterday, but the day before when Ryder was home.

Then with a kiss, and a hug, and not asking her if she were all right, Ryder left for Arizona.

Last night she didn't sleep. She tried everything from having the television on to having it off, to a cup of some herbal tea Ryder made her sometimes, to the total girl thing, burying her face in his pillow. None of it worked so she ended up watching a marathon of *Hollywood Stardust* and *Hollywood Starburst*, working on her presentation, and trolling the auction sites. Good news—she now owned an authentic poster signed by the entire *Hollywood Stardust* cast back in the day. She thought maybe Ryder would get a kick out of it. Honestly, for the price he better get more than a kick, he better get bowled over.

By the time she got to work yesterday, she was fine, got caught up at the office. Had a meeting about the meeting the next day, and then she came home to an empty apartment. Strange, before Ryder she never thought of her place as empty and she even had a pet.

Now at 3:01 she hugged Ryder's pillow to her and stared at Spike. Yes, Spike whom she allowed in the bed because the bed seemed empty when she used to be just fine sleeping by herself. The vision of contentment, Spike lay on his stomach, one ear down one flopped over his head. Not wanting his ear to get a draft she reached out and fixed his ear.

Spike opened his eyes.

"You don't have any trouble sleeping, do you?"

Spike rolled to his back an indication he would like some scratching. She indulged and scratched her fingers through his fur and closed her eyes one more time.

For several moments, she literally lay there wide-awake, staring at the inside of her eyelids. In fact, the more she attempted to sleep, the more she woke up.

"This is useless." At least when Ryder was here, she could wake him and have sex.

Great, now she was horny as well as awake and with nothing to show for anything. She flopped to her back and began reviewing her presentation in her mind. Today's meeting was a state of union, so to speak, with the current CEO of Ultracom, George and the CEO of News Now and other contender for her job, Albert.

She had done this meeting before, but this time the stakes were heightened. It would be the first time had seen either of them since the open position was even announced.

Yes, her numbers were on point, that was the main thing, but she knew she would be asked questions about *Hollywood Stardom*. She only wished she had one more thing to put in front of George to tie everything together.

Giving up on the whole sleep thing entirely, she sat up and turned on her television, scrolling through her on-line movie selections and stopping at one of Ryder's films, *The Label Maker*. It was a dramatic tale of a publicist who could literally make or break people's careers until he gets involved with one of his clients.

Cora pressed play. The night of the *Hollywood Starburst* party, he told her he would make a fan girl of her yet. She really hated when Ryder was right. Since the night of the play, he had been distant, and she didn't blame him. She just wanted things back to normal but didn't know what that meant anymore.

For a few minutes she watched the movie. The characters were engaging enough it could have been a series where the main character dealt with a different client every week.

Wait.

With newfound strength, she threw the covers back on the bed and got out. Though her lack of sleep caused her arms and legs to feel like rubber weighed down by anchors, she went to her desk, turned on her laptop and ran some old algorithms and reports on a possible scripted series for Chargge. Her company was a frontrunner when it came to streaming live entertainment news shows, and even dabbled in live events. Some other sites were doing scripted shows, but she wasn't proficient in production at the time, and scripted entertainment was as hot, and it was now becoming profitable. What would Ryder think? He had guest starred in some television productions.

When the hell, did she memorize his resume?

With a sigh, she clicked her chat application. Maybe he was up and on line. Before this whole dumb thing happened he told her to be ready for some video sex. Not that hit mattered, his box was grey, indicating he wasn't there or ignoring her or blocking her. For the woman who once got upset with his texts, she could go for some now. Right before she closed her laptop, the little ping went off indicating a message.

Damn her heart for speeding, and she clicked on the box, pursing out her lower lip when she realized it was Rodger not Ryder.

Can't sleep before your meeting?

The man had super-human powers. *Something like that.* I'm going to go in.

Her chest tightened at the thought of going to the office on her own at this hour, but she had to overcome it. Viktor arranged for her to text the guards when she was on her way, so she wouldn't be alone.

How about I come and get you?

She exhaled. *Thank you, I'll be ready in thirty minutes. I want to make some changes to the presentation.*

I know I could feel it. I'll bring your coffee.

Her anxiety ebbing a little, she shut the computer and dashed around the apartment, taking a quick shower and putting on a black pantsuit before hiding Ryder's pillow to make sure the house cleaners didn't wash it. She gathered up the rest of her items, summoned Spike, and rushed down to find Rodger right where he should be.

He handed her a coffee and they got in the car.

The man had a sixth sense, and they didn't really speak as they drove. She swore the hum of the car almost made her doze off, but with no traffic this time of day they basically flew to the office.

As they parked, she picked up Spike.

"Are you all right?" Rodger got out of the car, came around and opened the door for her.

"I told you not to ask me that." Pet in arms, she followed her secretary.

"This one time, I don't really care what you told me." As if he were a man on a mission, he looked around then got her and Spike into the elevator.

"I'm fine, I just want to make this change on the presentation." Once the elevator doors opened, she rushed to her office, rechecked her numbers, and added the couple of slides as she sipped her not-delicious-not-Ryder-created coffee.

After going through the presentation one more time, she glanced at the time. No doubt, Ryder would be on location now. More than once, she went to text him, but didn't want to bother him on set. Instead, maybe she would surprise him, work on the budget and have it ready for when she went out there over the weekend.

That was if he still wanted her there.

Also, on this fine Tuesday, the weekend felt extremely far away. On a positive note, maybe she would sleep some of the time away.

Though her body ached and more than once she caught herself staring off into space, she managed to get through a big portion of Ryder's so-called paperwork. Thus far, she deduced he was an unorganized mess and, rather than trying to make sense of the past, decided to move forward on the future, noting all her questions down, including the final cast count, locations, and she really wanted to see a script.

Her fingers twitched wanting to contact Ryder, but now with him not even giving her a good morning call or text, or asking how she was, the most unusual tense feeling took over every one of her muscles.

"Cora." Viktor entered her office and waved. "Everyone is arriving. Rodger took them to the conference room."

"I'm adding scripted streaming to my goals for next year." She handed Viktor a paper.

Viktor glanced at the document. "That's nice, but this is about Ryder's movie."

She snatched back the paper and, stealing a move from Madeline, gathered everything up on her desk into one horrible pile and picked it up. "Let's go."

Head held high, she marched across the office and into her conference room. She shifted the pile over to Viktor and shook hands with George, Albert and a few of their minions. "Good morning, gentlemen."

"Cora." George held her hand between both of his. "May I speak for all of us here and tell you that I'm happy you are all right."

"Thank you." She always liked George. The man served as mentor more than once.

Albert also nodded.

Everyone took their seats and Viktor set up her laptop.

"I thought we'd start with Albert and an update on News Now," George said and sat back.

The lights in the conference room dimmed, and the man began speaking about numbers, news feeds and returns on investments. Traditional, dry, he sailed right down the straight and narrow.

Her mind wandered and she reread her questions for Ryder. She really wanted to talk to him. Why didn't he call this morning or text or message?

"We're seeing a twenty-five percent increase in ad revenue." Albert droned on. "We also were the first to cover three major news stories."

With plenty of time before her turn, she clicked over to her email.

Her messages loaded and her stomach churned at the third one down.

From Starwatcher:

Seen any good stars lately or are you all alone in the universe?

A strange dizziness overtook her, and she forced herself to breathe and swallow. This was nothing, right? Just a crazy fan or someone trying to drive her crazy. It was nothing, she was fine.

She had to be fine. Ryder didn't even bother finding out if she was fine or not.

Once more, she clicked over to the notes she made on Ryder's movie. How on earth did he expect her to make a movie if he didn't give her the proper information and didn't even bother contacting her? She was getting control of this right now.

"News Now is expanding our global reach..." Albert continued.

After downing a glass of iced water, she scanned the room and caught Rodger's eye.

The man came to her and bent down. "What do you need?" He kept his voice low.

"Ryder. Go get him and bring him back here." She attempted to speak without moving her mouth.

"Of course." Rodger whispered. "Anything else?"

The others around the room clapped at the end of Albert's presentation.

She clutched the arm of the chair. "No. It's a beautiful day, so I'm sure you'll enjoy the flight."

Rodger put his hand over hers. "You're trembling."

George cleared his throat. "Cora, we're ready for you."

"Just get him. I have some important business that can't wait." She closed her email on her laptop and pulled up her presentation.

"I'm on my way." Rodger hurried out of the room.

"Cora," Viktor mumbled.

At last, she put her first slide up and stood. If nothing else, she was wide awake now. "Chargge is the definite leader as an entertainment portal..." This was her moment and straightened her posture. "We have seen a twenty-seven percent growth in ad revenue in last twelve months."

Albert sat back in his seat and crossed his legs.

She went to the next slide. "Our original content streaming for the website has been wildly successful. Ivy Alexander's show continues drive that division's ad revenue, but other shows are tailing it nicely." The little reporter who used to be scared of the camera now owned it, mostly due to the support of her husband, Logan, who tutored her. "During the time she's on set, she is featuring an all-inclusive report on the filming of *Hollywood Stardom*."

"The whole world revolves around this movie." Albert let out a laugh.

Oh, she knew this would come up. Cora turned to the table. "The proof is always in the numbers, and though this wasn't a meeting about the movie, Albert, I do want you to know that *Starburst* has already made millions for the studio and *Stardom* is projected to outshine expectations as well."

"Last I heard, the movie was running behind schedule and over budget." As if his words didn't really matter, he shrugged.

Cora faced George. "Sir, with all due respect, was this a debate I entered? If that is the case, I wasn't aware or I would have had some questions for Albert as well."

"How could you?" Albert leaned forward. "You were too busy talking to your assistant to even hear my presentation."

"Actually, I take that back, Sir. I don't have any questions for Albert, his set of data speaks for itself." A bit of adrenaline running through her, she switched to the next slide. "Everything is very predictable."

"Even with all your renegade tactics, you're only two percent above me. That's nominal," Albert countered.

"If we were speaking about a dollar I'd agree with you, Albert." She paced the length of the room. "However, on over a billion dollars, two percent can mean all the difference."

Even in her delirium, no one would take her in business. She only wished she was as savvy with Ryder as she was with Chargge. "Lastly, next year Chargge will be adding scripted streaming to its entertainment lineup. I've run the numbers, and it's now viable to have an in house production."

"Interesting." George jotted some numbers down.

"Maybe you can get some of the stars you're so close with to help you." Albert strummed his fingers on the table.

"If you're discussing Ryder Scott, then I'll have you know he only does film, but our connections with the studio will play in nicely with finding talent." She returned to her seat and turned off her presentation. Unable to resist, she clicked on her email again. At the sight of the message, she shuddered and put her hand to her head.

"Cora, are you all right?" George asked.

There was still nothing from Ryder. Well, he would have some explaining to do. She shut her laptop. "Absolutely."

"YOU'RE A PILOT?" Ryder wasn't sure why he even bothered asking Rodger the question since the man was clearly flying a plane. However, in this unbelievable, insane situation, he had to say something or he would put his fist through the window or Rodger or himself. Anything seemed a viable option.

"I think the answer to that is obvious." Rodger stared straight ahead.

"Is Cora all right?" Ryder shifted in his seat. The man showed up on set and told him to get on the plane that Cora needed to see him right away for a business meeting. With such a disruption, they decided to shut down production for the day, while he dashed off with Cora's secretary slash driver slash medic slash pilot. This man was annoying. This situation was annoying and he didn't like being summoned.

"Of course she's fine."

Rodger's answer seemed rehearsed and Ryder turned and gazed out the window as they made their descent into Van Nuys airport.

After a picture perfect landing, they made their way to the company car. "Is there any point in asking you any question to which I may get a real answer?"

"You can always give it a try." With precision Rodger drove toward the office.

"Why don't we start with why you don't like me?" Asking any further questions about Cora was senseless.

"I don't dislike you, Mr. Scott. I am merely reserving judgment." The man kept his hands at ten and two.

At receiving only another passive aggressive riddle of an answer, Ryder remained quiet the rest of the ride. When they finally drove into the office-building parking lot, he got out of the car before Rodger parked. Ignoring two people in the lobby who wanted an autograph, he stomped through the space, and made his way up the elevator without being bothered.

At last he entered her office and stormed inside. Not bothering to acknowledge the spinner girl at the front, he showed himself past the sacred door and went right for Cora's office.

Not caring if the door was closed or not, or who the hell she had in there, he threw the door open and found her in her usual position hunched around her three computer screens. "I'm here, your majesty." He slammed the door and waited for her to come running to him, tell him she missed him, and she wanted to go back to Arizona with him.

"Good." She stood. "I've been waiting."

What happened to her flinging herself at him? "Rodger did his best to get the air currents to bend to your demands, but even he's not that good."

"I've been working on your movie, and I have a question for you." She motioned for him to come over.

"And this was something you couldn't ask me on the phone?" He went to her and noticed she seemed a little pale. Maybe now some tears and hugs would take place. One couldn't lock lips remotely.

"I've decided that we just need to start over with the movie, therefore, I made this worksheet you need to fill out so we can plan correctly. I also would like a script." She handed him a printed piece of paper and a pen. Not one of her good pens.

"You pulled me off set and stopped production so you can hand me a spreadsheet and a pen?" He tried to keep his voice even.

"Oh, I have one more thing." She bent down.

Finally, he would get somewhere.

"Here, if you need something hard to write on." She straightened up and offered him a clipboard.

His heated anger ignited into an explosion. He snatched the clipboard away from her and threw it aside. Then he crumpled up the worksheet and tossed it across the room. "Are you serious?"

Cora jumped back. "Ryder!"

"Is that all you called me here for?" He tried his best not to raise his voice but it didn't work.

She raised her chin. "I have to know these things about your movie."

"You know what I think?" He headed toward the door.

Rather than answer she crossed her arms.

"I just think you want to see how far your control reaches. How many hoops you can get your boys to jump through? Well, Miss Caine, let me be the first to tell you I don't sing, I don't dance, and I don't jump. Find someone else." After everything he refused to be one of her staff at her beck and call, and he opened the door and left.

Head up, chest out, he pushed past Rodger and Viktor and a bunch of people he didn't know and returned to the elevator.

The night of the musical she said she didn't need him, wanted him to leave and he listened. He gave her what she wanted. When he found out about the attack, he wanted to die or kill someone for hurting his girl. Then he wasn't even allowed to ask how she was, and she didn't care.

Instead, she sent him off, only to order him back to fill out a form after she made fun of him for using such an archaic tool such as a pen when she ran the digital world.

Before hitting the button on the elevator he glanced down at the cheap pen still in his hand.

Stop everything.

The pen could practically write on the wall for him, but he needed to see it. She summoned him here, but not to fill out a form. In fact, she could have practically filled out the questions on the form herself. She summoned him as her way of saying she needed him, had to have him there. She was hurting and scared and didn't know any other way to tell him he was the one. His girl was talking he just didn't hear her.

"Cora." He turned on his heel and bolted back through the office, past spinner, Viktor, and Rodger. With his heart pounding full force, he collided with her door before he managed to turn the handle and barge back into Cora's office.

"Cora!" He scanned the room, but she wasn't behind her monitors or at the big table. With only one other choice, he ran across the space, opened the door and found her sitting on the marble floor in the corner of her private bathroom, knees pulled up to her chest. In less than an instant, he skidded across the floor, and gathered her up into his arms. "Baby."

Without a word, she buried her face in his chest, and her trembling vibrated through him.

"Am I allowed to ask you how you are?" He kissed the top of her head and breathed in the floral tinged sent of her shampoo.

She nodded.

"How are you?"

"I'm not fine." Her voice broke and the way her body wracked, he knew she finally broke down and started to cry.

For several minutes, they stayed there on the bathroom floor and he let her cry it out while he made a plan. They needed some time. Some time away from the drama, away from the set, and away from L.A. They needed some time to be couple. The fact she had to get him here under the guise of a business meeting was unacceptable.

"I got this, I got you, all right?" He stood and picked her up.

She only held on.

When he stepped into her office, he was met by Rodger, Viktor and Spike.

He addressed the men, "Cora and I are going to take a few days off. "I need someone to do whatever they need to do with her meetings, someone to square things for me on set, and I need the company car." They needed to just go, not care about clothes or anything else.

"I got the studio and corporate." Viktor patted Cora's head.

"Let's go out a different exit. The two of you attract too much attention." Rodger gathered up her purse and laptop then led them out.

"Come on, Spike," Rodger commanded and they followed Rodger down through a service elevator.

The secretary rushed ahead and helped get Cora and Spike get settled in the car. "Mr. Scott." He walked around to the driver's side and held up the keys.

Ryder took the offering.

Rodger stopped him before he slipped inside the car. "Please tell me if there's anything you need. I'll make sure you have it."

Ryder figured he might as well use the man. "We're going to my cabin. If there's a way you can get some food and necessities delivered, I'd rather us not have to go traipsing around town right away." For the time being, a little less time in the limelight was in order. This was precisely why his father told him to never let the cabin go.

"Consider it done." Rodger held out his hand.

Ryder shook his hand. "So now we're on the same side."

"You passed judgment." Rodger assisted him in the car.

Ryder put the key in the ignition and looked over at Cora. Spike in her lap, she leaned against the window with two tears streaming down her cheeks.

They had to escape and, for the first time in his life, he truly had to be a leading man, not just play one.

HOLLYWOOD STARDOM

FADE IN:

INT. LOS ANGELES - GRIFFITH PARK OBSERVATORY -
DAY

CHARLES - late thirties, hair combed off to one
side, dressed in khakis and a red polo shirt is
giving a tour of the observatory to some
schoolchildren.

He bends down and points up to a huge model of
the solar system.

                    CHARLES
               Every planet travels around
               the sun at its own speed.
               It takes Mercury only
               eighty-eight days to travel
               around the sun, while it
               takes Neptune over one
               hundred and sixty four
               years to make its way
               around our star.

The school children let out a collective gasp.

Camera pans over to ROXY. She's clutching her
purse and watching CHARLES.

                    CHARLES
               Can anyone tell me how long
               it takes Mars to travel
               around the sun?

                    ROXY
          (Rushes around the model and
          raises her hand)
               Almost six hundred and
               eighty seven days!

                    CHARLES
          (Nods)
               Who taught you that?

                    ROXY
          My best friend.
               (She bites her lip.)

CHARLES turns his attention back to the
children.

                    CHARLES
          All right kiddos, tour is
          over, your teacher will
          take you over the theatre
          and you'll watch a movie on
          the moon.

The schoolchildren cheer and follow their
teacher away.

                    CHARLES
          (Shoves his hands in his
          pockets and walks over to
          ROXY)
           What brings you here?

                    ROXY
           I wanted to see the stars.
          (She leans in and gives him
          a hug.)
           You look amazing.

                    CHARLES
           Thanks. I guess I finally
           grew into myself.
          (He pats her back.)

                    ROXY
          (Leans back but keeps her
          hold on him)
           Sometimes some planets just
           take longer to orbit the
           sun.

                    CHARLES
(Smiles)
 Touché.

              ROXY
 I did come for a reason.

              CHARLES
 I had no doubt.

              ROXY
 I thought I could take you
 for a coffee.

              CHARLES
 That's it?

              ROXY
 Yep.
(She winks at him)

              CHARLES
      (Nods)
 All right. Looks like
 little Roxy grew up.

              ROXY
 Yeah, I think I finally made
 my way around the sun too.
 It took a while.

Chapter Twenty-Three

"ONCE UPON A TIME." Ryder turned down an unpaved road and spoke his first words since they left her office.

Cora focused on the man who, over an hour before, decided to rescue her mainly from herself. Though he only said the beginning of every fairytale ever told, she longed to hear the story.

He glanced over at her, giving her a dramatic pause before continuing. "There was a man who gave his wife a little cottage for a gift."

With the lack of asphalt, the car bounced along the road, but she kept her eyes on him. Only drove two hours out of the city, it might have been another world. The higher they went, the denser the trees became, and the sky seemed to turn the most vibrant blue, almost as if someone decided to paint the scenery to provide them a storybook backdrop.

"Nine months later a beautiful child was born, and she had the distinction of growing up to be the mother to someone who would later become a very famous Hollywood actor." A slight grin made Ryder's lip upturn in the corner.

"Years later, the man and the woman, gave their only grandson the little cottage with the promise to keep it in the family and use it as a sanctuary, a place to go where he could clear his head." Ryder followed a bend in the road and suddenly a little wooden cabin seemed to sprout out of the forest. If she were in a fairytale, it would be made out of gingerbread.

He stopped the car, got out, and dashed around to her side.

In a move he no doubt got out of a movie, he opened her door, leaned down and picked her up right out of the seat. "To this day, no matter where the grandson is, he always keeps the keys to the cabin on his person, because one never knows when he will need a little retreat. It's a safety net of sorts."

Without the strength to protest, tell him she could walk, she wrapped her arms around his neck and allowed him to carry her into his little hideaway and continued to hang on every word of his story.

He let them inside and she didn't know if she should stare in wonder, laugh or burst into tears. "The grandson also made sure to keep everything the way it was when he first took over the cabin. He always thought it possessed a little bit of magic."

No truer words were ever spoken. If the outside was gingerbread, the inside was a sugar cookie, sprinkles and frosting all rolled into a picture perfect representation of a cabin in the woods. The entire place was wood, the kind of wood that had history, with knots and nicks that said people lived here, loved here, experienced here. Everything about the space was tiny, cozy and homey, with overstuffed couches and afghans.

Instantly Spike claimed his spot on a cushion by the flagstone fireplace. With her still in his arms, Ryder carried her right into the small bedroom. The sight of the four-poster bed with pillows and blankets was almost too inviting.

As if reading her mind, Ryder pulled down the green puffy comforter and laid her down among the bedding, and held up on hand telling her to stay in place. "Throughout the years from time to time, the grandson came up here, but he always made sure it was for all the right reasons."

He walked around the room, first putting her laptop and purse on the dresser, then pulling a pair of socks out of drawer, disappearing into what she assumed to be the bathroom for a moment, with more items in his hands, he went to the closet, pulled out a white button down and returned to her.

"The grandson has come here to get away and think, and even used the outside woods as a location shot for his movie." As he spoke, he removed her suit jacket and camisole. After removing her bra, he leaned in and kissed her neck, then stared at her while he helped her into his oversized white shirt.

His fingers grazed against her as he fastened the buttons, giving her the shivers. "In all the time he has been coming here, he has never brought a fair maiden into his world." He gave her a wink and kneeled down, removing both her shoes, taking a moment to treat her to a little foot massage. "Especially now that he has royalty with him."

Yes, she was relieved at his admission and her heart swelled at the way he continued his tale, his words and his hands. She couldn't help but let out a moan.

Once getting her out of her pants and putting her clothes aside, he slid the socks on her feet and kissed both her kneecaps. He took a hairbrush he brought from the bathroom and joined her on the bed.

When he went behind her, humming as he began to brush her hair, and she leaned against him, his sweet attention making her feel drugged, drowsy and safe. "Ryder." She spoke her first word since they left her office.

He braided her hair and kissed her ear. "Just in case you need to know, this grandson would slay any dragon for his princess."

"I got another email today." She shook her head, but she had to be honest with him.

"For your truth, you shall be rewarded." He got in bed with her, nestled them under the covers and held her tight. "I will now play my finest role, as human pillow for my royalty."

At this moment, she could think of no better prize. She turned over, settled down on his chest and glanced up at his glorious face. "Ryder?"

He dipped his head down and kissed her. "I don't care if I have to build a moat around us, if I have to slay a dragon and an ogre, or if I have to cast some sort of spell on someone, you will not be harmed again. Never. Do you hear me?"

Tears clouded her vision and reached up to touch him, make sure he was real. He might have brought her into a fairytale, but in a musical, this would be the point where the female lead would sing about her love for the unattainable male.

At her thought, she sat up.

"What's wrong?" Ryder's eyes widened.

She shook her head. Did she love him?

He pulled her back down. "My fair lady, you need rest. It seems to me someone needs her one and only to sleep properly."

Again, she lay back down, this time hooking her arm over him. The simple act of being back in her normal position calmed her. "Will you hum some more?"

"I, for one, didn't sleep a wink without you. I just want to be with you." He yawned and held her. "Right here, just you and me."

She shut her eyes and felt her body finally begin to succumb to sleep as his sweet humming filled the air. There was no sense denying she loved him, and now she could only hope for a happily ever after.

ANY GOOD HERO knew how to slay dragons. Ryder had the experience of not only playing the hero all his life, but about five years ago, he played a medieval superhero hybrid off some video game franchise, and everyone called him a natural.

While he bided his time on doing away with the real villains who terrorized his lady, two smaller, yet still treacherous, dragons needed to be dealt with post haste, and he approached the location where the evil lay in wait.

In one swift movement, he slid open his dresser drawer. There they were. Some called them miracles of technology, and in many ways they were, but in so many other ways they were messengers of pure horror. He faced his lofty opponents in the form of his and Cora's cell phones.

While he banned all use of those in his kingdom, or more specifically banned Princess Cora from all things electronic as part of their negotiation, at least he had to check her messages and calls. Or as he called it, the fire this particular dragon breathed.

On the flip side, the fact he had been trusted with such an act told him how far they had progressed.

His first encounter with the beast wasn't as successful as he hoped. After an hour, he realized that aside from the texts and messages to and from him, he had no idea what any of her work entailed.

However, he was now equipped with a second in command, so to speak, and he enlisted the help of one secretary.

At his own tactical excellence, he nodded and hit the button.

A message from Rodger filled the screen.

> *Ryder, everything is set up in the back for your campfire. Tell Cora, all is fine here, all taken care of. I can fly you up to Arizona when ready. Studio is at bay for now. Ultracom has agreed to let Cora video conference her meetings when you go to Arizona. Rodger.*

He typed back. *Thanks I shall knight you upon my return to the city proper.* Hey, he had to stay in character.

Before he put the dragon to rest, Rodger replied. *Thou art insane.*

He killed the first beast by turning it off and sliding under sock mountain and then went to the more ferocious animal, his own device.

We hope Cora is feeling better. Because of the extenuating circumstances and the fact we know production has been delayed, we are giving you two weeks for another collateral installment or sign the movie rights over to us. Your decision. Glen

Yes, this dragon would be a bit harder to deal with. A direct stab to the heart wouldn't do it in. This required more finesse, starting with the fact he had to respond and he typed back. *Duly noted.* Nothing would get in the way of his time with the princess, he needed to treat her like a queen. He temporarily disabled his enemy by switching it off as well, and continued on his mission.

With a gallant step, he went to the living room.

Curled up in his castle, sat Miss Cora, finally reading the script for *Working Title*. Rodger also proved an excellent resource on getting things off computers, having them printed and delivered to his cabin. Before Arizona, he had Madeline take one last look, and though he wanted to keep tweaking, he had to let his baby out of the nest. Yesterday when she awoke from her slumber, he decided to present her with the token. He understood she couldn't blindly give funds, and he hoped this would appease her.

The fact she had not moved from her position for the last two hours was either cause for concern or celebration.

Keeping his eye on his lady, he grabbed his grandfather's old cane, swiped it through the air, and marched toward to the front hall closet, peeked over at Cora, back in the closet and then back to Cora.

"*Darrien Dale Saves The Inner World.*" Script held up to her face, Cora chuckled.

The sound of laughter coming from her warmed his heart. At her using his character's name from the game movie, he leaned over and took her in. Lord, she was a beautiful woman. Made-up or au natural, she was perfection. "What do you know of that movie?"

"The couple of nights you were in Arizona were..." she kept her book up, but wrinkled her nose, "...let's just say those couple of nights were rough."

"Is that Cora code for she watched her man's movies?" He grabbed the blanket from the closet and held his hand out to her. "Princess, are you ready for your jaunt into the wilderness, or would you like to tell me what you think of the document I gave you as a tribute?"

Script tucked neatly under her arm, she took his hand, stood and snapped her fingers. Spike ran to her side. "I am ready kind sir. I have my knight, my steed, and my weapon at the ready. I will give you comment after our trek out yonder and I finish reading. I have but a few more pages."

"Then let us depart, as the road may be treacherous, but with you by my side I have no choice but to survive." He took her out to the back. One thing about being at the cabin was it took only a few steps to be surrounded by trees. With Rodger's expertise, Ryder already had a large blanket laid out, and a fire in the fire pit along with a picnic basket. "We are set with food and drink my lady." He bowed and joined her on the blanket.

Before he had a chance to sneak in a kiss, she opened the script and turned toward the fire to give her more light.

He started by opening the bottle of wine set by the picnic basket. "I take it you like the story?"

She held up one finger.

For at least a minute, he distracted himself with pouring the wine and handing her a glass. "Cora."

"Ryder, not right now." She lifted her knees and leaned closer to the fire.

As he waited for her to turn the page, he downed his wine and snooped around the picnic basket. Everything was exactly what he asked for—meats, cheeses, bread a little chocolate dessert. Rodger was magic like Cora said.

Right as he refilled his glass and was about to just put his mouth to the bottle, she sighed and put the script aside but didn't speak.

"Well?" Honestly, he was running out of runway to wait.

"I need to talk to you." She exhaled and looked up at the stars.

Oh Lord, she didn't like it. Most producers wouldn't back a flick they didn't like and in her case he knew she would still give him the funds, but could he take it? Wait, he didn't think that, of course he could take it, his kneecaps and movie depended on it, but what if she hated it. "Cora." He went for the second glass of wine.

"When you described this movie to me, I thought you were nuts." She didn't look at him.

Unable to find the strength to pour another glass of the sweet elixir, he gulped hers down. "Just say it."

"I need to know something first. Something that's been bothering me." She hugged the script to her chest.

"Anything." His heart speeding, and his head a dizzy from drinking three glasses of wine in a row, he waited in purgatory, having to complete a series of tasks before getting his answer. Well, just having to answer a question, but still.

"Did you ask your other women to back this film?" Her voice softened to almost a whisper.

Except for telling him to clean up his mess, she never mentioned his prior relationships before. "What do you mean?" He sort of wanted to forget about the other women.

"Did you or did you not show them this?" She lifted the script. "Did you or did you not ask them for funds specifically related to your movie?"

Unsure why it was important, he knew he needed to give her an honest answer, and he shook his head. "Why?"

"I wanted something from you that was just mine." She blinked and turned away. "Something that was never up on the auction block."

"What are you saying, Cora?" He crawled across the blanket to her.

"On our first night out you told me to forget the roles and I resisted, but somewhere in our journey, I did forget—" Her voice faltered and she cleared her throat. "I know this was part of our deal, and no matter what, I'll make sure you have a movie, but it's wonderful, and I want to be a part of it, and I only want to give it everything I have if it's only ever been mine."

Help him, she thought it was wonderful, she wanted to be involved. No better words had ever been spoken to him. "You know what else has only ever been yours?" He took her chin in his hand and made her face him.

One lonely tear trailed down her face. "What?"

"My heart." He stared right into her eyes. "I love you." The feeling overcame him, and he had to let it out.

"Ryder." She breathed his name.

He put his fingertips over her lips. "I forgot the roles as well. You're my life."

"Oh God, I love you." she said and wrapped her arms around his neck.

Unable to resist the woman in his arms who he loved and who loved him back, he kissed her. A soft kiss, a caress of their lips that he let take the time to grow.

She let out a little mew and opened her mouth.

They kissed. Over and over again, with the crackle of the fire in the background, the tang of wine on their lips and their bodies pressed together, they took their time and kissed.

Their kissing possessed the familiarity of two people who were together, combined with a newness, their admitted love, their closeness they had yet to explore, but had all the time in the world to discover.

As the chill of night came upon them, he laid them down on the blanket and covered them up with the one he brought with them. Her hands snuck under his shirt and she raked her nails down his back while he cupped her breasts and kissed and nibbled down her neck.

Out here in the forest, his sanctuary, now their sanctuary, there were no time constraints, no rush to the finish, only the slow buildup of two people who wanted to be together, share their lives, be there for the other. No, he never had that before. She owned it just like she owned the way her touches and attention aroused him like no other.

By the time they rid themselves of their clothes and their limbs tangled together, he knew if he didn't have her soon he would explode. "Cora." he whispered in her ear.

She moved to her back. "Make love to me, Ryder. I need you."

"I need to get a condom." Of all times to not have one.

"Do you?" She positioned herself underneath him.

"God, I love you." He knew she took the pill, but the fact she wanted to have with no barriers almost sent him over the edge right there.

"Then make love to me." Her voice came out breathy, sexy, dreamy.

"Yes." Being inside her with no condom was the ultimate bond, one he wanted to forge and couldn't take lightly. Rather than a show where he teased her, or they rammed their bodies together in a race to the end, as he entered her, he looked right in her eyes.

If being inside her with the condom on could be classified as magnificent, then having her body accept him, encompass him and allowing him to truly feel her tight desire around him would be spectacular.

Apparently, she felt it too. She closed her eyes and moaned, lifting her her knees and holding him tight.

Like their kissing before, they didn't rush, he kept his strokes slow and fluid and they moved in a coordinated flow. Instead of only seeking pleasure, they transcended to a different plane, one of unison and harmony that grew, reaching heights he never experienced. Soon he would have no choice but to give into his own need.

Beneath him, her pants quickened, she moaned and squirmed, indicating she was there as well, and this time more than ever before, they had to fall together.

In any attempt to prolong the pleasure, he fought the need to speed up, drive into her, and instead restrained himself. The euphoria built. "Oh God."

"Ryder." With her gasping and digging her nails into his back, he knew she was there.

That was all he needed.

His body contracted with pure ecstasy right as she tensed, with nothing between them, her pulses rippled over him, pulling him deeper and amplifying the rapture flowing through him. "Ah."

Together they reached their end, held each other, and resumed their kissing. For the first time, he didn't have to rush to pull away, he could stay embedded in her, and come down from the high.

Only this time the high didn't leave, it stayed. He loved her, she loved him, pure and simple. "Why me?" Not ready to let go, he turned to his side and kept her in his arms.

"Why you what?" There, in the great outdoors, she curled up against him.

He pulled the blanket up to their necks. "Why do you love me?" After he asked the question, he shook his head.

She paused and looked up at the sky. "You get me, and I miss you when you're not there."

"You ground me. I feel like I have a purpose with you." Lord, he had turned into the guy who came up with these lines, but in this case they weren't scripted, and he meant every word.

"I can hardly wait for *Hollywood Stardom* to wrap and all this corporate stuff to be over so we can concentrate on making your movie." Using her nail, she traced a little pattern over his chest.

He shivered and stared up at the stars, at last taking in everything that just happened. What he needed was money to make his movie, stop the thugs from nipping at his heels, but they would be there checking up, they would want the producer's credit. How would he explain this to the woman he loved? "It's going to be amazing."

<u>HOLLYWOOD STARDOM</u>

FADE IN:

INT. LOS ANGELES – GRIFFITH PARK OBSERVATORY – NIGHT

CHARLES and ROXY sit with the huge telescope in the observatory.

                    CHARLES
          Here, I got Saturn for you.
          (He moves back.)

                    ROXY
          (Leans in and looks in the
          telescope)
          That's my favorite planet.

                    CHARLES
          I know.

                    ROXY
          (Looks over at him)
          Your life turned out
          exactly as I thought.

                    CHARLES
          I'm nothing if not
          predictable.
          (He takes over the telescope
          and peers inside.)

                    ROXY
          That's my favorite part.
          You're like a planet or a
          star, I just look up and
          you're there.

                    CHARLES
          Maybe you needed to look
          more often.
          (He motions toward the
          telescope.)

ROXY looks inside and smiles.

                    CHARLES
          How's the acting?

                    ROXY
          Not what I thought, but I
          love Los Angeles, always
          have. I've been doing more
          coaching and teaching. If
          you need any pointers, let
          me know.

                    CHARLES
          Actually, I've been asked
          to do some spots on the
          local news. I've never
          been the public speaking
          kind of guy.

                    ROXY
          (Faces him)
          I think that makes you
          exactly the kind of guy who
          should be speaking to the
          public.

CHARLES shrugs.

ROXY straightens his collar.

                    ROXY
          You know I think the best
          advice I can give you is to
          be yourself and let your
          passion shine through. All
          those little facts you know
          are amazing and different
          and charming and exactly
          what everyone needs.

                    CHARLES
          What if I told you what I
          need is you there coaching
          me?

                    ROXY
          I would say just turn your
          head, and look off to the
          side, and I'll be right
          there.
          (She slides her hand down
          his arm.)

                    CHARLES
          Then that's where I'll be
          looking.

Chapter Twenty-Four

FROM THE TRAILER in Arizona, Cora stared out the window at the non-action on her movie.

"Cora." Coffee in hand, Rodger tiptoed toward her.

Before she even had a chance to ask what, the door opened and Viktor entered.

"Cora." Laptop open, Viktor charged toward her.

She opened her mouth.

"Cora." Ivy Alexander knocked on the open door and poked her head in the trailer.

Cora tore her focus away from the window over at her.

"Cora." Madeline snuck inside and practically crawled into the trailer on all fours.

"If one more person says my name and doesn't ask a question after it, they will be fired on the spot." She crossed her arms.

"*Mi Corazon*." Ryder bounded into the trailer.

Everyone else turned to her.

Cora huffed.

"Technically, he didn't say her name." Madeline snorted and laughed.

At least that's what Cora thought came out of her screenwriter.

Ryder waded past the crowd. "Why is everyone in here?"

Since she was going to ask that question too, she decided to cherry-pick who spoke first and chose the lesser of all evils and pointed at Ivy.

"I wanted to interview you for Chargge.com, talk about Erin's baby shower, and I have a personal thing." Ivy said, widening her eyes.

All right. Cora supposed girls had personal things, and how she got dragged into Erin's baby shower she would never know, but at least she was included. "Go sit down, I'll be there in a moment." She took in her options and looked at Rodger.

"I wanted to ask what you needed next." Roger handed her the cup of her favorite drink.

"Thank you." The coffee offering seemed like a pacifier. "Can you go make this movie?"

"Though my talents are vast, unfortunately I do not have the eye for cinematic greatness." Rodger shrugged. "We do need to go over your schedule, and I have a couple of personal things."

More personal things. "Take your seat on the couch next to Ivy."

Ryder cleared his throat.

"Viktor." With a nod, she chose her next victim.

"I have a work thing and a personal thing." Viktor raised his eyebrows.

"What's the work thing?" Her stomach twisted, but she wasn't sure at exactly what.

"It kind of relates to the personal thing." Without being prodded, Viktor walked by her and took his seat behind Rodger.

This was netting her no forward movement.

"CC," Ryder whispered in her ear.

She patted him and waited for Madeline.

Madeline was now leaning on the open door looking at her phone.

Apparently the screenwriter didn't know how this worked.

"Madeline!" Cora barked.

"Oh!" Madeline fumbled and dropped her phone along with everything else. "Sorry, I came in here to ask you a question about the script, but now I see that your sex photos are all over the Internet. Maybe I should come back."

"What!" Her entire body heated and Cora spun back to to everyone sitting on the couch.

In unison, Rodger, Ivy and Viktor all stood.

"No one move!" She put her hand over her eyes.

"That's what I was trying to tell you." Ryder's deep voice rumbled through her ear.

"Rodger." As if she weren't even in her own body, she lowered her hand.

Tablet at the ready, Rodger came over and turned the device to her.

There on the *National Reporter's* front page was a picture of her and Ryder under the blanket outside the cabin, but they definitely captured the essence of the moment, complete with her arching her back. At least it was under the blanket.

"That's a really good shot." Ryder nodded. "That was right after I told you I loved you for the first time."

Both Ivy and Madeline let out an *aww*.

"Read." She might as well face it.

"'The campfire was hot, hot, hot for Hollywood lovers Ryder Scott and Cora Caine,'" Rodger read the caption, "'we only wish we had the audio to go along with the images. At least we know why there was a delay on the *Hollywood Stardom* set. No one will ever know how much this little rendezvous cost the studio.'"

No sooner had Rodger finished than her phone rang.

"McAllister's office." Viktor held her phone up.

"Don't answer it. We need a plan first." Not an expert in crisis communications—and this was most definitely a crisis—she could only stand there.

"The plan better include what to do about the two advertisers Chargge lost this morning. One of them was Booming Baby Food, the other is that television station we may want to let go since we've had problems with them in the past," Viktor blurted out the words, but also guided her. "They cited the pornographic pictures."

"Those are hardly pornographic." Ryder took the tablet from Rodger and zoomed in. "We didn't even have a nip slip."

In no world would she talk to George McAllister, CEO of Ultracom, in the midst of an ad revenue issue. She would only call after it was resolved, and it was going to get resolved right now.

"Give me my laptop, get John from Booming Baby Food on the phone and get Drew and Erin in here." Needing some space to breathe, she walked to the far end of the trailer.

Rodger rushed the laptop to her and dialed the phone.

"Before I call George back we need to tell him that we have an ad revenue increase of at least one percent." She ran her advertising algorithm. "Ryder, what brand condom did we use?"

"Good thinking." Viktor came to her side.

"Cora, we don't use those anymore." Ryder joined her.

Viktor groaned, Ivy chuckled.

She gave him the look, the couple look, the one that told Ryder not to question her actions, just support her.

"Stallion Maxum." As if the whole world didn't already know about their sex life, he cupped his hand around his mouth.

"I got it. Let me call advertising." Viktor took the other end of the trailer.

Rodger held the phone out to her. "Cora. John is on the line."

"John." Cora breathed into the phone.

"I know why you're calling Cora, and I have to say I appreciate it, especially after everything, but I can't have the brand associated with those types of pictures." He hit her head on.

Good this wouldn't take long. "John, I am one keystroke away from pulling your ads and I will sweep my site clean of any reference to your baby food, but I'm going to give you a choice." Biding her time for one minute, she paused.

Right on time, Erin and Drew rushed into the trailer.

"Hold on one moment." She put her hand over the phone and went to the soon to be parents. "If I give you fifty percent off Hollywood Glow advertising on Chargge, once your little bundle of joy is born, will you say you love Booming Baby Food?"

"Oh, they make the organic baby food." Erin nodded. "But then I want to triple our ads."

Cora shook her head. "Quadruple the amount of ads, but I'll give you premium placement."

"On Ivy's show." Drew added.

The man was smart. "Deal." Cora just made up for one of the television account and held her hand out.

Both Erin and Drew shook her hand, and she turned her back to them. "John, as I was saying, I'm ready to pull your ads, but I will have you know that the second that Ivy Alexander has an exclusive story on those pictures cost per click will double, and I'll never give you back your old rate once I terminate you contract. On the other hand, if you add some revenue to the mix, I may be inclined to tell you that Erin Holland-Fulton is ready to endorse your baby food and we'll forget this whole unfortunate incident ever happened. I also need not remind you where babies come from, do I?"

The crowd in the trailer chuckled behind her.

"You bring up some major points, Cora. Hold on a moment," John said.

Ryder took her hand. "Did I ever tell you it turns me on when you go out for blood?"

At last she smiled, a lesser man would be threatened by what she had to do to make things work in her world.

"Cora." John returned to the phone.

She leaned against Ryder and cocked the phone for him to hear.

"I want to apologize about our kneejerk reaction to the situation. We are an old, family-run business, but under further evaluation, we have to realize we must stay with the times and what our customers want," John explained. "We will increase our spend twenty percent. Please have the ad department call me personally to set it up."

"Thank you, John." She hung up.

Ryder gave her a squeeze, but she wasn't done yet. She spun on her heel to Viktor.

Viktor tossed his cell phone aside and jumped up. "Make your call, you're one and a half percent up and we're all getting a year supply of Stallion Maxum condoms, as well as any other things to tickle our fancy."

Everyone in the trailer let out a cheer.

"If anyone is going to supply my daughter with sex accessories, it will be me." The voice of insanity entered her already crazy situation.

"Mother." She grabbed on to Ryder and turned.

"There they are, Tony." Arms wide open, her mother barreled toward them, wrapping one arm around her and the other around Ryder and bursting into tears. "Viktor!" The woman held her hand out. "Everyone hug!"

Viktor came over and Cora was suffocated in a pile people.

Her mother pulled back, kissed her twice, kissed Viktor and then took Ryder's face into her hands. "My, my, you are the gorgeous one, aren't you?"

For the first time ever, Ryder was rendered speechless.

"I don't know if you need any sex toys with this one around, he's just one huge plaything." Her mother pinched his cheek. "I'm Rita Cummerbund, otherwise known as Madame Sublime, or Cora's mother."

"Yes, you are." Ryder's face lit up with amusement.

Cora scanned the room for Rodger.

"That was the second personal thing I tried to tell you." Rodger shook his head.

Cora backed away. The woman and her living toy were here and now she had another thing to deal with. "I need to make a phone call."

"BOSS, I DID A FUNDRAISER for Ryder's Rescue," Ben's voice came through Ryder's phone. "Once news of Cora's attack hit the airwaves, the donations started pouring in. I deposited everything into the account we set up, and I got a shipment of tote bags with your logo on them. They're being delivered to the Sierra Towers." Ben finished his weekly report to Ryder on his charity.

"Wait." Ryder's Rescue had a logo? Ryder stopped in front of the door to his and Cora's suite at the hotel in Arizona. Something, maybe the pictures in tabloids, or watching Cora save her hide in the trailer this morning, or the fact he loved her told him he absolutely couldn't protest when she announced her mother and stepfather would be hosting dinner for them tonight. Still, he had his charity to deal with.

"What's wrong, boss?" Ben asked.

Part of dealing with his charity was refraining from divulging this information to Cora until later, much later, like when he had more to show for a charity than some cash and checks. More than ever, he had to make Cora look good. Every day he saw how she defended him, them, their movie, and after watching her go on a rampage saving face and part of her business, he knew he had to watch everything. "You can't ship them there, you should receive them. I mean Cora and I are out a lot and you're the one who has to make sure they get to the right location. Plus, you have to keep records." On the good Karma side of things, he was finally paying Ben for some of his work. It was the least he could do for the man keeping his charity afloat.

"Good call, Boss. I'll take care of it, plus we have some people asking about our next fundraiser."

"You're in charge. I have to go." Finally, Ryder opened the door to the suite. Hold on, was this his suite? At least he thought it was his and Cora's suite. For a quick second he leaned back to double-check the number. Yes, this was their place all right.

Their place but different.

Really different.

This morning when they left, the living area was a comfy living room with overstuffed couches and a chair where only last night Cora sat on his lap and fell asleep in his arms while he studied the shoot schedule for the next day.

However, now it was set up like a formal dining room in some mansion. Five, no make that six, uniformed waiters lined the walls, along with what appeared to be a private chef in one of those hats and everything.

Drinks in hand and in matching old-fashioned blue silk smoking jackets, Tony, Cora's stepdad and Viktor stood in one corner near a formal bar complete with bartender. Viktor lifted his chin in Ryder's direction.

"There he is!" In only what Ryder would call a bright blue formal prom meets ball gown, Rita, Cora's mother appeared from around the corner. "The man who took care of my daughter."

The woman snapped her fingers and one of the waiters came over with a glass of wine while a different one came over with another one of those blue jackets on a hanger. She took the wine off the tray while yet another attendant came over and lifted the train of her skirt. Together Cora's mother, the one waiter with the jacket, and the guy in white gloves holding the train, approached Ryder.

"Good evening," he said. Of course the one thing missing from this equation, and there was a lot to equate in the form of people in his suite, was his girl. "Where's Cora?"

"Help him." Rita scowled at someone, Ryder wasn't quite sure who, and someone came over, took his bag, bent down and helped him slip his shoes off. They put a pair of blue slippers on his feet and the guy with the smoking jacket helped Ryder on with his, including tying his tie. Rita handed him the wine and lifted her glass in his direction. "To the man who put my daughter on the map today. Those pictures were phenomenal."

Something about that comment seemed off. It wasn't that her daughter had a billion-dollar business she built out of a garage, or produced the movies that people waited two decades for, or maybe the sheer fact her daughter was the most gorgeous smart woman on the planet didn't put her on the map. But an almost sexy picture without even a nip slip that clearly upset her daughter made the woman want to get a pushpin and commemorate the moment?

"I need to find Cora," he said.

"She's finishing getting ready." Rita guided him to the other men. "Go play with the boys. I bought Tony a new toy because he's been so very good."

Something told him to play along so Ryder joined Viktor and Tony at a table with what appeared to be an antique chess set. Since he met Tony earlier, he felt like he had seen the man before but couldn't place him.

"Ryder, do you play chess?" His fingertip on one of the carved stone pieces, Tony quickly looked up at him and then returned his focus to the game.

Ryder's father would have told him life was a chess game and to get through in life all someone had to know was how to move the pieces. "I have dabbled." Right as he went to look for a place to sit, one of the servants carried a chair over to him.

"You know chess and tennis are a lot alike. You have to keep moving forward, you have to catch your opponent off guard, and when all else fails, you need to play right down the center." Tony made his move and sat back in his seat.

Tennis. That was it. "You're Tennis Tony!" About twenty-five years ago, the man was the star of the tennis circuit and was one of those athletes that all the women went crazy for with his long brown hair and perpetual tan. That was pretty cool.

"In the flesh." Tony bowed his head.

"Do you still compete?" Sports was never Ryder's forte. Neither was singing or dancing. He was an actor through and through, that and the owner of a charity.

"Not since Rita found me and made an honest man out of me." A smile grew over Tony's face. "Then I didn't have to."

Ryder nodded, and concurred. They had some things in common. Both celebrities both saved by their girls. "I hear you." With his wine in hand, he sat back and watched the game. Rarely did people just go about their business when he was around, and this whole thing was oddly settling, like he didn't have to put on a show.

"Yeah, she basically scraped me up off the tennis court. I was going through a rough patch. You know how it is, the money starts rolling in and then it rolls out just as fast." Tony made another move.

Ryder pushed his back into the chair. He knew that whole role all too well and ran his hand through his hair. "What do you do now, Tony?"

Tony studied the chessboard.

"My sugar face is kept plenty busy tending to the needs of his wife." Rita and her dress guy came over. She perched herself on the edge of Tony's chair and rubbed his neck.

Tony nodded, took Rita's hand, kissed the back and returned to his game.

"Yes, I was taken with him the second I saw him on the television, he was so beautiful. Once my company went public I promised myself I would meet him, and I arranged for a VIP room at one of his tournaments." Rita petted Tony's hair down and giggled. "Once he introduced himself, I knew I had to have him, and I practically asked him what I had to do to keep him."

"And keep me she did." Tony peeked over at him as if sending him a message. "I could do worse than end up married to a woman who researches and studies sex and toys for a living."

Ryder downed the rest of his wine and shifted in his seat. Was this how powerful women got their mates? If they changed a few details, they could easily be telling his story. Did Tony just give up, let Rita take over?

"Did you show Ryder what gorgeous husbands get when they treat their wives right?" Rita crooned.

Staring right into Ryder's eyes Tony lifted the sleeve on his smoking jacket to reveal a watch that anyone with any knowledge of brands and designers would know ten thousand miles away. "We added this to my collection on the way here." Tony leaned over to allow Ryder to get a better look.

Ryder admired the timepiece. No, Tony didn't give up, he just took the easy road. The same path his father told him to take, the same path he tried to travel down many a time. He had the easy road handed to him, but did he want it? Wasn't part of this whole gig to share things? His stomach tightening, he jumped up out of the chair.

"Ryder? What's the matter?" Rita made some hand motion, and no less than three men rushed over to her. "Mr. Scott needs some more wine, and he must be starving. He has to keep up his strength and eat."

"No, thank you, I'll be right back." As fast as he could, but not to appear as if he were running, he headed straight for the bedroom of their suite.

There, stuck in the middle of a big blue cloud was his girl hunched over her laptop.

"Honey, I'm home," he said.

Scowl firmly across her face, she glanced over at him. "I'm blue."

"I'm matching you." He went to her side. "What's the deal?"

"My mother is nuts, any more questions?" She returned her attention to her computer.

"Hey." He took her chin and turned her toward him. "You're working way too much."

"I could say the same to you." After giving the laptop one last look, she closed it.

"No." He shook his head. "My work is much different than your daily grind."

A little smile flickered over her lips and she pressed her palm to his cheek. "Well, if my daily grind allows me to see this gorgeous face at the end of it, it's all worth it." She leaned in and kissed him.

He broke the kiss and pulled her in for a hug. Yes, his whole life he was told to find the easy road, but just because one had the pavement to skate on, it didn't mean they had to glide through life. Rita's pet names and tokens to Tony made it clear how and why they got together, and maybe he and Cora started out the same way, but he didn't want to end up sitting in front of a chess set without having truly worked for anything.

Boy, would his father be disappointed.

Maybe his father was never truly in love.

Cora pulled back. "Ryder, are you okay?"

If nothing else, he needed to finish this movie and then really get to work. That was the right thing to do for him and for Cora. "Yeah, baby. I just love you." Somehow, he would break the rumor about him being a kept man.

HOLLYWOOD STARDOM

FADE IN:

INT. HOLLYWOOD - TELEVISION NEWS SET - EVENING

CHARLES is on the sound stage sitting with the
NEWS ANCHOR about the possibility of an asteroid
hitting the Earth.

                    CHARLES
          There are satellites and
          telescopes all over the
          world monitoring for any
          sort of danger twenty-four
          hours a day, seven days a
          week. The asteroid passing
          by the earth tomorrow will
          not come anywhere close to
          us, and there is absolutely
          no cause for alarm.

                    ANCHOR
          Well, I can't thank you
          enough. I, for one, can
          sleep tonight.

                    CHARLES
          Remember to look at the
          stars tonight.
          (He glances over to the side
          of the stage.)

Cut to ROXY standing on the sidelines. She
claps silently.

The music cues through the studio.

                    DIRECTOR O.S.
          Cut!

CHARLES takes his mic, stands and shakes hands
with the anchors before joining ROXY.

                    ROXY
          (Hugs him)
           You were perfect and you
           used your tagline.
           Remember to always say it.

                    CHARLES
           That was a great idea. I'm
           glad I listened to you and
           didn't rehearse too much.

                    ROXY
          (Pulls back)
           Well, I'm glad I listened
           to you now I don't have to
           live in fear of an asteroid
           hitting me.

                    CHARLES
          (Chuckles)
           I have connections. Never
           be afraid.

                    ROXY
           I'm not when I'm with you.
           You've always kept me safe.

CHARLES presses his palm to her cheek, leans in
but stops.

                    ROXY
          (whispering)
           What are you afraid of?

                    CHARLES
           This.

                    ROXY
           Don't be. I'm not an
           asteroid.
          (She presses her body to
           his.)

                    CHARLES
          No, but you could be more
          catastrophic.

He wraps his arms around her and bends her back
in a passionate kiss.

Chapter Twenty-five

"CUT!" RYDER YELLED and got out of his director's chair.

Though unsure why he stopped the scene, Cora somehow managed to ditch her mother and take a few moments to watch the man she loved at work. With all the chaos of the last few days, she barely got the chance to really observe him work this side of the camera. One thing was certain, his and Logan's styles were vastly different. In a shocking development, Ryder was more detail oriented than his co-star.

While she wanted the filming to get going, she also really liked his attention to every little nuance and took her opportunity to walk over to him.

From the set Logan lifted his arms. "What?" He barked out the word.

Without acknowledging Logan even spoke, Ryder lifted the script pages to his face.

In truth, since they returned from his cabin, she'd never seen the man as intense, and she gave his shoulder a light massage.

"Hey babe." He didn't even glance her way.

She frowned. "Everything all right?"

"Just working." He gave her hand a squeeze, stood and charged over to the lead camera man. The two men spoke and started switching lenses.

"Ryder!" Logan stomped over. "What are you doing?"

"Directing." Ryder walked past Logan and held his hands up as if framing the shot.

Cora bit her lip. The focused working Ryder was sexy, really sexy, but also a little aloof. Since her mother and stepfather arrived three days ago, he seemed unusually pensive, staying pretty quiet, especially for him, and working really late. When they did speak, it was about work. Worst yet, her cheeks heated when she thought about how long it had been since they made love. They had now gone longer than the two days they were apart right after her attack and she wanted to rip his clothes off and have him take care of her. Alternatively, she wanted to ask him if something was wrong. This was much easier before she loved him.

"The shot is fine." Logan continued to challenge him.

"Since we went through all this trouble to move everyone to Arizona, I want to do a set of shots with the wide angle lens so we can actually see the backdrop the studio is paying for." Ryder looked through the camera lens.

She would be lying if she said she wasn't impressed at how much Ryder knew about cameras and lenses. Maybe Logan did as well, but she didn't pay as much attention.

She tilted her head as he adjusted a light.

"Are we done yet, Mr. Meticulous?" Chest puffed out, Logan stood right in front of him.

Ryder straightened up, standing at least an inch taller than Logan. "Get back in the shot or it will take longer."

At Ryder's rough tone, she had no choice but to lick her lips. Still, she could go for a kiss. His attention last night and this morning was a little lacking. Focus was one thing, but she also wanted a little thrown her way. Oh lord, she was turning into what she hated.

Rodger came up behind her and slipped her a coffee. "I have two things to tell you."

"Please don't make them horrible." She shook her head.

"One is horrible one is not." Rodger laughed.

"Hit me." Might as well get it over with, it wouldn't go away.

"McAllister invited you to a golf outing with the men." Rodger patted her.

Unsure if that was or was not the horrible one, she glanced over at him. In case anyone forgot, she didn't know how to golf. "And?"

"Incoming." Rodger shrugged.

Fine, that was the horrible one. "You know, you'd be a much better secretary if you knew how to get rid of her." Cora snarled.

"I don't do parents, sorry, but she's leaving." Rodger dashed off with Spike in tow.

Damn boundaries from employees. Before she had a chance to brace herself, she felt the presence surround her, making the little hairs on the back of her neck stand up. For most difficult situations, it was best to face the situation head on. With her mother coming up behind her, she chose to keep her back to the woman. Maybe if she didn't see her mother, her mother wouldn't see her.

"He is a sight to behold." The woman found her. "Actually, all the men are. Too bad the other two are spoken for, or could have had quite a fantasy orgy."

"Mother." Cora shook her head and kept her eye on the prize. Namely Ryder.

"Oh, give me a break," her mother elbowed her, "I'm not the only woman who has thought it, trust me. I'm sorry I just showed up here, but you wouldn't have let me come any other way."

Out of the corner of her eye Cora glanced at her mother. They were different. Extremely different, but alike. Actually, once she joined the ranks of her mother with a successful Internet company Cora sort of understood the woman a bit more. Finally got the late nights, and never ending trips, and empathized with how the business came first.

"After I heard what happened, I had to come." Her mother gave her a hug.

Unfortunately, somewhere there was still that little girl who wanted her mom there after her dad died, and there the day she got accepted into both colleges she wanted to go to, and wanted her to answer the phone the day she sold her company.

More than anything, Cora was terrified she was more like her mother than she thought and if she and Ryder ever had children, she wanted her to be there for all those important moments, but even more so, be there for the unimportant moments.

Great, she was thinking about her and Ryder having children. The situation was truly hopeless. "Thanks, I appreciate it, but I'm fine, and Ryder is taking good care of me." At least he was, and she wanted him to continue.

"Then make sure you take care of him too." Her mother stared her down.

"Mother." No matter if her parent was Madame Sublime or not, she wasn't going to talk sex with the woman.

"I'm not going to leave until you hear me out." Her mother's tone was teasing with a backdrop of a parental threat.

"Come on." When Ryder returned to his director's chair, she guided her mother away from the action before he called action.

No way did she want them to be the reason for not having quiet on the set. At the moment he wouldn't notice her anyway.

"I like Ryder." Her mother laced her arm in hers, and they took their walk.

"You like Ryder's fame and looks," Cora corrected.

"So do you," the woman countered.

Not in any universe would she defend her relationship with Ryder to the woman that invented marrying the good-looking trophy. Cora stopped and crossed her arms.

"I wouldn't be having this conversation if I didn't think there was something more." Her mother tilted her head.

Once more they walked.

"If there's one thing I learned from Madame Sublime, it's to always keep them guessing, and become their fantasies." Her mother stood in front of her.

"That's two things." The second her mother opened her bag, Cora wanted to run. From time to time, she would get little gifts from her mother's website, and she never had the guts to use them.

"You know back in the day, Tony was quite the star. I know you've had issues with him, but we've been together a long time and that comes from a few things, like a commitment, and an understanding, and playing to one's strength." Her mother took a brown paper bag out out of her already oversized tote and handed it to her. "But along with all that, you have to keep things interesting."

Cora opened the bag and her jaw fell. What the hell was all this? She looked up at the woman.

A smile gracing her face, her mother shrugged. "Just a little bag of ideas created by someone who knows exactly what's like to be in your position. Don't ever get too comfortable."

She would be lying if she said the contents of the bag didn't intrigue her. What would Ryder think? Still, this wasn't her, this was her mother's arena. "I need to get to work."

"Of course you do, as do I." Her mother gave her another hug. "Tony and I are going to go check out some new products."

"I would tell you to have fun, but..." Cora shook her head and hugged the woman back. "Have a safe flight."

"Have a fun night." Her mother patted her and together they walked back to the trailers where they parted ways.

Bag shoved under her arm, Cora stared at the action on the set, or in this case the non-action. It gave her a safe moment to approach Mr. Director and she went to his side.

"Hey babe." Now he was hunched over a duffel bag of cables and whatnot.

"Don't we have people to do that for you?" They seemed to have people for everything else. Here's how it needed to work. There would be a person to look for the cord while Ryder looked at her. She tried to sound sweet, but in all honesty, her tone came out annoyed.

"I want to make sure this is done right." He continued digging through the mess.

"I'll tell you what can be done right." Fine, she stooped to blatant sexual innuendo.

"Yes!" Cord in hand he jumped up.

"So what's going on?" She put her hand on her hip.

"Working." Rather than looking at her, he studied the cable.

All right, if blatant sexual innuendo hadn't worked, then maybe pure sex would do the trick. She ran her nail up his arm. "How about we have dinner in the suite? Rather than blue smoking jackets and dresses, dress will be completely optional and discouraged."

"I'll be working late. I have to get us caught up." He leaned in and gave her a quick peck. "Love ya, babe." Duty done, he went to leave.

Before he could escape, she caught his arm.

"What's up, babe?" He returned to taking in his fabulous cord.

"Why don't you let me worry about the timeline? You can't work every second." She jutted her jaw out.

"What, don't you think I can do it?" At least he stopped looking at the cable and faced her.

"I think your talents are better served elsewhere." To make sure he understood her double meaning, she stepped closer.

"Is this what it's going to be like when we go into production on my movie?" His tone lowered and he crossed his arms.

"The producer produces the movie." With all the man knew about movie making, this should be obvious.

"Cora, let me get to work." He gave her a perfunctory kiss on the cheek and walked away.

For a moment, she stood there, wondering what to do and out of force of habit, she whipped out her phone to check her email, hating the way she breathed a sigh of relief at only her normal work messages. No one was cancelling ads, no sort of sexually explicit photos of her were popping up anywhere, no starwatcher was creeping her out.

Rodger waved her down. "Cora, it's time for your conference call with the advertising department."

"I'm a producer I produce." Bag clutched to her chest, she marched toward the trailer.

"What's wrong?" Rodger ran to keep up to her.

She shoved the bag at Rodger. "Go do something with this." Her mother was dead wrong. She didn't need to be a fantasy, she needed to be a boss.

THE SECOND CORA HEARD the telltale beep of hotel room door unlocking, she stood up, got in position, and waited for her star.

As she heard the door open and close, she yanked at the outfit, jutted her chest out and lifted her prop.

After what seemed like much longer than it took to walk from the main room of the suite to the bedroom, Ryder appeared.

"I'm ready for my audition, Mr. Scott." She lifted her fake cigarette holder and let her white silk robe trimmed with feathers fall open exposing her crystal encrusted corset and matching thong. Fine, she followed her mother's advice. After all, Tony seemed happy enough.

Ryder dropped his bag. "We're not taking any further casting calls."

Though she assumed he would rush to her, admire her body, and throw her on the bed, maybe the role-play thing required a bit more play or role. "I'm ready to do just about anything for a part, Mr. Scott." Doing her best version of a sexy strut, she went to her man, put her hand on his chest, and slid her palm down his flat, perfect stomach.

She didn't even reach the waistband of his pants before he caught her hand by the wrist.

They stared at each other.

"Perhaps I would do a better job on my knees." Not one to be stopped, and wondering if this was how all casting directors treated their starlets, she went to bend down.

"That won't be necessary. I'll pass thanks anyway. If you don't mind, I'll exit stage right." Ryder let go of her.

The sudden loss of his support caused her to fall flat on her behind in the stupid twenty-inch stilettos her mother threw in the bag. "Ryder! What is wrong with you?" When she tried to get up, she only succeeded in catching the heel of her shoe in her robe and repeated her performance of landing right on her derriere.

"I'm not going to be silenced by a blow job." He bowed and stepped over her, making his way to the closet.

"What the hell does that mean?" She ripped the shoes off her feet, practically tore the robe off her, and finally managed to stand up.

Rather than answer, he shook his head.

"Ryder, I demand you speak to me." She balled her hands in a fist.

"That's exactly it." He spun around to face her.

The man was speaking in riddles. "Ryder, you're not making any sense. I tried to make you happy, and now you're upset with me."

"I don't want to be placated, I want a partner." With his words out, he turned back to the closet.

How did this turn into such a disaster? "I just wanted to apologize for earlier." Not wanting to stand there like the desperate half-dressed woman she turned into, she chose the other escape route and stomped into the bathroom, slamming the door behind her.

Her mind took off in a million different directions. Maybe this was how breakups happened. He didn't consider her a partner? Didn't he want her anymore? Her eyes heated, but she refused to allow any tears to fall. All it would take was a snap of her fingers to get out of here. In fact, maybe she needed to do just that.

"Damn it!" She clawed at the stupid corset managing to get rid of the ridiculous thing along with all the stupid accessories and yanked on the hotel provided robe. Unfortunately for her, she left her phone in the other room. With her head held high, she opened the door, jumping back when faced head on with Ryder.

"Excuse me." In an effort not to sound like she wanted to burst into tears, she cleared her throat.

"I have a question first." As if caging her in, he put his hands out on the doorjamb.

"All right." She crossed her arms.

"Why did you want to apologize to me?" His voice remained hard, tense, angry, and he stared right into her eyes as if trying to detect any deception.

"Because somewhere between walking away from you on set and putting on some skanky outfit, I realized that I can't just conjure you when I want you, and we all have jobs, and I need to remember that, and..." She paused and inhaled.

"And?" He leaned down.

Unable to look at him anymore, she turned away. "I missed you and..." Again, she stopped herself.

"Tell me," he whispered.

"I wanted to make sure you still wanted me." Not sure if she was ready to hear what he had to say, not sure where to go, not sure what to do, she shut her eyes.

"Let's make one thing clear." He took her chin in his hand. "Look at me."

She did as he requested.

He gave her a light kiss. "There's never one second of any day that I don't want you."

The weight sitting on her chest for the last three days lifted a little.

"I was thinking a lot these last few days. I don't want to just be an accessory to you." His thumb grazed her jaw line.

Shivers ran through her. "You're the star."

He put his finger over her lips. "I think what I'm trying to say is that I want to be worthy of you."

At his words she couldn't resist and hugged him. "Ryder."

"Shh." He connected their mouths treating her to what she craved, a deep kiss, his arms around her, his body pressed to hers.

His taste took over her mouth, sweet, spicy, sassy like Ryder himself. There would never be anyone else for her.

He pulled open the tie of her robe, let the garment fall to the floor, and slid his lips down her neck to her shoulders.

As anytime they were together, her knees went weak and without skipping a beat, he picked her up and took her straight to the bed. Before joining her, he got rid of his clothes and came up behind her, spooning her, his thick erection pressing into her back.

She went to turn over, but he held her fast and pointed to the mirrored closet doors and threw the covers off the bed. "Watch us together." He lowered his face, kissing her behind her ear making her squirm as her skin heated.

His hands traveled to her front, his fingertips skimmed over her already tight nipples. She forced herself to look, take in how he tended to her. Once his hand snuck between her legs, she couldn't keep her eyes off them if she tried. "Ah." She let out a little cry as his fingers entered her.

"Someone likes watching." He pulled her back slightly and hooked her leg over his hip.

Her focus solely on the mirror and Ryder, she gasped as he filled her, slowly entering her, allowing her to see how their bodies merged into one. "Oh my god."

"That's so hot." He growled in her ear, and they both riveted on the mirror as he took slow deep strokes.

Dare she say they were beautiful together?

The addition of the visual aroused her, causing her end to come on quickly and she panted as the sensations built. "Ryder."

He knew her, knew her signals, knew what she needed and he sped up, treated her to harder thrusts, then pressed his hand where they were joined giving her something extra to grind into and take her over the edge.

"Let me feel it." His tone was demanding.

As he knew her, she also knew him, he was there with her, right there. "Ryder!"

"I'm there, baby." He tightened his hold her.

In the mirror she watched him drive into her then stiffen and stay embedded inside her as his orgasm hit. His throbbing resonated through her core.

That was all she needed to join him, and she arched her back as the pleasure consumed her, brought her to that place of ecstasy and calmness and oneness with the man she loved.

Ryder caught his breath. "Did you see that? Remember that whenever you think I don't want you or you have doubts."

"Ryder." She took his hand. "I am sorry about before and for what you walked into, I knew something was wrong and I didn't know how to fix it."

"I love you, baby. I'm sorry too, I just needed a few days to figure out how I'm going to achieve everything I want for us." His fingers played with hers. "I want to take care of you."

Rather than his reflection, she twisted around and chose to look at the genuine article. The thing was that she wanted him to take care of her. She supposed their arrangement was officially over so solving their issues wouldn't be as easy as putting on a costume and having sex. They were truly a couple and that seemed to only complicate everything.

HOLLYWOOD STARDOM

FADE IN:

EXT. LOS ANGELES – GRIFFITH PARK - NIGHT

CHARLES and ROXY lay on a blanket outside looking up at the stars.

ROXY cuddles up to CHARLES' side and CHARLES runs his fingers through her hair.

>   ROXY
>   What are you thinking
>   about?

>   CHARLES
>   What I've been thinking
>   about every day since you
>   walked into the observatory
>   and interrupted my tour.

>   ROXY
>   (Leans up on her elbow and
>   looks down at CHARLES)
>   What's that?

>   CHARLES
>   (Pulls her down for a kiss)
>   You.

>   ROXY
>   (Smiles and kisses him
>   again)
>   So what's your verdict on
>   me?

>   CHARLES
>   (Shakes his head)
>   It's still out.

                    ROXY
            (Looks down and plays with
            CHARLES' collar)
             If it means anything, I
             know what I want.

                    CHARLES
             Are you sure?

                    ROXY
            (Stares into his eyes)
             How can you ask me that?

CHARLES doesn't answer just moves her hair out
of her face.

                    ROXY
            (Whispers)
             Believe in me.

                    CHARLES
             I want to more than
             anything.

Chapter Twenty-Six

"HAVE YOU EVER BEEN to a baby shower?" As they drove up to Erin and Drew's house, Cora wrinkled her nose.

Ryder nodded. "I went to Logan and Ivy's for Curt."

"You went to a baby shower?" Cora crossed her legs and turned toward him.

"You've never been to a baby shower?" he asked. Of course, he also took his opportunity to watch her skirt ride up her legs.

She tugged her skirt down. "No, and I thought they were just for people who had the potential of having a baby."

"Are you saying I don't have the potential to have a baby?" For the first time in his life, he said the word baby when it related to miniature person and didn't feel like breaking out into hives.

"Do you have a uterus?" The same expression as when she bested someone in business overtook her face, narrowed eyes, slight smile.

"Yes, I do." At last, he had her, and he pointed to her stomach. "It's right there where I left it this morning."

Her eyes widened as the realization that he won hit her.

Since he had the newest and best car, he parked right in the Fultons' driveway. "We could have a baby." At his own words, he slammed on his brakes.

Her mouth open and complexion pale, Cora stared at him.

He had to go in for the save. "You know, we could totally have a baby." Rather than fixing it, he only repeated what he said and added the word totally like some valley dude. In his defense, they could have a baby. It was biologically possible.

Cora's expression didn't change.

"You know our baby would hit the genetic lottery."

By the fact she didn't move a muscle, he had the distinct feeling he wasn't making it better. He gave it one last go. "Smart, gorgeous, talented. We would have an actor or a CEO on our hands, maybe both."

At last she reacted in the form of letting herself out of the car and stomping up to the front door.

Wouldn't most women be all goo-goo eyed at the mention of creating offspring with him? He dashed after her and managed to put his arm around her right as Drew opened the door. "Welcome."

Ryder gave him a thumbs-up.

"We're starting the activities." Drew raised his eyebrows.

"Activities?" Ryder didn't think Erin could play drinking games.

"Come on in." Drew motioned forward. "You have to start by decorating a square for the quilt for the baby. Then you can present it to Erin."

They followed Drew inside and nodded then shook hands with the other guests, including Ivy, Logan, Madeline, some of the other crew members, and a couple of people he vaguely recognized from Drew's work the one time he took a tour of Fluent Words Laboratory. The entire place was decorated in old-fashioned pastel streamers and balloons with stork and baby decorations, and everyone huddled around a huge table with all kinds of arts and crafts things and squares of material.

"Well, this blanket will be worth a pretty penny one day." He picked up a yellow square and signed it with one of the fabric markers. "I will verify to the kiddo I did this myself."

Everyone around the table laughed, and Logan took a second square and signed it. Even Drew came over and signed one of his own.

Though this didn't really seem like a game, it was pretty cool, and he leaned over to see Cora's creation.

Sort of like in the car, she didn't move, only stood there and watched everyone decorating their square.

Figuring she might need a little help, he found a pastel green piece and a metallic marker and put it in front of her. "Here you go."

"I'm not a movie star," she shrugged, "my signature isn't worth anything." "At least on the open market."

Rather than argue the point on what her signature could be worth, he grabbed his pen. "How about we do one together?" He started by drawing the first thing that came to mind, a heart. "Now you add something."

She glared at him, then pursed out her lips, but finally bent down and began drawing. He held the square tight while she added in another heart and then a smile face. At last she put her name.

He put his name next to hers and lifted the square. Her name had really nice alliteration, but he had the last name to be reckoned with. "Interesting."

"What's interesting?" Now she stared at the little art piece with him.

"I was just wondering if we ever got married would you remain a Caine or go with Scott? I'm not sure if I love the hyphen thing, it's sort of clunky. Ivy went with Logan's name, as did Erin, even though she had her name. I think that's sort of cool." He held the square out to her.

Everyone around the table looked at them, then Logan nodded and let out a laugh.

"Whatever insanity that has entered your mind better stop right now." She snatched the square away from him, pushed past everyone and with fabric in hand, made her way to Erin sitting in an oversized chair under her lemon tree.

"Here you are, and here is something for the baby from me and Ryder." Cora dropped material on Erin's lap and thrust an envelope at her.

"Oh, should I open it now?" As with anytime Erin was presented with a gift, she sat up and smiled.

"Or wait and let the baby open it."

With Cora's flat delivery of her joke, it took Erin a moment to laugh.

At last, he went to her side. Cora was not an actress in any way, shape or form. The night she tried her roleplay was a disaster on many levels, but it was also endearing, and honestly, he didn't need an actress. He loved the fact she was genuine, and he put his arm around her.

Erin opened her gift and pulled out stock certificates to Chargge. "Oh my, Drew."

Drew went to his wife and studied the document. "Thank you, Cora."

A quick glance at the paper told him she gave them quite a tidy sum. If he and Cora had a baby, it would be set for life.

"If you tell your offspring to save that until he or she is old enough to ask what that is, it will be worth more hopefully." She nodded.

"Thank you again." Erin stood, gave Cora a hug, and then turned to him. "How do I look? I don't get to be pregnant on set." Erin rubbed her hand over her baby bump.

"Glowing, of course." Ryder bent down gave her a kiss.

"I wanted a traditional baby shower like all those regular things we never did." Erin winked at him.

Of anyone, he understood her sentiment. They both started acting at a young age and missed a few things. Sometimes having something seemingly unspectacular yet in its own way spectacular was all that was needed. "I get it." He gave his co-star a squeeze on the shoulder and vowed then and there that his and Cora's baby wouldn't miss anything. Even if their daughter wanted to act, he would make sure she had birthday parties and school and normal things. Daughter.

"We're setting up for lunch. Why don't you two go take a seat." Erin pointed to the long table decorated with all things baby shower.

Ryder took her hand and led her over to the table. "Would you rather have a boy or a girl?"

Cora stopped dead in her tracks, let go of his hand and faced him. "Are you mental?"

Choosing to ignore her question, he went on his own track. "I think a daughter would be good, or a son. Either way, I am good with it." Son could be cool too. Curtis was sort of awesome when he wasn't sticky or moist. It probably wasn't nearly as disgusting if you made the sticky and/or moist item. Some moist items could be extremely pleasant, and he winked at her.

Jaw jutted out, hands on hips, Cora turned back to Erin. "Will you excuse Ryder and me for moment? We'll be right back." Without giving him a second glance, she charged back into the house.

He followed her through the Fultons' kitchen and into their laundry room where she slid the door closed. Her back turned to him, she audibly sighed then spun on her heel toward him. "Explain yourself right now."

"What's the problem?" He leaned back on the door.

"What's the problem?" She took a step toward him. "What's the problem?" Along with another step, she raised her voice.

He pressed his back to the door.

"Comments about babies, changing my name, asking if I want a son or daughter." She got right up in his face. "Either you're making fun of me or you've gone utterly insane."

"I am not insane. I love you, and I started thinking about it and didn't freak out. In fact, I liked it." He held his ground and straightened up. "I love you, we're together, isn't this what we do next?"

"Is it?" Her teeth seemed to grind together.

Before answering, he truly thought about it. Something told him he better make one hundred percent sure before uttering his answer. "Yes." Let's see what she thought of that.

She paused, searched his eyes as if she were authenticating his words, then leaned in and kissed him. More accurately, she planted one on him, molding his mouth to his and slipping him the tongue.

He wrapped his arms around her and took in her taste, the way her breasts flattened against his chest, how she let out a little coo that told him if they were alone she would want him inside her.

The sheer thought of making love to her caused the normal reaction he had with her anytime or anytime thinking of her, and he took her hips in his hand and pressed their bodies together.

"God, I love that." She snuck her hand down, rubbing her palm over his ever-growing bulge.

"What?" He moved her hair aside and kissed her ear.

"How you get hard the second we kiss." A low chuckle escaped her throat and she kissed him again.

"Something tells me if I took a feel, I may find some wet panties." He cupped her bottom and got a nice handful.

"Then your intuition is dead on." She pushed back and looked around. "We should probably get back to the shower."

"You go be a girl and I'll follow, I need a second." After fixing a lock of her hair he slid the door open for her. "If I keep looking at you, I'll have no choice but to bend you over the Fultons' washing machine."

"Yeah, we should wait until we're in the car." As she left, she ran her hand over his shoulder.

Once closing the door, he leaned back and closed his eyes. Yes, this was what he wanted. Strange, how the most important things could come out of a small spark. Again, the insignificant turned significant, probably the most significant of all.

His phone vibrated and still heady from this whole afternoon, he pulled it out without even thinking about. Maybe Cora was trying to make his situation worse by sending a little sext.

The second he glanced down at the phone his arousal dissipated as fast as it came on.

Your movie is over schedule, and our movie is getting pushed back further and further, I wont remind you again that we need a little more on our end to keep it even.

For the first time since all this started he typed back with conviction. *I'll pay back the money in full, with interest lets just call it a day and part ways.*

His heart sped as he waited for answer.

No, we want the movie. You know this.

He squeezed the device trying to think of a comeback.

We want the movie and we want the cabin as collateral.

More than ever, the cabin wasn't on the table. Now his children and grandchildren would be in that cabin. He would never give the cabin up. *I already gave you plenty and I'm making the movie.*

Your plenty is not nearly enough. We need to meet.

He couldn't and wouldn't get rid of his movie. Like the cabin the movie was now part of him and Cora.

Cora.

His life had become forever entwined with Cora's, her place, his place, their jobs, it all melded into one. He shoved the phone back in his pocket. However, they weren't married yet, their property was separate.

His soon to be fiancée was in for an engagement present she didn't expect, and he didn't mean a ring. He would save the cabin and save the movie and at the end of the day, it would all come out in the wash anyway.

Before shoving his phone in his pocket, he made one last text.

Hey, I need you to do me a favor.

He had to protect everything that was his.

FADE IN:

INT. LOS ANGELES – NEWS STATION - DAY

CHARLES and ROXY sit at a news station office in a conference room with two of the station executives.

>   MAN #1
>   So, what we're proposing is
>   a bi-weekly segment on our
>   5:00 and 11:00 news.

>   CHARLES
>   (Reads over the contract and
>   hands it to ROXY)
>   Who picks the topics?

>   MAN #2
>   We will guide you, but you
>   have input. We just want
>   the segments to be timely
>   and trending.

>   ROXY
>   (Hands the contract back to
>   CHARLES)
>   What about the possibility
>   of turning this into a
>   full-fledged show? Space
>   is hot right now. Maybe
>   along with doing the
>   segments, we can try a
>   pilot.

CUT TO CHARLES WHO SMILES.

>   MAN #2
>   That is definitely a
>   possibility.

                    ROXY
              Maybe in three months if
              all goes well with the
              ratings?

MAN #1 and MAN #2 face each other, some soft
whispers are heard. CHARLES takes ROXY'S hand.
After a pause, the men face them.

                    MAN #1
              All right. We'll try a
              pilot with you.

                    MAN #2
              We will have some new
              contracts drawn up.
              (He points at ROXY.)
              You have yourself some
              agent.

                    CHARLES
              She's not my agent, she's
              my, my…

                    ROXY
              (Intertwines their fingers)
              I'm his.

Chapter Twenty-Seven

HUNCHED OVER HER ENEMY, Cora pulled the club back and took a swing.

Once more, she was bested. The stupid little white ball traveled maybe three inches off the tee. She threw her club down the driving range. The damn thing went much further than any of her balls. "Ryder!"

Ryder dashed over, picked up the club and put another ball on the tee. "You can do it, baby." He gave her back the tool of mass destruction.

"Golf hates me." She ground her teeth together and got back in position. Where on earth she got the idea that accepting George's golf invitation would result in her magically being able to play the game and getting some business done was beyond her. More than anything, she couldn't miss this. Both Albert, her competition, and Dane, the head of the studio, would be here along with George. She had to play with the boys.

"No, golf loves you, it wants you to meet it half way, relax and just hit the ball." Ryder walked around and stood in front of her. "Slow, even strokes. You're excellent at that."

She glanced over in his direction. From her position, she was now face to face with his crotch. Early morning training did have some advantages. Perhaps they shouldn't have waited until the day of the actual meeting to truly practice. Her mind was all muddled with Ryder and babies and wedding talk. Though nothing was official, it still got all her female atoms firing off. At last, she accepted she was a girl.

"I see where you're looking and it's all yours as soon as you become the pro golfer I know you are meant to be." He chuckled.

Heat overtaking her, she returned her focus to the ball.

"You can do it." He lowered his voice.

Not wanting to disappoint the man she was possibly going to marry, she inhaled and took another swing, this time missing the ball altogether, and nearly spinning around.

Rather than throwing a temper tantrum, she simply dropped the club and turned her back to the man who she wasn't sure was her fiancé or not.

"All right, this calls for an emergency contingency." He came up behind her and put his hands on her shoulders

"I'm going to call and tell them I broke both my legs. Hopefully someone at the studio can hook me up with some fake casts." Unable to look at anything, especially her own failure, she put her hand over her eyes.

"Cora, look at me." Ryder put his hands on her shoulders and turned her toward him. "I want you to have an open mind."

She let her arm fall and gazed into that face. "What?" Now that she thought about it, she was never good at sports.

"I'm going to do the golfing." He punctuated his sentence with that smile. That smile on that face.

"If you're golfing what am I doing?" she asked, confused. The man spoke his own language. "I have to be there."

"Oh, you will be there." He pulled her into his arms. "As my caddy."

And here was the man she was going to marry, at least she thought so. That man and the man who just suggested she be a caddy were the same man. "Please tell me the punchline."

"It makes perfect sense. You can't golf, I can golf, you need to be at the meeting, this will give you a chance to concentrate and, dare I say, give you the edge by having some extra star power behind you." He raised his eyebrows.

For a second she considered his proposition. It would be so easy to have him do the golfing. "I can't bring my...my...you." She pushed him back, picked up her club, put another ball on the tee and went for it.

This time the club slipped out her hands, knocked into the tee and the ball actually rolled backward.

Ryder plucked up the rolling horror show and held the ball up between two fingers.

"So this caddie thing, how exactly does that work?" As she walked by him, she tapped the ball out of his hands.

He gathered up the clubs and guided her into the clubhouse of the country club. "Well, first we have to look the part. The main thing about this is we have to own it and make it believable."

Twenty gasps, several pictures, and an endless amount of irritation later, she and Ryder emerged from the small clothing store at the clubhouse in matching purple golf shirts and khaki shorts.

As if they could be private at all, she pulled him over to a corner and spoke between clenched teeth. "I feel stupid."

"That's impossible." He leaned back and did that hand frame thing as if he were taking her all in.

"How can it be impossible, if that's what I feel?" She glanced down at her clothes and then over at Ryder. They looked like they were ready to attend a bad golf themed prom. All she needed was a corsage.

"Because you are the smartest woman in the world, which in turn, makes me the smartest man in the world." He put a khaki hat on top of her head.

Well, it wasn't a corsage, but it was just as obnoxious, especially when he put an identical one on his head. "I don't know how to caddie."

"I figured that when you didn't know how to golf." He kissed the top of her head. "Just do your business stuff and let me break some balls."

Before she had a chance to wrap her head around all of this, George, Albert and Dane entered the pro shop.

"There's our fourth." Huge smile, George came over, shook her hand and tilted his head at Ryder.

"Actually, here's your fourth." If she were going to do this, she was going to do this one hundred percent. "Mr. McIntire may I present Ryder Scott, my—" Not knowing what title to give him, she stopped. "Star of the *Hollywood Stardust* Series."

"And fiancé to one Miss Caine." Ryder held his hand out.

With Ryder's words, Cora gave a quick glance to the floor to see if her jaw dropped down there somewhere.

"Well then I say congratulations are in order!' George shook Ryder's hand and gave her a hug.

Dane and Albert gathered around.

"Congratulations." Dane parroted George's action, as did Albert.

"Well, not everything is official, so we want to keep it a little quiet." Somehow, she found her voice. "I think it's almost tee time."

"It's good to finally meet you." Dane looked Ryder over. "I missed you at our last meeting."

She felt that jab. Were they going to box or golf?

Ryder grinned at him. "Well, I always like to come in for the grand finale."

"You're not golfing, Cora?" Though Albert's facial expression remained stoic, Cora swore she saw a twinkle in his eye.

"Sometimes you have to know when to play a ringer." Something about this man made her claws come out. Most likely, it was the competition between them, but she felt that way since the first time she met him. Now wasn't the time to focus on Ryder and his newly dubbed title, though she didn't know how she wouldn't think about it.

"Well, if you don't know how to play." Laughing, Albert made a huge deal of putting on his golf glove.

"I can play with the best of them, Albert. One of the first rules of any game is playing your strengths, so today I'll play the role of caddie." Behind her, she heard a couple of the men chuckle. "Shall we get to our cart, gentlemen?"

"We abide by tradition here." George guided her out to where they country club kept the bags of clubs.

"Tradition?" Yes, she knew golf was steeped in tradition.

Ryder got their bag and slung it over his shoulder.

Dane took the bag from Ryder and handed it her. "We walk the course, and caddies carry the bags."

The weight of the bag practically toppled her over. What the hell was in there? Rocks with a boulder? She looked up at her...whatever, she looked up at Ryder.

"Let's buck tradition." He reached for the bag.

"No, I'm fine, just golf fast," she lied, then hoisted the bag up further on her shoulder, and slid her own personal ammunition out of her pocket, typing in a hurry. Thank god she had good Internet connection.

"You all right, Cora? Maybe we can get you a caddie?" Albert chuckled.

The men grabbed their bags walked toward first tee.

"I'm fine." She walked ahead of the men. "Isn't this great? Did you know that you burn off over seven hundred calories walking a course rather than just over four hundred by riding in the cart?"

"I suppose sometimes it's important to know when to bring in someone with more skill." George put his bag down.

"A little technology doesn't hurt either." Cora practically dropped their bag. Actually, if she had the strength she would have kicked it. When no one was looking, she did flip the thing off. She would get the best of the golf bag of terror. However, she did wonder how many calories she just burned walking the few feet to the first hole. If she were going to fit into a wedding dress, she had to consider these things. Wait. No one said she was getting in a wedding dress. Ryder could have just been playing along.

The men all congregated around.

"There's also something to be said for knowing every aspect of your business." Albert said, and followed George to the tee. "Not everything is technology and gadgets."

Fine, that was a direct shot at her. She watched the men choose their respective clubs, then she stared at the heavy collection in her and Ryder's bag. All she knew about being a caddie was she had to give Ryder a club. Maybe she could weed some of this out and just toss the unnecessary clubs in the garbage. Once more, she turned to her phone. She had three choices. The putter, she knew that wasn't right, the irons, also a no show, and the woods. However, not knowing how Ryder really golfed, beyond the way he held her from behind and helped her take a swing, and even after all her research on golf, she couldn't garner a guess.

"Better not let those technology and gadgets get in your way at over at News Now," she said. "Is the company's slogan, 'where news and technology converge?'"

Albert stepped back. "Back in the day, someone didn't get a job until they could do every job underneath them."

"Very true." George put his ball on the tee.

Ryder came over, wiped his hands on a little towel hanging there, and pushed one of the clubs at her, or should she say her fiancé basically bailed her out? He peered at her over his sunglasses and winked. "Get him."

With Ryder's guidance, she swiped the club out of the bag. "Next year I must be turning pro, since I'm starting off as a caddie."

Even through his sunglasses, she felt Albert's glare.

They all got quiet as George took his shot. The ball traveled down the fairway. When he did it, the act seemed so easy, but she still didn't see the allure of the game.

Dane went next much to the same result, as did Albert.

At last, Ryder approached the tee. With a swagger only he could possess, he put the ball on the tee, got in position, and without any pause, the other men showed, pulled back and made his hit. The man was a stock photo for a perfect swing and his ball sailed through the air. Once it landed past George's ball, Ryder shrugged. "I need to practice more." He handed her back his club and helped her with the golf bag.

"Maybe you need to film more as well." Albert picked up his bag.

They all took off toward their balls.

"I was wondering how you and Ryder had time to come out here this morning." Dane walked alongside her.

All right, apparently this was haze the new girl. She knew they only invited her golfing because of the political situation with the position opening up, and she only accepted because she knew they weren't expecting that move. Right then and there, she swore if she was selected as CEO she would open up a sewing circle or menstruation club or something else that traditionally the males didn't attend and ask the men to come.

"The script needed some adjusting, it's not unusual," she said. Out of the corner of her eye she saw Ryder's jaw tighten. Dare she admit she liked his protective side?

Fine, she would just come right out and say it, well actually think it. She liked him being all protective, but also appreciated he didn't say anything.

"Right, how's your timing with Erin Fulton's pregnancy? Dane hadn't let up. "I know that was a concern."

"We're fine and working around her changing figure. Ryder and Logan are good at camouflaging her." Trying to talk with the bag in tow was becoming increasingly hard. Of course, this conversation wasn't helping, especially since he already knew the answers to everything he asked. She decided to call his bluff. "I would be more than happy to not only show you the shooting schedule, but also show you some of the shots so you can see Erin's condition is in no way affecting the quality of the movie."

"I may take you up on that." Dane lobbed it right back to her.

"I think you should. You can take in how well everything runs now that we got rid of the rock in our millstone." She threw it back in his court and wished they were playing tennis instead, not that she knew how to play that game either. Maybe Ryder could play.

Finally, they made it to their respective balls. Thankfully, Ryder's was ahead of the rest and it gave her a moment to put the bag down. Between the interrogation and the weight of the game, literally and figuratively, she was out of breath by the time they stopped.

Ryder chose a club. "Which one of those assholes would you like me to beat up first?"

"I think they're just hazing me." Though part of her wanted Ryder to beat them up, she had to remember who she was, why she was here. While Ryder did the golf thing, she continued her research thing.

"One of them is going to end up with this up their ass." He took a couple of practice swings. "No one treats the woman I'm going to marry like that."

Though every fiber in her being wanted to ask how they went from discussing getting married to being engaged without him asking her, she refrained. Golfing, business and life decisions didn't mix.

Once again, everyone made their shots. All the men congregated and she lifted the bag, swearing she was going to have to go to a chiropractor after all this.

"So, when do you think the wedding will be?" Albert seemed to ask the question a bit louder than necessary.

"As I said before, nothing is official yet." She treated every question as a shot at her and prepared herself accordingly.

"It's an exciting time," Albert said. "I remember when Melinda and I got married, she was caught up for months with wedding plans and then the wedding, and of course we got pregnant right away." Albert strolled along.

His seemingly sweet and innocent remark was laced with corporate politics. A quick glance over at Ryder told her she wasn't off the mark. He caught her eye and gave her a slight shake of his head.

The fire within her raged. "Well, you must not be the best at multitasking then." She practically dragged the bag to catch up to him.

Brows furrowed, Albert looked over at her. "There's a line between multitasking and doing too much."

"Do you know where that line is?" She took on a purposely innocent tone.

Without speaking, Albert continued to stare at her.

"Oh, then you must have never overworked yourself." Wishing she could high-five someone, she chose to drag her bag along. When she almost tripped, she handed the bag to Ryder.

"Caddies carry the bags." Dane's tone teased her.

"Yes Dane, caddies carry the bags, but CEOs know when to get a team to help them with their work." She held up her hand and, as she predicted, all the men turned to her. "I'm not afraid to carry the bag, but there are ways to distribute the load. For instance, after a quick search of your past golf records, I now know you usually have a golf cart carry the weight for you. Gotta love technology."

With a nod and a bit of a grin, George went to his ball.

Dane gave her an extended look and did the same.

"There is something to be said for earning your spot." Albert walked away.

"I couldn't agree more." For a moment she watched Albert. If this were her call, who would she choose? The sure thing, the rock, the man who had the experience? Or the renegade who did things her own way, down to bringing her superstar man to a business function?

"So when are we doing this?" Ryder chose a club and bent down to line up his shot.

"What?" She stood by his side. All she saw was a lot of green with a little flag way off in the distance. The goal.

"Getting hitched." He stood and got in position.

"Nothing is official." Right now, her whole life seemed to be centered on little flags that were way off in the distance and too hard to reach.

HOLLYWOOD STARDOM

FADE IN:

INT. LOS ANGELES – GRIFFITH PARK OBSERVATORY –
NIGHT

CHARLES and ROXY walk through the observatory.

CHARLES stops in front of the huge model of the
solar system.

                    CHARLES
          And over here we have the
          solar system. Did anyone
          ever tell you it takes
          almost thirty earth years
          for Saturn to orbit the
          sun?

                    ROXY
          (leans into him)
          I have been told that once
          or twice from a very wise
          astronomer.

                    CHARLES
          Perhaps we should take a
          closer look at our favorite
          ringed planet.

ROXY lets go of him and looks up at the model.

                    ROXY
          (Points up to the model)
          There's something hanging
          from the rings.

                    CHARLES
          Really? Let me take a look.
          (Comes and stands by her
          side)

CHARLES climbs up on the railings and pulls down
a little string with a diamond ring at the end
of it.

                    CHARLES
               Whoever knew the ringed
               planet made rings?
               (He holds the ring out to
               her.)

ROXY puts her hand over her mouth. CHARLES gets
on one knee and holds the ring out to her.

                    CHARLES
               Marry me.

                    ROXY
               All right.
               (Stares down at the ring.)

Chapter Twenty-Eight

ONLY BECAUSE RYDER called and didn't text did Cora stop in the lobby of her building and answer the phone.

Since the day of the golf game, she had to admit she was in her own self-imposed purgatory. Her whole life was nothing but one big wait. Waiting for news on the CEO position. Waiting for the movie to wrap. Waiting for Ryder to—

She stopped dead in her tracks, causing Rodger to collide with her. Still, she managed to catch herself on the huge table with the gigantic flower arrangement and answer the phone. "This is Cora."

"This is Ryder." He chuckled through her phone.

Everything about the man was adorable, but she was still irritated. He couldn't say they were engaged and then not mention it again like the words weren't out there. While she wanted to say something, she couldn't bring herself to act. Part of being a good business person was knowing when to hold back.

Unfortunately, her heart didn't understand business all too well.

Her heart needed to go take a class and learn to toughen up. "So my caller ID said." There it was, her tough as nails attitude. "What do you need?"

"You." He answered fast.

Do not smile. She shifted her foot from one leg to the other. "Anything else?"

"Will you be at the office for a while?" His voice was a little too cheery.

"Yes, we discussed that this morning. I'll be at the set later." She took to tapping her foot. At this point, she would take a formal proposal over the phone. "Why?" There she opened the door up for him, left it wide open. Hell, she would even step aside so he had a smooth entrance.

"I'm trying to plan my day."

No doubt, she detected a teasing tone. "Well, then there you have it. Is there anything else?"

"Got it. Love you." He hung up.

"Cora."

Rodger's voice interrupted her staring at the screen waiting for anything to happen with Ryder.

"You know, I didn't even want to get married." She spun around and faced her secretary. "I am probably the only woman in the world who didn't enter into a relationship with Ryder Scott with wedding bells in my eyes, in fact, he was the one who brought it up."

The man nodded.

"You know, you can't just dangle the marriage carrot down to telling people you are my fiancé and then not finish." Frustration getting the best of her, she stomped her foot. "Now I'm a time bomb, do you hear me? A time bomb. Anytime he looks at me I think he's going to get down on one knee and propose, but no, instead all he's done is ask a series of dumb questions. Yesterday he asked me if I wanted a drink of water!"

"The cad." Rodger pursed his lips.

She frowned. "I never even thought about marrying him."

"Well, according to every website, including your own, you have not only thought about it, but accepted his proposal, with everything from a ten-carat diamond he dug out of a mine for you, to something he got out of a gum machine." He lifted his tablet to her.

The story of Ryder's proposal was strewn across the page. Sick, heated nausea coursed through her. "What happened to the sex shots?" She gasped for air. "I can't breathe."

"You can or you wouldn't be able to talk." Rodger put a hand on her shoulder. "Lean forward and take deep breaths."

"I think I'm dying." She stared at the marble floor, the lines seemed to move with her. "I think I'm dying, or I'm going to kill Ryder."

"Keep breathing." Rodger patted her back.

In an effort to not pass out, she listened to him, braced herself on her knees and inhaled. Out of the corner of her eye, she swore she something move. A person dressed in all black with blonde hair. "Rodger!" She shot up and pointed in the direction where she saw the intruder. "Someone's there."

Without hesitation, Rodger ran in the direction of the intruder.

Heart racing, knees week, with trembling hands she lifted her phone to call 911.

"It's all right." Putting his gun away, Rodger came around the corner with the security guard behind him.

"Miss Caine, I'm sorry if I startled you." The guard bowed his head, but he wasn't blond, he was grey.

"Are you sure there was no one else?" She glanced at Rodger.

"Not that I saw. Why?" Rodger buttoned his suit jacket.

She shrugged. Maybe she was wrong. "I'm sorry I overreacted."

Once more, her phone rang and without looking, she hit the button and lifted the device to her ear. "Ryder." She needed to call him and tell him what she saw. He needed to tell her it would be easy to mistake grey and blond hair, especially in such a quick flash.

"Congratulations!" Her mother's voice stabbed her right through her ear.

No, no, no, no. "I take it you saw the story on the Internet." Cora said and put her hand over her eyes.

"He's quite the catch. Reel him in good, wrap him up in twine, and make sure you take very good care of him." Her mother made a purring sound.

This whole thing was starting to make Cora's head throb.

"Since it seems as if my costume did the trick to make the superstar put a ring on it, I'm having some little toys delivered as an engagement present. Use the blindfold and handcuffs wisely, my daughter, and you will have a happy man." The woman cackled.

Dare she tell the woman the outfit nearly had the opposite effect? No, that would only make this conversation longer. "Mother, I need to go."

"I want to be involved in the wedding, so let's talk when the whirlwind dies down." Her mother made a kiss noise into the phone and hung up.

"Blindfolds?" Mouth half open, she faced Rodger once more. "My mother is sending me a blindfolds as an engagement gift. Does anyone really like that or is it just a fad?"

Rodger smoothed down the lapels of his suit jacket. "People do like it."

As she considered his words she bit her lip. "Don't people want to see what's going on?"

"Well, I do." Rodger's voice came out low and powerful.

Really? Intrigued, she tilted her head and opened her mouth.

He held his hand up, stopping her. "Don't we have to get to the office?"

"You know, you brought me condoms. In part, this whole thing is your fault." No sooner had she said the words, than her phone rang once more. Maybe Ryder finally saw the news.

Not one to make the same mistake twice, this time she glanced at the number, cursed the fact it wasn't her sort of betrothed, and answered. "Logan?" Along with her head pounding, now her chest tightened.

"Are congratulations in order?" he asked.

Of anyone besides Ryder who would understand, it would be Logan. "I think the tabloids may have gotten ahead of themselves." Damn she wanted to say yes, let the congratulations start. No she didn't, she didn't even want to marry him, she might love him, but he made her crazy. Who was she kidding? She wanted to marry him, but could she?

"I understand," he said. "I was only wondering because he hasn't shown up on the set yet and we sort of need him."

Though she wasn't looking at herself in a mirror, she felt the color drain out of her face. "What?" Was that why he didn't call Logan? Was he on the way to the set and something happened? "What do you mean he's not there?"

Before Logan had the chance to answer her nonsensical question, her phone beeped indicating another call. "Hold on!" Instantly she clicked over.

"Cora." Viktor said her name in the way that let her know something was serious.

"Oh my god, what is it?" She sank to her knees.

"I take it you've already seen the tabloids," Viktor said.

"Viktor, what's wrong?" Hated tears stung her eyes. Only minutes before, she swore she saw someone stalking her. What if they got to Ryder? What if there was more than one?

"You got an email from Stargazer saying congratulations and to focus on reaching for the stars." His tone came out flat.

The shaking that took over her body caused her to drop her phone.

"Cora?" Rodger rushed to her side.

"I swear I'm being followed and there's another email from that stargazer." She turned to Rodger and grabbed the lapel of his jacket. "Now Ryder's missing, he didn't show up on set!"

Rodger didn't move. No, he didn't do anything, only stared at her. The situation was dire enough that even Mr. Magic himself couldn't fix this with his incredible briefcase and gadgets.

"Where's Ryder?" she asked. There was no algorithm to deal with this one.

"Right here!"

At Ryder's voice echoing through the building lobby, she stood with just enough time to watch him dash through the space, and in a move only he could pull off, slid down on his knees and skidded to a stop in front of her. "Cora." He took her hand and slipped something metal into her palm. "I really love you. That crazy love that makes me forget my name, forget my lines, forget everything I ever was before you."

With everything else that happened that morning, she could only conjure the strength to stare at him and try to listen to his words. What was going on?

"I wanted to get you a ring, but then I thought that we should do that together. I had to give you a token only I could give you." He turned her hand over revealing a key then reached into his jacket pocket and handed her an envelope. "I would have asked you sooner, but it took me a couple of days to figure out how to complete the paperwork. Just like my grandfather gave my grandmother the cabin, I want to stay with tradition and give it to you. I want us to have our history there, our kids, our life, I want to give you our sanctuary."

"The cabin?" Her gaze darted between the key and his glorious face.

"Will you marry me?" He put his hand over hers.

Here it was, here was the moment. The perfect moment on every count. Not only had he told her he had been working on this for several days, which meant he wanted to ask before the story in tabloids, but when she thought for those brief few seconds he was missing, her thoughts hadn't gone to another woman or to something bad, but to his wellbeing. The fact he gave her his most prized possession said everything he felt about her. Above all else, the second he showed, she felt safe. She loved him, she trusted him, she wanted him, and he protected her. "You are the one, of course I'll marry you." Yes, she wanted to marry him.

A smile graced that face, the face of her future husband, and he stood and took her into his arms. "I love you, baby."

"I love you." No sooner had she said the words before he connected their mouths. She just signed up to be the wife of a superstar. In many ways she would be stargazing the rest of her life. She only hoped they continued to soar in the heavens and never crashed down to earth.

FADE IN:

INT. LOS ANGELES - COFFEE SHOP - DAY

ROXY sits in the coffee shop staring into a cup
of coffee. WILLIAM enters the shop, looks
around and joins her.

                    WILLIAM
              (pulls off his sunglasses
              and sits down)
               What's going on?

ROXY Holds out her hand and shows him the ring.

                    WILLIAM
              (Nods at the ring)
               I heard you got engaged.
               Why do I feel like I'm not
               supposed to say
               congratulations?

                    ROXY
               Is this right?

                    WILLIAM
               Don't you ask these types
               of questions to Charles and
               not me?

                    ROXY
               Exactly. What happens if I
               lose my best friend?

                    WILLIAM
               The day you fall in love
               you don't lose a best
               friend, you gain a partner.

                    ROXY
               That sounds like one of
               your songs.
              (Shakes her head)

CAMERA PANS DOWN TO THE RING ON HIS FINGER.

                    ROXY
              Was it like that for you?

                    WILLIAM
              When you know, you know.

ROXY looks at him.

                    WILLIAM
              Have you talked to STEVEN
              about it?

                    ROXY
              I haven't seen STEVEN since
              college. I just watch his
              movies. What does he have
              to do with anything?

                    WILLIAM
              (Pushes up from the table)
               I'm just asking.
              (He leans down and kisses
              the top of her head.)
               When you know you know.

                    ROXY
              (Watches William leave and
              she gazes down at her ring
              finger)
               I don't know.

Chapter Twenty-Nine

"SO TONIGHT, THE FUTURE Ms. Scott and I will be attending a function to support the indigenous wildlife in the rainforest." Ryder held out his hand to Cora and helped his fiancée out of the car. Dressed in a skin tight ruby red evening gown with a plunging neckline, his soon to be wife looked positively ravishing with a side of scrumptious for good measure. He kissed the fourth finger of her left hand. "I think I really need to put a ring on this."

"I have this though." A gorgeous blush gracing her cheeks, she lifted the key to the cabin she strung on a long gold chain and put around her neck. She let it fall and the key disappeared into her cleavage.

"While the key has never been happier, I think something more traditional may be in order." He gave her hand another kiss. "However, tonight we need to tend to our cause. Apparently, the power couple that will be Mr. and Mrs. Scott like animals."

She curled her arm around his and let him guide her inside the hotel.

As they wound their way toward the ballroom, he glanced over at her. Thus far she hadn't touched a door handle, she waited for him, and she kept her head held high with a huge smile. Only last night when they went to dinner, she kept her head down and in his shoulder, a perfectly appropriate move for some private time, and she recognized tonight was different. His wonder woman learned her lessons about being in the public eye, and it couldn't happen at a better time. With their engagement announced and their wedding on the horizon, media attention would only get worse.

He handed the man at the entrance their invitation and they made their way inside, and over to the table. *Hollywood Stardom* would wrap within the next two weeks and he would have to start right in on his movie. With Cora involved, things should run much smoother, and once he was sure everything was headed down the right path, he would have them set a date.

"Here you go, baby." He pulled a chair out for Cora.

In an advanced move, she nodded at the other people around the table as she sat.

"How about I go get us a couple of glasses of wine?" He leaned down and kissed her ear. Around the room he spied some people lifting their cameras and taking pictures and dare he say, his Cora was actually tilting her head toward the light? Apparently, engagement agreed with her.

"That would be great." She gave his hand a squeeze.

Right before he went to get the fortification, a familiar yet unwanted person approached in the form of the asshole who was up against Cora for her big position. "Cora." Ryder tapped her shoulder.

The second Cora saw the intruder coming toward them, she undid all his hard work and stood up from the table. "Albert."

"I hear congratulations are officially in order." The jerk first shook Cora's hand, then his.

Ryder put his arm around Cora and reminded himself he still needed to ask if Rodger carried cleaning wipes. Albert seemed oily through and through.

"My wife asked if I may get your fiancé's autograph." Albert pointed over at a table across the room and held up his invitation.

"You'll have to ask my fiancé." Cora's voice came out laced with a bit of mischief, and she looked up backward at him.

Though he assumed with the whole love thing and getting married thing their arrangement was officially over, as the future husband it was his duty to ensure Cora always looked stellar. They were truly a part of each other now. "Of course." He took the man's invitation and signed it with one of the pens he always kept on him.

"My wife was hoping she could see your ring later." Albert's focus traveled down to Cora's hand.

"She can see my key." Like earlier, Cora pulled the key out of one of Ryder's favorite place on earth or in the universe. "Ryder gave me his family cabin as an engagement present. It's a tradition."

Albert raised his eyebrows. "It won't be long now until the new CEO is announced. I suppose I will wish you luck."

"I don't think luck is part of this." Cora nodded.

"Then I'll say may the best man or woman win." Albert put the paper back in his tuxedo jacket, gave them a slight bow and left.

Cora gave Ryder the side glance.

"I'm going to go get that wine." Yes, he could take cues with the best of the best.

"You're going to make an excellent husband." Once more, she took her seat.

Head held high, he walked across the ballroom to the bar. "Two red wines, please." Before he the drinks arrived, someone tapped his shoulder and he turned.

"I'm sorry to bother you, Mr. Scott." An older woman in a gold beaded gown smiled at him.

He went to get his pen ready.

"I heard you would be personally accepting donations for your wonderful charity here. My husband and I wanted to make sure you had this." She pulled a check out of her matching handbag and handed it to him. "Our address is on the check, please send us the receipt."

Wait. She heard about him accepting donations? A quick peek over at Cora found her showing her key to some people at the table. He took the check and quickly tucked it in his pocket. It was all he needed in front of Cora. "Thank you. It will go to good use."

After another autograph on another invitation, she patted his shoulder, took her drinks and walked away.

At last, he retrieved his drinks and began walking back to his lady, only to be stopped by another couple. A huge older man held up a folded piece of paper. "My wife is a huge fan of your work and of your charity." Without even asking for permission, the man put the check in his pocket.

"Thank you." Drinks still in hand, Ryder hoped these people didn't ask for an autograph.

"May I get a picture?" The wife clapped.

Since these people paid, he nodded.

The woman handed her husband her phone and came up next to Ryder. He put on his signature smile while the man took a few shots.

"Oh, everyone at the club will be absolutely envious." She gave him a slight hug and the couple walked away.

Unsure what Cora had seen, he tensed as he made his way back to her. He set down the wine glasses and took his seat.

"That was quite an expedition." She turned her attention to her wine glass.

"But it all leads back to you." In hopes of deflecting any questions, he lifted his glass and tapped it against hers.

"Just remember that twenty years from now." She sipped her wine.

"Hundred years." Bullet dodged, with a deep breath and a grin he sat back and put his arm around Cora.

"Mr. Scott." A lady across the table waved at him.

He scooted up in his seat and got ready to have another invitation thrust at him for an autograph.

"Here is a check for your charity." The woman stood and went to his side. "I'm one of the chairwomen here, and I'd love to set something up to promote your cause. If you want to have my people call your people we could set something up for Ryder's Rescue."

As if in slow motion, his hand took the check. The amount alone would cover a couple of different rings for Cora, which would have been perfect had Cora not been sitting by his side.

"Ryder's Rescue?" Cora put her glass of wine down.

He folded the check and put it in his breast pocket with the other one and tried to figure out how exactly to answer the question without making either of them appear foolish.

"I just love helping new charities." Checkbook in hand, a round younger woman hopped up out of her seat. She wrote a check and thrust it at him.

In a scene fit for a movie, he was suddenly surrounded by no less than six people handing him checks and discussing Ryder's Rescue. It would have been so much better if he could breathe and talk to Cora.

"I heard about you rescuing a dog. You're such a good person Ryder." Another lady with copious breasts thrust more than a check into his face.

At Cora clearing her throat, he had a feeling he needed to clear the air. In fact, he could use some air, it was getting rather hot in here, and he tugged at his bow tie.

"We can all take a picture with him. His coordinator said he would be signing autographs and personally accepting checks." The chairlady leaned down, put her arm around him and leaned over to Cora. "You don't mind sharing him for a few minutes, do you?"

"Actually, if you ladies let me have him for one second to discuss a little detail, then I promise he's all yours." Cora stood.

On automatic he stood. Being the gracious check collector, he bowed to his audience and followed his future wife.

They went to one of the far corner of the ballroom, and with a smile on her face, she stared at him.

He grinned. "You know, you really got rid of that resting bitch face thing you had when we first started going out."

Smile still intact, she narrowed her eyes.

"Did you have something to say?" Her intense gaze caused him to shove his hands in his pockets and shift his weight from one foot to the other.

"I'm waiting for you." The smile never wavering, she tilted her head.

He had to let it out. "The day I rescued Spike, the words about a charity just fell out of my mouth, and suddenly I had all this money being thrust at me, and then I had this booming little side business. But don't worry, one of my buddies is helping manage it, and we give receipts. We even have tote bags." There he let it out, now they could go get a ring for every finger.

She blinked and took such a deep breath that her glorious chest heaved up and down. "You do know that a charity is not a booming little business, right?"

He sort of shrugged.

"Why didn't you tell me?"

Honestly, he was amazed she could keep that smile. Maybe there was a little actress in her after all. Since truth was on the table, he decided to go with it. "Yes, I know that, and that is why I chose to withhold that information from you at that time."

"Is there anything else you are withholding from me at this time?" The smile waivered.

Here was his chance, he could guide her out of the room and tell her about his issues with the mob. Hand balled in a fist, he willed himself to let it out.

No, he couldn't. Couldn't take the chance it would hurt Cora's running for the position. In this case, what she didn't know wouldn't hurt her. He only had to figure out how to deal with the producer situation, but they would be married by then and have to work it out. "Only that I love you more than anything."

"You're exasperating." She laughed and put her hand to her chest. "You know this whole time I thought there was some deep dark secret you held, and now I know it was the fact you opened up an illegal charity."

Lord help him, she could never know about Glen. He had even avoided Glen since his engagement. "Will you fix it?"

"You're not in charge of any more money." She put his hand to his cheek. "Give everything to Viktor tomorrow and we'll clean up your mess."

"I love you." He kissed her palm. Another disaster diverted. They said three times was the charm so maybe this whole thing boded well for him in the future.

No sooner did he go in for the kiss, than she tensed and the color drained out of her face.

"Ryder." She gasped and pointed. "That's him!"

"What?" He spun around.

"I'm done with this!" She shoved him aside and went running for the door.

Commotion broke out in the ballroom and he turned. "Please give us a moment." He held his hand out. No doubt all over the tabloids tomorrow would be a story of their breakup. He had to fix this, and he ran out of the ballroom into a scene fit for one of his worst nightmares.

There stood Ben, Cora and, worst of all, Glen. He should have told her when he had the chance. Something told him he was in the for the worst flop of his career, or worse yet, a tragedy.

So much for his perfect timing.

"STOP!" Heart racing and every muscle shaking, Cora caught up to the blond man. "Stop!"

The man stopped and held up his hands as if he were under arrest. "Cora."

"You know my name!" She pointed at him. This was the man, the man she saw the day Ryder proposed to her. The man who had been stalking her and she wasn't going to be the victim, she was going to deal with him head on. "I'm going to have you arrested."

"Wait." He took a step back.

"Ma'am, is something wrong?" An older man came to her side.

Refusing to let this criminal get away, she continued, "This man's been following me. He sent me emails, he attacked me." Throat dry, she grabbed on to the man's arm and bent forward in an attempt to catch her breath.

"Cora!" Ryder yelled to her.

"Ryder!" She practically pushed the kind man over and rushed to her fiancé. "This is the man who I saw." She pointed to the blond man. "We need to call the police." With her whole body vibrating from her shaking she dropped her handbag.

"It's okay, baby." Ryder took her into his arms.

Why wasn't he reacting? Beating the man up, calling someone? Why did the other man simply continue to stand there? Something was wrong. Something beyond finding her stalker.

"Boss, I'm sorry. I was just doing my job." The blond shook his head.

Boss? She pushed Ryder back and stared in the space between the two men. "What job?"

"Cora." Ryder whispered, but didn't look her in the eye.

The way he said her name sounded like an apology. Her chest tightened and she stepped back. "Please tell me this has to do with your charity."

"I'm Ben, I run Ryder's Rescue." The blond put a sick smile on his face.

"Is that why you're here?" The backs of her eyes heated, but in no universe would she shed a tear not in front of these people.

The blond glanced over at Ryder, then back at her and shook his head.

"He's a friend of mine. I hired him to watch you," Ryder blurted.

"Why didn't you tell me?" There was something more. Ryder might be a trained actor, but she was a professional through and through and when information was withheld, there was a damn good reason.

Ryder jutted his chin out. "I knew you'd say no."

"That's not true." She crossed her arms. Her heart beat hard enough to wrack her whole body.

"I had to protect you." Ryder's quick glance at the other man who simply stood there told her there was so much more to the story and none of it good.

"From me, no doubt," the other man finally spoke. "But I think what your fiancé is neglecting to tell you is that in this case he brought everything on himself," he said, as if filling in the blanks. "Allow me to introduce myself, I'm Glen, Ryder's business partner." He held his hand out.

"Don't touch her." Ryder took her by the shoulders and pulled her back.

At the man's cryptic words, she shrugged Ryder away and shook her head.

"I'm only introducing myself." Glen's smooth words were definitely laced with something sinister. "I had to meet the woman who finally stole your heart. Now with a wedding on the way, and lord knows what other delays, I had to protect my investment."

"Glen, not now." Ryder tried to step in front of her, but she stopped him.

"What investment?" She faced the man head on. Her instinct told her he would be the only one who would offer some semblance of the truth.

"Ryder's movie, of course." The man stared her right in the eye.

Her breath came in short gasps and she turned to Ryder. "Our movie?"

"I think you mean my movie." The man's voice reverberated behind her.

Ryder shut his eyes.

Once more, her business knowledge came into play and all the pieces lined up. "You backed his movie?"

"We more than backed it, we went into business together but unfortunately, Mr. Scott failed to deliver."

The man explained even though there wasn't any script needed to follow this plot line. Money. Always money. Even when she sold her business and said it was to make it grow, it wasn't that, it was for the money. "And the reason you haven't sued him?" Strange, how people asked questions, even though they knew the answers.

"In my line of work, we don't use courts and red tape. We have methods that are much more effective. You're a smart lady." Glen crossed his arms.

Ryder touched her shoulder. "Cora, let's go talk."

"We don't need to go anywhere." She thrust his hand off her. "When I asked you two minutes ago if there was anything else, the fact we weren't going to produce a movie together because you had sold yourself long ago never came to mind?" Somehow, she managed to keep herself together enough not to mention the words organized crime in public. Oh, she should have listened to her gut and not her heart.

"I wanted to do it with you." His voice shook.

"No, you didn't. You wanted me to bail you out. Make up for the money you spent, or lost, or used in some way. You didn't want to make a movie with me. The fact I thrust myself into role of producer only complicated your life." In hopes of finding an answer, she looked up to the ceiling. All that was there was a ceiling, a light fixture, probably a couple of cobwebs. No one ever did their job right.

"I complicated my own life." Ryder stomped to Glen. "Why are you here? I told you time and again I would make your movie. *Hollywood Stardom* is about to wrap, everything would be fine."

"And that is why you blatantly went against us and changed the title on the cabin?" Glen opened his suit jacket and pulled out a copy of the deed. "You knew what we wanted, and you betrayed us in every way."

Cora's breath caught. "The cabin." She pressed her hand to her chest. Just when she thought she figured it out, the puzzle pieces took on even more jagged edges.

"Yes, his family's cabin, the cabin you now own, and before your marriage I might add. How convenient." Glen narrowed his eyes at Ryder. "We only didn't burn it down because it's an icon."

"You bastard." Ryder inched closer to him.

Tears filled her eyes. Damn tears. She fought all her life and managed to keep them at bay except under the worst of circumstances. Ryder's engagement gift wasn't a gift, it was a way to ensure he kept what was his. Everything he did was an act. Everything. She pulled the key off her neck, the thin gold chain snapping.

"Cora, let's get out of here, and I'll explain everything." Ryder returned to her side.

"I don't need an explanation. I know everything." She shook her head and stared down at the key in her palm. What once represented her future, now painted a picture of her foolishness.

"No you don't." He took her by her shoulders and bent down. "I love you. I want to be with you forever."

"Why did you make me forget our roles?" She stared into his face, that goddamned beautiful face. Did every woman succumb like this? "For the first time in my life, I feel truly stupid."

"You're the smartest person in the world." He tightened his hold on her.

"No, I was smart when I wanted to keep you, and I was smart when I made our arrangement. I was dumb when I agreed to marry you." At realizing what she said, the tears finally escaped and rolled down her cheeks.

"What are you saying?" His skin turned the most unearthly shade of white.

"You don't really need me. Your producer role is filled." She let go of the key and her heart. They both fell to the floor. "I told you day one if you did anything to hurt my chances of becoming the CEO of Ultracom, our deal was over. I think this qualifies."

With the words out, she moved away, picked up her handbag and scanned the area. A crowd had gathered in the hall, including Albert. She always knew she shouldn't go to these charity events. In less than evening, she lost her love and her position. Would Chargge be next? "Go to a hotel tonight, you still have my credit card." She faced Glen. "Was it you? Did you follow me? You or your people?"

"I give you my word, it was not." Glen gave her a slight bow.

With a nod, she glanced at Ryder one last time and head held high, walked down the hallway. As Ryder taught her, one never knew who was watching. Without a doubt, they would be trending tomorrow. No musical had a song for this moment.

RYDER BENT DOWN and picked up the key to his cabin then looked down the hallway. On one side was the public, the other his love. She didn't get to walk away. Not like this.

His straightened up, but before he got the chance to run, Glen stopped him.

"I'm assuming there'll be no more distractions." The man stared him down. "We have enough collateral to last until the end of your latest film."

"Get away from me." Ryder shoved the man aside and, not caring about appearances, took off with Ben in tow.

"Boss, what can I do?" Ben ran alongside him.

He shook his head, only increased his speed through the hotel lobby and out to the front with just enough time to catch Cora slipping into the car. "Cora!"

Without even a glance in his direction, she shut the door.

Unwilling to accept this, he dashed over to the car and hit the window, only getting a glimpse of her silhouette. "Cora!"

Instead of the window rolling down or any hopeful sign from her, the car sped away. He stood in the middle of the valet parking at the hotel and watched the lights vanish.

In truth, he wasn't sure how long he stared, praying the car would return, and he would get in the car and everything would work itself out. It could have been a second, a minute, several hours.

A car drove up alongside him. "Boss?"

He didn't move.

Ben got out of the car and went to his side. "Boss, there's a crowd, let's go."

Somewhere between the ballroom and this spot in the cold night air, he lost his heart. Though he felt like he wasn't moving, he let Ben get him in the vehicle and they left.

Ben took his cue and for quite a while, they simply drove around the city.

"I need you to take me home." Ryder squinted at the streetlights turning them into nothing but white streaks. What on earth had he done?

"Boss," Ben whispered.

"I said take me home!" With his outburst, Ryder hit the dash. "I need to go home to Cora. Once we talk, I can make it right. I'm going to get married."

As they turned around, his phone vibrated indicated a text. It had to be Cora. She wasn't the type to drive away like that. Maybe she returned to the hotel and found him gone. He fumbled as he retrieved the lifeline to love and found not a text from Cora, but Rodger.

Mr. Scott, inform me where you end up and I will have your clothes and other personal items delivered to you.

His breath caught and he typed back. *I want to go home. I have to talk to Cora.*

Cora has asked all correspondence go through me. The electronic locks have been changed. She asks that you do not create any sort of disturbance as there is already too much publicity. I am personally asking you not make this worse on her.

Seriously she was shutting him out? This was nothing they couldn't overcome. *Rodger please I have to see her, I can make it better.*

I am personally asking you not to make this worse on her. Just tell me what you need and I will bring it, Rodger responded.

I need Cora. Ryder hit send and tossed the phone aside. "I can't go home right now."

"Where to, boss?" Ben kept his voice low.

"I need some stuff."

No need for directions, Ben turned the car around once again, and they headed to the only square of the world that would truly be one hundred percent his.

They parked and he moved in slow motion, hoping and praying that any second he would get a second text or call.

Ben walked ahead of him and turned on the light illuminating the small hallway. "Boss."

As he made their way to his door, he stepped on something, nearly tripped and bent down, picking up the pen he took the first morning he spent at Cora's. "What is this doing here?"

Pen in hand, he moved forward only inches and picked up a ticket stub from his first movie, then a patch from one of his sci-fi costumes.

He followed the sick trail of breadcrumbs, collecting a button and one of his 8 x 10's before stopping at his piece of red carpet rolled neatly out for him.

The red carpet that led right into his storage facility.

His empty storage facility. "It's all gone." His body went numb. If he closed his eyes, he could still visualize each piece. How dumb was he anyway keeping those dumb pieces of the past? What was the point when he didn't have a future?

"Ryder." Ben rubbed his hand over his face. "What can I do?"

Was it only this morning he was making toast for Cora and sharing a shower with the woman he was going to marry after making love to her? It seemed like a really long time ago.

Except for the pen, he dropped the few artifacts he collected, and walked out. Every memory he had with Cora was laced with that underlying anxiety of having his deceptions and lies discovered at any moment. He stole from her, not money, but himself, their memories and their life. "I need to go."

"Where?" Ben opened the door to the car for him.

He had nowhere to go. Here he was the superstar, the one of the bunch who made it, and he had nowhere, nothing, nobody. Cora told him to go to a hotel, but he couldn't go anywhere without being spotted even in his best disguise. Any of his former quote unquote homes made him literally sick in the stomach. And no way would he have Cora's name attached to more of a story than what would already appear in tomorrow's media. With only one last place to go, he found his phone and the location, then tossed the device to his one friend.

Exactly like the day Cora sent Rodger with him to clean up his messes, he ended up back in Pasadena. Unfortunately, none of them were equipped to deal with the disaster he created.

"I'll wait to make sure you get in." Ben parked in the Fulton's driveway.

"You're a good friend. One day maybe I'll actually make good on one of my promises." He patted Ben on the shoulder, let himself out, went to the door, and knocked.

"Ryder?" Erin looked the peephole then opened the door. "What are you doing here? Why are you in a tuxedo?"

He scratched his nails through his scalp. "I need a place to be."

"What?" She backed up and let him inside.

Drew came over. "What's going on?"

He looked at the two of them standing side by side. For twenty years while Erin waited for Drew, she always said she felt like her heart was missing the second he drove away and now Ryder understood.

"Ryder." Erin pulled him closer. "What happened to you?"

"You know how in just about every movie the villain gets his comeuppance?" He shook his head and stared at his friend's ever-increasing baby bump. They were wrapping just in time. Soon she would be too large to camouflage.

"Yes, what does that have to do with you?" Erin's voice rose her typical tone for concern and drama.

"Well, I got mine tonight." He didn't remember the last time a non-scripted genuine tear fell, and he turned his back to them.

HOLLYWOOD STARDOM

FADE IN:

INT. LOS ANGELES - GRIFFITH PARK OBSERVATORY - DAY

ROXY is waiting for CHARLES to finish up work.

CAMERA PANS to him in his office while ROXY walks around, looking up at the model of the solar system.

ROXY'S cell phone rings. She looks at the phone, glances over at CHARLES, and backs down one of the corridors before answering.

              ROXY
         (Puts her phone to her ear)
         Steven.

CUT TO STEVEN standing on location in Arizona.

              STEVEN
         A blast from the past.

            ROXY (O.S)
         Thank you for calling me
         back.

              STEVEN
              (Motions away one of
              the stagehands on set)
         Let me guess. You finally
         got up enough nerve to call
         me and ask me for a part.

CUT TO ROXY

              ROXY
         (Shuts her eyes)
         No, I know your wife is
         your muse.

                    STEVEN (O.S.)
          Strange how things work
          out. Charles called me.
          Congratulations.

                    ROXY
          Am I doing the right thing?

                    STEVEN (O.S.)
          If you have to ask, I would
          wonder.

                    ROXY
          (A tear travels down her
          cheek)
          You don't understand.

                    STEVEN (O.S.)
          He's the only one of us you
          haven't screwed over. Be
          careful.

The phone line goes dead.

ROXY walks back through the observatory and
waits for CHARLES.

Chapter Thirty

"CORA." Viktor tiptoed into her office and took his throne.

She sat up, smoothed her hair back, clicked off the auction site that had her enthralled for the last three hours, and took a sip of her cold brewed coffee.

Three days ago, she gave up trying to recreate the splendor that was Ryder's espresso and smashed the damn machine in her kitchen. Though she never picked up the pieces, the cleaning crew magically cleaned up any trace of the fallen appliance. Somehow, along the way Ryder's clothes vanished out of her closet and his toiletries out of her bathroom. In fact, every trace of him was gone except for the Ryder Scott memorabilia that continued to show up to her home. Rather than open the boxes, she just let them pile up in the dining room. There was plenty of room now without the broken espresso maker littering the floor.

"Cora," Viktor repeated.

"You know, I thought the emails would stop once the world found out Ryder and I..." She couldn't say the words. Instead, she picked up Spike and turned her chair toward the window. The email came from the same Stargazer and simply said it looked like her stargazing days were over. "I don't even care anymore." So much for living her life in the public eye. All it got her was a broken heart and a stalker no one could find.

"We need to care," Viktor whispered.

"It will go away just like everything else." She clicked over to Chargge. Even her own website covered the story of her and Ryder's last evening in painstaking detail. Pictures of her and Ryder and that mafia man littered every homepage, most even questioning why they were standing with someone who had a questionable background. The worst images were the ones of her walking away, Ryder chasing after her, and then running up to the car.

"We sent out the traditional celebrity statement about allowing you privacy during this difficult time, but the media is still hounding us for something." Viktor kept his voice low. "But it may be time to say something."

"Tell the media I bought and paid for something, and when it didn't fit, I had to return it." She stared into nothing.

After a knock at the door, Rodger entered.

Out of the corner of her eye, she saw Viktor and Rodger glance at each other and shake their heads, their code for the fact she still hadn't snapped out her funk.

"I have something for you." Rodger approached and straightened out a few things on her desk. "It's something you want." He pulled an envelope out of his jacket and waved it in front of her.

Unless Rodger produced an organized crime free Ryder out of his briefcase of tricks, she wanted for nothing, and she shrugged.

"In this envelope I have the all the information you need to decimate your competition and ensure your spot as CEO of Ultracom." He placed the envelope in front of her.

"What do you mean?" She turned toward her desk and lifted the envelope.

Viktor sat up.

"Exactly what I said. All you need to do is look, and you'll get all your answers. This information is all you need." He stared into her eyes.

For the first time since she left Ryder, her heart raced, a much better sensation than allowing the poor organ to sit there and shrivel up. Without even thinking, she reached for it, then stopped, but she still held on. What could it be?

"It's so easy, isn't it?" Rodger slapped his hand down on top of the envelope. "It's so easy when the carrot is dangled right in front of you, right? Who would know?"

As if the paper were on fire, she let go and held her hand back. "Rodger?" She knew what he was doing. He was comparing her situation to Ryder's, and it wouldn't work. She never put anyone in danger, she never traveled down that path, she did it right.

With a sigh, she leaned back in her chair. Did she? It was all too easy to succumb. "Since when did you become the advocate for Ryder?"

"This has nothing to do with Ryder." Viktor stood and pointed down at the information. "We need to see that."

"I don't know. He is everything I despise, but there's something there, something you need." Rodger slid his hand away.

Tears made her eyes blurry. She wanted her life back. The one where she traipsed through Ryder's trailer like she owned it, the one where the man she loved called her the smartest woman in the world, but then said that made him smart because everything had to lead back to him, the life that had some spark, even if they were just sharing a steak in bed watching old musicals. Hell, she wanted to hear Ryder sing, even if he thought he couldn't carry a tune. "He lied to me."

Viktor swiped up the envelope and tore it open. "He's scum."

"I know, and it was a big one." Rodger sat in the chair across from her desk. "You won't find anything in there except the ending to *Hollywood Stardom*." I know they're shooting the end tomorrow, but I'll go on record that I got you the end before it shot. Madeline didn't finish it until last night."

"You could have shown me then. I wasn't sleeping." The other night she fell asleep from pure exhaustion, but it didn't last long. Then housekeeping found where she was hiding Ryder's pillow and washed it. That was the end of the scant sleep she got since Ryder left, or she left Ryder, or whatever. Either way, her world ended that night.

Viktor held the envelope out to her right as the intercom on her desk buzzed.

She barely had to give Rodger a glance before he jumped up and hit the button. "Miss Caine's office."

Miss Caine. For the first time she cursed her own name. Already she had been referring to herself as Mrs. Scott in her mind, no hyphen as Ryder wanted.

"Mr. McAllister's office on the phone." The girl's voice imparting this information screeched through Cora's skull.

Cora motioned forward.

"Put them through." Rodger kept the call on the speaker. "This is Rodger, may I help you?"

"This is Debra from George McAllister's office. We'd like Miss Caine to come to the office for an unofficial informal meeting regarding the CEO position this afternoon. Lunch will be served."

Viktor nodded. She shrugged, took the envelope from the man she considered her brother and turned away again.

"She will be there, thank you." Rodger hung up.

"Let's get going!" Viktor yelled.

"No doubt my indiscretions and my association with those on the fringe of society has made this decision quite easy." She stared out the window wondering what Ryder was doing. Somehow, she had to get her life together. She glanced at the envelope. Inside was the information the world wanted to know. Unfortunately, she knew her own ending.

"Cora, if nothing else, you have to hold you head high and see this through." Rodger took Spike from her. Even her poor dog seemed more dour than usual. They both were sort of lost without the leader of their pack.

She stood, put on her suit jacket, grabbed her handbag and kept a death grip on the envelope. "Everyone in the car, this will be a working drive."

With Rodger leading the way, they hurried to the car. "What do we need to do?"

Once settled and on the road, she took out her phone and read a list she created one night when she couldn't sleep. It was finally time to face it. With this meeting, everything would have closure. "The car."

"I already have three offers on it. Do you want to sell it?" Viktor asked from the back seat.

"I think we should donate it." Maybe that would turn the karma around. Again, she glanced down at the envelope. Would knowing the end give her any happiness? She sort of pictured her and Ryder lying in bed sneaking a peek, being one of only a handful of people who had the secret. He made her bad. "Pick an animal charity and see what you can make happen. Do it in Spike's name."

"All right, what else?" Viktor turned back at her from the front seat.

Unable to say the next words, she took a breath and cleared her throat.

Thankfully, Viktor took the cue. "Do you want me to shut off the cards and cancel his insurance?"

Their lives were completely intertwined. She leaned down and grabbed the bridge of her nose.

"Let's not do this now, we're right near the offices." Viktor reached over and patted the top of her head.

"I have one more thing on my list." Maybe Roxy would have the answers. She opened the envelope, but didn't take the paper out. Not saying the words wouldn't make it less true, just like not saying she still didn't love Ryder. "The cabin needs to go back in Ryder's name."

They pulled into the Ultracom lot.

"So much for a working car ride." She sat up straight and tried to collect herself. Everything barreled down to Ryder.

"One good thing, he showed your human side." Viktor got out of the car and opened the door for her. "Do you need to bring anything?"

She glanced between him, Rodger and Spike. "This is all I got." They went up to the office building and were ushered into a huge conference room.

In truth, she expected to be called into a closed door meeting with her and George, then after some good-natured mentoring about cavorting around with the Hollywood set and the mafia would be sent on her way. She stopped short upon seeing Albert and Dane with their respective assistants in the room as well.

After some quick greetings, they settled into an uncomfortable silence until the door at the far end of the room opened and George entered, flanked by two more men.

George motioned to the table. "Everyone sit."

Albert jockeyed for the seat nearest George, while she took the one furthest away.

"As you know, I'm going to be retiring, and it is no secret that the two of you are the candidates to take my position." George took a sip of his water.

With no emotion left and the envelope still in her clutches, she sat back and waited. Across the table, Albert practically bounced in his chair.

"Any corporation would be proud to have either of you helm their ship, but in speaking with the board and reviewing where we see the future of Ultracom, we have decided that Miss Caine will take my place." George stood and clapped.

Her breath left her. Did the man just name her CEO of Ultracom? Really?

"Yes," Viktor whispered.

Everyone around the room applauded, everyone except Albert, who turned to his assistant and whispered something.

George's assistants stood, opened a bottle of champagne, and began passing out the glasses, starting with her. After all she won, she was the boss, this was now her domain.

Once the champagne was distributed George held out his glass. "Cora, would you like to say a few words?"

Part of being a CEO was knowing how to speak on the fly, put her personal feelings aside, and get the job done. She pushed out of her chair and raised her glass. "George, you have always been a mentor to me, I'm honored and humbled by your decision."

"Here, here." George took a sip of the drink. "I am proud of you, Cora."

She tapped her glass against both Viktor's and Rodger's and took a taste of her drink, trying not to focus on the dry rather than sweet champagne. No one except Ryder would have known her preference anyway.

"You did it." Rodger gave her a hug.

"Go say something to your opponent." Ever the teacher, Viktor spoke softly in her ear.

As if moving in a dream, she crossed the room, making small talk here and there, and not really hearing the words she spoke. If she had her life back, she and Ryder would have gone out on the town tonight, or better yet, stayed in with their dog and their movies. Who was she kidding? She never needed to celebrate around Ryder, because her life with him was one huge after party, fun and exciting and full of love. She would never have that again.

At last, she went up to Albert. "You were more than a worthy opponent," she said.

"Time will tell if the right decision was made." Without toasting her, he gulped the champagne. "I have to say I'm surprised, especially after that little stunt the other night."

"I'd rather not talk about that." She stared into her glass.

"I guess there won't be any more stargazing for you. You'll be too busy anyway."

His words barreled toward her, hitting her right in the chest, and nearly knocking the wind out of her. Unsure if he was tipping his hat and waiting for her to make a scene or had simply slipped, she managed to channel the little she learned about acting and showed no reaction other than taking another sip of the bubbly drink. "It will be a challenge." She spun on her heel and caught Rodger's gaze.

He dashed toward her. "What is it?"

The man always knew.

"It's Albert. He's the one. You and Viktor get the proof." She handed him the envelope. "As for this, I'll find out on set." Cora had to see Roxy get her ending. Maybe then, she could let go.

FADE IN:

INT. LOS ANGELES – GRIFFITH PARK OBSERVATORY - DAY

CHARLES is in his office. He types into the computer, hits enter, then stands up.

                    CHARLES
          I'm done, and I'm all
          yours.

CHARLES grabs his keys and joins ROXY underneath the model of the solar system.

                    CHARLES
          Are you ready to go taste
          cake?

                    ROXY
          (Crosses her arms and looks
          up at the planets)
          Do you really want to marry
          me?

                    CHARLES
          What's wrong?
          (He walks over and puts his
          hands on her shoulders.)

                    ROXY
          I'm scared.

                    CHARLES
          Roxy.
          (He turns her)

                    ROXY
          (Tears are streaming down
          her cheeks.)
           You're the only man. The
           only man who stood by me,
           the only man who
           understands me, the only
           one who I didn't screw
           over.

                    CHARLES
          (Stares at her with wide
          eyes)
           What are you saying?

ROXY slips the ring off her finger and hands it
to him.

                    ROXY
           I can't marry you. I'm
           going to ruin everything.
          (Sobbing, she runs out.)

                    CHARLES
          (Closes his hand around the
          ring.)
           Catastrophe.

Chapter Thirty-One

"I HAVE CALLED THIS MEETING because I think we should discuss the final shoot." Logan said and pushed a plate of food in front of Ryder. More accurately, a plate of vegetables.

Pen in hand, Ryder sat at the table inside Wilson's bar and debated which alcoholic beverage he should indulge in this evening. He reached across the table, stabbed several pieces of Logan's flank steak, plopped it on his dish, and shoved one in his mouth.

Everyone there, Logan, Ivy, Drew and Erin stared at him while he chewed.

Just to prove his point, he picked up another slice with his fingers and put it in his mouth. After chewing with much gusto, he chased it down with a soda and swallowed. "You know I'm not a vegan."

Erin leaned over and pinched his arm. "I was wondering where that pot roast was from last night."

Not caring about the pain or keeping up his half-truths, he faced his friend. "I snuck down and ate it all then put the empty container back in the fridge. I then topped it off with a hunk of cheese, the chicken from the night before, and some chocolate." In truth, he didn't really feel all too well. Cora would have never let him eat all that or, at least, he would have had a way to work it off.

"What are you, the truth brigade?" Erin stomped in front of him. "Since coming to live in my home, I've found out that you used a body double in *Charmed by Love*, that you sometimes drink water right out of the tap, and that you wrote a movie, didn't offer any of us a part, didn't make it, and then screwed your fiancée over." At her outburst, she burst into tears and flung herself into Drew's arms.

"You know, you're pretty dreadful." Drew told Ryder as he patted his wife.

He shrugged. Yes, he was a ball of shit, he knew it. Maybe he should have thought about jumping on the brigade of truth before he lost the one for him. He got up and went to the bar, spying a bottle of Moscato, Cora's favorite. "What have I done?" He grabbed the edge of the bar. "Time does not heal all wounds. Whoever said that really did not have that big of a wound."

Logan came to his side. "If you are this bad, just think how bad Cora must be."

"That's making it much better, and I thank you for that image." Ryder went behind the bar and read the labels on the bottles of scotch. Of course, if he got shit-faced no one would be there to take a shower with him, and he still had to show up on set tomorrow. Getting shit-faced wouldn't even be worth it without Cora. "I can't even get drunk properly." If he wanted to get drunk, Cora would have made sure he did it right. She would have had an inebriation plan, not some willy-nilly fly-by-night run-of-the-mill drinking out of a bottle until he passed out, hoping he could get rid of the sinking feeling in his stomach for even a few hours.

In a sudden move, Logan took him by the shoulders and spun him around. "Listen to me." Logan got right up into his face.

Somehow Ryder found the strength to look him in the eyes.

"This is it." Logan tightened his hold on him. "This is the finale of the series, one people have waited over twenty years for. This is the sendoff to one of the most beloved movie franchises of all time. You have to pull it together and let Roxy get her happily ever after."

"I can't be in anyone's happily ever after. I'm a villain, I'm bad. In one of Cora's musicals I would've gotten thrown off a cliff or run out of town while people around me sing some glorious song about redemption." Between all the food, little sleep, and hardly being able to breathe, the need to vomit crept up on him.

"Then, instead of dragging your ass around like the loser you've become, why don't you redeem yourself and try to get her back?" Logan lowered his tone.

"Am I redeemable?" He shook his head. How could he be redeemable when he put his love in danger? Even now he wasn't sure what Glen and his men would do until they got what they wanted.

"Every villain is redeemable."

The men caught gazes. Logan was once the villain in public, but now they loved him, embraced him. All Ryder cared about was one person's embrace. "I did you wrong all those years ago, I'm sorry."

Logan rolled his eyes. "You don't need to redeem yourself with me."

"I don't know if I'm redeemable, but all I know is that nothing matters without her, not this movie, not my career, not my movie." He froze and stared at Logan. Nothing mattered.

Nothing.

Adrenaline coursed through him.

"Then do something heroic." Logan tilted his head.

No matter what, he had to protect Cora. Even if he never had her again, he had to make sure she stayed safe. "I need go somewhere real fast, it can't wait it has to be done before we shoot the end." He went to leave, but Logan held him in place.

"What about Cora?"

"I need to do this first, and then I need to show her what I can be. I'll be back." He pushed back from his friend and dashed out the back door to a waiting Ben.

"What's up, boss?" Ben started the car.

Ryder slipped inside and pulled out his phone, texting the one person who in a major twist could put him on the path to redemption. Upon receiving his instant answer, his heart seized, but he had to go through with it. "Please take me to the storage facility."

They drove in silence, and he took his opportunity to finally look at what he already knew was adorning all the media outlets about his failed engagement. The pictures alone made him want to throw up, and he didn't even want to think about Cora's reaction. He betrayed her in every way and, though he couldn't take back what he had done, he could at least ensure her safety.

After weaving through major traffic, Ben pulled up to their destination.

"Stay here, buddy." He got out of the car and went to his spot. His footsteps echoed in the empty space, a location that used to be crammed with memories.

"I hope you're not going to ask for your items back." Glen came up beside him. "It had to be done."

"No." He didn't look the man's way. "I asked for it."

"Your father taught you well." The man patted his shoulder. "You asked me here."

Before continuing, Ryder took one last look. In his memory everything was there, but the one thing he wanted most was missing.

Strange, once upon a time, the storage space encompassed his whole life. However, gazing into nothing but a black hole didn't really upset him as it should. He didn't really need all those artifacts. Actually, he didn't need anything, not the car or the clothes, or the roles, or the money.

"Yes, I did." At last, he faced the man he went to for help, his enemy and, in ways, the man who represented his conscious. In order even to exist in the same universe as the one he loved, even have a spark that maybe one day he could possibly earn her back, he had to cleanse himself entirely. A rebirth of sorts. "I asked you here because have something for you."

"Oh, really." Glen chuckled. "What might that be?"

He swallowed. "My movie."

Glen widened his eyes.

"Do you have the contract? I'm ready to sign my rights over." Heat took over his body. Part of him prayed the man had the paperwork, part of him wanted to delay it a bit longer.

Glen opened his suit jacket and produced the papers. "You always were smart. Do you need a pen?"

"No." Ryder took the documents and lifted Cora's pen. He got down on the ground and laid both sets of papers out in front of him.

Glen stepped closer. "Why the sudden change?"

Rather than answer, he read the papers. Once he signed them, his movie would be gone. The little spark that made him start writing in the first place would belong to someone else. All the nights, all the years, his characters, they would not be his, and he would never be able to decide their fate. "Just swear to me you'll never ever harm her."

"I give you my word."

"The final script was in the filing cabinet, should you choose to use it. I had made some changes." He took a breath, signed and initialed in all the right spots, then stood. "I assume aside from my name as screenwriter, we are through as well."

"You will never hear from us again." Glen held his hand out.

He closed his eyes and handed Glen one of the sets of paperwork. "Do the movie justice."

When he opened his eyes, Glen and his movie were gone. Maybe it wasn't redemption, but it was a start, and for the first time in his life, he was completely clean. Next, he had to do something for Cora, something only he could give her. He had to play the role of hero and give it his all.

FADE IN:

INT. HOLLYWOOD – STUDIO SOUNDSTAGE - DAY

CHARLES is on the set. Behind him a huge
computer graphic of a black hole.

                    CHARLES
               A black hole is formed when
               a star dies.
               (He motions toward the
               graphic.)

CUT TO: The graphic illustrates the black hole.

                    CHARLES
               Some have theorized that
               the black hole could
               actually be a portal to
               which we can bend time and
               space, and that they hold
               the key to space travel.

In the background, the music becomes more
dramatic.

CHARLES turns to the side.

CAMERA PANS over to ROXY standing there.

                    CHARLES
               (faces forward once more)
               The gravitational force is
               so strong nothing can
               escape its pull, not even
               light. Nothing can escape.

The set goes dark.

CHARLES walks off set. ROXY catches his arm.

CHARLES stops and stares at her.

                    ROXY
          I was right on the side,
          waiting for you like I said
          I would be.

                    CHARLES
          What about all the other
          days?
          (He shrugs her away and
          leaves.)

ROXY watches him go and closes her eyes.

Chapter Thirty-Two

WE WANTED TO MAKE SURE you would be on set today.
Cora reread Logan's text as another one came in.
Hi Cora, you'll be here later right? Erin texted her.
Once more, her phone vibrated. Cora narrowed her eyes and read the simultaneous texts from Drew and Ivy both asking the same thing. Thus far, all her little hatchlings had checked in. All but one.

She supposed she should be grateful they wanted her there. Since that infamous break-up, she had video conferenced into the filming, but unable to watch it, she had Viktor or Rodger monitor the goings on in the land of make believe.

Rather than answer, she turned toward her desk and her three monitors. Systematically, she turned each one off, sat back in her chair and hit the intercom. "Viktor, Rodger, may I see you?"

After another two nights of no sleep, she was either delirious or she was about to save her sanity. All she knew was once she saw *Hollywood Stardom* wrap, she needed to end that part of her life as well.

Maybe her time with Ryder had ended in disaster, but it taught her a lot, a lot about herself, about being human, about love and passion, and maybe even going after a dream no matter what the cost.

Rodger entered first. "What does my CEO command?"

"I have the final report on how Albert not only terrorized you, but Franklin as well." Viktor took his throne. "How do you want to handle this?"

Once she discovered who was behind the stalking, she and Viktor traced Albert down as the perpetrator using exactly what Albert hated—technology. While he was smart enough to hide his tracks, once they had a starting point, it took only a few hours to unearth the DNA they needed.

"I want the information brought personally to George along with this." She opened her desk drawer and pulled out an envelope on her own personal stationary.

"What's this?" Viktor took the document.

"A long time ago I started Chargge because I loved musicals and movies and the industry. It's magic." With a deep breath, she sat back and looked at the men. "Somehow, by going public and being bought out, I lost the magic. When I was with Ryder..." She shrugged.

After a moment to collect herself she continued. "Anyway, I may not have everything, but I can have some magic. I don't want to be CEO of Ultracom. I want a life." What she wanted was her last name to be Scott with no hyphen and talk about babies and wear a key around her neck, but that was gone.

Viktor shook his head.

Before allowing him to react, she held up her hand. "I have decided that I'll stay with Chargge as a figurehead only, if that is what you want." She stared into his eyes.

Viktor stood. "Why are you asking me?"

"Because I'm going to recommend to the board they make you the CEO of Chargge. You deserve it and it's your turn." With the words out, the weight on her chest lightened a little.

"What are you going to do?" The man she called her big brother crossed his arms.

"I love production. I'm going to produce. Hopefully, you'll hire me for Chargge." No, she wouldn't be producing with Ryder, but she found something she loved to do, and right now that's what she needed. "I'm starting a new business, one that will never be for sale, and one that Rodger will help me helm." She glanced over at the incredible man.

"Of course." Her secretary dipped his head down.

She took a shallow breath. In time, she figured the breaths would deepen and she wouldn't constantly feel like something was missing. "Now, if you two amazing men wouldn't mind accompanying me and Spike to the final day of shooting on *Hollywood Stardom*, I would be honored."

"Are you sure this is what you want?" Viktor helped her out of her chair.

"It's as close as I'm going to get." After collecting her things, she headed toward the door, stopping short as the realization she was going to see Ryder for the first time since the incident hit her.

Rodger collided with her. "Are you all right?"

"I'm really thirsty." Her voice came out scratchy.

Out of his bag of tricks, Rodger pulled out an ice cold bottle of water. "Here."

How he kept it ice cold, or why he had water on him at the most convenient time kept her attention until they got in the car and she studied the bottle. "You gave me alkaline water."

"That's what I had." Rodger started the car.

"If you're so incredible that I am taking you with me to start my new company and you seem to always have everything on you, I demand I have something other than alkaline water." Her throat still parched, she thrust the bottle back at him.

He took the bottle, stared her down and then opened up his briefcase where he produced, of all things on this planet, some fresh lemon slices. Keeping his eyes on her, he twisted the lid off the bottle, squeezed the lemon inside, gave the bottle a shake and gave it back to her. "Well, if it was alkaline before, with the addition of the lemon it should be neutral now."

Fully irritated, she sat back. "Do you think you can learn to braid hair?"

"Not for you." Rodger drove to the studio.

They drove though the studio gates and parked in their spot. On shaky legs she made her way near the set, coming up behind the back of the Hollywood Stardust façade. A flash of the day Ryder showed her the panel where the actors all wrote down their dreams went through her mind. The rock star, the director, the actress and the astronomer. All four came so close to what they wanted. If she were to add her name to that list today, she would have said producer and wife. Only one of those things was going to come true.

Her breath came in short gasps when she finally made her way around toward the director's chairs. Instantly, among the crowd of people on the set, she spotted Logan, Ivy, Erin and Drew, but no Ryder. She swore she didn't know what she would do if he spoke to her, but she wouldn't deny herself knowing the fate of Roxy. Maybe somewhere, somehow, she would get some guidance.

Logan came jogging up to her. "I'm glad you're here. We had a slight delay and have to reshoot a quick scene with Ryder, and then we're going to do the end."

"Should I come back?" In all honesty, she didn't know if she could sit on set too long and watch Ryder without flinging herself toward him.

"No, we're ready to roll." Logan pushed her toward her director's chair with her name.

Strange, they were never ready to roll anything. Always there was a delay where they had to set up for the next shot. They should have just invited her back tomorrow. Still, she sat down and took a sip of her neutral water. The beverage really was lacking.

Without time to protest, Logan dashed away, then yelled, "Okay, everyone on your mark? The boss lady is here and we want to get this in one take and make it last forever."

That was weird. Logan never said all that fanfare before any other scene. Maybe they were all giddy from being so close to the end.

The guy with the clapperboard came out. "Ryder's song, take one."

Ryder? Did they mean William? They were only on take one? They could be here another week. What the hell was going on here? She handed Rodger her water and sat up, clutching the arms of her chair.

Out of nowhere, the music to the song Ryder sang in the movie boomed through the area.

Wait. He didn't sing his song in front of the Hollywood Stardust façade.

Before she had time to think, Ryder, followed by no more than at least twenty people, came dancing out.

Yes, dancing.

Her breath caught at the sight of him, and she widened her eyes taking in everything about him. Handsome didn't even come close to describing him. There would never be a more beautiful man in the world. He wasn't in his William get up with that molded hair she didn't care for. Rather, he was in a tuxedo. This wasn't for any shoot.

He did his best to keep up with the steps, actually did a great job and, in coordinated steps, he and the rest of the dancers made their way closer to her.

Then Ryder came front and center and burst into song.

Since the day we met I knew it would be us two.
The love we have together is experienced by so few.
What started out as business, blossomed and it grew.
Then you became the one and everything was new.

The song started as like William's but he changed the last two lines.

I wanted it easy, I wanted it fun, I wanted to have it all.
What I didn't expect was how in love with you I'd fall.
The day you said you loved me too, I knew I had a gift.
If I could only turn back the clock and get rid of this rift.
Because...

Fine, the tears started. Still, she watched him dance, sing and basically give her a musical.

You're the one, you're the one, you're the one I can't live without.
You're the one, you're the one, from every rooftop I will shout.

As he sang his way into the chorus, the dancers disappeared, the set cleared, and he came closer.

You're the one, you're the one, I'm sorry for everything. In front of her, he dropped down to one knee.

You're the one, you're the one, will you wear my ring? With the last line out, the music stopped, he put the microphone down and pulled a red leather box out of his tuxedo jacket.

Panting from his exertion, with a shaking hand, he opened the box revealing a not only a gorgeous round diamond fit for any Hollywood wife, but her key on her chain.

"Ryder." Her voice cracked.

"I love you. There is no one else for me on this earth. I'm on my knees begging you to forgive me. You're not in danger, I made sure of it. I gave them the movie, and if you'll have me, maybe we can produce something together, just us?" He held the box up to her.

"The movie is gone?" She shook her head. That was his ultimate sacrifice, a true test of his love. She knew what that meant to him.

"I'll talk to anyone I need to about what happened, and I'll make sure it doesn't affect getting your job." He reached forward and moved a curl away from her face.

"I got my job." Beyond her control, the tears flowed.

He looked up into her eyes.

"I got the job, and turned it down, and quit Chargge to open up a production company," she reached for her key, "with you."

"Marry me." He pulled the ring out of the box, stood, and took her into his arms. "Please."

"Yes." She put the chain around her neck and held her hand out.

He slipped the ring on her finger and kissed her. Their bodies and minds as one, they would conquer the world together. She pulled back and took his face into her hands. "I love you, Ryder."

"I love you." He gave her another light peck. He picked her up and headed toward his trailer. "Now it's time for you to be in the movie. We have one more happily ever after to get through."

She held on to the man who would be the one forever.

<u>HOLLYWOOD STARDOM</u>

FADE IN:

EXT. HOLLYWOOD, CA - OUTSIDE HOLLYWOOD STARDUST
THEATRE - DAY

                    ROXY
          I have to go.

                    WOMAN
          Just tell me.
          (She grabs Roxy's hand.)

                    ROXY
          Sometimes you find love in
          the most unexpected places.
          (She smiles at the woman.)

The camera pans back as ROXY walks to STEVEN,
WILLIAM and CHARLES.

ROXY gives WILLIAM and his wife a hug and kiss.
She then turns to STEVEN, kisses his cheek and
hugs his wife, and lastly she goes to CHARLES.

CHARLES pulls her in and places his hand on her
pregnant stomach and kisses her. The camera
scans down to find the ring CHARLES gave her on
her finger.

ROXY closes her eyes and rests her head on
CHARLES' shoulder.

FADE TO BLACK.
ROLL CREDITS.

Chapter Thirty-Three

"ARE YOU READY, future Mrs. Scott?" Done up in her hair and makeup for film, Cora gave Ryder her hand, and he led her out of the trailer. For the first time he got to be with his fiancée without a horrible cloud of secrets and anxiety hovering over him.

Upon their appearance, everyone began to clap.

While he bowed, Cora hid her face in his shoulder, but this time there was no doubt her shy demeanor was authentic. They had the rest of their lives for her to be the strong business mogul, but today she was his wife-to-be and fledgling actress. With everyone's spouses in the movie, he and Logan decided if, in fact, she accepted his proposal, she would appear in the final scene along with the rest of them.

They all gathered around the famed Hollywood Stardust façade and after everyone admired Cora's ring, Madeline rushed forward.

"Roxy is going to deliver her last line and then join everyone at the theatre and come hold the hand of the man she ended up with." Madeline handed out the final page of the script.

"Steven and his wife." Ivy leaned into Logan.

"William and his wife." Cora stared up at him.

"Roxy and Charles." Erin dropped the paper and hugged Drew.

"Sometimes you find love in the most unexpected places and that is where Roxy found hers." Madeline bowed and backed away.

Ryder pulled Cora into his arms. "Looks like we all got our happily ever after."

THE END

Read the Series!

Available on Amazon from Kindle Press (A Kindle Scout Winner)

Typecast

What's Your Fantasy?

Twenty years ago, the movie *Hollywood Stardust* defined a generation of teens and changed the four actors' lives forever.

Typecast as the villain both in front and behind the silver screen, Logan Alexander has purposely allowed his star to fade. Now with the 20th Anniversary of the movie on the horizon, he is the only one fit to step into the spotlight, deal with the unwanted publicity, and make sure that things meant to be left on the cutting room floor remain there.

Ivy Vermont has always longed to be a leading lady, yet her paralyzing stage fright has relegated her to stay behind the scenes as a fact checker for Chargge.com's entertainment webcasts. However, when her one-time poster-boy crush walks in to the studio demanding only she be in charge of his story, she knows she must take advantage of her big break.

Now, Logan tightropes between old loyalties and new love, while Ivy struggles to stay in reality with her ultimate fantasy.

An Excerpt

"THERE IS ABSOLUTELY NO WAY I am going out there and interviewing some B-list has-been bad boy." Julia Davis, the lead entertainment reporter for Chargge.com crossed her arms. "Your little fact finder screwed up again. Seriously, Craig, how can I be expected to work this way?"

Heat encompassed Ivy Vermont, but she met Julia's crossed arms with a set of her own and glanced between Craig Stockton, her boss, and Julia. "Technically, Logan Alexander is not a B-lister. He doesn't even act anymore."

"Your ridiculous details mean nothing." Julia's nostrils flared.

"Ivy, what happened to getting Ryder Scott or Erin Holland from *Hollywood Stardust*?" Shaking his head, Craig approached. "It's a little hard to do a story on the twentieth anniversary of the movie without one of the stars. You told me everything was set."

With facts, rather than stature on her side, Ivy stood up straighter and lifted her chin. "Logan Alexander was as much a star in the movie as the other two of them, well three."

"Last week, rather than getting that little boy in the hot dog commercial with the catchy line, you brought me the dog." Julia stared her down. "How can I interview a dog?"

"The trainer was there. Some say dogs have the mentality of a two-year-old, and it did tricks." No one ever saw the potential. If she could talk as eloquently in front of the camera as behind, she would be the reporter. Actually, she would have been an actress and the interviewee. Even the camera on her phone terrified her, not a flattering trait coming from a family of actors. "A few fetches and atta boys would have been perfect for your report."

"I am not doing this interview." The click of Julia's heels on the wood floor of the conference room grew louder as she approached. "What? Are you scared to face me?"

Though she tried not to look directly at her, Ivy gave in, swallowing back any mention of the tiny mascara smear above her left eye. Julia should meet Mr. Alexander with such an imperfection. "The agent promised me Ryder or Erin. Only, two hours ago, he called to say Logan would be here instead."

"He was one of the major stars." Craig wiped his brow.

"Stop defending your personal pet." Julia turned her back to him.

Ivy held out the note cards she made for the wicked reporter. "Logan Alexander is an excellent person to interview. The villain is always the most interesting. Even after all the scandals, *Hollywood Stardust* is one of the most beloved teen movies ever made, and changed the genre forever."

"I don't need your details. Did you spend your life studying this movie?" Julia grabbed the cards out of her hand and tossed them to the floor. "He was arrested and personally responsible for getting the sequel canceled. He is as bad in real life as he was in the movie."

"Don't forget that I ran off innocent Drew Fulton and no one has ever heard from him again."

At the unexpected male voice, Ivy turned. Her breath caught as her ultimate teen fantasy stood before her.

The heat in the room intensified, but she froze. Mr. Logan Alexander leaned in the doorway—more like filled up the doorway. He lifted a cigarette, twirled it between his fingers, and placed it in his mouth.

Unlike someone who lived the hard-knock life of a disgraced actor, time had kissed him, leaving him looking much like his teen dream self, only a little more rugged. While his other two male costars from the movie possessed more of the good and wholesome image, Logan Alexander personified the conniving character. He was the one who lured people with looks that could only be described as remarkable.

As if this whole thing were nothing but a bother, he pushed away from doorjamb and entered the room, glanced at Julia, turned his back to Craig, and faced Ivy. "So, you think the villain is the most interesting?" The cigarette bounced between his lips.

Interesting? Interesting as in the way he pulled his dark blond hair into a ponytail that hit the nape of his neck leaving one long strand to hang down the side of his face? Maybe interesting in the way his light blue eyes seemed almost translucent, half-closed, and definitely naughty? Of course, also interesting in how the slight bit of stubble highlighted the angles of his face, and the way he managed to keep his cigarette balanced. Then the answer was yes, he, or the villain, was the most interesting.

"The villain always needs to go under the most transformation." She managed to squeak out the words and pointed to his cigarette, unsure if she needed to tell him about the no smoking rule. Did fantasies follow rules?

"Don't worry. I'm not going to light it." His gaze scanned down to her shoes and back up to her face.

Interesting. She licked her lips. The man was more glorious in person than on the silver screen.

"What if the villain hasn't undergone a transformation?" Julia tapped her foot.

Ivy ground her teeth together. If anyone needed to change, it was Julia.

"I suppose I'll get more hard-hitting questions than asking a dog trainer if Rover, the hot dog hunter, is potty trained. You sure know how to dig deep." Though he answered Julia, he continued to look at Ivy. "I liked the dog, a much better choice than the obnoxious little boy."

Transfixed, she continued to stare at him.

"Just because the villain can change, doesn't mean they will." Julia moved over as if trying to get his attention.

He exhaled, but the cigarette stayed in place. "How can I do an interview with you when I know you are team Ryder all the way?"

"*Hollywood Stardust* was the typical love triangle." Julia raised her chin. "Today's teen movies are better developed than movies decades ago."

"Oh, that reference to my age really does pain me." He pressed his hand to his chest. "Tell me, did the villains of your era wear pompadours and leather jackets, or perhaps suits of armor?"

In an effort to stifle a laugh, Ivy bit the side of her mouth. There was something to be said for the villain getting their comeuppance, and she didn't mean Mr. Alexander.

Julia narrowed her eyes and spun toward Craig. "I am not playing her game of bait and switch. If Miss Details loves villains so much, Miss Details can do the interview. Call me when you get a real star." She stormed out.

"Well, that is one thing your runaway hostess and I agree on." Mr. Alexander's smile revealed a perfect set of Hollywood teeth.

"What would that be?" Craig wiped his brow.

"Miss Details should do the interview." In a swoon-worthy move, Mr. Alexander bowed to her.

The spotlight shined down on her and the same stage fright she battled every second of her life took a strong hold over her body, made worse by being presented with her teen idol in the flesh. "Craig." How she managed to utter even one word was beyond her, but she took it as a good sign.

"Oh, no. No, that won't do at all." Craig shook his head. The first and only time she was on camera at Chargge.com, she ended up running off set and throwing up in a trash can. "I am sure Julia will be right back."

"Don't bring her back on my account. I'm Team Details all the way." Logan raised his fist as if he were about to begin cheering and, with a wink, lifted his chin in her direction. "She is clearly an expert on the movie and knows story structure."

His gesture, though probably insignificant to him, served to ignite her courage as well as her body. She chose to ignore them both. All she needed was to throw up on one of the *Hollywood Stardust* stars.

Craig cupped his hand over his mouth. "She is an expert on every movie."

Yes, fine, but she was mostly an expert on *Hollywood Stardust*. She remained silent.

"I refuse to be interviewed by anyone who is not an expert in cinema." Mr. Alexander picked up one of her note cards, gave it a quick scan, and sauntered over to her. Yes, it was a total saunter. His walk may have also included a bit of a swagger as well. "Miss Details is the only one for me. It seems she has found something to talk about other than drugs, Drew, and sequels, since I won't answer those questions anyway."

She fought the need to hug her prepubescent crush, bury her face in his chest, and breathe in what could only be the smell of cologne and cookies. Later, they could go back to her apartment, and she would confess she used to write his name in her notebook and practice kissing him on the back of her hand. In her dreams, she could interview him and then they'd conquer the world together. In reality, she knew he was only playing a role and she would never be able to utter a sentence. Dumb reality.

"Either she interviews me or you can call the company that owns not only *Hollywood Stardust*, but your website as well, and tell them the video blog they expect to make waves won't air today. I'll be in the lounge not lighting my cigarette." He handed her the card and walked out the door.

She leaned forward, bracing herself on her knees. "Oh God, I want to do this."

Her boss paced across the floor. "You would be the perfect person if you could just learn to calm down. It's what we hired you for."

Though Craig never admitted it, she was the bane of his existence. He hired her as a favor to her father, and they gave her the job as a reporter. Technically, her current job as fact-checker and scheduler didn't even exist. The reporters were supposed to do their own research, but Julia sort of snatched her up as a personal assistant. Both her parents who possessed multiple acting awards between them, looked at her with wide eyes and pity every time they discussed her career. Even they weren't good enough actors to hide their disappointment.

She crumpled the note card in her fist and straightened up. "I'll do it. I will interview Logan Alexander." Part of her expected a spotlight to shine down on her signifying her strength of conviction. The other part was thrilled she didn't live in a world where spotlights randomly illuminated at key life-changing moments. She would end up living in the bathroom with the lights off, shaking.

Craig shook his head. His skin had turned the most unusual shade of red.

"This is the movie of a generation, the one that spoke to that specific time. The story should be told by someone who truly loves everything it represents." For once, she needed to be her own spotlight. "This is the movie that pushed the boundaries, didn't rely on the happily ever after, asked the questions." Maybe the movie that meant the world to her could also cure her.

"We need this story, Ivy." He crossed his arms. "Seriously, we need the story. Other sites are competing with us. We need something to go viral. The advertising dollars are not coming in as they should, and you know what that means."

Yes, it meant cuts, starting with the person who technically didn't have a title. She might as well go big or go home, literally.

"Do the interview, but make sure you ask about Drew Fulton and the arrest and the sequel."

"He said he wouldn't answer those questions." The swirl of anxiety circled around her stomach.

"Ivy." He rubbed his hand over his face. "You can do this. You were made for this. Go to wardrobe, ask them for something more contemporary and fashionable, and ask the questions. We need you."

For once she wouldn't disappoint. She stopped herself from saluting and gave him a strong nod. "I got this." As she walked out, she made a mental note to have a trash can put near the set.

Available from Amazon

Limelight

Worth The Wait...

Twenty years ago, Drew Fulton was made famous in the genre-changing movie, Hollywood Stardust and fell in love with his costar, Erin Holland. Left heartbroken and fed up, he played his ultimate role and walked away from his life, taking on an entirely new persona. Now he wants everything back, from his place in the limelight to the love that made him leave. He only needs to make sure he can leave the past in the past.

Known as the spoiled, has-been star of Hollywood, Erin Holland has spent the last two decades pining away for the one love she cannot have. Blindsided when Drew Fulton appears in her life as mysteriously as he disappeared, she is torn between acting on her heart and using Drew's reappearance to relight her star.

Together for the first time in twenty years, their true passion consumes them, but the sparks of old wounds still threaten to burn out of control before they can decide if their love was worth waiting for.

Limelight is a Hollywood Stardust novel. All books are stand alone, no cliff hangers, with their own central couple. They can be read in any order.

An Excerpt

Flashes from the cameras created lingering silver, glowing starbursts in Drew Fulton's eyes. The media frenzy started almost instantly, derailing the 20th anniversary screening of the one and only movie he filmed, *Hollywood Stardust*. For someone who successfully remained hidden for two decades, he chose the ideal subtle moment to come out of his self-imposed exile, or maybe not.

"Drew, where have you been all these years?" called out one of the reporters gathered for the gala.

Once the studio executives realized what happened, they stopped all the festivities and with a bit of movie magic, made the stage into a spot fit for a press conference in record time.

Before showing up at the shindig, he promised himself to go for it. Now was the time for full disclosure and he leaned down to the microphone. "To encapsulate two decades into one sentence, I changed my name, went to school, earned my doctorate and opened up a small nutraceutical laboratory." All right, it wasn't the world's best sentence, but it would suffice. In the next two days he would have to show up at his business and do a lot of explaining, something he sort of pushed aside when he made his snap decision to come here to find her.

A woman waved her hand. "Why did you feel the need to change your name and disappear?"

Drew wasn't sure if she was part of the media or not, but if he didn't answer her, someone else would force the issue.

He searched for her in the studio set converted to look like the inside of the Hollywood Stardust Theatre, the destination for the four characters in the movie. In the film, their quest took them across country. The road a metaphor for the trip one takes to transition between adolescence and adulthood.

In real life, he and the other actors faced the same challenges.

Once more, he looked for her. With her knowledge of all things smoke and mirrors, no doubt she managed to squirrel away where she could watch everything, yet not be seen. For the first time since he met her, she shied away from the limelight.

He swallowed and took hold of the microphone stand. While he wanted to offer the fans of the movie the truth they sought for all these years, the answer as to why he disappeared was better left unspoken, at least in public.

"Sometimes you need to just get away from everything and everyone and start over." More lights went off, leaving him blinking to see.

"But how did you hide your identity?" The question came from a male in the crowd.

An easy one. "During the movie I wore prosthetics to appear more like the producers wanted the character and they asked me to stay in costume for public appearances. It was very easy to fade away once the costume came off...and the weight came off."

Some chuckles went through the audience.

Yes, he was the chubby kid. During filming he lost weight, causing a whole host of issues for the movie. They had to keep adding padding to his costume to keep the consistency. He hid for a while, let the fanfare of the movie die down and then went abroad for college. By the time he returned with a different name, no one ever put it together. He still found it incredible that he pulled it off at all. Maybe he was a real actor after all.

"Have you kept in touch with your cast mates?" Another question barreled toward him.

He glanced off to the side. While he might not be able to find her, his best friend, Logan Alexander, was always there. Logan nodded, giving him the okay to answer. "Only Logan Alexander." The quote unquote villain of both the movie and of real life was one of the best people he knew. One might even say a hero.

Some mumbles went through the crowd.

"Drew, why did you decide to come back now?"

Again, he looked for her. Where did she hide herself? On the other side of the stage he located Ryder Scott, their leading man. The poster boy for a movie star, he always had everything. After the film, Ryder went on to a successful career and now also dabbled in directing and producing. However, he couldn't locate the last of their four. The reason he came out of hiding.

"I have some unfinished business." He needed to go find her. "I can take one more question before we should probably let you all get back to the movie."

"Can we get a picture of the four of you together?"

Well, the promise of a picture that would be all over the world should bring her out. He turned left and right. Ryder joined him first, shaking his hand and taking center stage to thunderous applause. Logan, who only moments before proposed to his fiancée on this exact stage, came out next and the clapping grew to the point where it vibrated the building.

Logan shook his hand and raised his eyebrows.

"Where is she?" Drew attempted to ask the question without moving his lips.

"She'll be here." Logan patted his back and took his place.

The crowd stilled as if holding its collective breath, waiting for the one female of the group.

He ground his teeth together. After everything he just did, would she not reveal herself?

And then she appeared.

Damn him to hell for his breath catching at the sight of her. Though he followed her career, watched her in her movies, her television appearances, even clips of her in a stage play, nothing compared to her in person.

She stepped to the edge of the stage and the applause began once more. Yes, even with his news of showing up after twenty years, Erin Holland would always steal the spotlight.

The color that overtook her cheeks would be gorgeous in the pictures, but he knew better. He knew the blush came from her being flustered, unsure and taken off guard. If they were alone, away from the scrutiny of the public, she would be crying. Not that it mattered. Crying, flush, with or without makeup and even with twenty years behind them, he had never seen a more beautiful woman.

Instead, she nodded toward the audience and made her way to them. Her silver form-fitting dress moved like liquid metal, fluid and flowing. She wore her blonde hair down, smooth and cascading over one shoulder, but pulled back from her picture perfect face. Her doe-like blue eyes and heart shaped lips were all natural and the envy of many a teenage girl way back when.

She stared into his eyes, asking questions, shooting accusations. In short, being Erin through and through. The one woman he couldn't stand, but couldn't get out of his mind. He could never move forward if he only looked back and the second she came within reach he held his hand out to her.

"Drew." She licked her lips, put her hand in his and gave him a hug. Her trembling betrayed her cool outward demeanor.

"I came here for you." He inhaled. Her perfume might have changed, but the aroma enveloping him was the same. It was just her. "We need to talk."

Without a word, she pulled back and took her position between Logan and Ryder. The three made up the love triangle of *Hollywood Stardust* while Drew's character was always left standing on the edge, just like him.

Again, the flashes went off and he found himself posing with the rest of them. Old habits returned, subtle changes in his position to catch the light, show off a better angle, allow the photographers to get the ever-important shot.

He needed to get to the person he came here for and raised his hand, the universal signal for stopping the show.

"Drew, one more question before you leave," a woman called over the mumbles, the claps and the oohs and ahhs.

He waited.

"What unfinished business brought you back? Is this a publicity stunt for the movie or was it something, or someone, else?"

"It wasn't a stunt. In fact, I didn't even know I was going to do this until about an hour before I arrived." He turned, wanting to catch her before she ran away licking her self-perceived wounds.

As usual, he was too late. Erin had already vanished and he almost fought a laugh. Once more, he changed his life for her, and again she wasn't around. "As for the rest, stay tuned."

TO BE CONTINUED...

On the Dotted Line

A signature can change everything...

Rather than silver, Randolph Van Ayers III was born with a platinum spoon in his mouth and plenty of strings attached. Faced with a list of specific goals he must achieve in order to earn control of his family's banking empire, he's accomplished each task and triumphed. One item remains on his list. He must marry by his thirty-third birthday and stay married for one year. However, when his so-called fiancée leaves him on the courtroom steps only hours before his deadline, he realizes he might lose for the first time in his life, and a Van Ayers never fails.

Taught to rely on the universe for answers, Willow Day has always struggled in the material world, specifically her lack of material. With her small holistic store near foreclosure and without a home, she must do anything within her power to make the business work and take care of the woman who raised her. When the rude, yet gorgeous, Randolph the Third offers to fix all her troubles in exchange for one year of her life, she opens her mind and takes a chance.

It's the battle of the mystical over the money. Between a hidden pet who looks more like a cotton ball, performance artists with wings, and a woman who spouts advice like a living fortune cookie, everything from restaurant reservations to a trip to celebrate the winter solstice create clashes for the couple as they learn how to fit into each other's worlds.

With both their futures at stake, they must learn to accept reality, what the fates have dealt them and the consequences of falling in love from the moment they decided to sign on the dotted line.

On The Dotted Line is a full-length (90,000 + Words) stand-alone novel

An Excerpt

"Don't get married for love." Randolph Van Ayers III pressed two fingers to his left temple. The throbbing in his head reverberated throughout his body. Though he wanted to go home and lie down, if he came home with anything his mother considered an ailment, he would end up quarantined in one wing of the house no matter how many times he told the woman headaches weren't contagious. The Mitchell Art Gallery presented him with a definite upgrade to being a medical pariah.

"Maybe you should look inside yourself for love." The owner of the gallery, Slate Mitchell, stopped in front of a photograph of the back of a man's head staring out into space. "However, I am still reeling that I didn't get an invitation to your wedding, love or not."

"Don't spew your rhetoric at me." It took all his effort to shake his head at the oversized, overdone image. The print wouldn't be worth anything in his lifetime. "I didn't even want to attend, not that it matters since I didn't get married today for love or otherwise. However, I do thank you for the party in my honor."

"Nothing like an impromptu birthday party to blunt being left on the courthouse steps with no bride." Slate patted him on the back.

"I appreciate how you've kept this low key as I asked." His life had been reduced to a frat party in an art gallery. Earlier a keg was delivered.

"It's only small if the police don't get called. I have some better ones over here." Slate guided him through the wide-open space designed to be a showcase of the latest local artists. Anyone in the city with seven figures behind their name wanted to be the next person to discover the artist of the second, and the gallery was in the perfect spot in LA to make waves without the cost per square foot of more trendy or upscale areas.

They stopped in front of another wall of photographs. "These would go with the sculpture of the birds you bought last month. Different artist, but similar feel. I can get you a discount for your special day."

He assessed the black and white photograph of a little bit of nature left in the Greater Los Angeles area. Mountains, clouds and birds in perfect juxtaposition of smog and the city. "A discount. Happy birthday to me."

"Well, it's the least I can do for the man whose bank made it possible for me to become the new go-to gallery for poor little rich boys such as yourself." Slate motioned toward the next photograph.

"Remember until you pay off your mortgage, my bank owns you." Randolph took a breath in an attempt to focus on the potential of the picture. "Maybe you should default on the loan, after midnight tonight it will no longer be my bank and I will no longer be rich." While he considered Slate one of his better friends, he knew once the money ran out the friendship would follow.

"Come on, that story you tell is just a pick up line. You can stop now." Slate stopped and motioned toward the next piece of art, namely his girlfriend, Jade. "And here is a masterpiece."

"The story is totally true. Randolph told me the story when we were dating, it's incredible, and true." Dressed in a nude body suit with a hat made up of flowers Jade uncoiled her body, stretching her arms out and taking her time standing up. She came over, kissed them both on the cheek and hooked her arm in Slate's. "I'm blooming."

"Baby, it's a story designed to make girls have the expression on their face you have right now. You didn't really date him, you only went as his plus one to that finance event when he was desperate." Slate chuckled and kissed the top of her head. "You make a beautiful flower."

Randolph met the little piece of living art a few years ago at a financial conference when she donned her other persona as a property manager. Her parents owned some select buildings throughout Los Angeles and she took care of them when they retired. He invited her to accompany him to an event, but rather than a kiss goodnight he ended up with a friendship instead. However, the slight blush and smile on her face spoke volumes. Women loved his pathetic all too true story.

If only it were a story.

"Unless he got married by his thirty-third birthday and stayed married for a year, he would lose his inheritance." Jade pressed her hands to her chest. "He signed a contract and everything."

Both he and Slate groaned.

Jade let go of her boyfriend and flung her arms around him. "I'm so sorry. I would help you if I could."

"Can I borrow you for twelve months?" A plus one was better than nothing. He needed to face the fact he was never going to have a relationship for anything other than money. Hell, he probably got left at the courthouse for a man with a larger trust fund.

"No, you may not. She is not on loan." Slate pulled her away. "Plus, he doesn't want to get married for love."'

"Well, he may not want to get married for love, but getting married for money isn't working for him either." Jade returned to Slate and wrinkled her nose.

"It doesn't matter. It's over unless a bride drops into my lap in the next five minutes." Since he created the situation, he would live with the repercussions. In the end, his father's entire scheme had been built around his failure. At least for once he would prove the man right.

"Can we study the art?" Slate walked backward, corralling them to the next piece.

"I need to finish getting ready for the party and Willow's here. She said she wanted to talk to me so I invited her." She waved her arm. "Come here and say happy birthday to Randolph."

An ethereal cloud of yellow and white swirls materialized out of the corner of his eye.

He tightened his jaw and finally did Slate the favor of staring at the next work. Maybe Willow Day would vanish if he didn't look directly at her. Everyone knew ignoring the problem made it go away.

"It's Randolph's birthday?" she asked.

Her voice brushed over him, as soft and supple as her name. If only the rest of her matched. A new tenant in one of Jade's buildings down the street from the gallery, he crossed paths with her a few times in the last couple of months, but the encounters were always the same. No, pretending a problem didn't exist never made it go away. He squeezed his hand into a fist.

"We're having a party for him." Jade dragged her over.

With the woman standing directly in his line of sight, he needed to look. The way she gazed at him always made him think she was intrigued or interested. Again, her appearance didn't match her attitude. Long, straight blonde hair literally floated around her as if she managed to get someone with a fan to follow her around. Unlike most women in Los Angeles, she wore little makeup, only enough to enhance her light blue eyes, petite features and glowing skin. He suspected she had a nice little body under all the flowing layers of clothes. She didn't stuff herself into her wardrobe leaving little to the imagination. Someone would have to really search and discover. No, nothing on her was man made or artificial, everything natural. A rare find.

"Well, Happy Birthday." She graced him with a smile.

The same smile sucked him in the first time he met her. Though it lit up her face, he sensed something beneath her upturned lips, something he wanted to get to know until he actually spoke more than two sentences to her. "Thank you."

"Scorpio." She tilted her head. "I should have guessed."

Case in point. He swallowed. "I hardly think a bizarre alignment of planets and stars millions of light years away from me on the day of my birth have anything to do with my personality. Wouldn't that mean anyone born on my birthday should be exactly like me?"

"Let's hope not." While her voice came out soft and sweet, her words were hard and cutting. She gave Jade one of her multi-layered smiles. "Sorry I'm late."

"It's fine. I'll meet you back in Slate's office." Jade pointed.

Without any more well wishes, Willow walked through the gallery.

Jade glared at him. "I'll be back for your party." She spun on the ball of her bare foot and left.

"What's your poison?" Slate motioned toward the photo.

"I want something different, something with some bite." Everything presented to him seemed trite, done before. He longed for something unexpected.

"I think you have enough bite for everyone." Slate shook his head. "Especially Willow."

He exhaled. "She called me a Scorpio."

"How dare she call you your own astrological sign?" Slate tucked his notepad back into his pocket. "She's such a meanie."

"It was the way she said it." He stopped in front of the next photo. The artist quite literally took a picture of nothing. A big black square hung on the wall, creating a hole in the middle of the show. With a bit of metallic paint it might have potential, as long as the artist had the vision.

"Aw, did Randy get his feelings hurt?" Slate raised his voice as if he were talking to a baby. "She's having a hard time."

"What's wrong with her?" He stared into the nothing. Maybe the artist was trying to depict potential rather than emptiness.

"Everyone goes through ups and downs, some downs are just lower than others."

Damn it. He glanced at his friend. The few times he met her, their encounters were always the same. She would materialize, he would try to speak, something strange would come out of her mouth, leaving him no choice but to comment and she would walk away. "She's back in your office, meeting with Jade." In his distraction with his own situation, he neglected to pick up on the significance of the Jade meeting, especially if Jade was interrupting one of her art performances.

"Yeah, Jade, her landlord. Go grovel, it will do you some good."

Money woes, one of the world's great equalizers. "I'll take this one. It speaks to me." He strode through the gallery, stopping short outside Slate's office at the sound of her voice.

"I don't have any money left, and you can't keep extending my rent payment," Willow whispered. "It's not right, everything is off balance."

He put his back to the wall to listen.

"Don't worry about the rent, it's fine." Jade's tone was one of compassion and authority. "Right now we are working on the barter system. Just keep me in products and tea and we are fine."

"I can't do that. I just need to sell a little more at the shop." Her voice was broken but not destroyed. "I did a little research."

At the rustling of papers he inched toward the doorjamb trying to spy what she would produce.

"What's this?" Jade raised one of the documents.

"There are companies who will give loans to people in need." She let out a nervous chuckle. "Funny the people who need the loans the most are the ones who can't get them."

"Willow, these are loans designed so that no one ever pays them off." Jade shook her head.

A shudder ran though him at the thought of the interest rates alone. Those loans were no joke and lured in desperate people who needed money fast and under the most dire circumstances.

At his realization, he glanced at the time and resumed his eavesdropping.

"Hey, I didn't mean for you to spy. What are you some kind of creep?" Slate came from the other direction and pushed him into the office. "Look at what I found lurking about."

He stumbled into the room and his head spun. Once he regained his footing, he gave Jade a half-hearted wave and glanced at Willow. If possible, her light complexion was even paler, almost translucent. He recognized her pallor. It was the same look he saw whenever someone honestly needed funds. Somehow he needed to tell her he had her stay of execution, and it would only require one year of her life.

Jade narrowed her eyes at them.

"I wanted to grab something to show our peeping Randolph." Slate went to his desk and picked up his tablet computer.

Both Jade and Willow focused on Randolph.

"I don't believe Willow should take out one of those high interest loans." With all the attention on him, he did the only reasonable thing and brought sanity to an insane situation. The vice around his head seemed to tighten and he rubbed the back of his neck. "She needs to create as much inventory as possible for her shop because that is the only sure way she will have money coming in."

"I need the loan to buy the materials to make my inventory." Willow lifted her chin.

"Not if Jade is letting you take a break on the rent." He returned his hand to his temple swearing he felt the pulse of pain through his fingertips.

She hugged her papers to her chest. "My supplies are very expensive."

"Willow's morning tea actually works. I feel great." Slate looked up to the ceiling. "What's it called?"

"Activi-tea." Jade went to Slate and hooked her arm in his. "We also loved the one you call Boo-tea."

The vision was a bit too nauseating and he returned to the matter at hand. "There are many grades of materials, just change some of it up to save money. It's done all the time. I think the issue lies in not knowing your true profitability and not having a focus on your product offering."

"Some say when you are out of quality you are out of business." Willow's eyes widened.

"There are others that say the same about money," he countered.

Silence encompassed the room.

"Slate," Jade whispered.

"Hey, I really did want to show you something, and wanted to talk to you about the artistic co-op. Look at this." Slate basically shoved the tablet in his face. "Remember that artist who creates those murals in the middle of the night in little hidden spots? They call him the Mural Man."

He nodded and restrained any reaction to the article and the picture. Instead, he kept his focus on Willow.

"Whoever it is struck again last night and painted over some graffiti." Slate stood next to him and enlarged the picture. "Wonder what this art would be worth. It's different. I definitely need to get someone like him involved in the project."

"I may have another way to help you." Without acknowledging Slate, he lifted his chin toward her. "A different kind of proposal."

"Honestly, Mr. Van Ayers, I'm not interested in anything you have to offer." She reached into her bag, pulled out a little jar and held it out to him. "I do believe you need this though. Rub it on your temples for your headache, and later you can tell me if I skimped on my ingredients."

He took the jar. How did she know he had a headache? "Maybe we should talk in private."

"Or not at all." She spun back around to face the desk.

"Come on Birthday Boy, let's go get your party started." Slate corralled him out of the office.

"I'll be right there." He watched Slate stroll down the hall and resumed his position with his back pressed against the wall, once more glancing at Willow and at his watch. They needed each other and he had only a little more time before his life had insufficient funds.

"Let me run some numbers and some options." Jade straightened the pile of papers on her desk. "Why don't I see if I can find you a less expensive apartment in one of my other buildings? If not, I can ask around."

Since Willow's move to Los Angeles and opening up a small shop for holistic healing, Jade and her boyfriend, Slate, had been nothing but kind to her. Somehow the universe took care of her by allowing her to meet Jade at a metaphysical faire during one of her friend's performances. Afterward, they got to talking, and she helped her get into the building only a few doors down from Slate's gallery.

Jade and Slate understood her vision and always referred customers, but it wasn't enough. Though everyone loved her teas and wellness elixirs, she couldn't sell enough to catch up. Whenever she started to make any money, she needed to buy more materials and could never quite get things to even out. As a last resort, she even took something from the one person who had given her the most without telling her. "Jade." She chewed her lip trying to figure out exactly how to say what she wanted.

Jade continued to read the papers. "Yes?"

"Nan and I moved into the upstairs of the store a few weeks ago." She dug her nails into her palm, but she promised Nan, the woman who raised her, she would tell Jade the truth. With the words out, the weight on her chest lightened a bit.

Jade looked up from the documents.

"I'm sorry, I should have said something." Her mouth dried out. "If we can just stay a little longer."

"Is Nan okay going up and down the stairs?" Jade winced.

Leave it to Jade to be concerned with Nan and not call attention to the fact they didn't have a real home. "Yeah, it takes her a minute, but she needs the exercise."

"Please be careful, and if there's anything you need--"

"I'll figure it out." Not wanting to take one more thing from her friend, Willow cut her off. "The universe will make its decision, and if we can't get caught up we will leave."

"I'm fine, seriously." Jade gave her a smile and held her arms up. "I am a work in progress and I'm blooming. Just work on it okay?"

"I have something for you." She smiled at Jade's costume wishing she had the ability to bloom as well. While she may have received a reprieve, she didn't get the pardon. Her friend and landlord gave her an incredible deal on the rent. She looked inside her oversized bag in search of her meager offering. Not that she wanted or expected one. "Hold on." One day she would remember to carry a flashlight, but she would put it in her purse and it would end up at the bottom. She turned her bag over onto her lap. Her wallet, crochet project, various stones she picked up along the way, pictures and more paperwork tumbled out.

"Wow," Jade gasped. "Amazing what that bag holds."

She rifled through the assortment and held a piece of jade she made into a necklace out to her. "It seemed fitting."

"You don't have to."

She gave her the gift. "Jade is green, the color of healing and hope. It is also for luck, though I already think you are pretty lucky." Karma, the universe, or the gods blessed Jade with a great career and parents and a wonderful boyfriend. The woman fit her name. Maybe one day her own energy would change. Nan kept telling her to be patient, she was paying her dues. The only problem was she already had too much debt and needed a windfall. All her troubles came from the material world or the fact she had no material.

"I think I should change into something more befitting Randolph's birthday." Jade took off her hat of flowers, stood and put the necklace on as she headed for the door. "Thank you."

"Thank you." She scooped everything back into her purse and joined Jade.

"Absolutely." Jade nodded. "You're going to stay for the party, right?"

With nowhere else to go, and reluctant to face Nan yet, she shrugged.

"At least go have a drink or something, and give Randolph something to look at." Her friend winked.

She tensed. "Maybe I'll sneak away and let him have his day."

Jade headed toward the door. "I think he likes to tease you so he can get your attention."

Her cheeks heated.

"Someone's blushing." Jade raised her eyebrows. "I'll see you out there."

She stood in the small hallway by herself. Music and laughter echoed through the building and all around her. Not in the mood for a party, she decided maybe the best course of action would be to take a walk and clear her head before returning back to her makeshift home.

Wanting to make a clean getaway, she tiptoed toward the exit. The noise indicated the party was in full force with food, drinks and a ton of people.

In a self-indulgent moment she stopped and glanced around, instantly spotting Randolph. The man stood out in his tailored suit giving him an air of power, but his blond curls and mischievous green eyes gave him a playful air and were equally as fun to look at, the same way she would stare at teen idols when she was younger.

All she knew about him was his family owned a bank, actually banks and he was exceptionally, incredibly irritating. Irritating in the same way a clothing tag would scratch at someone's skin but it couldn't be ripped out. The few times she talked to him only ended with him being condescending, and her saying something to try to match it. The man was in no way good for the psyche. Yes, he was irritating and he also was coming her way.

She turned away, wondering how bad it would appear to go running. With fleeing from the scene not an option, she straightened up.

"May I get you a drink?" He flashed her a smile of perfect pearly whites fit for any pre-pubescent girl's wall.

Okay, if he was going to be nice, she would return the gesture. Maybe it would even out all the bad energy. "Thank you. I think I'm just going to go, but I do wish you a happy birthday."

"I wanted to talk to you. I think I can help you." The smile didn't waiver one bit.

"I'll be fine. I would rather not have any more business advice." She took a step backward.

"It wasn't business advice, but rather a dose of reality." Still the smile, but he glanced at his watch.

"Reality?" Why couldn't he leave them be at a happy birthday and a disobedient curl falling on his forehead?

"Yes. I know you live in an alternate universe, but I wanted to bring you back down to earth." He put his arm out as if to guide her to do what he wanted.

Her heart seized and she broke out into a sweat. She longed to slap him across the face, but held back. "One day I hope you regret the fact you never visited an alternative universe, but I'm sure by then it will be too late for you. Enjoy earth." She swallowed back the burning bile in her throat and rushed out of the gallery into the alley.

Nan always said all she needed was fresh air and a night sky to be happy, her way of explaining how material things didn't matter. However, when rain started or the temperatures soared or sank, it was pretty nice to have a roof over her head. After everything the woman had done for her, she needed to figure out some solution before they ended up on the street.

"You left before cake." Randolph's voice seemed to fill the alleyway.

She wrapped her arms around her shoulders and stared up at the stars wondering if up there somewhere a female on another planet gazed in her direction with some jerk banker bugging her from behind as she tried to figure out how to fix her life and her credit score. Did they even have FICO in other galaxies? "I think I've watched you blow enough hot air for the duration. I can picture it just like I was there."

"I didn't know you were clairvoyant as well." He chuckled.

Shivers overtook her with each inch he came closer. "I'm not, but I still see you leaving me alone."

"I deserved that, and I do want to apologize for my comments earlier." He stood beside her and glanced at his watch. "Also, as I said before I wanted to talk to you."

"Is this a timed conversation? Can it be less than ten seconds?" His aura clashed with hers making it impossible for her to concentrate and causing ugly words to leave her mouth.

"I may need a little more than ten seconds." Once more he looked at his watch.

"But not much more." She turned to him.

"Now that hurt." He lowered his arm, then, as if he couldn't control himself, he lifted his wrist to his face again.

"What could you possibly need to talk to me about when you have something so pressing going on with your watch?" The acid of negativity Nan spoke of built up in her blood, singeing her skin. "I'm sure my paltry little problems aren't enough for you to miss an appointment or party over."

"First, your problems are huge. Let's make no mistake about that." He shoved his hands in his pockets and leaned back on his heels. "Second, you're not the only person in this alley with huge problems."

She studied him. All her life she had been reminded not to judge on outward appearances and material possessions, but the man's shoes cost a small fortune, his cufflinks a large one. What did this man even know of problems? Also, who wore cufflinks anymore?

"May I tell you?" He glanced at her.

"Fine." She swallowed, preventing herself from letting loose another insult.

"What if I told you I was supposed to get married today?"

Only because his voice lowered as if it wanted to fall on the gravel and be run over did she manage to forgo the comment about a ten-second honeymoon. "I would say check your watch again, you only have a few hours left."

He paced in a circle ending up back in front of her. "She cancelled on me at two o'clock, right before I was supposed to meet her at the courthouse."

Though nothing appeared funny, she sucked in her cheeks and waited for the punch line. She refused to succumb and ask what happened only to have him make a snide comment about numerology or something. "Well, look at the bright side, you got to buy some art instead. Something much quieter with lower maintenance." She slighted a woman she didn't even know as if his situation were personal. It wasn't like she was planning on marrying the man. Somehow he brought her to new lows.

"All my life I had these goals I had to meet. My father actually has a checklist and every time I meet one of the milestones his personal assistant notarizes the list." He seemed to be speaking more to himself than her.

"What kind of goals?" She balled her hand in a fist not wanting to become engaged in his tale.

"Valedictorian in high school, charity work." He counted the items off on his fingers. "Summa cum laude graduate in college. I had a 4.0 average."

"Ask a banker a question and he gives you his numbers." She bit her own tongue to stop the laughter.

"I had one more item on my list, something my father added and then I was done." He straightened up. "One more and my trust fund, the business, everything would be mine. My life would be mine."

"One more thing?" She crossed her arms. His gaze intense, those green eyes darkened turning almost black as if they wanted to absorb everything and give nothing in return.

"I had to get married by my thirty-third birthday. Stay married for at least a year, and on my thirty-fourth birthday I would be free." He turned to the ground.

For a moment they didn't speak, only the music from inside the art gallery interrupted their silence.

"Now who is living in the alternate universe?"

"I wish it were me." He repeated his action of walking around in a circle.

"You're not kidding about this list are you?" She stepped toward him.

He shook his head. "I'm completely serious."

"So what happens if you don't make it?" Fairytale or not, she wanted to know the end. At least the story was an amazing distraction from her issues.

He rubbed his hand over his face. "I don't lose. I can't lose. I won't lose."

"Do you have a bride in your pocket and a Justice of the Peace around the corner?"

"I have a charter plane at my beck and call." He lifted his head. "And I have you."

Everyone had their certain moments in life they would always remember. Some of these moments were shared with the world such as man landing on the moon. Other moments like special birthdays or life changing events one was supposed to keep forever. Then there were the moments, little flashes that stuck with someone for the rest of their lives but would be meaningless to anyone else.

Randolph mentioning her, marriage, and a charter plane together qualified as one of those moments in her life.

She forced herself to take a breath, move, react in any sort of way to his idiocy. "I think the fever is getting to you. Maybe you need to go home."

"Actually, I feel surprisingly better. I think what you gave me worked." He tilted his head, his curls tumbling off to one side with the motion.

"So says the naysayer." No one was ever surprised when a prescription worked, but everyone was amazed when what nature doled out did the job. Actually, she was amazed he gave her remedy a shot.

"Maybe you're on to something." He pointed at her. "At last my head isn't pounding. You did that."

"Then I need to go home. I think I'm going to be sick." She needed to go anywhere deemed a Randolph-free zone. She walked down the alley toward her store, the gravel digging into the bottom of her sandals.

"Lest you forget you don't have a home." He called after her.

"Don't let him get to you," she mumbled and forced herself forward. He must have continued to eavesdrop on her and Jade.

"How much longer are you going to be able to put off not paying your landlord?"

His words hit her, and nearly knocked her over.

"You know you may have something I need, but the street goes both ways." He followed her down the alley.

Not wanting to hear whatever argument he spewed, she continued her trek.

"What is it you want Willow? What if I told you I could make it happen?"

"I just want to be happy." Her steps slowed.

"You know, if you married me I would get the rent current within three seconds of saying yes and you would never fall behind again." The man continued. "I could also make sure you never had to buy anything but the best ingredients for your store. If your headache remedy is any indication, they work."

Her mind yelled for her to keep walking. At the end of the alley she would be at her shop, go up the flight of stairs, make a cup of tea and get rid of his bad vibes.

"I can make you happy. I have the money and the connections. You would be set, all for only three hundred and sixty-five days of your life."

Some force beyond her control made her turn to him.

"You know, I'm thinking that living in mansion may be a better alternative to your cramped quarters above your store." He inched toward her. "Think about it, all your expenses paid, time to concentrate on anything you like, luxury living, and at the end..."

Once again she found herself face to face with him.

"This time next year, your own business is perfectly set up and you'll have seven figures to do with what you please."

Seven figures? Images of stacks of money, stacks and stacks of money like a cartoon appeared in her mind. She barely ever had three figures to her name let alone seven. Still, she opened her mouth, inhaling to get the power to tell him exactly what she thought of his offer, how she couldn't be bought and sold.

"Don't give me the line about money not buying happiness." He leaned forward. "It may not buy happiness, but it buys security, wellbeing and potential."

Maybe the man should have been an attorney instead. She almost believed him. Almost. "I am sure if you have all that money you could find a different girl much better suited for your needs." She pointed toward the street. "Hollywood and Vine may have what you're looking for."

He held his hands out as if tossing the ball into her court.

Curiosity alone made her ask the next question. At least she told herself it was curiosity and not consideration. "What would this marriage entail?"

"Funny you should ask. I happen to have a prenuptial agreement I can tweak rather easily." He reached into his suit jacket pocket and pulled out a folded paper. "For the duration of the year we would need to live at my family's mansion. We would have our own wing."

"Of course, and I'm assuming a chef, maid and butler as well." The minute she returned home she needed one heck of a cleansing to make everything she heard go away.

"Five maids, maybe six, one butler, several various assistants, a chef, and a chauffeur." He flicked the paper. "We need to be in the same bed every night. We must be together by midnight."

"What happens if we're not? Will you turn into a monster?" She tapped her foot. "Actually, I think you're already a monster, so maybe we'll all turn into pumpkins."

"I never want us to appear anything other than happily married." He went on without a hitch. "We spend the holidays up with my grandparents in Vermont."

"You have grandparents?"

"We all have our shortcomings." He shrugged. "I am not to compensate you for your year of service."

"But..." She swore before this conversation finished she would slap him or herself for thinking about the monetary gain and she forced the visions of those perfect piles of money out of her consciousness.

"However, there's a loophole even my father didn't consider." He raised one finger. "I am allowed to be involved in your line of work, and every decent husband gives his wife a monthly allowance. How else can you do all the things that make you a good wife?"

"I don't think anyone could make you a good wife, least of all me." She curtseyed. A long forgotten tingle in the back of her nose indicated tears might be on the way. "I bid you goodnight Mr. Van Ayers, and thank you for my bedtime story."

"You know, until I saw you tonight I gave up. I never give up."

A nuance in his voice, a small shake, a fault in the perfect timbre made her pause. Nan always told her to look for the subtle signs. The truth and the beauty would be found in what most people overlooked. She lifted her head. Any semblance of amusement or a smile vanished from his face. "Why me? Just because I don't wear a suit doesn't make me your fool."

"I don't think you're a fool." He held his hand out as if to stop her. "I thought above anyone else on the planet you would be open-minded to helping us both out."

A breeze whispered through the alley. Chills ran through her and she hugged herself since no one would be around to do it for her. "You're serious."

He remained silent.

"The story, the list, the marriage, the money, you're not joking." She stomped her foot. "Swear to me you're not joking."

He put his hand over his heart. "I would take an oath if I could. You can notarize my words."

She closed her eyes needing to block out everything and think. The answers to her problems couldn't be as easy as a year penance with some snarky, albeit gorgeous, banker.

"Starting the second after you sign the marriage license you will never have to worry again about any of your so-called material things again. You will be set for life." Randolph's words vibrated through her. "So will your Nan."

At the mention of her only family, she opened her eyes. A life where Nan could relax, do her work, teach her and never have to scrimp for the little she needed. An opportunity to give back a small bit what Nan gave to her. Their future would be assured, and they could buy a house, a real house. "I'm not sleeping with you." What was she saying?

He cleared his throat. "You must sleep with me, but you don't have to *sleep* with me. I will have you know there will be a fidelity clause in the contract."

She decided not to mention there was no need for such a thing. Her life was a fidelity clause.

"If you agree, I will draw up your official contract on the plane. We will spend the night in Las Vegas and tomorrow you will need to move." He returned the paper back to the secret pocket in his jacket.

"Nan needs to come with me." Was she saying yes? Her heart stopped, skidded to a halt. "She gets full use of the kitchen."

He narrowed his eyes and stared off as if thinking.

"Nan comes or you are out your business, your trust fund and your sleeping only partner." Though she knew she should walk away and forget this whole deal, she stood her ground, unsure if she wanted the deal or only wanted to win. Randolph the third brought out Willow the terrible.

"You're a tough negotiator." He put his hand out for a shake. "If Miss Nan moves in and creates havoc in Chef's kitchen, do we leave now to get married?"

She stared at his offering, a large hand with long fingers and perfectly manicured nails. Karma and prayer wouldn't provide for her or Nan, they were days away from not being able to afford food. They needed a miracle, and as Nan would say, sometimes miracles happened in the most unexpected places. One year for the rest of her life.

She glanced up at the stars, took a breath and put her hand in his.

About the Author
Kim Carmichael

Kim Carmichael began writing nine years ago when her love of happy endings inspired her to create her own.

A Southern California native, Kim's contemporary romance combines Hollywood magic with pop culture to create quirky characters set against some of most unique and colorful settings in the world.

With a weakness for designer purses, bad boys and techno geeks, Kim married her own computer whiz after he proved he could keep her all her gadgets running and finally admitted handbags were an investment.

Kim is a PAN member of the Romance Writers of America, as well as some small specialty chapters. A multi-published author, Kim's books can be found on Amazon as well as Barnes & Noble.

When not writing, she can usually be found slathered in sunscreen trolling Los Angeles and helping top doctors build their practices.

To find out more about Kim Carmichael visit:

Website: www.kimcarmichaelnovels.com

Facebook: http://www.facebook.com/kimcarmichaelnovels

Twitter: @kimcarmichael4

Follow Kim on Amazon.

www.ingramcontent.com/pod-product-compliance
Lightning Source LLC
Chambersburg PA
CBHW070346260626
47161CB00001B/33